THE SEVEN: UNFORGIVEN

THE SEVEN: UNFORGIVEN

JOHN G. HARTNESS

FALSTAFF
BOOKS
WWW.FALSTAFFBOOKS.COM

CHAPTER ONE

ot much of a town, the young man thought as he climbed down off his horse and stretched his back. *Certainly not the kind of place I'd expect to find him. But maybe that's the point.* He took in the meager buildings as he walked down what passed for a main thoroughfare. To his right was a smithy with a huge, green-skinned half-orc beating a horseshoe into shape. The peals of his hammer rang out in a rhythm that the man found himself unconsciously matching with his steps. He gave a wry half-smile and slowed his pace. There was no reason to hurry.

Next to the smithy was a general store with a wide porch. Two old men sat across a weathered oaken barrel from each other, not nearly as intent on the game of Kings & Pawns as they might want it to seem. The younger of the two, a whippersnapper of barely seventy years, cut a wrinkled eye at the man as he passed. He gave it no serious mind. People liked to stare at anything different, and this did not seem like a town where men often wore steel in the street.

A pair of women leaned out the windows of the "boarding house" across from the store. One a red-headed human with freckles scattered across her impressive bosom, the other a lissome elvish woman, carrying the air of ennui and sadness that always enveloped the fey folk when they were away from their trees, either by their own doing, or by circumstance beyond their control. The elf caught his eye, her hand straying down to

1

her thigh as she sat perched on the windowsill, a dress of gossamer green silk flowing in the slight breeze. The man noted the slight bulge of a blade strapped to her thigh. This willowy forest-dweller was not without her defenses, it seemed.

He allowed himself another slight smile as he focused his attention on his destination. The town's only inn and tavern sat at one end of the "street," more a wide dirt path beaten down between the buildings than anything constructed with intent. A wide, two-story building, six sturdy posts held up the shallow porch covering the front door. A low wall sat atop the porch, just about the perfect height for a crossbowman to kneel behind and take some cover while still seeing the approach of anyone coming from town. Large windows blanketed the front of the building, but anyone looking closely would no doubt see the large shutters hinged to the top of each window. The traveler gave a slight nod as he saw this. No doubt there was a release mechanism inside that would drop each shutter simultaneously.

He may have left the life, but it certainly hasn't left him. His heavy boots thumped on the steps leading up to the porch, and the man paused. That wasn't right. His footsteps were too loud, with too much echo. An amused huff escaped him. *He kept the space under the steps hollow so it would be harder to sneak up on him. Anyone running onto this platform would announce their presence.*

The doors were unlocked, of course, but they opened out instead of in, another nod to defense. He pulled the door open and stepped through, blinking his eyes against the sudden dimness.

He took in the gaming tables, the small stage in the corner by the fire where bards and traveling minstrels would play for their supper and a warm spot to lay their head. The steps leading to the guest rooms were enclosed in a narrow corridor instead of the usual open staircase. But this proprietor wouldn't be renting out girls, so there was no need to display their wares to a drunken clientele, and narrow hallways were much better for defenders and much, much more difficult for attackers.

He strode across the room to the bar, feeling every eye upon him as his boots clomped across the worn wooden floor. The man pulled out a stool and said, "Ale." He didn't look up. It wasn't time yet. He wanted to make sure his quarry was close enough before he revealed himself.

A meaty brown hand with brutally scarred knuckles pushed a tankard across to him. A little foam ran down the side of the battered pewter mug, and the nutty scent of home-brewed ale wafted up to his nose. *Someone has developed a new skill in the past few decades,* he mused.

"First one's on the house for newcomers, but I'll need to see the color of your money before I'll pour a second," the bartender said. His voice was a low, rumbling baritone that seemed to come from down around the bowels of the earth.

The man said nothing, just reached into a purse hanging from his belt and withdrew a small gold disk. He placed it on the bar and slowly drew back his hand, revealing the coin.

The bartender kept a tight rein on his reaction, but not tight enough to hide the sharp intake of breath as he recognized the token for what it was. Not a coin of any realm, but a token. A symbol of a very special organization that the world thought long dead. Only seven coins like this had ever been made, and thanks to a very particular piece of magic in the smelting process, only seven *could* ever be made. They were only supposed to be in the possession of seven very specific people.

The young man sitting at the bar sipping ale was not one of those people. And the bartender knew that fact only too well.

"I'm afraid that won't spend, stranger," the burly bartender said, drawing closer and leaning over to wipe up the drops of foam from the bar's immaculate surface. "How did you come by that coin, and how did you come to be in my tavern?"

The bartender's voice was low, too soft to be overheard by any of the other customers, but there was no mistaking the cold determination behind his words. If he didn't like the man's answer, the threat of extreme and immediate violence was very real.

The man looked up at him, finally meeting the bartender's gaze. This time the thick-shouldered man didn't even try to hide his shock. He took a step back, his eyes widening in shock, or maybe fear. "Who-who are you? I know those eyes. I know them like I know myself. But they don't belong in a child's face. Who are you, boy? Tell me who you are and what you're doing here, or I swear by all the gods I'll split your skull open right here and root around in your brains for an answer myself."

"My name is Qabil. My mother was Eltara. She gave this coin to me, saying I would know when it was time to use it. It's time, Leshru of the Broken Blade. It is time for The Seven to ride again."

The big man sat down, his shoulders sagging as if the mass of an entire continent rested upon them, and looked at the newcomer. "Qabil, you said?"

The young man nodded. They were in a small room off to one side of the tavern, probably the place where the important men of the town played cards, if the lingering aromas of expensive whiskey and old pipe smoke were any indication. He sat with his hands folded in his lap, making very sure to keep them in sight at all times. If this Leshru was half as powerful as the warrior in his mother's stories, he was not someone to be trifled with.

Or at least he had *been* someone to be feared, in his time. That time seemed long past, however, and while the hands of the man sitting across the small round table from him bore the scars and the callouses of a lifetime of letting his fists do the talking, the slight limp in his step and the squint that he gave the coin on the table in front of him made him seem more like a slightly dotty grandfather than one of the most fearsome warriors the continent of Watalin had ever seen.

Until you looked in his eyes. Those deep brown eyes—killer's eyes, his mother used to call them—peered deep into Qabil's soul, appearing to rifle through his life and memories, assessing him. Finally, after draining a tankard of his homebrew, the big man scratched the still-dark stubble on his chin and leaned forward, picking up the gold token again.

"I haven't seen another one of these in close to thirty years, boy. I put that life behind me, opened up a tavern, and settled down. I found a nice woman who didn't mind my snoring too much, married her, raised a daughter, married her off, and buried my Adeline three years ago. This—" he held up the coin. "This is a reminder of a life best left behind us. That's what we agreed. What we all agreed." He looked at the young man again, searching, waiting for a reaction.

"Not all of you agreed," Qabil said, leaning forward to pluck the coin from the old bartender's fingers. He held it up between their faces, right in the line of their eyes, his hazel to Leshru's brown. "One of you decided to stay in the life all this time, and took over the port city of Lennox, ruling there as Lord Mayor. He's not afraid to snap a neck or two to get what he wants, and he's still strong enough and fast enough to keep his band of thugs and cutthroats in line."

"Walfert," the big man said, his voice low and his mouth twisted into a snarl, as if he stepped in something unpleasant. "Never could trust that wiry little prick. He was the one you wanted when it was time to deal with locks or traps, but you tried real hard not to leave him behind you when things got ugly. You could find your back unguarded in a heartbeat, or worse."

"Now he focuses purely on 'worse,'" Qabil said.

"Still, that's no reason to drag me into his affairs. I'm out of the life, like I said. Go to the sheriff, or the duke, or the king. Hell, go to the High Priest of the War God for all I care. Walfert's dreams of ruling his own kingdom have nothing to do with me. Or you, either. I can tell by watching you walk into my place that you aren't a sailor, you don't have the walk for it. And you aren't a merchant, you don't have the slick tongue for it. You aren't an adventurer, or that blade on your hip would be hung right."

The young man reached down instinctively to touch the hilt of his short sword, and Leshru favored him with a grin. "See? Your sword is fine, boy. But any man who's made his life at the hilt of one would know that without reaching down, just like I know, even now, how many things there are within arm's reach that I can use to bash your head in before you could stand and draw steel.

"So who are you, boy? Who are you, walking into my tavern, into my *town*, bold as brass and wearing Eltara's eyes. You say she's your mother? Prove it. Describe her."

The young man stiffened, then forced himself to relax. The old man was poking at him, probing for weak spots, just like his mother said he would. Qabil decided that enough was truly enough, and pulled a wicked curved dagger from a sheath at his back. He laid the knife on the table between them, spinning it so the hilt faced Leshru. "Describe my mother? Well, the last time I saw her she was lying on the floor of our kitchen with this knife stuck between her ribs, just under her shoulder blade. Her hair was mussed, and when I tried to brush it out of her face so I could get one last look at her, all I managed to do was smear blood all over her cheeks and forehead like some kind of demented war paint.

"She was still beautiful, if that's what you're asking. She still looked almost the same as she had since I was born, although she was well past her ninetieth year before she was murdered."

"Did Walfert...?" Leshru asked.

Qabil held up a hand. "No, of course not. He doesn't do his own dirty work anymore. He's much too important for that. No, it was his head of security, a dapper elf who went by the name of Bothun. That's who

5

plunged the blade into my mother's back, but you can see whose blade it was. He sent it with his man—a message. His mark—"

"Aye, lad. I see the mark," Leshru said, picking up the dagger. "I see the mark on the pommel, and I know this blade. He carried two of them. Named them, of all ridiculous things to do with a knife. Called one Mercy and the other one Judgement." He turned the knife over in his thick hands. "Look here, at the cross guard. See how it's square over the fingers but round over the back of the hand? The guard on the other blade is rounded front and back, as they were meant to be. He always said this one was called Judgement because it was flawed, just like his own." He handed the knife back to the younger man.

"You've got one of Walfert's blades and Eltara's eyes, to be sure. But what makes that proof? I haven't seen Walfert in nearly three decades. Wouldn't surprise me if he sold his knives and you bought them off a broker in some random town. And you may be Eltara's get, but who's to say? Could be you're just some quarter-elf with pretty eyes."

"What about this?" Qabil held up the golden token, and Leshru snatched it from his fingers, moving with a speed that belied the wrinkles around his eyes and the thick white hair covering his arms.

"*This* is why you're back here, instead of out there. Because if your answers to how you came to be in possession of this coin aren't satisfactory, then I don't want my paying customers to see what I do to you."

No fear showed in the young man's face. Rather, a frustrated expression sat there for a moment, until he let out a heavy sigh and said, "Fine. Here. If I don't at least *know* Eltara, how would I know you always called her the Fairy Princess?"

Leshru sat back in his chair, his breath whistling out in a long exhalation that ended in a curse. "Damn me, boy. We never called her that outside of camp or someplace safe. Only one of us would know we called her that."

He locked eyes with the young man, and both of them saw the other's were full near to overflowing. "That's what we called her, teasing her because she was half-elf. Our little fairy princess. Any time she griped about doing camp chores, we'd tease her about it. She didn't mind the teasing. Hated cleaning up after meals, though. That woman would do almost anything to get out of scrubbing pots."

"That never changed," Qabil said with a sad smile. "As soon as I was old enough to see over the washbasin, the scrubbing up became my job.

She loved to cook but hated to clean up the mess. I guess she was a little bit of the fairy princess, after all."

"Alright, boy. Put it away," Leshru said, tossing the coin to the boy. "I believe you. Enough to go poke around at Walfert and see what that old schemer is up to, at least."

"And if we find proof that he was behind my mother's murder? That the elvish assassin was working on his orders?"

Leshru rolled his neck from side to side, eliciting a series of cracks like snapping branches. He looked down at his hands, turning them over and flexing his fingers as if remembering how the implements of his former trade worked. "Well, if that turns out to be true, then I suppose me and Walfert are going to have some words. I don't expect he'll enjoy the conversation very much."

CHAPTER TWO

The two rode into Talberg, passing beneath the notice of the guards who saw only an old man on a swaybacked plow horse and a younger man, maybe his son, maybe grandson, leading the oldster into town for an outing. Nothing stood out about them. Their horses were poor, but not so poor as to be worth remarking. Their tack was worn, but serviceable, the kind owned by someone who rides regularly, but doesn't count their life on their time in the saddle.

Their clothing was typical for that part of the country—thick gray cloaks, treated to keep the worst of the rain off, boots coming up the calf to protect from branches, or snakes when they walked. Both men wore heavy pants and long shirts, with knives hanging from one side of their belts opposite their thin coin purses. Anyone watching them pass by might only remark at the extraordinary ordinariness of them, as if an artist painted a portrait of the most unremarkable men he could imagine.

As long as they kept their eyes pointed to the ground, that is. Even the guards at the gate took an involuntary step back as they met the old man's gaze. He had the thousand-yard stare of a man who had walked through the fire and wasn't entirely sure he'd come out the other side. His eyes told tales no sane man wanted to hear, and the guards waved them through with haste before retreating to their watchtower for a quick nip at the bottle they kept on the shelf for cold nights. It was midday, and a warm spring afternoon at that, but both men, grizzled veterans them-selves, felt a chill when looking in the eyes of the brown-skinned man.

"Where did you say he was?" Leshru's voice was gravel rolling down a rocky slope. He kept his eyes locked on the back of his horse's head, never turning to look at his traveling companion.

"The last word Mother received had him running a small shop in the Merchant's Quarter. He specialized in rare stones and jewelry, apparently."

"That fits. Nip was always a bit of a magpie. Lead the way." He slowed his horse, allowing the younger man to pull ahead as they rode single file through the crowded streets.

Qabil flicked the reins, and his horse, a dappled mare he traded for when he set out on this latest leg of his journey with Leshru, pulled smoothly in front. She was a steady beast, calm and stout if not fast. Qabil didn't mind the lack of speed. This was not the part of the journey where he would need to run. He hoped.

He tried to keep his attention sharp as they rode through the town, tried to take in everything around him and note any possible threats, but there were just so many people, far more than he had ever seen back in the village where he lived with his mother...

His attention wandered, and he found himself back on the farm, his hands and shoulders aching from walking behind their old plow horse shoving the blade down through earth still tough from the last hints of freeze. His mother's voice floated around him, weaving a song of joy to spring, a melody of growth and life and love that she sang as she tossed seeds into the rows he made with old Bettle the horse.

The smells of his old life surrounded him in memory, the freshly turned earth, the breeze coming over the fields, the gifts he had to dodge from Bettle with what seemed like every step. Qabil felt a smile stretch the corners of his mouth and he looked up, only to snap his attention back down to a scruffy young man who bumped into his leg, then looked up in apology.

"Oh! Sorry, milord. My deepest apologies," the boy said. "Wasn't looking where I was going. Entirely my fault. Please forgive the—*urk!*"

The boy, who looked to be maybe twelve or thirteen years, let out a strangled cry as a thick hand reached down and wrapped itself in the shirt at the back of his neck, turning the collar into a noose and yanking him to his tiptoes. Qabil looked back at the old tavernkeeper in shock.

"Lesh, what are you doing? Let him go! He apologized, and it's not like he even hurt me or the horse. What are you doing?"

Leshru ignored his protests and leaned down, putting his face right next to the frightened young man's ear. "Give it back and I won't strangle you here in the street and leave you to rot in the gutter with all the other turds." The menace in the older man's voice froze Qabil's blood, and from the look on the smaller boy's face, came very close to thawing the would-be pickpocket's bladder.

The boy reached under his shirt and held a leather pouch up to Qabil, his trembling hand making the coins jingle. Qabil reached down to his hip, astonished to find his purse missing. His eyes wide, he retrieved the bag from the thief's outstretched fingers and tied it to his belt again.

"Good. So you're clumsy, but not stupid. That might keep you alive a little longer," Leshru growled. "We need a guide. Nod, and you can earn some of what you tried to steal. Or I can let you run off like the frightened little rabbit you are. But if you run, you'll never know what gave you away, and you'll be dead in a fortnight." Leshru released the young thief's collar, and he dropped to his feet, eyes darting this way and that as he evaluated the best route for escape.

"The offer stands, boy. Come with us, keep the rest of the rabble away and guide us to the man we want to see, and I'll pay you. Then I'll tell you how you got caught. Or you can run. But if you run, you'd better be down in the deepest hole you've got in this city for the next three days, because if I see you, I'll assume you plan to rob us again. I won't be this generous a second time."

The boy gaped up at Leshru. As Qabil took a closer look at him, he marked the young thief's slight frame and noticed the slight point to his ears that told of his partial elven ancestry. That accounted for his youthful look, and Qabil adjusted his estimate upward. The boy was his age, nearing seventeen maybe, but not more. He was dirty, and skinny, but the light in his eyes was shrewd, and the look he gave Leshru was assessing behind the open-mouthed expression. His hair was dirty and hung down over his eyes, but Qalib was willing to bet they held a similar almond shape to his own.

"You going to stand there and gawp, boy, or you going to grab Qalib's reins and lead us to the nearest pawnbroker that deals in pretties and shinies?" Leshru reached out with a foot and prodded the boy in his shoulder.

The lad shook himself, as if coming awake from a long sleep, and nodded to Leshru. "You two are interesting. Haven't seen anything interesting in Lowtown for a long time. I'll run with ye for a bit, 'til you get boring. Or 'til you get dead." Without another word, he reached up and took Qalib's reins. "You'll be wanting Old Stinno, I guess."

"Why's that?" Qalib asked.

The boy shot him a grin, and the teeth shining out from his dirty face were white and clean. "He's about the same age as your old friend here, so I reckon they rode together. The other magpies in the Quarter are either *really* old, or the worthless sons of noble fathers put into business where they can't fuck up too much. Or bastards that proved themselves too smart to be sellswords, so their dear old da thought they could make themselves useful to make up for the embarrassment of them drawing all that inconvenient breath."

He looked up at Leshru. "Besides, you look like you know your way around a fight." He raised an eyebrow, turning it into a question.

"Seen one or two," the old barkeep grunted.

"Then you probably know how Stinno got all them nicks and dents in that big stick he keeps leaning in the corner behind the counter. Nobody tries to lift stuff from Stinno. Not more than once, any count."

"Wise decision," Leshru said. "He's not got my patient and caring disposition."

The boy chuckled and turned, pulling Qalib and his mount through the crush of people. "Hold on," Qalib called. "What's your name?"

The boy looked over his shoulder. "My friends call me Thallis. My marks usually don't call me nothin' because I'm gone before they know I've ever been there."

"And what does the City Watch call you when they come looking?" Qalib smiled as he said it. There was something charming about this brazen young cutpurse. He was certainly different from anyone he'd ever known back on the farm.

"They call me Ghost, when they know to call me anything," the boy said, returning Qalib's grin.

It took nearly an hour of shoving, dodging, and cursing to get the two horses through the press of humanity in Lowtown. Twice Qalib felt hands, feather-light, trace the outline of his purse before Thallis spun around and leveled a dagger at the face of the would-be thief. Both times, the pickpocket's eyes widened as they recognized their escort and they backed away with their empty hands raised.

"You seem to have something of a reputation in these parts," Leshru said after the second such encounter.

"You whittle enough ears into points in the same neighborhood and people develop ideas about your willingness to gut anyone who offends you," Thallis replied, not bothering to look back at the big man.

"You...whittled their ears?" Qalib asked, leaning forward a little.

Thallis did favor him with a glance. "Some people hold some silly prejudices," he said. "Not everyone is accepting of my elven heritage, including a few elves. So I 'made my point' right on the side of a couple of heads. Round ears got points, pointy ears got rounded off. Four or five of those settled any discussion about my worthiness to walk the streets unmolested." The thief grinned at Qalib, who sat back in his saddle. Things were *very* different here than back home, it seemed.

After a little further shoving, they came to a nondescript storefront with a sign over the entrance that read, "Stinno's Curios."

"This is it," their guide said, looping Qalib's reins through a metal ring mounted by the door. "Stinno takes an early lunch, so he oughta be minding the counter. If his shop boy is in there, just tell him you're a friend of the family. He'll go get the man right enough."

"Shop boy?" Leshru asked, dismounting and passing his reins to the thief.

"Yeah, Stinno's an old softy, in spite of his crust. He takes a boy off the streets, teaches him his sums and letters, keeps the older street rats away that might have a taste for young flesh, makes sure the boy's fed and stays warm and dry. In exchange, the boy keeps the place neat and sleeps above the shop to keep people like me out." His green eyes took on a distant look as he talked about the kindness of the old man, and Qalib thought he might know more about Stinno's tendency to rescue urchins a little more intimately than he was letting on. "Anyway, I'll stay out here and mind the horses and your packs."

"I know every coin in that pack," Leshru growled.

"I'd expect nothing less," Thallis replied with a grin.

Qalib looked back and forth from the gruff former adventurer to the cocky young thief, feeling a lot of unspoken words passing between the pair. After a moment, he shrugged his shoulders and pushed the door open.

A small bell above the door jingled with his entry, and an emaciated old man looked up from the counter. His bald pate was ringed with tufts of white hair, and his long, hooked nose protruded from a wrinkled face, providing ample shade for the pursed lips underneath.

"Who sent you, lad? Was it that ample-bottomed twit Horst? Or the idiot Priest of the Light? Well, speak, boy, don't just stand there waiting for the flies to come in and fly straight down your gullet!" His voice grated like two stones grinding together, but despite the sharp tone, he saw a glint in the narrow eyes peering back at him from a wrinkled face.

Those eyes widened as a rumbling voice came from behind Qabil. "Numar's tits, Nip. If I thought it was possible, I'd say you sound like even more of a prick now than thirty years ago!"

"Lesh? Is that you?"

The big man stepped around Qalib. "It's me, Nip. How have you been?"

"Well, I suppose I'm well and truly fucked, if you're here. How bad is it?" All mirth was gone from the old man's eyes as he stretched one arm out to the side, hand open. A staff flew from the corner of the room to land against his palm with a solid *thwack*.

"Bad," Leshru replied. "This boy is Eltara's. Walfert's gone and murdered the fairy princess and taken over some shit town to the east. Boy wants our help murdering the bastard right back."

"Walfert's gone dark, eh?" The old man leaned on his staff and nodded. "Can't say I'm surprised. He was always the type with more ambition than skill. But to kill Tara? Why the hell would he do that? He had to know that would be about the only thing we'd all ride together for."

"I expect that's it," Leshru said. "He thinks if he can become known as the man who slew The Seven, he can ride that fame right to the throne. Or at least Princess Risande's bed."

"Well, the little bastard's soon to learn that even without his knives or Tara's bow, The Seven will take a lot more killing than he's man enough to do. Come in and bring that ratty thief in from outside. We may as well sit down to one last meal before we go murder an old companion."

13

CHAPTER THREE

After a filling but unremarkable meal of boiled potatoes and roasted pork, Nipural pushed his plate away from him and picked up his mug. He waggled the empty vessel at Thallis, who looked back at him with a blank expression.

"Don't behave like you've forgotten where the wine is, boy. Get the jug and refill the glasses," the old man grumbled.

"I don't live here no more, Stinno," Thallis said, but he stood and walked over to a small counter where a wine jug sat. He brought the jug over to the table and refilled the shopkeeper's drink, then poured a slug of wine into his own cup. He set the leftover wine downing the center of the table and gestured to the other men, indicating they should help themselves.

"That's not how we treat guests in this house, Thallis," Nipural said, but stopped when the young thief held up a hand.

"*We* don't treat guests here any way, Stinno. Like I said, I don't live here anymore. It was *decided* I was big enough and swift enough to take care of myself, so that's what I been doing. Why you tryin' to act like I ain't never left?"

"And why you tryin' to talk like you ain't never learnt nothin'?" Nipural shot back, his cultured accent falling away into the gruff patois of the streets. "You aren't in one of Doran's rabbit warrens now, boy. These men...well, the big ugly one anyway, are honorable men who deserve to

14

be treated as such. So act like I taught you something when you lived here and pour the thrice-damned wine."

Qabil looked across the table at Leshru, who gave an almost imperceptible shake of his head. Whatever was going on between the grizzled old shopkeep and their young guide, it was best they stay silent. Qabil returned his attention to chasing the last potato around his plate with a knife and fork, then running the quartered chunks through the thin gravy before popping each bite in his mouth.

"Now what's gotten into you, boy? You've been prickly ever since you strolled back in here." Nipural took a long drink of his wine, gazing at Thallis over the rim of his cup.

"Who are you?" the boy asked. Qabil's eyes shot to the thief, amazed to see fear dancing behind them.

"What do you mean, who am I?" the old mage asked.

"I mean, who are you? Long as I can remember, you been Stinno the pawnbroker, the man you went to for a fair shake on your goods, so long as they ain't too easy to identify or too dear to the owners. No weapons, but trinkets and gems can be turned into coin at Stinno's place. Old Stinno's a grumpy bastard, but he takes good care of his boys, don't never lay a finger on them like some of the other masters, and teaches them a trade if they want to learn it."

"A generous offer *some* of his boys have an unfortunate tendency to ignore," Nipural said, and it was obvious from the grumble in his tone which camp Thallis fell into.

"But now I bring this oldster and this half-elf no older than me through the front door and you don't even try to sell them nothin', you just greet this bald goon like he's your long-lost brother, even though he ain't called your right name once since he's been here."

"Quarter," Qabil corrected.

The young thief whipped around, a snarl curling up the corner of his mouth. "What?"

"I'm only a quarter elf. Probably only one generation closer to the forests than you are. My mother was half-elven, but my blood is too diluted with humanity to gain any of the benefits of that lineage. But there's too much elf in me to be considered human, either. You've probably felt much the same."

"I ain't talking about me," Thallis growled, turning his attention back to Nipural. "I'm talking about Stinno, and why he answers when you lot call him by the wrong name."

"You know why," the shopkeeper said, his eyes kind.

"I do, but I want you to say it," the boy shot back. "Say it out loud, that you been lying to me and everybody in Lowtown for all these years."

"Of course I have," Nipural said, his face completely bland. "Why would I advertise the fact that Nipural Wyrmrider was setting up shop buying and selling stolen goods in Talberg? All that would buy me is more attention from the City Watch and a steady stream of young morons bursting through my door, eager to prove they were more than a match for the battle mage that slew an entire nest of wyverns with one blast. I moved here to retire, boy. Not to make the reputations of young mages with more balls than spell-sense."

Leshru let out a sharp bark of laughter, drawing a raised eyebrow from his old friend. "Sorry, Nip," the big man said with a wry smile. "I just seem to remember Eltara using those exact words to describe you back when we were first starting out."

A wistful look passed across the older man's face, and he nodded. "Aye, that she did. I've been waiting a long time to find the right moment to drag it out and slap it on some new young idiot." He looked to Qabil. "Your mother had a sharp turn of phrase. Something about her bardic training, I think."

Qabil's eyes widened. "Her what? My mother was trained as a…bard?"

Leshru laughed again and reached across the table for the wine jug. "Oh, lad! You didn't know your mother was one of the finest musicians in all of Relhye? Heh. I wonder what else she didn't tell the child, Nip?"

"I'd hope she didn't tell him anything," Nipural grumbled.

Leshru shook his head. "He found me, so she must've told him something. He knew where you were, too, leastwise what city. Took a little work once we got here, but not much to speak of. You getting sloppy in your old age?"

The mage arched an eyebrow at his old friend. "And I suppose you're at the top of your game, pouring home-brewed ale to goat farmers and bowing and scraping to the local lordling who wouldn't have been able to afford a day of our services back when we rode."

"Goat farming is an honest living. That's what we all said we wanted. An honest living. I don't mind a little goat smell, but not so much that I want to wallow around with them. That's why I bought the inn and not a farm of my own. What was Eltara doing all these years, boy? Other than raising you, I mean."

Qabil's face tightened, the pinch of buried sorrow narrowing his lips.

"Raising me was most of it, I guess. I never knew her to have a job, but we were never poor. She just…seemed to be able to pay for things. We had a farm in Narim, a small fishing village south of—"

"We know it, lad. We slew a band of orcs that set up shop in a little cave down on the beach about three hours' ride from town. The town fathers were so grateful to us, and so scared the orcs would come back, that they deeded us the land the cave was on. I never did know what happened to that deed…" Leshru's voice trailed off.

"I guess we know now," Nipural said.

"I reckon we do," Leshru agreed. He motioned for Qabil to go on, and took another long pull from his mug. "This wine is good, Nip, but is there any ale in this place?"

"Ale makes me piss too much. I'm old now, friend. I get up in the middle of the night enough without adding sore kidneys to my list of complaints. But go on, boy. Tell us more about Eltara and her quaint fishing village. I'd like hear what became of one of the best blades I've ever ridden with." The smile that twisted the corner of Nipural's face was wry, but warm.

"Not much to tell, really. Narim isn't a big place. Most people either fish, sell fish to traders, carry fish to markets in bigger cities, or sell ale and whiskey to men that either fish, sell fish, or transport fish. It…" A small smile flitted across the young man's face, and Nipural could almost see the boy he had been not so very long ago, with his shaggy curls grown long to hide the tips of his ears and the corners of his eyes, his infectious grin and deep copper skin charming the local girls into a hayloft. Then a shadow passed over his face, probably the memory of why he left Narim, and he aged a decade in an instant as the hard lines of his jaw set, and determination filled his expression.

"We had a good life. I worked our farm and was setting money aside to buy my own in a couple years. I was walking out with a girl, Linnea. She was the blacksmith's daughter, and we were starting to talk about…about a future. Then that bastard Walfert came and brought it all crashing down." The fury in his eyes warred with the grief on his face as the young man fought for control of his emotions. Leshru looked over to Nipural with a raised brow, unsure of what comfort to offer the boy.

"I watched my ma get killed when I was a little boy." The words were quiet, but strong. All eyes swung to Thallis, who sat leaning forward, his elbows on the table and his eyes locked on Qabil. "She served ale and food at the Prancing Lion, just on the edge of the Merchant's Quarter and

Hightown. It was about as good a place as you can get a job without being a noble or getting the attention of one, and most times it's best to not get the attention of a noble."

Thallis reached out and picked up his mug, then set it down with an empty *thunk*. "I washed dishes to pay for my meals. I was probably five or six, and I wasn't quite tall enough to reach into the basin we used for scrubbing the pots, so I had an old milk pail with a hole in the bottom that wasn't no good as a bucket no more, and I turned it upside down and stood on it while I did my work. I was real proud of working so young, of contributing. I was a sucker."

"It wasn't right to make you work that young," Nipural said. "That kind of thing should be reported to the Watch."

Thallis let out a sharp huff of laughter, blowing the air up into his hair and moving it across his brow. "Who do you think eats and drinks every meal at the Lion? The bleeding Watch and their shitbag captain Moreen." He locked eyes with Qabil. "Moreen. That's the bastard I think about like your Walfert. One day I'm going to cut that bastard's liver out, fry it up, and feed it to him before he dies staring into my eyes."

"A captain of the City Watch killed your mother?" Leshru asked, his face grim.

Nipural reached out and put a hand on the big man's forearm. "Put the mug down, Lesh. I don't want to replace my dishes over the lad's tale. Go on, Thallis."

"She was just working. Serving drinks and slices of roast pig, just like every night. And like every night, the place was full to the tits, and at least half the men in there were Watch. So of course when one of *them* puts his hand on my mother's ass, nobody does anything but laugh. Of course when one of *them* pulls her down to sit on her lap, everybody thinks it's hilarious, even though Ma spilt ale all down her good shirt, and now she was going to have to stay up late heating more water to wash it, then hope it dries before lunch tomorrow. But when she slaps the piss out of one who tries to run his hand up her skirt, *that's* not so fucking funny, now, is it?"

Nipural shared a glance with his old friend. They both knew how this story turned out, even if they hadn't seen the outcome sitting right in front of them with unshed tears standing in his eyes.

"So she rang Moreen's bell, right in front of all his men. Well, the big bad guard captain couldn't have that, could he? He had to teach the uppity bitch a lesson, didn't he? It wasn't his fault if she hit her head on the hearth when she fell down. It's not even that he struck her so hard, just a little backhand to remind her of her place." The bitterness in the young thief's voice wouldn't have been out of place in a man of sixty years, rather than a boy barely a quarter that age.

"So I lost my ma and the roof over my head in the same night, thanks to that dripping sore of a man. And someday, he'll die by my hand. I understand what you're after, Ears, so if you'll promise to help me get my revenge one day, I'll help you get yours now." He stood and pushed back his chair, then leaned over the table and held out his hand.

Without a word, Qabil rose and clasped the offered hand. "I'll help you kill Moreen after we let Walfert watch his guts spill out and pool around his feet."

Leshru looked over at his old friend. "We may be the legendary Seven, but these kids might show us a thing or two about bloodthirsty before this mess is all sorted."

Nipural stared at the two grim-faced boys. "There's still a thing or two I remember about how to murder a man. I think I'll remind our old friend Walfert that he's not the only one who can get his hands bloody when the job requires it."

"Does that mean you're with us?" Leshru asked.

"Was there ever really a doubt?"

"Not about you, maybe. But some of the others won't be as easy a sell."

"No, they won't. I expect there's one in particular you'll be wanting me to open the negotiations with?" Nipural's eyebrow crept so high it seemed to almost get lost in an expedition to find the back of the skinny old man's head.

"Well, she is your baby sister," Leshru said, the corner of his mouth twitching as a grin fought to escape.

"Yes, that's why she hates me most of all, you prick. She swore she'd cut my throat and drain me like one of her deer if she ever saw me again."

"Good thing you told me you never believe a word she says." Leshru reached out and clapped the old mage on a bony shoulder.

Nipural leaned forward, rubbing his arm. "Just my luck this will be the time Prynne decides to take up honesty and murders me on sight."

CHAPTER FOUR

They spent the night in the rooms above Nipural's shop, with Qabil and Thallis sharing the apprentice's old room, and Leshru and Nipural bedding down in the old man's broad bed. It wasn't the first time the old adventurers had shared a bunk, but they were both considerably older and more accustomed to their space than they were when they'd traveled the lands with five of their boon companions, bringing some semblance of justice to what pieces of the world they could reach.

Leshru lay awake for a long time, staring at the ceiling. What in all the Hells was he getting himself into? Haring off like he was a buck of twenty summers again, thinking he could just charge through the countryside and pull The Seven back together. Well, more like The Five now, if he could even get everyone else to agree to fight Walfert. Prynne would come, of course. She'd bitch, and she might take a shot at her brother just for old time's sake, but she'd eventually come down from her trees and ride with them. Torgan would start packing armor the second he laid eyes on them, but Xethe…

Did they even really *need* Xethe? The god-touched drunkard was good at many things, but he wasn't a masterful fighter, like Leshru or Eltara. He wasn't a mage of awe-inspiring skill, like Nip, or the blessed of the gods, like Torgan. He couldn't shoot the core out of an apple from a hundred and fifty yards like Prynne. He was really only good at a few things:

drinking, whoring, and getting the lot of them into trouble with his big mouth.

"Thinking about the others?" Nipural's dry voice broke the stillness of the night.

"Aye."

"Wondering if we have to take the songbird along?"

"You know me too well, Nip."

"We do."

"Why? All he's ever done is get us into trouble."

"He's also the one among us Walfert liked best. So he might be the only one with a quick enough tongue to keep Walfert from slaughtering us on sight. We aren't the legendary adventurers we once were, Lesh. We can't go rolling up on a fortified town, especially one that little cutthroat owns lock, stock, and barrel. In the old days all we'd have to do would be ride up to the gates and demand entry, and people would be falling all over themselves to surrender. But those days are almost as old as we are, my friend."

"I know. We need him and his irritating ability to talk his way out of almost as much trouble as he talks us into. Doesn't mean I have to like it."

"If it makes you feel better, make him ride with Torgan. A few days of Dwarven prayer songs should be enough to get even Xethe to rethink his life choices." The old mage's laugh turned into a wheeze, and he sat up in the bed, pounding his chest with a fist.

"What is it, Nip?" Lesh asked, sitting up behind his friend.

"Just a cough I can't seem to shake. It's nothing." He stood up and walked across the bedroom by the light of the moon.

Leshru could see how his friend, always thin, had veered off into the territory of "old and frail" sometime in the decades since they last rode together. He wondered for a moment what he looked like to Nipural, or to Qabil for that matter. Did the boy see anyone in them that could help avenge his mother's murder? Or did he just see a pair of broken-down old men trying to relive their glory days one last time?

"Are we going to be able to do this, Nip? Are we going to be able to fight Walfert and avenge Tara?"

Nipural looked back at his oldest friend and saw worry writ large across his broad brow. Leshru was not one to think on tomorrow, at least not when he last knew the big man. But this Leshru was not the fiercest brawler Relhye had ever seen. This Leshru was a bartender and tavern owner slipping on his gauntlets one more time to aid the son of a fallen friend. The Leshru hadn't bathed in the blood of his enemies for a long, long time.

"I don't know, Lesh," he said, reaching for a bottle of wine on his desk. He pulled out a sturdy wooden chair and sat. With a wave of his hand, he summoned a floating globe of dim yellow light, bathing the room in warm illumination. The old wizard poured himself a glass half-full of the rich, red wine from far off in Kroy, a southern country where he had studied magic as a boy. The smell of familiar grapes always took him back to a time when the world felt less complicated, and when his knees couldn't foretell a change in the weather.

He looked out the window at the moon, just a sliver of a thing, barely casting enough light to pierce the shadowed street between the buildings. A thief skittered across a faraway rooftop, gait as sure along the slick tiled roofs as most people's were on level ground. The old mage wondered how many of his friends would ride home from this adventure. He wondered if he would, then shook his head. No, he wouldn't see this place again after he left it tomorrow. No matter what happened with Walfert, Stinno the pawnbroker died the moment that little brass bell announced Leshru's entrance. The only question remaining was how long Nipural himself would survive his alias.

It had been a good place, Talberg. Big enough to hide from searching enemies, yet small enough that he knew every shopkeeper for three blocks. Burl the Butcher, with his long strings of sausage and his hanging sides of pig. You never asked what went into the making of those sausages, but there were never any stray dogs or cats hanging around the back of the butcher's shop begging for scraps. Findle the Bookseller, who might sell one dusty tome in a fortnight but made his real money forging documents for wealthy and unscrupulous patrons. Patents of nobility were his specialty, but he also did a brisk trade in deeds to faraway lands and letters of ownership of horses whose brands were curiously missing.

Findle was a good enough sort underneath the surface, if you knew where to scratch. Many was the night he stayed up nearly 'til dawn creating papers declaring slaves to be freemen, then appearing out of thin air at the edge of the Slavers' Market auction, holding a sheaf of papers and earning the ire of every man there to sell or buy. Nipural had crafted more than one new set of wards on Findle's doors when a powerful slaver decided the old bookworm's interference had gone too far.

All their faces flashed through his memory as the old man stood looking out over the moonlit cityscape, all her scars and blemishes hidden in the shadows, only the beauty shining through the night. He would miss the girls selling flowers on the streets, blowing into his shop all sweet smells and wide smiles in the winter to get warm. He'd miss the fat baker Olaf, who never failed to pop his head in as he trundled his cart home each night, handing off a loaf of bread or a pair of sticky buns that he couldn't quite manage to sell that day.

He'd even miss Guard Lieutenant Torres, the fastidious twit. The bandy-legged man had stood more than once in front of Stinno's counter, his mustache quivering with fury and demanding that his men be allowed to search the premises for one light-fingered urchin or another, claiming he knew Stinno was hiding the boys, teaching them to be thieves and cutthroats. Nipural never let him past the front counter, only having to resort to calling Watchmaster Dugger twice in all his years in Talberg. Torres never knew why his superior, the man in charge of all city defenses, bowed to the will of this stooped old shopkeeper, and "Stinno" never saw need to tell him.

No, he didn't need to tell the funny little overwrought man about rescuing a small boy from a pair of hungry wargs some three decades before. He didn't need to tell Torres how a mage and his companions were too late to save the boy's parents, but deposited him with an uncle, swaddled in giant blood-soaked wolf pelts, his tears dried but his smile forever dimmed. He didn't need to explain to Torres why the Watchmaster wore a cloak made of black wolf's fur, and always treated the pawnbroker with the utmost respect, even a hint of fondness, and more than a touch of fear. No, he just stood before the self-righteous chaser of footpads, arms folded, and never budged as whatever boy stupid enough to draw the attention of the Guard cowered in the bolthole under the floor waiting for Stinno's all-clear, knowing that the dressing-down he was about to receive from his mentor was perhaps worse than the flogging he'd get from Torres.

Yes, he would miss this place, he thought. Then he looked over at a now-snoring Leshru and realized something else: he'd missed *this*, too. A part of his life he thought long over, a part of himself he thought dead and buried, and he hadn't even known he was missing it until it showed up on his doorstep carrying Eltara's eyes and leading Leshru around like trouble barely leashed. He'd missed the rush of his pulse when he saw his old friend, the flush of blood to his muscles when he hefted his staff again after all these years, the sharpening of his senses as he realized this was no social call. He'd missed being Nipural. He'd missed being a hero.

23

Now he had one last chance to be one, before his body, devastated by years of pouring more magic through it than any sane person could handle, finally gave out. One last chance to make a difference, and he wasn't going to miss that for the world.

$$\cancel{||||}\,||$$

A steady drizzle had all four of them soaked and chilled to the bone before they made it to the city gates the next morning. Qalib rode up front with Thallis and bit his tongue as the nimble thief fidgeted and shifted in his saddle with every clop of his horse's hooves.

"Be still," he chided. "You'll annoy the horse."

"Bugger that to the Hells," Thallis replied, water rolling off his hood to drip down his nose. "The damned animal is annoying my arse!"

"Just wait until tonight," Qalib said, guiding his horse to the side as Leshru moved forward.

"I'll deal with the gate guards," the burly man said. "You two stay quiet and don't stick your noses in anything that doesn't need you. And nothing that gets said until we're clear of town is going to need you." He clucked his tongue and pulled ahead of the trio.

"What's he on about?" Thallis asked, sneering at Leshru's back. "He acts like I ain't been dealing with the guard around here since I was barely big enough to find my own pecker to piss."

"Shut your hole, boy," Nipural said, leaning over his horse's neck to thump Thallis on the shoulder with his staff. "The guards won't give us any trouble leaving, but in weather like this, a shared skin of wine between a traveler and the men watching the gate might be plenty to get us news of the road ahead."

"What kind of news?" Thallis asked, his affected guttersnipe accent gone and his eyes bright with the opportunity to learn something new. Qalib thought as he looked at his new companion that there were more layers to the young thief than he wanted anyone to know.

"Bandits, mostly," Nipural answered, straightening in his saddle. "They'll know if the people coming in the past week or two have seen any increase in robberies or 'unofficial tolls' on bridges or narrow passes through the foothills. But they'll also have any stories about monsters, or press gangs, or slavers working near the city."

"Conscription and taking slaves is illegal in Relhye," Thallis protested.

"So is picking pockets," Nipural replied. "Does that stop you?"

"If I don't get caught, is it really illegal?" Thallis replied with a smirk.

"You and the slavers learned ethics from the same place, apparently." Thallis's smile disappeared at the old man's words, but he pulled his horse forward to get closer to where Leshru stood next to one guard, a portly fellow with a thick beard and a broad, double-headed axe strapped to his back. He looked as much bear as man and let out a raucous laugh at something Leshru said.

"You're a right laugh, Rulesh," the guard said, clapping Leshru on the shoulder. "And a stout one, at that. Where are you headed with two boys and a narrow-assed old fart like Stinno?"

"We have business to the west," Leshru said. "An old friend has started a smithy in Lennox and needed some seed capital. Stinno had a few gems on hand, and a debt to my friend to repay, so I agreed to help the oldster out, keep his back covered as we traveled. The boys want to get out of the city and test the edge of their swords, or maybe get their swords wet some other way, if you know what I mean." Leshru slapped the guard on the shoulder at his ribald remark, and the big man laughed.

"Aye, don't I know it. Some of those farmer's daughters can be fine teachers in the softer arts, and it's a lot cheaper than the pleasure houses. As long as you can outrun their father's plow horse!" Both men laughed, and Leshru passed over his wineskin to the guard.

"Anything we need to be worried about out there?" he asked the guard.

"Been a few more bandit attacks than we're used to seeing this close to town, so I'd be careful once you can't see the city walls any longer. You'll come to a little village not long after nightfall so long as the skinny boy can keep his saddle all day. I'd push on to there and lay out the coin for a spot in the barn. It's rough, but it's a roof and a damn sight better than waking up with a dagger at your throat."

"Aye," Leshru agreed, taking back the wineskin and drinking from it. "I've had that happen once or twice. It's not an experience I care to repeat."

"I'd think not. One thing to note, though. I'd have the boys keep their hoods up and eyes down in some of the smaller towns. Some folks don't like elves lately, even ones a couple generations removed from the forest."

"I've heard that," Leshru said, a lie given that he and Qabil had avoided speaking to anyone between his tavern and Talberg. "Any idea what it's about?"

"Not really. There are some going around saying the elves are just trying to infiltrate our cities so they can eventually wipe us out. I even heard one idiot yesterday saying we should make everyone with any elf blood register with the guard when they come to a city. It's like he didn't even know Queen Joelle was half-elven herself. It's stupid, but prejudice is on the rise, so I thought I'd say something before your boys run into it unawares."

"Thanks for the warning. And keep the wine. I've at least got a hope of riding out of this storm today. You're stuck standing right here." Leshru swung back up into the saddle and walked his horse over to where the others waited for him.

"You all hear that?" he asked.

"Yeah," Thallis said. "People don't like elves. What else is new?"

"What's new is that it isn't stupid kids saying stupid kid things or old men muttering into their cups," Leshru said. "It's adults saying them out loud and in public. People have always had their stupid fears of anything different. But at least they used to try to hide it. If they're open enough and violent enough that he thought to warn me for your sake, things are getting bad out there."

"Should I glamour the boys to hide their ears?" Nipural asked.

"No," Leshru said after a moment. "Let's see what happens in this first village. If it's as small as the guard says, we won't have a problem dealing with any trouble that raises its head." He gave the old mage a cold smile and everyone in the party was suddenly reminded why dukes and lords paid homage to The Seven when the band of mercenaries rode through their lands.

"Let's go then," Nipural said after a moment. "We're not getting any drier standing here in the rain."

CHAPTER FIVE

W hat happened in the first village was...nothing. A few sharp looks and one or two men making the sign against the evil eye as they rode past, but no one attacked them, tried to sneak into the stable to harm their horses as they slept, or even said a cross word to them. If they charged a silver more for a mug of ale than Leshru was accustomed to, he couldn't say if it had more to do with the boys' ears or with the simple fact that they were likely the first people in months to stop in the tavern that didn't live within a mile of the town square.

The story was the same in the next village, and the one after that. They encountered nothing worse than scowls for several days, but on the fifth day, things took a darker turn. They rounded a bend to find a large oak laying across the road, blocking passage from either direction. The tree stretched from a deep ditch on one side of the road to a hastily constructed barricade on the other. The barricade, a series of boards nailed together and affixed to a post hammered into the ground on the edge of the forest, was manned by a fat brigand with a rusty halberd who sat on a stump with a brown jug beside him.

As Leshru and the others rode into view, the rotund man heaved himself up, wobbled a little before planting the butt of his polearm in the ground for balance, then waddled over to stand at the side of the road.

"Halt in the name of the Black Rangers," he said, his voice booming through the dense woods surrounding the road. It was the perfect place for a toll barrier, if Leshru was being honest. The tree was too big for a horse to comfortably jump, and Gods only knew what was scattered on the other side of it. He could see foot-long stakes whittled into points on the near side to deter riders, and he assumed the other side was similarly booby-trapped. On the right side of the road, a steep ditch had been further excavated to make it completely impassable without riding far into the woods, and the trees were close together on both sides of the road. A column of riders could weave through the forest single file, but looking at the setup, the old adventurer had no doubt there were traps scattered throughout the woods.

He reined in his horse and slid to the ground, holding up both hands as the sentry lowered the axe head of the halberd to aim at his throat.

"That's far enough. Don't go getting no ideas about swordplay, old-timer. I've got a big damned axe, and I know how to use it."

"At least half that is true," Thallis muttered, earning himself a sharp look from Nipural.

"Just getting down to reach my saddlebags better," Leshru said. "Who are the Black Rangers and by whose authority do you stop us?"

"We're the unofficial rulers of these parts, you could say," the man replied. "We handle some of the duke's less centralized tax collection." He laughed and lifted his halberd, once again leaning on the long haft of the weapon. "Toll's five silvers per horse. Or we can take the horses. Your choice."

"Five silvers!" Thallis exclaimed. "That's highway robbery."

"I believe that is exactly what it is," Leshru agreed, his dark face splitting open in a wide smile. "This being a highway, and this fat slob being a robber, or at least what passes for one this far out from anywhere a civilized criminal wants to make a living."

Thallis looked around at the trees and dirt road with a sneer. "Got that right. I wouldn't be caught dead out here if I didn't want to see what kind of trouble you lot are going to get into."

"Oi!" the pudgy guard said, his face flushing red. "You just call me a fat slob? I'll cut your balls off, old man!"

"And so it begins," Nipural said, reaching behind him and pulling his staff from where he had lodged it beneath his packs. "Again."

Leshru turned back to the would-be robber. "Look, tubby. I'm going to give you one chance here. You can either open the gate and sit down on your stump until we pass, then try to milk the next poor farmer out of his last brass pennies in an hour, or you can push your luck with me and end up with the handle of that polearm shoved so far up your arse you'll be picking splinters out your ears for a week. It's your decision, lad, but I know which side I'd be on if I were you."

The big man's friendly expression never wavered, but his smile didn't touch his eyes, which were colder than midwinter snow. While he talked, he reached down to his belt and pulled off a pair of heavy banded gauntlets and slipped them on, then tightened the wrist straps with leather thongs. The gloves were massive, ferocious-looking things with wide iron bands across the knuckles and thick padding on the inside to protect his hands from the impact. It had been many years since Leshru wore them, but they fit as well as the first day he'd had them made. It felt good to put them back on. Good, and final, like some part of his life was coming to a close. *Ah well,* he thought. *It was good while it lasted. Should have known I wasn't going to die a bartender.*

"What's it going to be, boy? You going to get out of the way, or am I going to lead my friends over you?"

"What if I say my friends are going to even up the odds a little, grandpa?" the guard asked, then let out a sharp whistle. Four men stepped out of the trees, bows in hand with arrows nocked. A mountain of a man with braids down his back came around the opposite end of the tree, and a slight man with a thin-bladed sword in one hand and a dagger in the other vaulted the tree to stand before Qabil's horse.

"I'd say you're still outnumbered, idiot," Leshru said as he stepped forward, slapping away the halberd as it came down. He brought a gauntleted fist up on the point of the fat brigand's chin, and the chubby bandit dropped to the ground.

"Well, shit," Nipural said, turning his horse to face the pair of archers to the right of the road. He raised his staff and a globe of white energy streaked out of the tip, exploding in a blinding flash before the two men. "Qabil?" he called.

"I've got the other two," the young man said. "Thallis, can you deal with our two-bladed friend?"

"Anything to get off this fucking horse," the thief said, joy suffusing his voice as he kicked his feet free of the stirrups and slid down off the back of his mount. He dropped to the ground, rolling to his left, and came up with a throwing dagger in hand. He let fly with his blade, only to watch it bounce harmlessly into the dust as the swordsman swept it out of the air with his rapier. "Nice one," he said. "Looks like I might have a fight after all."

"Don't worry, boy," the black-clad man said, slashing through the air a few times with his sword. "You won't have a fight for very long."

Tearing his gaze away from his new friend, Qabil spun his horse and unslung his bow from around the saddle horn in a smooth motion. He yanked two arrows from a quiver by his leg, put one between his teeth and nocked the other. Without hesitation, he drew and released before the first archer even selected a target. The man dropped to the ground, gurgling around the arrow sticking out of his throat. Qabil put his second arrow in the other man's shoulder, rendering his arm useless but missing any major arteries. He spun the horse around to check on his friends.

Leshru, after making short work of the halberdier, strode across the packed earth to the braided man, who unlimbered a long-handled hammer from his belt. "Fat Garth is stupid and slow, but he's Her Lady's little brother, so I'm gonna have to kill you now. We got orders not to let anybody hurt him."

"Your orders should be to make sure he doesn't engage with anyone more capable than you lot," Leshru said. "You're down four archers and we haven't even tussled yet."

"Four?" the big man asked, turning to look behind him. "Shit."

Nipural stood by his horse at the side of the road, leaning on his staff. The two archers he blinded were sitting on the ground with their feet stretched out before them, vines growing up from the ground and holding them fast.

"Oh well," the big man said. "Orders is orders. You hurt Fat Garth, so I gotta kill you."

"I know about orders," Leshru said. "I did more than one thing in my time that I didn't want to do on account of them. Come at me, then." He raised his fists, and the big man grinned, then paled.

He took a step back and lowered his hammer. "I know you. Ain't but one man ever took to a fight with nothing but gloves and a grin. You quit the life before I was even born."

"Aye," Leshru replied. "But it didn't quit me. We going to dance, or you going to bow out?"

"Fuck this," the giant said, tossing his hammer to the dirt. "Drop 'em, boys! This is Leshru Brokeblade. He's the baddest son of a bitch on Watalin. I don't know who his friends are, but if they ride with the Brokeblade, they ain't no one to fuck with."

"You sure, Ram?" the little man with the two blades called over his shoulder. "I'm pretty sure I can gut the kid without him getting a cut in on me."

"Maybe," Qabil said from where he sat astride his mount with an arrow aimed at the man's chest. "But you'll be dead before the first drop of his blood hits the ground."

"Don't worry about me," Thallis said. "I'm harder to gut than I look." He spun the daggers he was holding between his fingers, and the knives seemed to disappear into thin air. "So we ain't gonna fight? Does this mean I got to get back on the gods-damned horse?"

"No, we aren't going to fight. Yes, you have to get back on the horse. But first cut every bowstring you find. I trust this big one to keep his friends from riding after us, but let's not tempt fate by showing our backs to an arrow."

"Still remember that time outside of Lethes, eh?" Nipural said, chuckling.

"That scar aches every time it snows," Leshru said, taking off his gauntlets and hanging them once more from his belt. He walked over to the big man and stuck out his hand. "Leshru of the Broken Blade. Thank you for not making me kill you."

"Ram. Not got any kind of fancy last bit to go with it. Thank you for not making me and my friends all pay with our lives for our insult," the big man replied.

"What the fuck is this?" the little black-clad man said, stalking over to where the two men stood shaking hands. "First you don't let me gut the kid, now you fucking *apologize* to this oldster? Who the fuck do you think you are, old man?"

Leshru let go of Ram's massive hand, then spun on his heel, back-handing the little swordsman across the face. The slender man spun completely around before sitting straight down on his ass in the middle of the road, looking for all the world like a poleaxed steer. "You should respect your elders, little man," Leshru said. "Some of us only lived this long at the expense of mouthy little pups like yourself."

Then he reached down, pulled the man to his feet by his sword belt, divested him of his blades, and punched him right between the eyes. The already-dazed bandit's eyes rolled back in his head and he fell straight back, unconscious before he hit the ground.

"They said you hit harder than any man alive," the giant brigand said, a tone of awe in his voice. "Now I believe it. I've seen trolls that couldn't shut him up."

"I'm stronger than most trolls," Leshru replied, without a hint of braggadocio in his tone. "Now I'm going to leave you your hammer, and your men can keep their blades. But no bows, like I told the boy, and this little popinjay was rude, so he gets his toys taken away. That seem fair?"

"I think you should take his and Garth's purses, too. They deserve it."

"I already lifted the black-clad idiot's the second he turned his back on me," Thallis said, jingling a leather purse in his hand.

Ram looked him up and down and nodded. "You ever get tired of riding behind a legend, boy, you come back here and we'll find you honest work robbing travelers."

"No thanks," the young thief said. "I live through this shit, I'm going back to Talberg to murder a guard captain. After that, I plan to never see another tree as long as I live."

"Good to have goals," the big bandit said, picking up his hammer and dragging the small bladesman back to where the archers sat bound by tree roots. "How long will they be stuck like that?"

"About an hour," Nipural said. "You should bind the other one's shoulder. He won't die if he gets attention, but no promises otherwise."

"Let him bleed," Ram said. "He cheats at cards. Safe travels. I'll send word ahead to all of The Lady's men that you're not to be disturbed. Can't count on all of them being smart enough to listen, but it should help."

"Thank you," the mage said, mounting his horse. "Come along, gentlemen. I believe our work here is done." He waved a hand and the barricade rose.

As they passed the huge fallen tree, Thallis leaned over to Qabil. "This is the strangest crew I ever worked in."

"Just wait until they run up against a challenge," the almond-eyed boy said, his eyes lingering over the body of the archer he'd killed. He knew as he rode by that the young bandit's round face and open staring eyes would hang in front of his memories for a long time before he slept that night.

CHAPTER SIX

W hat's got you so damned jumpy, Nip? How long has it been since you saw her?" Leshru asked as they led their horses off the road and onto a deer trail that Nipural claimed would lead them to his sister's home deep in the woods. The day was bright, but the trees dense and the forest floor carpeted with thick pine needles that muffled the sound of their mounts.

It seemed to Qabil that Nipural wasn't the only one nervous. There was an edge to Leshru's voice that was unfamiliar, and Thallis... Well, Thallis hadn't looked comfortable since the gates of Talberg fell out of sight behind them, and Qabil thought it unlikely that would change until he had cobblestones beneath his feet and a maze of buildings to get lost in again.

"Fifteen, no...seventeen years," the elderly mage replied, his gaze darting about like a bird on a slate roof in midsummer. "It didn't go well."

"You two always fought like cats and dogs," Leshru said. "What happened this time?"

"I may have insulted the man she had taken up with, and she may have threatened to shoot me if she ever saw me again."

"She used to threaten to shoot you once a week at least," the burly fighter replied.

"Yes, but she didn't mean it then. This was different."

"How so?"

"She'd already shot me once in my left arm." Nipural rolled up the sleeve of the black shirt he wore and held it up. Qabil saw a two-inch red scar just above the old man's wrist. "She said if she ever saw me again the next one would go through my neck."

"She actually shot you?" Leshru said, chuckling. "You must have really made her angry this time. What did you do, sleep with the man? No, Prynne's not enough of the jealous type to shoot you over that. Did you ensorcel his privates so he couldn't perform? *That* would make her mad."

"I did nothing of the sort. I didn't think he was trustworthy, so I may have...investigated a little."

"You snooped," Leshru corrected, a scowl contorting his dark features. "I told you that your curiosity would be the death of you." He paused. "What did you find?"

"I was right," Nipural said. "The bastard had been bought right out from under Prynne's nose. He was working for the baron to see if Prynne and her group of foresters were really bandits pretending to tend the forest and chase down poachers."

"Which, of course, they were."

"Well, yes, they were, but they weren't like that bunch we saw a few days ago. They were more judicious in their targets."

"Meaning?" Thallis piped up, his interest piqued once the subject of thievery was broached.

"Meaning they robbed the tax collectors, wealthy merchants from other lands, and had been known to shoot at the local sheriff if he was meting out justice in a way Prynne felt was too harsh," Nipural replied.

"So you uncovered a traitor in her crew, and she got pissed at *you* for it?" Thallis said, scoffing. "Women, am I right?" He looked around, a smirk on his face.

That smirk vanished as the air flew from his lungs. The young thief looked up from where he lay flat on his back in the middle of the woods. "Hey! Which one of you did that?" He sprang to his feet and drew his dagger, glaring at Leshru and Nipural.

"That was Nip," Leshru said. "You disrespect his sister again and it'll be my turn. Then you'll know that he's the gentle one between us. Now get up and grab your horse before she wanders off. And if another snide word crosses your lips about Prynne... Well, it's hard to talk with a broken jaw."

Thallis stomped over to the big man. "I'll slice off your ears and nose before you can blink, old man. You think I lived this long on the streets on account of my looks? Not a chance. I'm faster than almost any man alive, and you lay a finger—" His words cut off as Leshru did just that. He stuck out one sausage-thick finger and poked the boy, just once, at the place where his armor bent in the middle. He jabbed his finger into the boy's belly hard enough to drive all the air from his lungs again, even through the leather armor he wore. Thallis dropped to one knee and looked up at the old warrior, something like respect in his eyes.

"What will you do if I lay a finger on you, boy?" Leshru asked, his face stony. "I suggest you stay down there until you decide if today is the day you die. I don't want to hurt you, but yours won't be the first grave I've dug in a copse of trees in my day."

"I...I'm sorry," Thallis said, sheathing his dagger and getting up slowly. "I let me temper run away with me. Won't happen again."

Leshru smiled, and his white teeth gleamed through his thick salt-and-pepper mustache. "Don't make promises you can't keep, boy. You're a hothead, and young besides. You'll lose your temper again before we finish this journey, and that's to be expected." His smile vanished, and the stone-faced killer once again stood before the shaken thief. "But you draw steel on me, or any other member of this party again, and you'll die without ever seeing Talberg once more. This I promise you."

He held out a hand to the boy, who shook it and nodded. "I understand. Don't kill any of this crew. Got it."

"I'm fairly certain that he just showed you that what you really mean to say is 'don't *try* to kill any of this crew,'" Nipural said. "Now if you two are finished dancing, can we get on with finding my sister?"

"I don't think that will be necessary, sir," Qabil said, deciding to err on the side of too much respect rather than too little.

"Why not, son? We need her bow if we're to have any chance of dealing with Walfert."

"I know that," the young man replied, pointing all around them. "But we don't need to find her. I'm pretty sure the men with bows mean she's found us."

He gestured to the woods in front of them, where two men in green and brown mottled leathers stood with arrows nocked to longbows. Two more men appeared on either side of them, also with arrows to string, and a final pair stepped out from behind trees in the direction they'd come from, effectively cutting off their narrow avenue of escape.

"Well, I hope this is the right forest-dwelling bunch of armed men,"

Thallis said, raising his hands above his head. "Otherwise, this could be downright embarrassing."

"Don't worry, young man," said a ringing female voice. "It's almost certainly going to get embarrassing regardless, at least for my brother."

"Hello, Prynne," Nipural said, making sure to keep his hands in full view.

"Hello, Nip. Lesh, what are you doing here? I thought you swore off stupid adventures and opened a bar."

"I did," said the big man. "But we've got a situation that needs dealt with, and it's the kind of thing only The Seven can handle."

At the mention of The Seven, there was a sharp gasp from one of the archers and a quiet murmur from some of the others. Prynne sighed. "Yes, yes. These men were once part of the legendary Seven—adventurers, heroes, villains, and holders of the least original name for a party in history. We had a perfectly serviceable bard. Why didn't we let him come up with a name for our group?"

"Because that idiot would have either had us named something lewd that would get us thrown out of every town in Relhye, or something so flowery and convoluted no one but a bard would be able to remember it. Now can I put my hands down or are you going to have your lackeys shoot me?" Nipural asked with a growl.

"I promise you, *brother*," the woman said, her voice grim. "If anyone here is going to put an arrow in you, it will be me."

"Good enough," the wizard replied, putting his hands down. "Now take us to your camp; we have business to discuss."

"The only business we have to discuss is how much I'm going to tax you for trespassing in my forest," said the woman. "I'm not going anywhere with you, ever. Maybe Lesh if he asked nicely, but I don't know these boys, and I don't like you. So go home, Nip. Sit by a fire and warm your old bones. It's pushing on toward winter and I know how your knees hurt when it gets cold."

"Would that I could, sister," Nipural said. "But Leshru had the right of it. We have a problem that needs solving. Permanently."

She let out a sigh and turned, walking back into the woods. "Fine. If you're not going to leave, and I'm going to have to listen to you drone on about changing the fate of the world, I at least want to do it with a drink in my hand."

"It's not the world," Qabil said, and Prynne froze in mid-stride.

She turned back to the boy, one eyebrow climbing heavenward as she stared at him. She didn't speak, nor did she make any threatening moves, but Qabil knew as surely as he knew his arse ached from riding for weeks, that if he stepped wrong here, it would likely be his final mistake.

After an interminable stretch of silence, Qabil swallowed hard and said, "The world is not in danger. At least I don't think so. I don't know if anyone is in danger, if I'm being honest. Well, I suppose I am, because it's me that's brought this whole thing on in the first place. I need justice, you see. He murdered my mother, and I mean to see him dead for it."

Prynne studied him, her blue eyes calculating. She looked far younger than her brother, but whether that was from actual age or the toll the magic had exacted from Nipural's physical well-being, no one could say. "You look familiar, boy. Who was your mother?"

Before Qabil could speak, Leshru cut in. "You know whose child this is, Prynne. Look at his eyes."

The archer's eyes narrowed, then she drew in a sharp breath. "Tara? You're Eltara's son?"

Qabil held her steady gaze. "I am. She was murdered by her former companion, a bastard thief named Walfert, and I plan to see him dead by my hand for it."

"Is this true, Nip?" Prynne asked, turning to her brother. All the anger and verbal jousting was gone. Her eyes brimmed with tears, and a flush of anger crept up her pale cheeks. "Did that backstabbing rodent kill the princess?"

"Aye, Prynne. He did. He's decided he's the Lord Mayor of Lennox now. We're headed there to remind him that we were more than just some fools who rode together killing and pillaging."

"We were family," Leshru said, his deep voice rumbling through the small clearing.

"We are family," Prynne said. "And no one hurts my family. No one but me, anyway," she added, with a glance at Nipural's arm. "Does the arm hurt much?"

"Only when it's cold." He let out a wry chuckle. "You're right, though. At my age, everything hurts when it's cold, so I barely notice your little parting gift. Most of the time."

"I still have yours, too," Prynne said, patting a knife at her side.

"That come from the traitorous little shit?"

"I found it. It was like a rose in winter, just growing from between his ribs, a solitary bloom."

"Never knew you for knife work when you could avoid it, Prynne," Leshru said.

"He fucked me, Lesh. He fucked me, and then he planned to fuck me more by handing me over to that corpulent worm Baron Dusen. He was going to help that thieving scum hang me in the market square. I wanted to see his eyes when he realized he was dying at my hand."

"I always knew you were the dangerous sibling," Leshru said.

"I never argued that fact," Nipural agreed.

"Come on, you two. Bring your squires and let's get something to eat. There was a fat turkey on the fire when Roland told us of a pair of geriatric idiots tromping through our woods."

"Geriatric?" Leshru said, following the willowy woman as she turned and walked away.

"Squires?" Thallis asked, shooting a questioning glance at Qabil.

"Don't argue with her," Qabil said. "She shot her brother, and she mostly likes him. Think what she'll do to you."

"I heard that!" Prynne called back over her shoulder. "He's not wrong, by the way."

CHAPTER SEVEN

S o what's the plan?" Prynne asked as she passed a jug of wine to Leshru. They were seated around a fire in the middle of Prynne's camp in the woods. It didn't look like any bandit camp Qabil ever imagined, more like a village sprang up in a clearing beside a stream. There were two long bunkhouses, low-slung buildings with roofs covered in branches that made the structures almost disappear into the woods around them if you weren't looking closely. Apart from the bunkhouses stood a small cottage where Prynne and a couple of her lieutenants slept. The cottage stood out, but what appeared for all the world to be run-down and deserted from the outside, was actually very cozy and well-built once you stepped inside. The cooking was done outside, on a stove cut out of the side of a massive boulder, with a curtain of vines that could drop down over it at a moment's notice.

A few quick words from sentries and messengers as they passed through the camp and Qabil realized that Prynne was "the Lady" that the first bunch of bandits they encountered were talking about. He wondered how far her reach extended, and how much of the countryside belonged to the rulers in name only.

They sat on stumps and rocks to eat, and as Qabil took in the encampment, he thought that it was entirely possible for someone to ride right into the middle of the place, with two dozen men and women in their homes within a stone's throw, and see nothing but an abandoned hovel with an overlarge fire pit out front and a privy bigger than the house warranted. It was ingenious camouflage, really. They provided almost exactly what someone wandering through the woods expected to see, and most people wouldn't look just below the surface to see the truth of the matter.

"Plan?" Leshru asked, his face a picture of innocence as he took a deep draught from the jug. "You know me, Prynne. I'm not the planning type. I'm the punch things until they stop annoying me type. You and Nip always were the deep thinkers of the group."

"Yeah, see where that got us," Prynne muttered.

"Alive and wealthy, if I recall," Nipural shot back. He let out a long sigh. "Let it go, sister. I am sorry for the way I handled things with your traitorous lover. It was petty of me to announce to the entire crew that he was setting you up. I shouldn't have been such a prick."

Prynne looked at him with her jaw set. She stared across the fire at her brother as if looking for the lie on his face. Then she relaxed and sighed, matching her brother almost precisely. "I'm sorry I shot you. I shouldn't have expected anything different. You've been a prick your whole life— why would you change?"

"That may very well be the worst apology in history," Qabil mock-whispered to Thallis.

Everyone laughed at that, and the tension around the fire lifted. "Now," continued Prynne, "about that plan?"

"We get the remaining members of your band together, and you help get me close enough to Walfert to slit his throat," Qabil said.

"Have you ever slit anyone's throat, boy?" Prynne asked. Her posture was relaxed, leaned back against the bole of a giant oak tree, but her blue eyes pierced the gathering dusk. She regarded Qabil coolly, one long arm stretched over a massive brown dog that lay next to her, its tail thumping against the dirt as she scratched between its ears.

"I've killed people," Qabil replied, his voice rising to match the color on his cheeks. "And I watched my mother die at this man's hands, so it will be an easy thing to watch him die at mine."

"I hope that's not true," Prynne said, her voice soft. Qabil leaned in to hear her next words. "It shouldn't be easy, boy. It should never be easy. I'm an archer. I've killed men from over a hundred yards away, so far away I couldn't even tell what he looked like. I couldn't see the pain on his face as the arrow pierced his throat, the confusion as he fell to the ground wondering what happened to him and why it was getting dark. I couldn't see the light go out of his eyes as his blood spilled out onto the grass along with everything he ever hoped to be. But it wasn't easy." She took another long pull from her wine jug and continued, staring into the fire as she spoke.

"It's easy for men like Walfert. Small men. Jealous little rodents in man-suits that value only their own wants and desires. Bastards like that think only of what they want, what they can get, and how they can put one over on someone else. They don't think of the wife of the young soldier falling to her knees in the doorway, or the child looking at the stone-faced man who made her mother cry. They don't think that the person they killed has value, maybe even more than they do, and that makes it easy." She lifted her eyes to meet Qabil's across the flame.

"The moment it becomes easy is the moment you become one of them. That's when you're no longer one who hunts the wicked, but one that we hunt. Don't let it be easy, boy. You ride with this crew, you'll soon take a life. Hell, the look on your face tells me you already have. Remember that life. Remember what it felt like to watch that man die and watch every desire, every laugh, every tear, every smile fade from his face. Remember that, every day, and don't ever let it be easy."

Qabil held her gaze for one, maybe two heartbeats, then he sprang to his feet and dashed off into the woods. Leshru stirred, but Thallis held up a hand. "Stay, grandpa. I think he's listened to the voice of experience enough for one night." The young thief stood without a sound and slipped into the darkness beyond the trees, following Qabil's noisy progress through the woods.

"Well, Prynne," Nipural said, reaching for the jug. "I'm so happy to see you still have your charm."

The morning dawned clear with a new crispness to the air, as if Fall were approaching from some distance but wanted to send a messenger along ahead to let everyone know it would be there soon with its sister Winter in tow. Leshru rolled his head from side to side, trying to loosen up neck muscles unaccustomed to sleeping on the ground after years of softer, and safer, living. He spied Nipural sitting cross-legged by the fire, meditating as he did every morning to restore his connection to the magic, and he could hear the grumbling of Thallis and Qabil as they rolled out of their tent and staggered into the woods to relieve themselves.

This doesn't feel the same, he thought as he began a series of stretches and slow movements designed to limber up his massive frame. *Some of the players are the same, but it feels different somehow.* He bent at the waist, pressing his palms flat to the ground before leaning forward until he balanced on his hands with his body parallel to the packed dirt of the clearing.

"Looking good there, granther," Thallis said with only the slightest hint of mocking to his tone. "Not many thick ones like you can do the *Vallar-dun.*"

"Not many street rats recognize martial arts from half a globe away," Leshru replied, slowly lowering himself to his feet.

"A priest of Tenriyu spent some time last year in the market. He did his exercises every morning before he set up his basket weaving. It looked interesting, so I learned a bit." The boy stepped in next to Leshru and began to follow his motions exactly as the old warrior went through his morning exercises.

"If he taught you this, he was more than just a wandering priest," Leshru replied. "These forms are how the priests teach their initiates to focus their minds and attune themselves to their bodies." Back on both feet, he raised both hands to the sky, shoulder width apart, then brought them together, exhaling slowly as he drew his hands down in front of his face.

Leshru went through the motions of the *Vallar-dun* for the next quarter hour, watching out of the corner of his eye as the wiry thief matched his every movement. In silent unison they stood, bent, crouched, and contorted themselves, every movement in agonizing slowness as they focused on the awakening of each muscle used to bring their bodies to full wakefulness.

As they reached the final pose, Leshru wondered if the boy really had learned the entire cycle, or if he would cut his routine short. He bent once more at the waist, palms flat on the dirt, and leaned forward. Slowly, almost painfully slowly, he shifted his center of gravity over his arms, flexed his elbows slightly to take the weight, then straightened his legs over his head, inching toward a perfectly vertical handstand, but making the transition so slowly as to leave his arms screaming with the effort and sweat beading on his forehead from the focus.

At long last the old warrior stood, perfectly inverted, then drew himself downward, leaned his face back, and pressed his lips to the dirt, completing the ritual of greeting the morning sun and thanking the earth for relinquishing death's embrace upon him for another day. Then he exploded upward, pushing off the ground with all his strength, and landed on his feet, sweat streaming down his face.

He heard the *slap* of boots to his left and turned to see Thallis grinning over at him. "Never saw the old priest do *that*," the boy said, a slight pant in his voice. "Fun, though. Good warmup. Thanks, granther. I needed a stretch after sleeping on the dirt all night. Time for a wash and a nosh, eh?" The boy turned and jogged over to where Qabil stood with his arms folded, watching the two of them practice. The boys said something to one of Prynne's rangers standing nearby, then headed off into the woods, presumably to scrub off in a nearby stream.

"Warmup," Leshru grumbled. "I'm over here sweating like I've carried a mule up a mountain and the pup calls it a warmup. I never should have lived this long."

"I remember a few times we almost didn't," Prynne's voice came from behind him, and Leshru turned to see her holding out a sausage roll and a mug of water. "We really going after Walfert, Lesh?"

The grizzled warrior looked at her, tall and whipcord-thin as always, but with gray streaking her hair and crow's feet nestled in the corners of her eyes. "Aye, Prynne, we are. I don't know if we'll kill him, but we owe it to the princess to try."

"And the boy? What do we owe him?"

"First crack at the rat, I guess."

"You know Walfert will carve that boy open and wear his guts for a necklace."

"Probably," the big man said with a nod. "But maybe that'll distract the dirty little bastard long enough for you to put an arrow through his eye."

"You're horrible, Lesh."

"Never claimed to be anything else, Prynne. Never claimed to be anything else. Let's wake up Nipural and get the horses saddled. We've got a long way to go if we're going to find Torgan before it snows."

"Snows? What the Hells, Lesh? It's months until the first snowfall."

"Sure it is. Here. But Torgan ain't here, is he?"

"Oh bugger a duck. Don't tell me he—"

"Aye. He went home. We want the Steelhammer, we've got to go get him. Last I heard, and this was a couple years back, he was mining diamonds near the Dragon Peaks."

"I hate the mountains, Lesh."

"And I hate people killing my friends. Now you have to put up with the mountains so I can get revenge on the foul little weasel what killed my friend. Now go wake up your brother while I get cleaned up. And see if there's any more of them sausage rolls left. That was good."

CHAPTER EIGHT

I hate the cold, Lesh," Nipural grumbled as he leaned as low to his horse's neck as he could and stay astride, trying to break some of the chilling wind.

"At least you've got that stupid hood," his companion replied, raising his voice over the driving snow. "I'm stuck with practically nothing."

"I also have hair, old friend," the wizard said with a chuckle. "But it's only helping so much. How much longer are we in this weather?"

"No idea until your sister gets back," the big warrior replied. "I think we should try to find some sort of shelter, though. The boys are looking worse than us, and that's saying something."

"The boys," Qabil and Thallis, were indeed looking thoroughly miserable in the sudden snowfall. Qabil had his cloak wrapped around himself as tightly as he could manage and was hunched over the saddle in a formless lump of gray wool, while Thallis was nothing but a long pointed nose protruding from a hodgepodge of random fabrics hastily yanked from both young men's saddlebags when they realized that while the short oiled cloak Thallis brought from Talberg kept him dry enough, his supple leathers did nothing to keep him warm in the freezing mountains.

Qabil looked ahead, marveling at how Leshru just plodded along, no concession to the driving weather but a small knit cap pulled down over his bald head and ears. The old warrior was either mad or really was incapable of feeling pain, as the legends said. For himself, he was near the

45

point of feeling nothing at all. His legs were completely numb from the knees down, and the only reason he knew he still had fingers was he could see his gloves frozen to the saddle horn in front of him.

The quartet of miserable adventurers rounded a bend in the narrow mountain pass, putting them momentarily on the leeward side of a rock outcropping. Leshru held up a fist, and Qabil gratefully snapped his ice-covered reins to bring his horse to a halt. Leshru slid off his mount and trudged back to stand between the boys.

"We'll stop here until Prynne gets back. Thallis, grab two ridgepoles and stick them in the ground over there." He indicated a spot about eight feet from the rock face. "Qabil, unload both tents and roll out the fabric."

"What are you doing?" Thallis asked, ever-curious.

"I can tell you about it while we freeze our dicks off, or we can do it and get thawed a little. Which would you prefer?" Leshru snarled.

Thallis half-slid, half-tumbled from his horse, the thick fabric encasing his limbs making the movements stiff and slow. He snapped together the ridgepoles of the two tents they carried and jabbed them into the ground, leaning on them to make sure they were planted sturdily. When he finished, he turned to where Qabil had the tents laid out flat on the snow-covered ground, and watched as Nipural jabbed his staff into the ground and closed his eyes. With a muttered phrase and a brief jolt of energy through the air, the two panels of canvas inched closer together until they were one huge woven sheet.

As all this was happening, Leshru scaled the rockface some ten feet, and with a small hammer on his belt, drove four spikes into the cliffside. He motioned for Qabil to pass him up one corner of the fabric, and in a matter of moments, he had one side of the now double-sized tent fastened to the mountain. Thallis saw what he was doing and snapped the large brass rings Leshru tossed him to the grommets on the far edges of the tent fabric, then clipped them to the tops of the ridgepoles. In a matter of moments, they had erected a small lean-to sloping from the rock face to the poles jabbed in the ground, with the sides of the tents hanging down to block the worst of the wind.

"Bring the horses in here and hobble them along the sides," Leshru called. As Qabil and Thallis did this, Nipural walked into the center of the shelter and slammed the end of his staff on the ground three times. With the third strike, Thallis felt that *rush* of magic coming from the old man once again, and his mouth fell open as a circle of grass appeared around the magician, widening until, in seconds, the ground in a ten-foot circle around Nipural's feet was clear of snow and steaming with newfound heat.

"This'll keep us from freezing to death until Prynne gets back," Leshru said.

"And when she does, we can decide if we rest here for the night or move on," Nipural said with a nod.

"That'll be resting here, then," said Prynne, leading her horse into the already crowded shelter. "I made it another few leagues, but the snow shows no signs of stopping, and I turned back when I couldn't tell where mountain stopped and canyon began."

"Aye," Leshru agreed. "Then we stop. We can't ride where we can't see, and one step off these trails and no one will find our bodies until spring. But look on the bright side, boys," the grizzled warrior said with a broad grin splitting his dark face.

"What's that?" Qabil asked, knowing he wasn't going to like the answer but deciding to get it out of the way already.

"You don't have far to go to fetch water for supper!" Leshru said with a grand gesture at the snow surrounding their meager shelter.

"I hate you sometimes, old man," the young man grumbled, but started shoveling snow into waterskins and setting them near the pit where Prynne was building a fire.

"Just wait until you know him better, kid," the ranger said. "Then you'll hate him all the time."

"Nip!" Leshru protested. "Your sister's being mean to me!"

"Better you than me," the old wizard said, pulling saddlebags off his own horse.

It was short work to make a close camp under the stretched fabric, and even shorter work to throw jerky into a pot with melted snow and a handful of vegetables for stew. After they had all eaten, Leshru pulled out a flask and leaned back on his saddle, sipping his whiskey.

"So what have you been up to all these years, Prynne? Living the outlaw life, robbing the rich, giving to the poor like some legend?" the bald man asked as he wiped a few errant drops of amber liquid from his whiskers.

Prynne looked up from where she was unstringing her longbow and wrapping the weapon in waxed cloth to protect it from the weather. "Aye, a bit of that. I worked as a caravan guard across the Nurani Desert for a few years, but I got bored. After three or four years, no one robbed any of our caravans anymore."

"You killed every bandit in the Nurani?" Thallis asked, holding out his hand for the flask. He scowled when Leshru pointedly ignored him, but lowered his hand.

"Not by a long road, boy. They just wouldn't attack *our* caravans. The spies in Qal'peth and Simall knew us too well, and whenever I or any of my lieutenants signed on for a crossing, they told their rats out in the desert to leave us alone. I guess they were tired of losing so many men." Her weapon stowed, the ranger pulled a pair of long knives from her belt and a whetstone from her pack and began to sharpen the blades.

"Ha! You got too good, Prynne. Probably shot one bandit captain too many through the eye." Nipural's voice was proud, and when Qabil looked over at the wizard, he saw a warm smile illuminating the man's face. The smile vanished like heat lightning when Nipural noticed him looking, though.

"Probably," Prynne agreed. "So I sold most of my interest in the mercenary company I founded and moved back north. Heard there were some nobles who were a bit heavy with taxes and with the whip, so I thought I might spend a little time changing attitudes in Gunreland."

"How's that working out for you?" Leshru asked, one eyebrow lifted.

"It's not," she replied, her voice flat. "I was about a season away from just killing the baron myself."

"And then what?" Nipural asked. "Is the baron's heir any better?"

"I don't know," Prynne replied. "Figured if he wasn't, I'd put an arrow or two in his gut, too."

"That's your problem, little sister," the wizard said, the corner of his mouth curling up. "You never think things through. You kill this baron and you don't make things better for the people there, you make them worse. Taxes aren't going to go down just because one idiot royal chokes on an arrow. You have to make sure that the ones you put on the throne after him are an improvement. Otherwise, you could spend your whole life doing nothing but murdering nobles."

"Heard of worse jobs," Thallis said, taking a huge bite out of an apple he'd fished out of his saddlebags.

"Don't you start, you little ruffian," the wizard snapped. "I taught you better than that. You can't just cut off the head of a region. You have to lay the groundwork for what comes after. Otherwise, you could be causing more harm than good."

"Isn't that what we're doing, though, *big brother*?" Prynne asked, the *shick-shick* of her blade along the stone a crisp counterpoint to her words.

"Going in to kill Walfert and destabilize all of Lennox? Aren't we just going to leave that city in chaos when we drop the little rat-faced bastard face down in the center of the town square?"

"I was thinking we'd be a little more subtle than all that, Prynne," Leshru said, his words calm and slow, a perfect counterpoint to the whip-crack of the siblings' argument.

"Oh, shut up, Lesh," Prynne snapped. "You're about as subtle as a siege engine and you know it."

"You're not wrong," the warrior agreed. "I was counting on your brother and the little thief to handle the sneaky bits. I was just going along in case the boy couldn't gut Walfert on his own."

"You mean me?" Qabil asked.

"Aye, boy. Unless you think you're a master sneak thief all of a sudden."

"No," Qabil said, shaking his head. "I just... I don't know, I..."

"Hadn't thought quite so far as what happens when we actually get to Lennox?" Nipural asked, his voice softer now as he looked at the boy.

"Yes. I mean, no. I mean..." Qabil took a deep breath. "I've been so focused on getting you all together, The Seven, that..."

"That you thought once you had us by your side Walfert would see us coming, shit himself, and fall down on his knees in fear, then you could just walk up and slit his throat? Is that what you thought, boy?" Prynne's words were as pointed as the dagger she sharpened, and Qabil flinched as if stung by a wasp.

"No, but..."

"Oh, leave him alone, for shit's sake," Thallis said, leaping to the defense of his friend. "He ain't never planned a caper of any kind before, much less one where there's a dead body at the end. But we've seen him fight. Hell, we've fought with him. When the time comes, he'll do what's got to be done. And if he can't, I can."

"Why?" Prynne asked.

"Why what?"

"Why are you willing to kill a man you don't even know for murdering a woman you never met?"

"He didn't murder *a woman*. He murdered my friend's mum. You don't do that. You don't hurt somebody's mum." The young thief's eyes went misty for the barest of instants, then hardened to chips of flint with fire-light dancing across them.

"Yeah, but he's just your friend. What's so important about that?" the ranger pressed.

"How many friends you got, archer lady?" Thallis asked, his jaw tight.

Prynne looked at Leshru, then Nipural, and shrugged. "These two, Torgan, yeah, even the songbird. Couple of the men back at camp, and Tine, my second in the Nurani caravans. So five or six. Why?"

"I got two," the young thief said. He pointed at Nipural. "That old asshole right there, and this one." He jerked a thumb at Qabil. "That's it. Two. This ratfucker Walfert killed my friend's mum. So I'll see him dead if it's the last thing I see before I leave this world."

Prynne stared at the young thief, then silently nodded and went back to sharpening her knives.

Leshru sat up and passed the flask over to Thallis. "Good speech. But you got one thing wrong, kid."

"What's that, granther?"

"You *had* two friends. You got four now."

CHAPTER NINE

A dmit it, old man, you're lost!" Prynne called from the rear of the string of horses and rider. Her voice was muffled from the layers of cloth she had bound across her face to protect her from the cold, but her words were no less biting for being muted. The morning was bright and sunlight blazed off the snow covering the ground. Everyone, not just Prynne, had strips of fabric wound around their heads to keep them warm and to prevent them going snow-blind from the dazzling whiteness that surrounded them. The storm had broken the night before, and the road was passable, but just barely.

"I'm not lost. I just can't find the entrance," Nipural growled back from his lead horse. "And stop calling me old! Or have you forgotten that we're twins?"

Qabil looked to where Leshru rode alongside him. "They're *twins*? But Nipural looks so much older. How is that even possible?"

"I hear you, brat!" the wizard called from the front of the party. "I may be old, but my ears are sharp as ever!"

Qabil raised an eyebrow at Lesh, silently repeating the question.

"Everything in life has a cost, son. I was a fighter, so I paid in scars and broken bones. Prynne is the finest hunter I've ever seen, but she paid for that skill by forgetting how to be with people much. She's far more comfortable surrounded by trees than men and women. Your friend Thallis is a thief, and he paid for that by sacrificing trust in people."

"So magic…made Nipural old?"

"Aye. Every spell cost him minutes, days, even years if the working was complex enough. It's why mages don't just go around using their power to light candles and cook food. It's easier to do those things the normal way. Doesn't cost as much in the long run."

The old warrior chuckled at the boy's stunned expression. "Don't feel too bad for old Nip. He doesn't always have to use his life. Sometimes he can borrow a little here and there."

"What's that mean?" Thallis asked. The trim thief had ridden up so that his horse's head was right on Leshru's flank. "He can leech off other people?"

"Other things, usually. Animals, mostly. Trees and plants can give a little, but from what he's told me through the years, it's not enough to fuel any big spells. For that it's got to come from a person."

"But it can come from anyone?" Qabil asked. "It doesn't have to be the mage himself?"

"That's right, boy," Nipural said, having slowed his mount to a stop. He stood in the stirrups and looked from side to side, a hand shielding his eyes. "I can draw on the life force of anything around me, including other people. But I won't. That's how a mage goes dark, sucking the life from others to fuel his workings. That's where you hear these old wives' tales about nasty wizards sacrificing virgins to summon up demons, or other nonsense."

"So none of that's true?" Thallis asked. "You ain't never sacrificed no virgins?"

"No, but I like to keep my options open. Why else do you think I brought you along, boy?" Nipural growled.

Thallis flushed and scowled at the old man. "I don't qualify then. Not for a long time."

"Well, then I guess Qabil will have to suffice," the old wizard said, a grin tweaking the corners of his mouth.

"Guess we'd better find an inn with a lusty barmaid so I can take care of that, then," Qabil shot back, smiling. "But have you? Ever used someone else's life force to cast a spell?"

A shadow flitted across the old mage's face, and he hesitated a long moment before answering. "Yes. Never without their knowledge, and never lightly. It's one of the most personal things you can do with a person, taking a part of them into yourself. You know them after that, better than you know yourself in some ways. I've only done it a few times, and only when circumstances were truly dire."

"Who?" Thallis asked. "Who'd you leech off?"

Leshru chuckled and swatted at the boy. "You have no sense of what's proper and what's private, do you boy?"

"I spent the last couple years stealing rich folks' lace underthings and selling them for a place to lay my head. Respect for privacy ain't something in too much demand in my line of work, basher."

Nipural didn't answer or look back at Thallis, but after a moment, Leshru said, "Me, for one. There was a time we was in a tough spot and Nip was our only chance at getting out with our skins. So I gave him a bit of my life force to charge up a thunderbolt and blow the doors off a jail."

"Usually it was Tara, though," Prynne said from behind them.

Qabil whirled around, his hand straying to the hilt of his sword. Prynne reached up and grasped the hilt of a throwing knife on the bandolier she wore slung across her chest. "Don't make a mistake you can't unmake, boy. I like you, but not enough to let you draw steel on me and walk away unblooded."

Leshru leaned over from his mount and put a hand on the younger man's shoulder. "Easy, boy. That's the one warning she's ever going to give you. The next time you piss her off, she'll start carving off bits."

"Then how do you still have all your parts, granther?" Thallis asked, his tone mocking. "Can't imagine you ain't never stepped wrong and found your foot in your mouth."

Leshru looked at the young thief, his hand still heavy on Qabil's shoulder, and said with a stony face, "Where do you think the tip of my left ear went? That's Prynne's idea of a second warning."

"Never given a third," the ranger added. "But it was Tara told my brother to bleed her for power. Being half-elven, she had more years to give than the rest of us, was how she put it. I always thought she just didn't like seeing her friends hurt, so she took the pain on herself. Either way, kept Nip from using me in his mad experiments, so I was good with it." The ranger's voice was cold, but there was a haunted look in her eyes that belied the hard words. Qabil got a very real sense that this hard-bitten ranger missed his mother more than anyone else in their little band, save only himself.

The boy's shoulders relaxed, and he nodded at Prynne. "That makes sense. Explains why she seemed to age something like a regular person, too. Not that I know all that much about how elves look when they get old."

"You ever see any of your mother's people?" Leshru asked. The old warrior straightened in his saddle, shifting this way and that to get his bulk evenly distributed across his mount's broad back.

"No," Qabil replied. "She said her family was all dead, or scattered to the winds. Really, she said her blood family was all dead, and her family of choice was scattered. Guess that was you. That's why she was so happy when Walfert came to see her. Why she let him into our home, why she trusted his lackey when he returned. That's why she died."

"What did happen with that, Qabil?" Nipural asked. "All you've told us is that Walfert sent his man to kill her, and he left her lying with a blade in her back. But why? Walfert is a bastard, but he and Tara always got on well enough."

"Better than the rest of us. I never liked the twitchy little bastard," Prynne muttered. "Walfert, not your mum. I liked Tara fine."

Qabil gave the ranger a little smile as she corrected herself. "I don't know, if I'm being honest. He came to the house several times through the winter, and he was always pleasant enough. I didn't care much for him, though. He was just a little too fine for Narim, if you know what I mean. He had the hands of man who never mucked out a barn, or pulled in a net full of fish, or drove a plow horse. His boots were always too clean. That's the thing I most remember about him. I remember because he insisted on putting them up on the table after he shared a meal with us. He'd lean back in his chair like he was lord of the manor or some such shite and prop his shiny boots up on the table I had to clean."

"I'd have knocked him ass over teakettle into the floor and seen what he thought of that," Thallis muttered.

"I thought about it more than once, but he was quick. And shifty. It was like he could tell when I was thinking about smacking him one, or saying something about how he acted. I'd blink, and there'd be a blade in his hand where it was empty a second before, and I never saw him draw it. I never even saw where he carried his blades, except for the skinny little thing he wore on his hip."

"Skinny thing?" Nipural asked, snapping his reins and pulling his horse to a halt. "Tell me about this blade, boy." The mage's eyes were flint, boring holes into Qabil's face, his gaze was so intense.

"It's a rapier, I guess. A sword, for sure, long, and barely two fingers wide. The belt and scabbard were nothing special, just plain black leather.

Well-crafted, from what I could see, but no jeweled buckles or trills like that. I never saw the blade. He never had cause to draw it in our home, but the hilt was ornate. There wasn't a crosspiece, like I'm used to seeing. Not like mine. There were just bands of steel that joined the blade and the hilt and looked like they formed a cage around the hand of whoever held it."

"It's called a basket hilt," Nipural said. "It provides a little more protection to the hand than other swords have. What else? Was there anything else you saw about the blade?"

"Not the blade itself," Qabil said. "But there were three stones. One on either side of the blade, and one down at the bottom, where all the wires came together. I don't know what kind they were, but they were all alike. Black, but different. There were flecks of all kinds of colors inside, and it seemed to swirl together. It reminded me of a comb set my mother used to have. She said it was made of mother-of-pearl."

"Black opals," Prynne said. "Those stones are black opals. The ones on either side of the blade were oval, and laid down atop the hilt, and the one at the pommel was round, and much larger. If you looked at it for very long, the colors seemed to move of their own accord, didn't they?"

Qabil looked at the woman and was stunned by the expression on her face. If he didn't know better, he'd say that Prynne was...afraid. "Yes, that's right."

"Well...balls," the ranger said. "That complicates things a bit, doesn't it, brother?"

Nipural gave her a steady look. "It certainly does. Will this be a problem?"

"Just more reason," Prynne said.

"Makes things a little more challenging, though," her brother replied.

Prynne opened her mouth to speak, then closed it again, nodding.

"Look here," Thallis said. "I don't know what you're all scared of about this sword or these gems in the sword, but I'd appreciate the living hell out of it if somebody would fill me and Qabil in on whatever it is got you all so stirred up."

"That's going to take more telling than we have time for before nightfall," Leshru replied. "But we may as well set up camp since Nip's gotten us good and lost again."

"We're not lost," the wizard protested. "I just can't find it!"

"Find what?" Qabil asked. "What are you looking for?"

"The path to Torgan's mine. I know it's near here somewhere, but in all this thrice-damned snow I can't find the route."

"You think that sign'll tell us?" Thallis asked, pointing to a board nailed to a tree a dozen yards farther along the road. The young thief rode forward and used his sword to knock the snow and ice from the board. An arrow appeared, with the words "Steelhammer Mining and Antiquities Extraction" written below.

Thallis rode back to the group, grinning like a cat with a belly full of cream. "I think we go that way," he said, pointing up a narrow path off to the right side of the road.

"I hate children," Nipural grumbled, snapping his reins and heading off in the direction the sign pointed.

Thallis looked at the old man's back with a fond grin. "You're welcome!"

CHAPTER TEN

The ringing of hammer on steel announced the forge before the sight of smoke and the stench of molten iron. Leshru led them around a bend in what barely amounted to a trail, more a narrow stretch of packed snow tight to the side of the mountain on the right and dropping off into clouds and certain death on the left. Qabil noticed Thallis moving even more slowly than his norm and spoke, keeping his voice low so as not to draw attention to his fear and embarrass the city boy.

"You can let the horse have its head on a path this narrow," Qabil said. "No point in trying to steer it anyway. There's only one way to go, and a horse is smart enough not to walk off into thin air, long as nothing spooks it."

Thallis whipped his head around. "What would spook it?"

"Probably nothing, this time of year," called Prynne from directly in front of the young thief. "Snakes are hibernating, and anything else that would look on a horse as prey will have heard the din you all raise and gone off in search of a more peaceful meal. Not that a snow leopard or mountain lion is likely to stay too near anything that raises such a racket as Torgan, anyway. That furry idiot is a one-man cacophony, waking or sleeping." She clucked her tongue at her own mount, and it picked up the pace, moving forward to the wide area where Leshru and her brother were dismounting.

"What did she mean about a cacophony?" Qabil asked moments later as the boys were tying up their own mounts.

"I reckon she meant he snores. That's what I got out of it, anyhow," Thallis replied. He noticed the downcast expression on his friend's face. "Something about that bother you?"

"How did you know that?" Qabil asked.

"What do you mean?"

"Cacophony. How did you know what that was?"

"I dunno. Reckon I read it somewhere. Probably summat Stin—Nipural gave me to read. He always made all of us what lived with him read every day." He shook his head. "Sorry. I start talking about the city and I start talking like I did when I lived on the streets. Dunno why."

"You talked like that because that's how everyone around you talked. I don't talk like a fisherman around all of you because you're not fishermen. You're all... Well, you've all read a lot of books. A lot more than me, anyway."

"I got a bunch of books in me at Nipural's place, but once I moved out on my own, wasn't time for that. Sounds like you didn't have a lot of time to read either. You never said much about your life before you decided to be a murderer. Were you a fisherman?"

Qabil let out a sharp laugh. "Not anywhere near. My mother would've had kittens if I even talked about going out on a boat. Especially after what happened to my da." His expression darkened briefly. "He was a fisherman. Went out one morning and didn't come back. A storm came up that afternoon and took three boats. One of the men washed up on shore three days later with part of his face and both legs chewed off. Da and the other five men that went missing were never heard from again."

"Shit," Thallis said. "I'm sorry, pal. That's brutal."

"It was the worst day of my life. Until Walfert made one even worse. Is your dad still around?"

The young thief blushed, something Qabil hadn't even known he was capable of. "I dunno. Never met him. Ma said she knew who it was, it wasn't nothing like that. She wasn't no whore. Just said she was young and stupid and fell in love with the wrong man, and he didn't love her enough not to be a right bastard when he found out she was carrying me. So she never told me who he was. Always promised she'd tell me when I was older. But now I'm older, and she ain't. So I reckon we're both orphans. Two of a kind, that's us."

"It's the way of things, boy," Leshru said from the other side of his horse. "We all become orphans if we live long enough, or tragedies if we don't. Either way, nobody gets out of this life alive." He tossed his saddle-bags over his broad shoulders and turned toward the ringing sound of the forge.

A massive sign with STEELHAMMER carved into granite spanned two huge ten-foot posts driven into the ground marking the entrance to the forge, mine, and oddly appointed storefront. The sign was hewn from one solid piece of stone, as far as Qabil could see, and was less fastened to the posts than resting atop them. It looked solid, but he quickened his steps as he passed under it regardless, and noticed the others doing the same. The road opened up into a huge expanse of cleared ground, a massive circle some two hundred yards across. The smithy was set into the mountain near the gate, with a complex set of wooden sluices running up the stone walls collecting snow to be melted by a similar construction of chimneys that ran from the roof of the building alongside the sluices, leading to a pair of massive wooden cisterns that fed water for the forge.

Directly before them was a gaping hole in the mountain that could be nothing other than the mine itself. It was a huge black maw that Qabil felt even from that distance yearning to swallow him whole and never spit him back out into the light. He shuddered involuntarily and heard Thallis chuckle from beside him.

"Now you know how I feel out here among all this sky and trees and open spaces. I'm at least as skittish out here where there's not a wall to point my back to as you would be in that rocky hole with no view of the sky and not a blade of grass for miles. Your elf is showing, Ears."

"Oh, piss off, city mouse," Qabil replied. "You can't tell me you want to go cave-diving?"

"Not a chance," the thief replied. "I no more want to go into that over-inflated tomb than you do. I just found it funny, is all."

"Let's see how funny anything seems once Torgan gets sight of this motley crew," Prynne said, making Thallis jump a little as she appeared beside him almost as if out of nowhere. "You know, for a thief, you sure are easy to sneak up on," she said to the boy.

"I wasn't paying too much attention while I was surrounded by my friends," he shot back.

"She shot her brother in the arm and took off part of Leshru's ear," Qabil said. "I expect too many friends like her and you'll need a healer on the regular."

The ranger favored him with a wry smile and nodded. "You should listen to him. Keep your friends close."

"And your enemies closer, I know. I've heard that one," Thallis said.

"That last part is bullshit," Prynne said. "I favor my enemies out of arm's reach but within arrow's range if possible. That way I can kill them without worrying about them bleeding on my boots. Ah, looks like the welcoming party has arrived. Keep your blades sheathed, boys. They just want to test us."

"They" were a half dozen dwarves and men all striding across the open ground toward them, the leader a stout dwarf with a jet-black beard and a cudgel in his hands. All his compatriots were similarly armed, with no blades in evidence, but plenty of iron gauntlets, staves, and clubs close at hand.

"Who challenges the sovereignty of Clan Steelhammer by marching uninvited up to our door?" bellowed the leader.

"I am Leshru of the Broken Blade, the best brawler to ever strut across Watalin, the man who has bedded more women than hairs in your beard and cracked more skulls than your ugly friend there has pimples on his arse! I once bit off a shock dragon's ear and pissed lightning for three days, and five times have I strode across the blood-soaked sands of the Great Arena of Nurani holding up the heads of my foes as trophies before the God-Queen Pil'xana herself placed the laurel on my brow! I am the most dangerous thing to walk through that gate since the Steelhammer himself came home from his battles, and any man, dwarf, or giantkin that wants to test me can grab their balls in one hand and their blade in the other and step up, because Leshru of the Broken Blade accepts all challengers!"

The crowd of dwarves and men stopped and the leader grinned, then let out a huge laugh. "Well said, Imposter of the Broken Blade, but the real Leshru retired a long time ago. Now let's see if you fight half as well as you lie. If you seek audience with Clan Steelhammer, you must win past our door in the old way, by defeating our stoutest warrior in single combat. Do you accept the challenge?"

The barrel-chested dwarf stood a little over five feet, and his hands and face bore the marks of one who had been through many fights, and won most of them. His nose pointed off to one side of his face and had the blooming red bulb of one that has been both broken many times and blown up from years of cheap ale in large quantities. His legs resembled tree stumps more than anything, jammed into a stocky body with thick arms and no discernible neck. If someone had told Qabil that this walking obstacle was no living creature, but a simulacrum of stone and mortar, he would have found it believable.

"Alright, then. How do you want to do this?" Leshru asked, loosening his belt and slinging it, and the two knives hanging from it, over his horse's back. "First blood, unconsciousness, surrender, or death?" There was no fear in his dark eyes or hesitation in his rumbling voice. He asked the question the same way one might ask a neighbor if they thought it would be a particularly cold winter.

"You are the interloper, you can choose the weapons," the black-bearded dwarf replied.

"I don't give a shit," Leshru said. "No blades or pointy bits and I'll be fine. I'm going to use these to pound your face into pudding. It you want to use your little stick there to tickle my chestnuts, go ahead." The big man took off his wool cap to reveal his scarred bald pate, then drew on his banded gauntlets. He took three steps toward the dwarf and looked down at him. "If you just fall down after the first punch, you won't have to take the next one. Wouldn't be the first time I've dropped an opponent with one shot."

"Might be the first time that opponent had the opportunity to get up again," Prynne muttered. "I watched Lesh punch a half-orc in the side of the head once wearing those damn steel fists of his. His skull burst like an overripe melon. The dwarf should take the out."

"He won't," Nipural said.

"Of course not," his sister replied. "And Lesh doesn't want him to. That's why he made sure everyone in the square heard him make that offer. So the dwarf will try twice as hard to make a challenge out of it."

"Is Leshru really that good a fighter?" Thallis asked. "I mean, I've heard, of course, but you all quit fighting a long time ago."

"It's like fucking, boy. Once you get good at it, you never forget how it works," Prynne replied.

Thallis blushed and turned away, all his bravado melting in the face of the ranger's sly smile. Qabil returned his focus to the men before him, who had begun to circle each other, eyes locked.

A bead of sweat rolled down Leshru's ebon pate, and he dashed it away before it could get in his eyes. That was the opening the dwarf thought he wanted, and he lashed out with his club, aiming a quick strike at Lesh's nose. Leshru slapped the cudgel aside and took a step closer, putting himself at an awkward distance for the longer weapon. He formed a knife edge with the fingers of his left hand and jabbed it into the dwarf's torso, just above his belly where his ribs came together.

As the smaller man been over, retching, Leshru slammed his right hand into the hinge of his opponent's jaw, dislocating it with a *pop* that was audible to everyone watching. The dwarf dropped to one knee and swung an uppercut at Leshru's groin, but the wily old brawler caught his wrist and slammed a fist into the dwarf's face, breaking his nose again.

Blood cascaded down the man's face, and Nipural leaned over to his sister. "Blessing in disguise, really. Lesh might have straightened out the bend in his nose."

"Or just put another twist in it. Like a short, rounded, river," Prynne replied.

The dwarf staggered to his feet and took a few steps back, one hand clutching his broken nose. Leshru followed, keeping pace but making no attempt to corral his opponent. After a few seconds, the dwarf stopped, blew a huge gobbet of bloody snot into the dirt, and lowered his head as he charged at Leshru, screaming at the top of his lungs.

Leshru dropped to one knee, cocked his right fist back, and punched the dwarf in the side of the face as he stood up, straightening the dwarf and lifting him straight off his feet and onto his back, unconscious in the dirt. The old brawler looked around at the stunned circle of dwarves and asked, "Anybody else want to go a round?"

"Aye, but I'll choose the weapons, you bald-headed prick," came a gruff voice from behind the ring of welcoming party. A shorter dwarf with red hair bushed out all over his head and a red beard down almost to his belt pushed his way through the crowd. "Why is it whenever you lot show up, people start bleeding?"

"I have strong people skills," Leshru replied. "Good to see you, Steelhammer."

"Good to see you, too. Wait. No, it isn't. If you're riding again, and with these two, it means something's fucked. Get inside. I'm not talking apocalypse without a beer in my hand." He turned and walked off toward the largest building in the camp, presumably the tavern or common house. Leshru, Nipural, and Prynne all followed without a word, and Qalib shared a quick look with Thallis. Thallis shrugged, and they hurried after the rest of their party, hoping to be inside before the disgruntled dwarves decided to avenge their vanquished friend, and to use the youngest and most likely targets to do it.

CHAPTER ELEVEN

Torgan Steelhammer looked across the sea of empty tankards that covered the scarred and pitted surface of the long table the party sat around. Night had fallen, and it lay heavy upon the room as voices became hushed with weariness, drunkenness, or just apathy. Thallis snored gently from where he sat with his head down on the table, a pillow made of his cloak and his folded arms. Prynne stood by a window on the far wall, looking out at what, Qalib had no idea. The side of a mountain, he supposed, but she seemed as though she was a woman who could close her eyes and see any number of distant lands and lost acquaintances. Leshru sat at the bar, comparing notes with the brewmaster on the best grains, the freshest places to get water, and other esoteric brewing shit that only someone who cared far more about the making of beer than the drinking of it could possibly care about.

That left Nipural sitting at the table with Qalib and a resolute dwarf. "No," Torgan said, for perhaps the thirtieth time that night. "Not just no, but Hells no. This isn't the stupidest idea you've ever had, Nipural—that cake was taken the night you decided to bind a fire imp into a tattoo and affix him to Lesh's arse while he slept. I thought I was going to piss myself when he farted and set his blankets ablaze!"

"Well, that's not so bad, then. See, I told you it wasn't the worst idea you'd ever heard." The wizard puffed on his pipe, a habit that seemed more affectation than anything, given the miniscule amount of tobacco he deigned to put into the bowl. It seemed that Nipural was more concerned with the fact that wizards were *supposed* to smoke pipes than with the actual smoking of it.

"It's not," Steelhammer said, scratching at his chin. "It's not the second worst, either. That one goes to the time Xethe tried to convince the mayor of that little shitpot town up the coast of Kroy that he was a physician and should be allowed to 'treat' his oldest daughter unsupervised. That ended up with us taking on an entire garrison of the town guard."

"We won, though. There were a lot of them, but they weren't very good."

"True." The old dwarf's eyes narrowed. "No. It's officially the third worst idea I've ever heard, and I swore to Celia that I wouldn't go off on another stupid lark with you lot, no matter what. I'm not crossing that woman. She scares the red out of my beard."

This was not the first time Torgan had referenced his wife, Celia. Apparently she was, by turns, the sweetest, most beautiful hellcat in the bedroom the dwarf had ever met, the most pious daughter of Karlasta, dwarven goddess of strength, fertility, and unarmed combat, or perhaps the most terrifying harridan to ever swing a hammer, with a temper hotter than the forge and a backhand more deadly than a broadsword. It seemed to depend entirely on how much beer the dwarf had consumed, and whether or not he wanted to stay home with his wife out of love and adoration, respect and adulation, or just sheer terror.

"Why not bring her with us?" Qabil asked, and both the dwarf and the wizard whipped their heads around to gape at him. He turned slowly around, just to make sure there wasn't a wyvern standing over his shoulder, because judging by the looks on their faces, his companions were horrified at the mere suggestion.

"Take Celia? On a revenge quest? Are you mad, boy?" Torgan's mustache quivered in either rage or fear, and he slid out of his chair, somewhat unsteady on his feet, stomping over to Qabil while keeping one hand on the table at all times.

"Probably," Qabil replied. "I am trying to round up a bunch of retired adventurers to murder the ruler of a city-state who has a small army at his disposal. But why is asking your wife to join us any more mad than making the attempt in the first place?"

"Because..." Torgan turned and looked at Nipural. "You tell him!"

The old wizard slowly took the pipe out of his mouth and laid it down gently on the table. Then, using his staff for balance, he stood up and walked the three steps down to Qabil at a pace that could at best be described as glacial and uncharitably as wobbling. "Because... Well, it's just not done, that's why. Men do not take their wives on adventures. And women do not take their husbands. Or their wives. There are a fair number of pairs of adventuring men that would likely be wed if they ever stayed in one place long enough to do so, but that remains the exception rather than the rule."

"If Torgan was married to a man, it would be fine?" Prynne asked. "That seems a bit unbalanced, dear brother. Although, to be fair, so do you."

Qabil had no idea when the ranger had returned to the table, but it seemed that more often than not, Prynne simply was wherever she wanted to be, without actually *going* from place to place. "See? I think you should ask Celia. See what she says about it."

"See what Celia says about what?" asked a massive shadow that stood behind Prynne's right shoulder.

Qabil leaned back to get a look at the newcomer and found that he had to lean back almost to the point of falling off the bench beneath him. The flickering light of the lamps set in the tavern walls illuminated the strangest being he'd ever seen, although he had to admit to himself that did not encompass much before this trip.

The being was female, at least judging by the long auburn braids she wore and the massive bosom that stood out from her like the prow of a ship. Everything about her was massive. She was nearly seven feet tall, with broad shoulders, a head like a boulder, thickly muscled arms, and hands that looked as if they could pulp apples into juice without any effort at all. But none of that was what captured Qabil's attention. No, what held his gaze most firmly was the light green tinge to the woman's skin.

"You're a half-orc," he said, then covered his mouth as a slight belch escaped.

"You're apparently the smart one," the newcomer said.

"But you also seem to be half-dwarf," Qabil said, noting the distinctly rounded cast to her features. "Not half-human."

"And you seem to be quarter elf, quarter drunkard, and half idiot. Which puts you a half sight ahead of most of the men in this place, my fully idiot husband included. So what do you want to ask me?"

There was an almost audible click in his mind as the pieces fell together, and Qabil said, "You're Celia!" He grinned, very proud of himself for figuring that out all for himself. Then he considered that perhaps he was less sober than he had initially thought.

"I am well aware that I am Celia, child. Who exactly are you? Who are any of you, now that I look around and see half a dozen unfamiliar faces. This is a banner day for Clan Steelhammer, husband. Why did you not tell me we had guests?" The edge in her voice was sharper than Qabil's sword, and he began to see where some of Torgan's respect, or possibly fear, came from.

The dwarf began to stammer out a reply, but Celia held up a massive hand to silence him. "We'll talk later," she said to her husband, and it sounded like a death sentence. She turned her attention back to Qabil. "Now, what was it you wanted to ask me?"

"Ummm...I...thought that if Torgan was so reluctant to leave you behind, which I can now understand, having met you, that we should just bring you with us on our journey," he replied, wiping away an errant bead of sweat from his brow.

Celia reached down and lifted Thallis by his armpits, slid him a few feet down the bench, and set him back down. She was exceedingly gentle with the snoring thief, until she came to the point where she let go of his armpits and let his face fall forward to smack into the table. He jerked up, looked around, saw the mountain of verdant femininity beside him, and hurried off to the door, muttering something about needing to find a restroom.

"And where are you going, youngling?" Celia asked, turning her attention back to Qabil.

"Lennox. I have business with the so-called duke there."

"Ah, Walfert. Yes, I'd heard of him even before I met Torgy. As I understand it, he either created or took note of a vacancy in the city's leadership and set himself up as the local ruling body. What is he to you?"

"He killed my mother," Qabil said, his voice flat. "Or he sent a man to do it. But either way, it happened on his orders."

"And if you're a piece of an elf, and you're traveling with some of Torgy's old companions, that means..."

"Aye," Torgan interjected. "He's Tara's boy."

"He murdered Eltara?" Celia asked, her face like a thundercloud.

"You knew my mother, too?" Qabil asked.

"She came to our wedding. It was a little more than twenty years ago, probably a few years before you were born. She was a lovely person. Gentle, kind... I liked her."

"We didn't get an invite to your wedding, Torgan," Prynne said.

"I was living under a new name," Nipural said to his sister. "And I doubt it would have been easy to get a message to you. Was he supposed to send it by squirrel courier? Just wander Watalin from tree to tree until it found you?"

"He found Tara," Prynne said, giving the dwarf an accusing stare.

"I didn't have to find her," Torgan said. "I knew where she was all along. Narim, right? Little place on the ocean where everyone stinks of fish?"

"It's a fishing village," Qabil said, coming to the defense of his home. "Everyone there either catches, sells, or transports fish for a living."

"Doesn't mean they need to stink up the whole countryside," the dwarf replied. "I guess from what you're saying none of the rest of you had heard from her."

"Or you, or any other of these louts," Leshru said, returning to the table with a pitcher of beer, a long-stemmed glass, and a bottle of red wine, which he set down in front of Celia. "Bartender says you don't drink beer."

"I do not. It doesn't agree with me," she replied.

"Gives her gas that'll peel the paint off the walls," Torgan muttered. Everyone in the room winced at the sound of the meaty *thwack* Celia laid on the side of his head.

"Be polite, Torgy. Just because you used to be a murderer and a thief doesn't mean you can still act like it. You're a respected smith and a priest now. You might consider behaving as such."

"Never marry a woman who'll live as long as you, boy," the dwarf said to Qabil. "There's no hope of ever finding peace this side of the grave."

"This trip goes sour and he won't have to worry about that," Leshru said. "We don't do this smart, the boy won't live long enough to dip his wick for the first time, much less marry."

"What exactly are you planning to do when you get to Lennox, young man?" Celia asked, one eyebrow raised.

"Find Walfert and show him what my sword looks like. Preferably by shoving it through his eye."

Leshru grinned. "Bloodthirsty little bastard, ain't he? But that's the plan—we find Walfert, and we convince him he's better to the world dead than alive. Won't take much to convince the world of that, but getting the thief to buy into it might be a little more of a challenge."

"Sounds reasonable," Celia said. "I liked Eltara. We're in." She slapped a giant hand down on Torgan's shoulder and held it there, kneading the muscle in a massage that did not look like it was intended to relax anything.

"Now wait just a moment, love..." Torgan began to protest, then stopped as Celia squeezed his shoulder.

"No, Torgy," she said. "The matter is settled. We ride tomorrow right after breakfast. Now I suggest that the rest of you get some sleep before our journey. Vengeance is a rough road, and a long one, so you'll need your strength." Then she stood up, half-dragging Torgan to his feet, and hauled the dwarf up from the table and out the front door.

Nipural looked around the gathered party and said, "I don't think we'll need nearly the strength that Torgan will."

CHAPTER TWELVE

Q abil's head only felt two sizes too big when he awoke to the sound of chairs scraping across the common room floor. He looked around, memory of where he was and why he was on the floor coming back to him as his bladder reminded him that he had drank quite a bit of beer the night before. He staggered to the side door, stepping over Thallis and around Leshru on the way. Nipural was in a chair by the fire, his head bowed to his chest and pipe dangling from one hand.

He walked out into the chill morning air and loosened his pants, letting out a huge sigh of relief as a mighty stream of piss arced out into the snow. Today was the day his journey really began. His party was assembled, the remaining members of The Seven were together, and it was time to hunt down Walfert and make him pay for his crimes. He closed his eyes as thoughts of revenge battled regret at drinking the last tankard fought for dominance in his head.

"You going to write your name in the snow, boy?" Qabil's eyes snapped open, and his stream cut off at the sound of Prynne's voice. He started to turn, then froze, tucked himself away, and looked at the ranger.

"What are you doing out here?" he asked.

"Same as you," she replied. "Pissing. I just chose to do it in the privy instead of on the wall of the common house. But you mark your territory however you like, Fairy Prince."

"Fairy what?" he asked.

"Prince. Tara was our Fairy Princess. You're her get, so you must be the Fairy Prince. Not near so pretty as your mum, though, sorry to say. Was your father powerful ugly? He must have been to drag Eltara's beauty down enough to make a child that's barely a slice above cute. You're alright, child, might even be handsome before you're done, but not near pretty enough to really favor your mother."

Qabil opened his mouth, glaring at the woman, then froze at her upraised hand and her laugh. "Oh, stop, boy. I'm playing with you. You're perfectly attractive enough, for an infant. I just wanted to see if you inherited your mother's temperament. You didn't, by the way. Nothing fazed Tara. She could be chatting up a king or staring down a troll and she had the same placid look in her eyes. Like everything was going to be okay. And whenever she put her hand on that sword's hilt, it was. You've got her eyes, lad, but more fire. I don't know if that's your father's or your own, but it'll do us well where we're going. Walfert's a bastard, and it takes a bastard to kill a bastard."

"Then we should be fine, sister dear," Nipural said as he stepped out the door and wrinkled his nose. "Why didn't you use the privy, boy? It's rude to just piss all over the side of the building like that." He walked away toward a small wooden structure some yards away, one that Qabil had failed to notice when he first came outside.

"Was she really that good?" Qabil asked, opening the door for Prynne.

"What do you mean?" she asked, stepping into the common hall.

"My mother. Was she really a good swordswoman?"

Prynne turned to him, mouth open. "Boy, do you know who we are? Who we were, at least?"

"You're The Seven. You were the most legendary band of adventurers to ever roam Watalin. You fought men, monsters, and anything in between. There are even rumors that you once fought a god to a standstill."

"It was a demigod, and we beat his ass," Leshru said as he knelt on the floor tying his bedroll to his pack.

"Your mother wasn't some hanger on, lad. She was one of us. She stood beside us in every fight—"

"In front of us in more than one," Leshru added.

"How can you not know how good she is? Did she not teach you how to swing that stick?" She pointed at the blade on his hip.

"A little, but just the basics, she said. She always told me that if I lived right, I'd never need to draw a sword, and I never thought I would. Until..."

"Aye, that's how it goes, mate," Thallis said, stretching and trying to tame the wild nest of hair atop his head. "Nobody ever thinks they will. Until they do. Until some prick kills their mum."

"Until someone kidnaps them as a babe and sells them to an arena to fight and die for the amusement of the masses," Leshru said, his voice a low rumble.

"Until they push your brother one time too many," Prynne said.

"Until four of them are holding your sister down as she thrashes and curses," said Nipural as he closed the door.

"Until your god tells you to put down your pickaxe and take up the hammer, that there's work to be done," said Torgan from the door.

"Until the friend of your love is dead and deserving justice," Celia said from beside him.

"None of us came into this life willingly, son. Certainly not your mother. But once we were in it, we knew we had two options open to us." Leshru held up a meaty fist with his index finger extended. "We could be half-assed idiots traipsing around the countryside and end up getting killed by the first thing bigger than a hobgoblin we ran into." He added a second finger. "Or we could be the best goddamned warriors this world has ever seen and make the fucking heavens tremble at our approach. There are only two ways to go, boy. You can live a quiet normal life, long and happy in some village by the sea. Or you can be a fucking legend."

"Needless to say," Prynne said, bending over and tossing her pack over her shoulder. "We chose to be legends."

"You don't think you're leaving here just like that, do you?" The voice was gruff, and loud, and familiar. Qabil turned from where he was fastening the pack onto his saddle and saw the same angry dwarf from the day before, but today he had a bandage stretched across his nose and both cheeks, and instead of a rough club, he held a war hammer with a wicked spike on the back of its head. He also had half a dozen friends.

"I think we're leaving here however we damn well please, Nardov," Celia said as she stepped around her horse, a thickly muscled gray that

71

looked like it could pull a plow for three days straight without even stopping for water.

"Stay out of this, woman," the dwarf, Nardov, growled. "This is words between men."

"It's going to be words between more men than you if you disrespect my wife, you pug-nosed jackass," Torgan said, stepping up beside his wife.

"Is this where we all say something witty and form a heroic line, all determined and steely-eyed?" Thallis asked. "Because nothing comes to mind, so why don't you just bring it, you bunch of half-sized half-wits?"

Qabil groaned at his friend's words because Nardov and his companions, all armed and armored like they were going off to storm a dragon's lair, did just that. With a roar, the cluster of dwarves charged, eager to redeem their friend's honor. What kind of honor, Qabil had no idea. He'd never been much for the kind of friends that needed to beat each other's heads in to prove who was the toughest, or the stoutest, or the whatever-est. So this idea of worth being measured by who you could beat up was unfamiliar.

But the concept of a brawl was nothing new, and that's what was coming at them. All the hammers and swords were still hanging from belts, so he hesitated to draw steel on their opponents. But he didn't give a second's pause to kicking the first dwarf that came near him right in the nose. The onrushing dwarf, a thickset young male by the length of his blond beard, stopped cold when he ran into Qabil's foot. The dwarf's legs, however, didn't stop, and he found himself lying on his back staring up and the steel-blue sky.

"Please don't get up," Qabil said. "I really don't want to put a sword in you."

"I'd really rather not have a sword in me, so I'm just going to roll over here out of the way," the dwarf said, and began to do just that.

"'Ware the horse apples," Qabil called after him before moving over to distract a tall dwarf with his hair shaved into a thin ridge running down the center of his scalp.

The spike-haired dwarf was advancing on Nipural, who fended him off with the occasional poke to the stomach with his staff. As Qabil approached, the dwarf slapped the mage's staff to the ground and rushed forward, only to stop, swatting at his face and coughing as Nipural blew a thick stream of pipe smoke in his face. The dwarf turned in circles, pawing at the air with his eyes squeezed tightly shut, slapping himself in the face again and again as if he were surrounded by a cloud of gnats. Nipural observed the dwarf spinning round for a moment, then stepped forward, wrapped his long arms around the dwarf's thick neck, and in a matter of a few seconds, choked him unconscious. Then the mage picked up his staff and leaned against his horse, calmly watching his companions battle the rest of the dwarves.

"Why didn't you just hit him over the head with your staff?" Qabil asked.

"That could have caused serious injury, or even killed him. Any time you hit someone in the head with enough force to render them unconscious, you run a very real risk of killing them. He hadn't tried to kill me, so it would have been rude of me to try to kill him."

"He looked like he was trying to kill you."

"Oh no, if he wanted to kill me, he would have drawn a weapon. He just wanted to thump one of the tallfolk. It's something of a pastime among the Steelhammer clan. Any non-dwarf entering their camp must be prepared to fight their way in. Once inside, you can enjoy their hospitality for as long as you like. But you will almost certainly have to fight your way out. Now pay attention, boy. I want to see how Torgan's wife handles herself in a scrap. It could be important soon." He stretched out a spindly arm to where the massive female half-orc stood before two smaller opponents.

"Boys, you know how this is going to end," Celia said. "I've tussled with both of you before, and it doesn't go well for you."

"But you've never tried to handle us both at once," said the shorter of the two, a young dwarf with his brown beard split and braided into two lengths down his chest.

"I don't think that sounded the way you wanted it to sound, Narren," said the other, a relatively slender blond dwarf with a broad grin across his face. He looked up at Celia. "You know how to works, Cee. You wanna stay? Ya gotta fight. Ya wanna leave, ya gotta fight. Life's all about the fight. It's all about—*urk!*" His words cut off abruptly as Celia lifted her right foot between his legs with enough force to lift the dwarf completely off his feet. He dropped back down, both hands clasped firmly over his jewels, and toppled over, his eyes bulging from his skull.

"Now, Narren," Celia said, clapping her massive hands together. "How *exactly* do you want to be handled?"

The double-braided dwarf looked up and up at Celia, all the color draining from his face. After a long moment of gazing into her stern face, he lowered his head and said, "Just make it quick." Celia obliged with one mighty blow of her fist.

Qabil looked over to Nipural and cocked his head to one side. "I think she handled herself pretty well, don't you?"

"Aye, lad. I think she'll do just fine."

CHAPTER THIRTEEN

For the gods' sake, Lesh, let me see that," Prynne said as they sat around the campfire that night. She stood up from the chunk of firewood she was using as a crude seat and knelt in front of the big warrior. She held out a hand and glared at Leshru until he stretched out his big right hand and laid it in her palm. Prynne twisted his wrist this way and that, wrinkling her nose as she examined the knuckles.

"You're an idiot, you know that, right?" she asked without looking up.

Leshru didn't hesitate in his reply. Qabil could see this was a dance they both knew the steps to very well. "I know."

"If this gets infected, your hand will swell to the size of a pumpkin again, and it will be worse than the time you got bit by that giant spider in the cave near Simall."

"It was Randath, not Simall," Nipural corrected. "You're getting the Nurani confused with the Talmot again." He leaned over to Thallis. "My sister can find one specific acorn in a hundred acres of oak trees, but she can't keep her deserts straight to save her life."

"They all have sand, snakes, and assholes," Prynne retorted. "What more do I need to know?"

"It's often useful to know exactly what kind of assholes they are," Leshru said, smiling down into her face. "That way you know if you're going to have to kill all of them or just their headman."

Prynne looked up into his dark brown eyes, and Qabil saw something pass between them that hinted at perhaps more of a bond than just companions. But it was gone as quickly as it came and left no trace. Then she dug her thumbs into a swollen knuckle and the big brawler winced. "Hold still, you big baby," she grunted, squeezed again, and Leshru's hand gave a *pop* that was audible to everyone around the fire.

"There. Now you don't have to worry about that finger staying dislocated. Idiot. Now follow me to the stream and we'll get it cleaned and dressed." She stood up, walked over to her pack, and pulled out a small leather pouch that clinked like glass when she hefted it. "I've got some lady's bower to take down the swelling, and a little salamander tongue to keep the infection out of that cut on the back of your hand. Why weren't you wearing your bashers? The whole damn point of you getting those things was to keep you from breaking off parts of your hands."

Her diatribe continued as she practically pulled Leshru to his feet and across their rough camp, then down a narrow trail that led to the stream where Qabil had fetched water for their mounts earlier.

Thallis looked around the campfire and said with a cheeky grin, "I know Leshru used to be married, but I didn't know it was to her." His grin quickly shifted to a look of dismay as Nipural's staff bounced off the back of his head with a *bonk!* "Hey! I was just making a joke. Come on, old man!"

"Don't you old man me, boy. Just for that, you get to deal with the washing up." The old wizard pulled out a pouch of tobacco and waved Torgan over, clearly intent on sharing a post-meal smoke with the dwarf.

"Come on," Qabil said, picking up his battered tin plate and Leshru's at the same time. "I'll help. Let's *not* follow their path to the creek exactly, though."

Thallis gathered the other plates and the stewpot they had cooked in, and the two young men headed down to wash up. They had spent all day riding down the mountain and moved below the snowline just about two hours before time to stop and make camp. Qabil had been a competent rider when he set out from Narim two months back, but now he felt like he could ride circles around anyone in his old village. Of course, none of them had ever ridden every day for weeks on end, through countryside, cities, and now a snow-capped mountain range.

He's always been fit, but he noticed traveling with Leshru and the others had scoured away any of the pudginess left on him from his relatively easy life before. It felt like years, that "before" time, but it had not even brought the change of seasons yet. So much had happened, and yet it felt like their journey had only begun as they set off that morning. Maybe it was because they finally felt like a complete group. They were all together. Not the band he'd hoped to bring together, but this was the band he had, so this was the band he'd ride with, and perhaps die with.

The Seven. All his life Qabil had heard whispered tales around campfires and songs around tavern hearths about the legendary group of adventurers. Some called them heroes, some called them mercenaries and murderers, but if there was one thing all the stories agreed upon, it was that they were the fiercest warriors to ever take up blades. Or, in Leshru's case, to shatter one.

It wasn't until the first time Walfert came to visit his mother that he had ever heard anyone mention The Seven with regard to her. She wasn't some great hero. She couldn't be. She was just Mama, who bandaged his skinned knees and kissed his bruises better when he fell. She was Mama, who cried in the night sometimes when the storms blew in off the ocean and she thought he was already asleep. He knew she cried for Papa, but he also knew she didn't want him to know how the loss cut her, how much of the light went out of her life when he was lost.

But then Walfert swaggered in, all brocaded black leather and velvet, dripping with silver rings and chains with a sapphire winking from each ear. He wore cuffed boots and a broad-brimmed hat over a long black coat that seemed too long to be practical but which swept majestically when he turned. His hair was always oiled to perfection and his beard trimmed down to a precise triangular point. His palm, when he extended it to Qabil, felt like he had never even met an honest day's work, and certainly never shaken hands with one.

In short, he was a prick and Qabil loathed him from the moment he laid eyes on him. But the strutting little thief did do one good thing—he made Eltara remember who she was, and talk about it. After the first time he came to visit, Eltara sat Qabil down and told him the story of her youth. Some of it, at least. She told him about riding with Walfert, and Leshru of the Broken Blade, and all the rest. She told him of Nipural Wyrmrider, the most powerful wizard she'd ever seen, and his sister, Prynne, the best archer on three continents. She spoke of Xethe, the bard that could spin tales and songs that would keep an entire room focused solely on his tune while Walfert the Shadow-Touched crept around to every table and stole the entire tavern's weapons. She told him about Torgan Steelhammer, whose arm was almost as strong as his faith, who could call lightning forth from clear skies and rain bolts of fire down from the heavens when he beseeched his goddess for her favor.

And she told him of herself. She told him how a young half-elven girl, trapped between two worlds and accepted by neither left her village at the age of sixteen with a hunting bow, a few arrows, and a bedroll, and rode back in ten years later in gleaming mail as the Eltara the Sword Dancer, one of the legendary Seven, and nothing like the girl they remembered. She sounded nothing like the woman Qabil knew, either. Thinking back on those tales, he could see that she studied with a bard somewhere and wondered when that happened. Was it before The Seven? During?

"Penny for 'em," Thallis said, jolting him out of his reverie.

"Just...thinking," Qabil said.

"Well, less thinking and more washing, else we're going to get back with supper dishes just in time to wash up after breakfast." The grinning thief splashed a handful of water at him, and the two engaged in a brief, if soaking, water fight before settling down and scrubbing up the plates and pots.

They worked together in easy silence until they were almost finished, then Thallis looked over at him. "Is this what you thought it would be like?"

"Like I thought what would be like?" Qabil asked. "I never spent much time pondering my quest to avenge my mother's murder before she was killed, if that's what you mean."

"No, stupid, but you were a kid once. You have to have dreamt of riding the roads with The Seven or some other legendary band of outlaws, or heroes, or both. Was it anything like this?"

Qabil thought back. Those days seemed so far in the past, those innocent days spent daydreaming and staring at clouds, talking with the other village children about the adventures they'd have when they grew up. Fewell, the miller's son, always said he was going to ride off one day and explore the world, nothing but his wits and his blade to keep him safe and prosperous. Samara, the baker's daughter, wanted nothing more than to open up a sweets shop in a city and have a little bell over the door that jingled all day as customers came and went. Tomar and Ramos, twin sons of a fisherman, loved horses. Tomar wanted to become a blacksmith and spend his days making horseshoes, and Ramos dreamt of being a messenger, riding from town to town all his life.

Then Fewell's father brought him into the mill and showed him how to run the business, and Samara's parents made a match for the baker's daughter and the miller's son to be betrothed, their children's fate no more than a logical business arrangement. Tomar fell overboard in rough seas the year before Qabil left home, and Ramos became just another taciturn fisherman with rough hands and dead eyes, as though half his life died with his brother.

And himself? Qabil wanted to see the world, and here he was, seeing it. Seeing the bottom of a lot of dirty pots, to be sure, and more dead bodies than he had expected in his childhood dreams, but seeing the world. He just wished he hadn't had to see his mother's grave first.

"No," he said. "It was nothing like this."

"Me neither," Thallis said. "A lot less shitting in the woods, if I'm being honest. And on that note, I'll be back in a moment."

Qabil waved at his friend's back as the lithe young man vanished into the woods, his hands already at the drawstring of his pants. He gathered up the rest of the plates, piled them all into the stewpot, and sat down at the base of a tree to wait for his friend to finish wiping his arse with a fistful of leaves, or a handful of moss if he was lucky.

No, none of his dreams of the grand adventures his life would take him on were ever like this.

CHAPTER FOURTEEN

Qabil sat by the campfire sipping coffee as he watched Thallis and Leshru go through their morning routine of stretches then shadow-dancing. The ground had thawed considerably since they had come down from the mountains, and the warm sun on his shoulders made him sleepy and wish he could crawl back into his bed. But he couldn't. They would be back on the road in an hour, as soon as everyone got their morning exercise out of the way and the camp struck.

"How far to the nearest town, Torg?" Nipural asked.

"There's a village half an hour west of here. Day and a half to the next place big enough to have an inn, if it's a real bed you're missing," the dwarf replied.

"I am that, don't doubt it," said the wizard. "But more to the point we're almost out of feed for the horses. I think we need to detour to this village and resupply, or we may not make it to the next."

"I thought we had plenty of provisions when we left Crag Steelhammer," Prynne said.

"I did, too. But apparently our horses are burning more fuel than I expected." He gestured wordlessly at Celia, who was, of course, looking right at him.

"You know I'm watching your every move, don't you?" the half-orc asked. "I'm a load for a horse, but we still should have had enough on the pack animals to make it to Destrir."

"That may be my fault," Qabil said. "I fed the horses the first two nights, and when Torgan helped me on the third—"

"Aye, lad, you were giving them half again as much as they needed, and the stupid animals were happy to just eat every bit of it. We're lucky none of them ate themselves sick. You're right. That's probably why we're short. Ah well, we were all young once. I could tell you about the time—"

"I'm sure you could, Torg, but instead of telling us about it, why don't you and I ride over to this village, get a couple bags of oats to carry us down the road, and be on about our way. Prynne, want to come with?" Nipural asked.

"No, I think I'll stay here. You figure this village is about an hour away?"

"Yes," Celia replied.

"Good enough. That gives me an hour for training and an hour for healing. Get up, fish-boy. Let's see what your mother taught you." She prodded Qabil with her foot.

He looked up at the ranger, standing there with two matched wooden poles in her hands and a smirk on her face. He stood and took one of the sticks from her. It was roughly sword-length, so he gripped it and held it out in front of him.

"Gods above and below, boy! Have you actually ever *held* a blade before?" Prynne asked, her eyes wide in astonishment.

Qabil looked down at his feet, then at his arm. His form looked just like he was taught. Feet shoulder-width apart, knees slightly bent, arm outstretched but bent at the elbow, blade up but not too high. "What's wrong? What am I doing wrong?"

"You look like you're waiting for the music to begin so you can dance with a fucking princess, not fight for your life!" She stepped in front of him, standing normally, her "blade" down by her side. Then quicker than Qabil could see, she stepped to the side, cracked his wrist with her "sword," causing him to drop his own stick, then took one step and lightly touched the tip of her faux sword to his throat. "You're dead."

"I wasn't ready!" he protested.

"Was Tara?" Prynne asked, and her eyes were as cold as her words. Qabil felt heat was over him in a roil of emotions: rage, shame, then fear as it dawned on him just what he was planning to try. "Now you begin to see. You aren't going to shoot this one, and he won't be some stupid bandit who hasn't even grown in his full beard yet. Yes, they told me about the men on the highway. You did well with a bow, but you've probably been hunting as long as you've been fishing, haven't you?"

Qabil nodded, not trusting himself to speak. How could he have thought he could take on one of The Seven? Walfert was going to carve him to bits, and the best he could hope for was that Leshru or one of the others would avenge his stupidity.

"So the bow is natural to you. But the sword obviously is not. Where did you get the one you're wearing, then? Tara didn't give it to you." It wasn't a question.

"No, she didn't. I...found it among her things after she...as I was leaving."

"Give me that," Leshru said, walking over and holding out a hand. Qabil unfastened the sword belt from his waist and handed the blade over, scabbard and all. The big man's brow furrowed as he looked at the hilt, then the crosspiece. "There's something under this cheap leather shit," he said as he picked at the cording on the hilt. Then he abruptly turned and stalked off, waving Thallis to follow.

"So you don't know shit about sword work," Prynne said. Her words weren't cruel, just matter of fact. She might have been commenting on the color of the sky, or the taste of the coffee. "Can you fight otherwise? Can you throw a punch at least? And take one?"

Now it was Qabil's turn to smirk at her. "I'm part elf from a shitty fishing village in the middle of nowhere and my mother was the prettiest woman for three days' ride in any direction. Do you think I got in a fist-fight or two over one or both of those things?"

She laughed. "Good point, boy. I bet you might have been punched in the nose once or twice, and probably punched back just as hard. Come at me." She held up her hand and waved him toward her.

"What?"

"Come at me. Hit me. Let me see what you can do." She beckoned him forward again, but Qabil just stood there, hands at his side.

"I can't hit you. You're a..." He didn't want to call her a lady because the hawk-faced ranger was anything but that, in her leather armor with her limbs wreathed in long, corded muscle. Qabil knew nothing of the ladies of court, but he couldn't imagine any of them wearing their hair hacked off at the jaw and slicked back with grease to stay out of their eyes when they fought. But he very much did not want to offend her, for a myriad of reasons, not the least of which being that he was still terrified of her, so he didn't want to *say* she wasn't a lady.

"I'm about as much a lady as you are, boy, despite the lack of anything hanging down from between my legs. I've fought men and monsters, armed and bare fisted, and now I'm going to see if you know anything about how to stay alive, or if I'm going to have to teach you from scratch. So hit me!" She yelled the last and stepped toward him with her fists raised.

Qabil reacted instinctively, raising his own fists and stepping forward to meet her. When he saw she wasn't backing down or stepping aside, he swung a left hand toward her face. She slapped it aside with her right hand, and Qabil took advantage of her focus to snap her head back with a jab right to her nose.

She staggered back a step, and for half a second, Qabil wondered if he had actually hurt her. Then he saw the grin on her face and heard the low chuckle coming from her throat. She came at him in earnest then, and the fight was on.

It wasn't much of a fight, although Qabil managed to land one more good punch, this one on the side of Prynne's head. She batted away most of his shots with an open palm, and her slapping against his forearms hurt like he was being beaten with a baton. Her hands were like wooden staves themselves, and when she stepped inside his guard and punched him in the gut, it felt like being kicked by a mule, a sensation he'd experienced once and had hoped never to repeat.

He dropped to one knee, working valiantly to hold back his breakfast. After a few sketchy seconds, he managed to take enough deep breaths through his nose that he felt fairly certain the contents of his stomach were going to remain where they started. He stood up, clutching his aching gut, and squared his shoulders, raising his fists to the grim-faced woman. "Okay, let's go again."

Prynne laughed, not the sideways snort she gave when she threw some barbed comment at her brother, but an honest, surprised laugh. She threw her head back and grinned like a fool as she howled her amusement. Finally, she pulled herself together and looked Qabil in the eye. "You've suffered enough for one morning. We'll take this up again tonight after we make camp."

"What do you mean, again?" he asked.

"Did they not tell you what I did for The Seven?" Prynne asked.

"You were the ranger. You tracked, found trails through the wilderness, and could shoot better than any man alive."

"All true. I can still shoot better than any man I've ever met. Don't ever make the mistake of thinking you're the best alive, though. I've seen too many make that claim and be proven wrong. Usually because they end up no longer alive. I have no doubt there's some scrawny little elf wandering through the Gaugrin Forest who has to down his dinner on the wing every night through thick cover that can outshoot me. But as I'm not likely to run afoul of his hunting, I can still lay claim to being the best archer alive. Because everyone who chooses to contradict me ends up dead." She smiled at Qabil, and he suppressed a shiver at the ice in her eyes.

"But I also taught them how to fight. Not Lesh, of course. He was the toughest bastard I've ever laid eyes on before I met him. But Torg, and Xethe, and Walfert, and Tara. I taught or sparred with them all. Even Nip, not that it did any good. My brother would rather spend ten minutes weaving a spell to render a guard unconscious than to knock him out with a ten-second rock to the skull."

"You taught my mother how to fight?"

"Some. She knew a lot from before she joined up with us. They teach bards how to defend themselves in most of the civilized schools, and that's what she thought she wanted to be." She got a faraway look in her eyes remembering her fallen friend.

"Why didn't she?" Qabil asked.

"Why didn't she what?"

"Why didn't she become a bard?" His mother had never told him she had any bardic training, never even played an instrument in his sight. Every once in a great while he would come upon her singing as she hung out laundry to dry, or keening a lament over his father's grave marker, just a simple stone in their back yard since there was seldom a body when a fisherman is lost in the storm.

"Something about a friend of hers that was killed on his final journeyman's tour. Maybe more than a friend, I never asked. But the girl was dear to Eltara, and when she was killed, Tara put away her lute and pipes and took up a blade in search of justice. Or maybe vengeance. I can never tell the difference between the two." She gave him a level stare. "She found the man who killed her friend, and she killed him. I asked her if it helped."

"What did she say?"

"No. She said it didn't take away any of the pain, so now she was in the same agony without anything to do about it."

"I suppose you think I should see the parallels between my mother's story and my own and abandon my quest for revenge and wander the countryside preaching forgiveness? Because if it brought my mother no peace, it obviously will bring me none as well."

"Not in the least. I think you should find Walfert, cut him open from his nuts to his nose, and splash around in his entrails like a child in a mud puddle after a spring rain. I plan to make a skipping rope out of his intestines if you leave enough length intact, myself." She wasn't smiling. There was nothing about her that made Qabil think she was anything but sincere.

"It might not make you feel better for long is all I want you to know. But if you don't learn which end of that sword goes in the other guy's guts, you'll be dead before Walfert gets so much as a skinned knee, so when we stop for the night, you'll practice with me. And again in the morning, and when we stop every night, until either I think you're good enough to last more than a handful of seconds against the ratfucking bastard I used to ride with, or until we're sitting on his doorstep and you don't have a choice."

"You think I'm going to die, don't you?" he asked.

"I'm certain you're going to die, boy. But since we'll already be there to avenge your mother, I'll stab him one extra time for you as well." With that, Prynne clapped him on the shoulder and steered him back toward the campfire. "Now get those pots scrubbed clean. Torg will be back soon, and we need to have the road under out feet."

85

CHAPTER FIFTEEN

Qabil stared across the bare patch of short grass at Prynne, his practice "blade" held out in front of him, point low as she had taught him. He watched the lean woman as she shifted her weight from side to side, passing her own three-foot wooden "sword" from hand to hand as if it were nothing more than a small knife, the kind one would peel an apple with.

Her eyes flicked toward his right knee, the one he had forward as he stood sideways facing her, and lunged. He knew her tricks by now and shifted to his left, picking his right foot up and catching a solid "thwack" on the side of his leg instead of a blow to the knee that would have left him limping for days. But he'd learned a great deal practicing with her for the past week, and he knew that such an obvious attack wouldn't come without a sneakier follow-up, and as he pushed off his right foot, he bent his left knee, dropping his face under the elbow she threw at his nose as she closed with him.

He slammed the end of his stick into the dirt, barely missing her toes as she scampered back, then spun quickly to his right to avoid her counterstrike. Then he charged, taking the offensive for a change, striking at her head again and again with his stick. She blocked his blows easily, but his flurry of heavy strikes left her no chance to retreat, and with every swing, he drove her back another step until finally her heel caught on a rock and she went down hard on the unforgiving ground.

With a guttural yell, Qabil drove in, thrilled to finally be on the verge of besting the legendary archer when suddenly he found himself airborne, then crashed to the ground on his back, the air rushing out of him in a loud "Oof!"

In a blink, Prynne had pushed herself off the ground, flipped over backward, and sat astride his chest, faux sword pressed to his throat. "Yield," she said with the same saucy smirk he'd been looking up at morning and night as she thrashed him for the past week.

"You first," he said, grinning like an idiot missing a village.

"Pretty sure this blade at your throat means I win, fish-boy," Prynne said, raising one eyebrow.

"Pretty sure that thing you feel pressing into your kidney doesn't mean I'm happy to see you," he replied with an eyebrow of his own.

Prynne twisted around to see his practice sword wedged against her back, tip poised for what would be a lethal strike with a real weapon, and a painful death at that. She moved the "blade" from his throat and stood, holding out a hand to help him to his feet. "Well done. Mutual death is sometimes the best you can hope for. If you can't survive a fight, at least avenge yourself on the way through Death's door. Good work."

Qabil smiled. That was the first sincere compliment he'd received from the woman. Everything else had been backhanded at best, if not purely insulting. "I'll take a draw. It's better than I've done up to now."

"You're improving, there's no doubt. You'd have to, or I'd have beaten you so black and blue you wouldn't be able to ride by now." Prynne held out her hand for his practice blade. "Now that I'm at least partly certain you won't cut your own jewels off, it's time to step up to live steel. Go get that blade off your horse."

Qabil froze. "Are you sure? I mean, I'm getting better, but..."

"Don't worry, lad. I won't cut off anything of yours that won't grow back, and if you manage to give me anything more than a flesh wound, then I'll know I was too damned old to come on this little jaunt in the first place. Now go get your sword."

Qabil hurried over to his horse, a placid mount named Daisy that he had traded for back at Torgan's camp. His old plow horse was tired, and making her go all the way down that mountain had seemed unnecessarily cruel. The miner he traded with promised him that Daisy was a solid mount with years left on her, and that the animal he left on the mountain would have a peaceful life pulling ore carts up from the mines. Qabil had gladly paid the difference in the animals' worths to have a horse under him that both Prynne and Leshru assured him would be strong enough for their journey and likely fast enough for anything they would encounter. She would never outrun a pack of wolves in a sprint, but neither would any mount bearing the massive Celia, so at least he'd be in good company for his last meal, even if he was the one being eaten.

He pulled his sword belt off Daisy's saddle and strapped it around his waist. He made sure the weapon hung properly on his hip, where he could walk or run without becoming tangled in his own blade and draw it without any awkward fumbling. It felt right, the sword, a comfortable weight on his side, as if he'd been missing something there for balance that he never knew he needed before.

He returned to the practice ground, really just a little area of shorter grass a few yards away from where Torgan and Celia were preparing the evening meal. The couple had taken over for preparation the moment they joined the party, thus sparing the rest of them from either the tough, bland meat that Leshru barely softened in the stew pot before serving, or the colorful and unpredictable concoctions that Nipural created. Prynne had never even taken a turn at cooking, informing Qabil and Thallis that the others had eaten her cooking before and sworn that the world was safer if she never prepared food again.

"Are you sure about this?" he asked again.

"Torgan can heal anything short of a mortal wound, and you'll have to be more hapless than my brother to screw up bad enough that you fall that far on your own sword," Prynne said, her smirk locked back onto her face. "That doesn't mean I won't bleed you a little, so draw that pigsticker and let's dance!"

She drew and cut at his face almost faster than he could see, but the week of practicing with her literally morning, noon, and night had taught him that her shoulder always went up just an instant before an attack, so he had enough warning to duck under her stroke and roll forward. This was a move they'd been working on, as it would be the last thing anyone would expect from a less experienced opponent—to rush toward the better swordsperson.

He came up onto one foot, still empty-handed, and swept his leg around to try and catch Prynne in the back of the knee. She knew the move well, since she was the one who taught it to him, and hopped straight up into the air to avoid his kick.

But that gave him just enough space and time to draw his sword and get some separation from her, which had been the whole point. He knew he wouldn't take her off her feet; he just wanted to change the plan of attack and get his sword in his hand before she decided it was time to put him on his arse in the grass. Again.

He heard a laugh from Thallis and brief applause, then the sound of drumming reached his ears. Celia had put aside her dinner preparations to watch his first attempts at fighting with a real blade in his hand. Great. An audience. Just what he needed. Qabil gave himself a mental shake and admonished himself to ignore the distractions and focus on the onrushing ranger.

Prynne came in with her blade twining through the air in short, tight loops, forming both a defensive and offensive shield of steel. Qabil couldn't get near enough to close with her, and any time he thrust at her body, he risked his sword getting tangled with hers and spinning off into the growing dusk. She stepped forward; he stepped back. She stepped forward again; he slid to the side to keep from getting pinned against a tree or tangled in the horses. Another advance, another retreat. They fell into a rhythm, and Qabil felt the drumming in his feet, as if the music was telling him when to move. *Dum-dum-DUM-dum, dum-dum-DUM-dum, dum-dum-DUM-DUM*—step, step, shift, step; step, step, shift, step; step, step, shift…

As if the pulse of battle had infused his every muscle, Qabil felt the flow of the music take him, and suddenly he was moving in perfect rhythm with the drumming, which was itself in perfect rhythm with Prynne's movements. She stepped; he faded back. She stepped; he stepped back. She stepped; he shifted. She stepped again, and this time he lunged, reversing his movements and batting her blade to the side. In an instant he was inside her guard and pressing his blade to the side of her throat.

"Yield," he said, then looked down to see if she had a dagger to his groin. He wouldn't put it past the sneaky warrior to have baited him in just to prove a point. But her off hand was empty. He looked back to her face, and her eyes were wide.

"I yield," she said, and stepped back from him. She was pale, and there was a trembling in her arms. "What the fuck was that, fish-boy?" She almost shouted, but it seemed like she pulled herself back at the very last moment.

"I don't know," Qabil said, confused. "I fell into the rhythm of your movements, and the drumming, and…"

"Oh, fuck me running," Prynne said, sliding her sword back into the scabbard at her side. "Lesh! Did you know this little shit was a Dancer?"

Leshru looked over at her and shrugged. "Thought it likely. Figured if he was, you'd find out for us soon enough."

Prynne looked back at Qabil, muttering "Prick" under her breath. She walked over to the confused young man. "You have no bleeding idea what I'm talking about, do you?"

"Not in the least. Leshru called my mother a Sword Dancer once, but I've never heard that before. What is it, and what makes you think I'm one?"

"Come on, boy," she said, walking over to the cookfire. "This is going to take some explaining, and I hate giving history lessons on an empty stomach."

"Or a sober one, eh, sister?" Nipural said, holding out a wineskin to her.

"That's the damned truth," Prynne replied, taking a long pull at the wine. She waved Thallis over. "Come on, little thiefling. You might as well hear it, too. You'll just eavesdrop if I try to keep you out of it."

"Too right you are," Thallis said, folding his legs under himself and sitting on the grass. "I love story time, Granny." He gave Prynne an impudent smile, which was not returned.

"This granny will wear you balls for earbobs if you piss her off. Remember that."

Thallis paled and nodded as Qabil sat next to him. "Alright, then," Qabil said. "What the hell is a Sword Dancer, and what makes you think I am one?"

CHAPTER SIXTEEN

Prynne took a long draught off her wineskin and leaned back against the wide trunk of a massive oak. She gave Qabil a penetrating look, then let out a sigh. "How much do you know about your mother? About her before your memories start?"

"Not much," he admitted. "She didn't talk much about anything that happened before she came to Narim. I never even knew she was one of The Seven until the first time Walfert came to call."

"Did you ever see her with a sword in her hand?"

"No. I…" His voice trailed off as he touched the hilt of his weapon. Blinking back tears, it felt like he was looking in on himself as he sat on her bed, afternoon sun streaming in through the window, still wrapped in his funeral finery, just staring off into the suddenly murky future.

Just three days before, everything had been clear. He would marry Linnea, if he could ever master a trade sufficiently to gain her father's approval. Winning her mother over had been easier than snagging Linn's attention. A blacksmith's daughter was a catch in a small village or town, even one like Narim where shipwrights and net-menders were in more demand than smiths, and the most complex thing Linnea's father was likely to craft were fishhooks. But Qabil loved her, and she loved him, and for her, he would learn to pump the bellows and sharpen fishhooks, if becoming a blacksmith's apprentice was what it took to convince her father that he was a serious man and not some flighty child.

Three days before, the world made sense. His mother had been sitting by the fire humming softly to herself as she knit a blanket, her favorite way to pass the evening hours. Qabil had been where he was after every meal: elbow-deep in a washbasin scrubbing clean the pots and plates. He often joked that if he didn't take up smithing, he could earn a good living for himself and Linn as a scullery maid.

Then the door opened, and Bothun stood on the threshold with three shadowy figures behind him. They rushed into the small cabin, the elvish "security chief" and two of his men sweeping his mother out of her chair and toward the door, and the other corralling Qabil in the kitchen. He fought, as well as he could, but one untrained almost-man was no match for an experienced guardsman, even if they were unwashed, poorly outfitted mercenaries.

Qabil rushed the one stalking him, a thick-shouldered man with a patchy chin beard and sparse mustache. The mercenary had a pock-marked complexion and cold, flat eyes, and when Qabil came at him, he just stepped to one side and lifted a knee into his gut. The boy dropped to his knees like a stone, and the mercenary took two steps forward and slammed a fist into Qabil's temple. He crashed to the floor, his arms and legs no longer taking orders from his brain, and lay there, watching as the men surrounded his mother.

Bothun had his men hold Eltara's arms, and when she struggled, he slapped her hard enough across the face to split open her lip. Qabil never saw her shed a tear, just glare at the elf with a hatred like he had never seen before.

"You dare come into my house and lay hands upon me? Run away now, Bothun of No Land, and perhaps you can burrow you way deep enough underground before I catch up to you that you'll live to see the sun rise." Then she spat a glob of blood in the assassin's face and brought her right heel down hard on the arch of one of her captors' feet. The man on her right let go of her arm, and before Qabil could even register what happened, his mother had spun around the man holding her left arm, drew a dagger from his belt, and sliced him open from his belly to his chin.

The dying man fell backward, vainly trying to hold his guts inside, and Eltara flipped the blade around in her hand, whirled to the right, and buried the dagger in the chest of her other captor. Then she drew the mercenary's sword as he fell to the ground and turned to face Bothun.

"It doesn't have to be this way, Eltara," the weasel-faced elf said. He put the lie to the myth that all elves were graceful and lovely. Not just because of the trio of wide scars running down the left side of his face, as if someone dragged their fingernails from his brow to his jawline, but he just seemed to be an ill-assembled cluster of features that might be beautiful on their own, but meshed into a whole that was just somehow a little off and disconcerting.

"I won't marry Walfert," Eltara said. "I said no the first time he asked, and the second, and all the subsequent times. I won't say yes now just because he's managed to steal himself a throne somewhere. I had a husband. One I loved, and lost. I won't take another."

"But you will," Bothun said. "You'll marry Walfert, and you'll sit beside him, and you'll lay with him. Or I'll do unspeakable things to your boy. I'm already going to build a special cell in the dungeon, just for him. But if you don't do as you're told, I'm going to make him mine just like Walfert is going to make you his. My master and I will *own* you both, body and soul."

"Not fucking likely," Eltara said, and Qabil drew in a sharp breath. He'd never heard his mother swear like that before, but if ever it was warranted, this was the night. "Do you remember who I am? *What* I am?"

"I remember what you *were*," the elf said with a cold smile that didn't touch his eyes. "I suppose now we'll see if you're still anything like the woman you used to be."

Qabil watched from the floor as his mother and the elvish assassin dueled throughout their cramped living quarters. Bothun would feint forward; Eltara would parry. Eltara would make a slashing cut at his face; Bothun would block and spin to stab at her midsection. Through it all, Eltara kept up a steady rhythm, her heels thudding into the floor in time with her movements. It seemed as though she had a song playing in her head and her body was moving to a rhythm only she could hear.

Bothun waved the last surviving guard back, keeping him out of the fray. Even inexperienced as he was, Qabil recognized the wisdom in this. They weren't used to fighting together, so they would almost certainly get tangled up, and his mother would dispatch them as fast as she had their fellows. He watched his mother and the assassin circle each other, pulling chairs and end tables over to foul the other's steps, neither one able to maneuver in the tight quarters. Through it all, Eltara kept the beat, and whenever her path brought her near Qabil, he could swear he heard her humming under her breath.

They danced. That was the only way to describe it because that's what it was more than anything. Their steps seemed almost perfectly rehearsed, and neither one put a foot wrong. Qabil felt like it was only a matter of time, though. It was *their* house. That had to give Eltara an advantage. He pulled himself up to his knees, fighting to keep the dizziness and nausea at bay as his head swam from the blow to his temple. He swayed a little, but stayed upright, then his eyes widened as the last guard came over to him, dagger in hand.

"Drop the sword or I'll cut the brat's throat," the mercenary said. He was a stout man, with close-cropped hair and a thick beard, and he smelled of onions and grease. He yanked Qabil's hair back, and the boy twisted around just enough to jam an elbow into the man's groin. He doubled over, loosening his grasp on Qabil's hair, and as the boy stood, he twisted the dagger out of the mercenary's hand, slicing open his palm in the process. But once he had the knife, he wasted no time, just buried it to the hilt in the man's guts, twisting as he did. The would-be killer's eyes went wide, and he gripped Qabil's wrist in a viselike grip that slowly, ever so slowly, went slack as his gaze grew blank and he slumped to the floor, his lifeboat streaming down Qabil's arm.

He turned away from the dead man to see his mother staring at him, a look of horror on her face. It took him half an instant to realize her expression wasn't for him, but rather herself, and at the blade Bothun had slid into her midsection. The assassin stepped forward, driving his sword deeper and finally through Eltara's abdomen, and the elf held her up until there was no light left in her eyes. Then he shoved her to the floor where she lay on her back, eyes open but unseeing, as a pool of blood spread beneath her.

"Mother!" Qabil screamed, and ran toward her killer. All he saw was rage, all he felt was pain, and all he wanted was to feel the scar-faced elf's life rush out on his blade. But Bothun stepped aside and rapped him on the head again with the butt of his sword, and Qabil sprawled over his mother's cooling body.

"Too bad," Bothun said. "I would have enjoyed breaking you body and spirit, boy. But I can't bring back a toy for myself and leave Walfert's prize lying in the dirt, now, can I? Don't worry. This will hurt a great deal, but not for very long."

Qabil felt a hand grab his shoulder and roll him over, and his throbbing head got the better of him. He vomited straight up into the air, spewing bits of fish stew into the elf's face. Bothun staggered back, wiping at his eyes and cursing, then the door to their house burst open.

"What in all the hells is going on here?" Came a thundering bellow, and the door was filled with the massive form of Yablod, Linnea's blacksmith father. "Qabil? Are you in here, boy? What the fuck is all—*urk!*" His words cut off as Bothun slammed a shoulder into the man's gut and knocked him to the floor.

"Gods damn it," the elf said, turning back to Qabil. "What a fucking mess." Then he drew a dagger from his belt and pulled it back to throw. Just as he released the blade, Yablod punched him in the knee with his massive fist, and the dagger tumbled end over end, burying itself in Eltara's stomach rather than Qabil's throat. With another muttered curse, the elf shoved the blacksmith back down and ran off into the night. Qabil watched him go through swimming eyes, then pain, and grief, and fear swept him away and everything was black.

That was three days ago. Today he watched as four men lowered the box that held his mother into a hole in the ground, and he threw the first handful of dirt onto her himself. Then he came back to his empty house, where the door still hung off its hinges, but the village women had at least come in to scrub the floors while he lay in his bedroom and alternately wept and screamed.

It was quiet now, empty. All the well-wishers were gone, and he was alone with his thoughts, his memories, and the dark stains on the wooden floorboards that were all that remained of his mother. He went into her room, sat down on her bed, and just...looked. He really *looked* at the room for the first time, taking in everything he had seen all his life but ignored because it was home, it was his mother's room, it was...familiar.

But no more. His mother hadn't just been a fisherman's widow. She'd been one of the most famous warriors the world had ever seen, and after seeing how she dueled Bothun and his men, he knew the stories were not exaggerated. If anything, they undersold her abilities.

But this room, these were the things that would tell him who Eltara really was, and how to avenge her. The answer was here, in front of him, he just had to find it. He looked around, trying to push down the grief and the fury and look at it with a dispassionate eye. His mother's voice came back to him, soothing him when he would fight with other boys.

"You must always stay calm. Fear and anger cloud your mind, and your eye. They do not serve you, or any purpose of yours. They exist only to destroy you," she said as she cleaned his bloody knuckles with a damp cloth. "If you must fight, then fight to win. But do not fight out of anger, for when you raise your hand in rage, you have already lost."

He couldn't hunt down his mother's killer with pure righteous anger. That would just leave him buried next to her when Bothun gutted him like a fresh flounder. He needed help, he needed allies, he needed...The Seven. He knew his mother had been part of the famous band of mercenaries, heroes to some, outlaws to others, but legends to all who heard their tales. Before he saw her fight, he thought she was just a friend to the adventurers, but now? Now he knew that she battled alongside these titans, these wizards and warriors, and they would help him find justice for her murder.

Now to find them. He walked over to the small wooden dresser where his mother kept her clothes, a modest, scarred hunk of pine that he had looked at for years, but now saw must have had many lives before it came to their home. It was rough-hewn and scuffed, with scratches on the top and sides, and one drawer missing its handle.

If Eltara was a famous hero, why did they live so simply? Why didn't they have a palace, or at least a manor? And servants. Servants would have been nice. Then he wouldn't have had to wash so many pots and plates in his life. But his mother wasn't like that. She wanted a simple life, maybe *because* she had seen so much of the world with her friends, she wanted to have something of a normal life as she raised her son.

"Well, Mother," he said to the empty room. "You got so much normal it was downright dull. But now that I've seen how much blood comes alongside excitement, I'd rather return to boring." He opened the top drawer of the dresser, feeling uncomfortable looking through his mother's things but knowing he needed any information he could find on her old companions.

The top pair of drawers yielded nothing but clothes, as did the next two. But when he pulled out the bottom drawer, it slid right out into his hands, much shorter than the ones above it. There was nothing of interest in the drawer, just a few brightly colored summer dresses his mother seldom wore after his father died. He knelt on the floor and bent down until his head was almost level with the floor, peering into the dark recesses of the piece of furniture.

Seeing nothing, he stretched one arm back into the recess where the drawer had sat, and after not nearly enough distance to reach the back of the dresser, felt his fingers meet resistance. He ran his hand across the surface—a wooden panel hiding a hollow space behind, if the sound from his tapping fingers was any indicator. He pressed the panel in the center, then at the corners, then felt around blindly for some type of trigger to release it, until finally he found a small hole carved into the wood. He hooked a finger through it and pulled, and the panel popped free with only the slightest resistance.

Pulling the false back out of the way, Qabil reached into the recess behind, feeling a cloth bag, something metallic and yielding, and something long wrapped in fabric. He pulled the items out of the dresser and sat back on the floor, looking at what he'd found. The bundle of loose metal that he found was in fact a chain shirt made of a lightweight metal woven into interlocking rings of bright metal. He'd never seen it, but recognized the elf-crafted chain shirt from stories he'd read about The Seven and their near-miraculous arms and armor.

The long cylinder was a sword in a scabbard, a slender double-edged blade nearly two feet in length, with a blue gem set into the crosspiece and a hilt and pommel wrapped in brown leather. The scabbard was brown leather as well, with silvered flowers decorating the length of it. Qabil drew the blade and swung it through the air, marveling at how light and quick the weapon was. He resolved to ask Yablod if there was anything special about the metal, or if it was perhaps enchanted in some way.

The last thing he examined was a small pack, fit for carrying over both shoulders or one as the bearer chose, bulging with something heavy and lumpy that clinked as he moved it. Qabil opened the pack and dumped its contents out onto the floor, his eyes going wide as dinner plates at the gold and platinum coins that spilled out. More money than he had ever seen in one place scattered across the floor in front of him, and mixed in with the metal coins were gems of all colors and pieces of jewelry in gold, silver, and platinum, plus a few in metals he didn't recognize. The last things to tumble out of the pack were a smaller pouch, which landed amidst the pile of coins with a heavy *thunk*, and a leather-bound journal, which he snatched up excitedly. Perhaps this would answer some of his questions. Perhaps this would lead him to the rest of The Seven and to vengeance on the bastard who killed his mother.

CHAPTER SEVENTEEN

The journal told me of her companions, and how to find Leshru. It was like she wrote the book just for me, as if she knew that something would happen to her and I would need to find The Seven someday. The next morning, I took some of the money, gave the rest to Yablod for safekeeping, and rode off looking for Leshru." Qabil looked around and noticed that the sun had set and the rest of their party was now sitting in the circle with them, staring into his face.

He also noticed that his stomach was becoming very insistent that he put something in it, so when Thallis handed him a bowl of stew, he nodded and began shoveling it into his mouth without even really tasting it.

Prynne nodded, as if that were her cue to begin talking. "So that's how she died, and I can guess from that tale how she lived as well. She never behaved like she was the wealthiest person in that town, or likely county, and never even told you she had a sack full of riches tucked away somewhere in the house, did she?"

Qabil didn't stop eating, just shook his head at her and took a long drink of the waterskin Thallis offered.

"Sounds like Tara," Torgan said quietly, looking up at his wife. "She never was much of one for riches."

"She didn't have to be," Prynne said. "When you grow up wealthy, you don't think about being wealthy. It's only us poor bastards who think about getting rich. Tara was rich from the start, so anything she got with us was just icing."

"What do you mean, she was rich?" Nipural asked. "She never said anything about that to me."

"Nor me," Torgan said.

"She didn't have to say it, numbskulls. Eltara's breeding and status showed through in everything she did, from the way she was useless in the kitchen to how she walked into a room and stopped, as if waiting for someone to announce her. You may have called her 'Princess' as a joke, but I'll bet it wasn't far off the mark," Prynne said.

"Prynne's right," Celia said. "I only met her briefly, but even someone raised as an abomination and an exile could see that she was a proper lady. Not like the bitches who ran the village where I was raised."

"I don't know anything about that," Qabil said. "She never really talked about her time before coming to Narim and meeting my father. I mean, she was just my mother, you know? She wasn't anything extraordinary. Until…"

"Until she wasn't there and you realize how extraordinary she was," Thallis said, passing him a fresh waterskin. "That's how it is for a kid. Your parents, if you've got the whole pair, they're just there. It ain't 'til one or both of them is gone that you know how precious what you lost truly was."

"She wasn't a princess," Leshru said. Qabil looked across and saw the firelight playing across the big man's dark skin, creating deep shadows around his eyes. "She wasn't a princess, but she was some kind of bastard daughter of an elf lord."

"When did she tell you this?" Nipural demanded, leaning forward. "And why are we just learning about it now?"

"She told me when we traveled together, before we were seven. When it was just me, and Tara, and Xethe, the shiftless fuck. I met the pair of them in a tavern in Dital, where I'd been fighting in the pits for money. I used a sword then, and I was good with it. Damned good. But I had a bad habit of drinking up everything I won fighting, so then I'd have to go back and fight some more to make more money to buy more drink. Nobody in Dital would fight me anymore, on account of I hurt too many of my opponents, so I was looking for a way out of town. That's when I ran into Tara and Xethe."

"Hold up a minute," Thallis said. "You had to stop fighting because you were too good?" He looked around the fire. "Does that seem like subtle bragging to anybody else? What do you mean you hurt too many people?"

"The fights in Dital were mostly civilized. They were to first blood, unless the fighters or their sponsors had some kind of grievance. But like I said, I drank too much. And not always after the fight, either. I cut off about three too many sword hands, and my sponsor couldn't find anyone willing to stand across from me. So I found myself without a sponsor. Not a big problem, it's perfectly legal for a fighter to pay their own entry if they can afford it, and then they don't have to split the purse with a sponsor. Problem was, if nobody will fight you, there's no point in entering the contest. So it was time to leave Dital and go somewhere, hopefully far enough away that nobody would have heard of Leshru the Light-Footed."

"Leshru the...*what?*" Nipural's eyes bugged out, and he almost spit wine into the fire.

"Shut up. It was a long time ago. I was a skinny lad, if you can believe it. Sword work uses different muscles than brawling, and it benefits you to be fast rather than powerful. I was both, back then."

"That's been a while," Torgan said under his breath.

"Can still beat you in a footrace, Stumpy," Leshru shot back with a grin.

"What does this have to do with my mother?" Qabil asked.

"Like I said, I met them in a tavern. They were playing and passing the hat, and I was drinking and keeping my ear to the ground for any caravan or merchant that might need an extra guard. Some fat slug decided that your mother's arse looked like it was the right shape for a squeeze when she came off the stage to take a break, and when she slapped the piss out of him, the whole bleeding place erupted in a brawl. Seemed like they'd all just been waiting for an excuse to beat the shit out of each other, so Tara's ass was the excuse they needed. Sorry to be talking about your mother's—"

"Let's just...not anymore, okay?" Qabil asked.

"Fair enough," Leshru replied. "There I was, sitting at the bar minding my own business, which is a complete lie, since I was eavesdropping on every bastard I could find who looked like he might have two coins to rub together. But a fight breaks out around me, and I'm not one to let an opportunity go to waste, so the first fool that comes within arm's reach, I bash him in the jaw and take his purse."

"You just robbed him?" Thallis asked, a shocked look across his face.

"I was a drunken pit fighter who punched people in the face for money. I just considered it brief employment—I punched him in the face, then I took his money. I did that a few more times until I figured I had enough coin to buy myself passage in a caravan bound somewhere they'd never heard of me, and headed for the door. I almost made it, too. But your mother stopped me."

"How did she do that?" Qabil asked.

"She got thrown across the room by an angry half-orc and landed on top of me," Leshru replied. "I went down like a ton of bricks, Tara came to her feet with a sword in her hand and blood in her eyes, looking for something to stab, and I was lucky not to be her target. I wasn't so much upset as being felled by a woman, but I thought it was unseemly for the bastard to have thrown somebody at me, so I waded into the fight. I didn't want to kill anybody, as that would probably delay me leaving town while the locals decided whether or not to hang me, so I just walked over and calmly punched the orc a few times until he went to sleep."

"You say that like it's nothing to beat an angry half-orc unconscious," Celia said with a smirk. "I happen to know for a fact that my people have notoriously hard heads."

"Truer words have never been spoken," Torgan said with a chuckle. His wife mock-glared at him, then motioned for Leshru to continue.

"Well, I may have needed to punch him pretty hard, but eventually he went down. I figured that was enough to keep my reputation as a tough bastard intact, so I tried to leave again, but your mother was blocking the door."

"How was she doing that?" Qabil asked.

"By fighting two men and a dwarf at the same time, all the while humming a tune to herself as she parried their blades. I'd never seen anything like it, boy. It was like the music had hold of her and she was only partly present. She seemed to see the swords before they were even swung, and ducked, or spun, or twisted away from everything she didn't block. And she never struck back, either. It was like she knew they wouldn't be able to hurt her, so she shouldn't hurt them. It was a thing of beauty."

"Only you would find beauty in a bar brawl, Lesh," Nipural said.

"You know I'm right. You saw her later on. Whenever shit went sideways and we were in the thick of it, Tara would start tapping her foot, or humming, or even whistling, and you knew that we were going to be alright."

"He's not wrong," Prynne said. 'That's what Sword Dancers do—they turn music into motion and translate that motion into nearly unstoppable fighting. You said your mother never taught you anything about the sword, but did she teach you to dance?"

Qabil looked confused, but said, "Yes. She always loved to dance, and she taught me to dance beside her. She always said that her dances weren't meant to be danced holding your partner, but rather facing them and dancing around them."

"Because they're meant to be danced while each of you are holding a sword," the ranger said. "Sword Dancing is an ancient art, perfected by elves far from here and brought to Gaugrin Forest thousands of years ago. Tara must have learned it from her father, long before she ever went on the road with Xethe."

"That's what she told me the morning after the fight," Leshru said. "After she knocked out the three morons fighting her, she and I bolted out into the night. Xethe grabbed their instruments and met us on the edge of town, and we walked half the night before making camp. We wanted to make sure if anyone from the town was interested in settling any scores, that we made it as difficult as possible. The next morning, we agreed to travel together, and over a shared breakfast, I asked her where she learned to fight like that.

"I'd seen a lot of different fighting styles in the pits, but nothing that used rhythm in that way. It was very fluid, and incredibly graceful, and I was pretty sure I couldn't master it if I had centuries to learn, but I wanted to try."

"Did she teach you?" Qabil asked.

"No," Leshru replied with a rueful shake of his head. "Not for lack of trying on either of our parts, but even for Leshru the Light-Footed, I was too thick and slow to learn it. I got better, and it made me a better fighter overall, learning to look for the rhythm and patterns of an enemy's attack, but she would have had to start teaching me when I was a child for it to stick."

"Like she did with me," Qabil said.

"Aye, like she did with you."

Qabil took a long breath and let it out slowly. "So what does that do for me? Is it going to keep me alive against Walfert? Bothun? The dances she taught me were pretty, but I can't imagine they'll do me much good against a trained warrior."

"What am I, boy?" Prynne asked. "Remember, I yielded to you. I didn't do that out of charity. I did it because I was beaten. If we can take the 'dances' your mother taught you and move them into swordplay, we might be able to keep you alive long enough to stick a knife in Walfert's guts after all."

"And if not, you'll fight real pretty before you die," Thallis said, clapping Qabil on the shoulder. Somehow, that didn't make him feel any better.

CHAPTER EIGHTEEN

Qabil rode apart, head down, allowing the warm drizzle to soak into his hooded cloak and occasionally form one long droplet of water that grew and grew until it plopped down off the tip of the hood, barely missing his nose before it splashed onto the horn of his saddle. The gray sky matched the gloomy expression on his face as his horse plodded along. The weather wasn't bad, so much as it just wasn't good. It wasn't a real rain, nothing worth stopping over, and barely enough to put one's hood up for, but after riding through it all morning, he found himself soaked to the bone and wondering how exactly he felt so much water sloshing around in his boots when it has barely rained.

"Penny for 'em," Thallis said, pulling his horse up to ride alongside Qabil. When he received no response, the young thief leaned over and poked Qabil in the shoulder. "Ay! I'm bothering you, so be bothered!"

Qabil smiled at his friend, not the most unlikely of companions, but definitely close to it. "Just thinking."

"I can see that. The smoke from your ears makes it hard to see if I try to ride behind you. What about?"

"Walfert. Mother. This whole Sword Dancer business."

"You think he's going to kill you?"

"Probably."

"Then we're going to need a plan that isn't just 'walk up to him and start with the stabbing.' Have you given that any thought?"

"Not really. Mostly I've just been trying to figure out how I feel about this new side of my mother, and of my life, really. I mean, it seems that every game I played as a child, every dance she taught me, was really meant to be performed with a blade in my hand. What does that say about her? About the life she thought I would lead?"

"I don't know what kind of life she thought you'd have, but I think what it says about her is that she loved you and wanted to protect you. And the best way she could do that was to make sure you could protect yourself. Look, you ain't no little squirt like me, but you ain't the biggest guy I ever seen, neither. I'm betting there were plenty of kids growing up bigger than you, and a few meaner."

"Most were meaner," Qabil said. "If Mother had ever heard of me being cruel to anyone, she'd have flayed me alive."

"Aye, figured as much. So you probably got your fair share of shit handed to you when you was a kid, right?"

"Yeah, I suppose. No more than everybody else..." His words trailed off, and his friend pounced on the opening.

"But that ain't true, is it? You got pounded a few times when you were younger, but then it all stopped. Probably after one of them tried something and found you weren't as easy a target as you once were."

Qabil thought for a moment, then nodded. "You're right. There was one fight where I gave as good as I got, and after that, nobody really came after me anymore."

"I'm going to guess that happened not long after your ma started teaching you those new dances, eh?"

Qabil smiled. "Aye. She knew what was going on, but she didn't want me fighting, so she taught me without teaching me. I didn't win that fight, but the other boy knew he'd been in a scrap when were done."

"Bullies can't abide that shit. Once you weren't just going to stand there and get your face bashed in, they stopped messing with you."

"I guess you're right. Maybe I did learn more from her than I thought. And maybe that, coupled with what Prynne's been teaching me, will make the difference against Walfert."

Thallis's eyes narrowed as he looked over Qabil's shoulder. "Might get put to the test sooner than that, if the smoke I see up ahead is any indication. Looks like that village we're trying to get to before dark is on fire. We'd better ride."

Qabil glanced over to where his friend pointed, then saw the rest of their band picking up the pace. "How far to Radsford?" he called out.

"About an hour at a walk," Celia replied. She pulled a short horse bow from its place on her saddle and bent it to string as her stout horse began to trot forward. "A quarter of that if we run. Go ahead, we'll catch up to you there." She gestured to her thick-bodied mount, more plow horse than trotter, and Torgan's short-legged pony.

Prynne took the lead, her horse off at a gallop with Leshru close on her heels. Thallis and Qabil followed suit, with Nipural behind them. Hooves pounded and dirt flew up in a cloud as they raced to the small village, barely more than a few shops and an inn from what Celia had told them about the place. They crested a small hill, and the scene ahead made them all draw up short.

"What the fuck?" Leshru swore.

"Bandits," Prynne said. "Probably some local shitheel who decided to play at being a warlord. The town likely got tired of paying his 'taxes' and told him to bugger off, so he's decided to teach them a lesson."

The "lesson" was being written in blood and fire, as the inn, the central feature of any small village, was engulfed in roaring flames. A two-story building, wide enough for the whole village to gather when need be, the inn obviously had doubled as a meeting hall, tavern, and lodging for any travelers seeking refuge along the road.

There was no refuge to be had today, just flame as what looked like the entire town was gathered in the square in front of the building, watching in horror as a gaggle of rough-looking men in mismatched armor and ragged cloaks erected a trio of large X-shaped frames of wood in the space before the burning inn. A fat bald man was tied to one, his limbs splayed out and strapped to the frame. A woman of similar age was strapped to another, and a boy a little younger than Qabil occupied the third.

"That must be the innkeeper and his family," Thallis said. "We've got to do something!"

"What do you want to do, boy? Run down there in the middle of a dozen men with nothing but we five and get yourself cut to ribbons?" Leshru asked. "Oh wait, I meant we four."

Qabil looked around, and sure enough, Prynne was nowhere to be seen. "Where?"

"Just watch, son," came Nipural's soft voice at his shoulder. "Watch, and do whatever Lesh tells you to do, as fast as he says it. Faster, if you can." Qabil looked over at the old wizard and was surprised by what he saw in the man's face. The slightly dotty oldster he'd been traveling with was gone, but this time it wasn't replaced by the nostalgic old wizard looking back on his life that often appeared around the campfire at night, or the waspish grump who rolled out of Nipural's tent in the morning before his coffee. No, this was a stern-faced adventurer, with eyes full of secrets and a countenance of clouds. This man carried a wealth of years in his gray hair and lined face, but his eyes were sharp, and his jaw was set. This Nipural was ready for a fight.

"You understand me? Wait here. Do what Lesh tells you. Thallis, follow me." Nipural's voice cracked like a whip, and even the normally quick-tongued Thallis had no reply. The wizard and the young thief peeled off from Leshru and Qabil and rode off to the right, toward another small road leading into town.

"What are we going to do?" Qabil asked.

"We're going to ride in there and ask very politely what the fuck is going on," Leshru replied.

"And if we don't like the answer?"

"Well, then I suppose someone is in for a bad afternoon." The big man clucked at his horse, and Qabil fell into step behind him.

It only took a few moments for them to ride down the hill into the village, but by that time, the man and what was presumably his family were stretched across the trio of wooden structures. The men were turned away from the crowd, facing the still-burning inn, and stripped to the waist. The woman's frame was carried off to the side, and she was positioned where she could see both the men and the fire.

A tall man with lean arms and legs walked in front of the men, then turned to address the crowd. His armor was a little better than the other thugs, his boots a little shinier, his sword a little finer. He held a whip coiled in his right hand, and he slapped it into his left palm with every slow step. The man raised his voice to be heard over the crackle of burning wood, and when he spoke, a cruel smile stretched across his face.

"Bear witness, my neighbors, to the punishment of those who dare to cheat our Lord Untrek! This man, Everette, your friend, your innkeeper, your kinsman...this man has held back on the taxes rightly due our lord. He has shorted the tax collector for three moons running, and now his bill must be paid in full! He will be an example for all of you of what will happen if you do not do your part. We must all contribute to the workings of our great community. It is selfish of Everette to withhold the funds that our lord so desperately needs to defend you from the beasts of the forest, to keep the roads safe from bandits, to push back the rising tide of refugees from the war-torn lands to the east!"

Qabil stared at Leshru. "What the hell is he talking about? There's no war to the east. At least, none close enough for people to be coming here."

"I know that. You know that. The prick holding the whip knows that. But these farmers don't know that. All they know is someone is standing in front of them telling them to be afraid, and if they aren't afraid enough, he'll give them something to fear." The big man's face was stony, his jaw set and his eyes narrowed. "I count eight here in the square. Did you mark any others as we road in?"

"I saw no sentries, if that's what you mean."

"Then probably less than a dozen. Pretty simple, long as none of them have bows. Come on." He slid from the saddle and strode forward as he strapped the familiar metal bands across his knuckles. "Much more of this and I'm going to have to go back to just wearing these fucking things all the time."

Qabil tied off both horses to a post by the smithy to their right and hurried after his companion. He loosened his sword in its scabbard, feeling his blood begin to pulse in his ears.

"Stay calm, boy. I'm going to try to talk this down, but I don't have high hopes for that."

"And if you can't?"

"Then it gets interesting." Leshru reached the edge of the gathered villagers as the slender man continued to shout about oncoming hordes of refugees who would steal their crops, rape their women, and befoul the land. Just as he reached a crescendo of fear mongering, with the crowd beginning to mutter angrily at the innkeeper and his family, Leshru stepped through the front ranks of the assembled people, Qabil close at his side, and began to clap loudly.

The whip man faltered, his words tumbling over each other, and he actually stumbled as he spun to look at the grinning bald warrior applauding him. A broad smile split Leshru's stubbled face and he applauded more furiously as the man turned his attention on him. "Bravo! Well played, sir! You almost had them believing that pile of horseshit. I guess it's like a bard I once knew always said—if you lie big enough, and loud enough, people will believe even the stupidest tale."

"Who are you, old man? Do you want to be flogged alongside your friends here? We can always build another cross," the thin man said, letting the whip uncoil in his grip.

"I'm just a traveler," Leshru replied. "My name doesn't matter. But I just came from the east. There's no war there. There are no refugees coming here. No one is trying to take these people's crops or fondle their children. Except you and your raggedy bunch of bullyboys."

Instead of engaging with Leshru, the man turned to the crowd. "Who will you believe? This stranger, who you've never seen before today? Or me, the duly appointed representative of the lord of this region, Untrek the Bold!"

"Yes," Leshru addressed the crowd, pitching his voice to match the indignation in the other man's tone. "Who will you trust? A stranger, who rides in with no weapon in his hand, asking you for nothing, gaining nothing from his words, or the scrawny prick who robs you blind, burns up your liquor, and whips your friends?"

"That's your idea of diplomacy?" Qabil hissed.

"I'm not very good at the talking parts," Leshru whispered back. "I usually just go straight to the hitting people parts."

"Well, it seems that we've reached that point. Again," Qabil said as the "tax collector" and his thugs drew their swords and formed up in front of them.

"Told you it would get interesting," Leshru said with a grin.

CHAPTER NINETEEN

I'll give you one last chance," Leshru said to the assembled bandits purporting to be tax collectors. "If you throw down your swords now, we won't kill any of you."

"You? Kill us?" one of the men jeered. "I don't know if you can count or not, old man, but there's a lot more of us than there are of you."

"Aye, you're outnumbered," Leshru replied. "That's why I'm giving you an out. No shame in backing down from a superior force."

"The day an old man and a boy are superior to me and my men is the day you can throw dirt over me," said the leader as he raised the whip over his head. He brought the lash down, but Leshru just stepped to one side, stuck out his arm, and let the whip wrap around it several times. He grabbed the leather weapon with his left hand and jerked hard, pulling the bandit leader to him. A fist to his jaw and the skinny man went down in a heap.

"Now," Leshru said, looking around at the rest of the bandits. "You could still run."

As one, the other thieves drew steel and charged the unarmed man. Qabil pulled his sword and stepped up beside his friend, noticing how quickly the villagers vanished once the weapons came out. Would have been nice if someone at least stayed behind to untie the prisoners.

A stocky man with graying stubble and two missing teeth in the front of his mouth turned from Leshru to run at Qabil, a wicked curved dagger in each hand. Qabil let his mind go blank, as he'd practiced every night with Prynne, listening to a song only he could hear. He let the memory of music fill his ears, and as the rhythm flowed through his bones, he spun to the right, out of the path of the bandit's charge. The man whirled about faster than Qabil would have expected, lashing out behind him with one dagger, but Qabil was already somewhere else, stomping his feet on the dirt in time with the song in his head.

The bandit lunged at him, but Qabil parried his blade. The man came in with his left hand high, only to find there was no one there, as Qabil ducked under the oncoming blade and twisted around to the left. He slashed with his own sword and opened a deep gash on the back of the bandit's leg. He wasn't deep enough to cut the hamstring, although the man had a good limp starting. The bandit rushed forward as best he could on one good leg, his knives flashing in the afternoon sun, but his movements unconsciously fell into rhythm with Qabil's, driven by the pounding of feet onto the hard-packed dirt of the village square. Lunge, dodge, slice, parry, punch, block, lunge, spin, strike, riposte—Qabil felt the music well up within himself and found himself moving through space with his eyes closed, just *feeling* where the man was going to strike next. He envisioned the next three moves—lung, block, spin, and…slice.

He opened his eyes to see the bandit fall face-first into the dirt, his throat open from ear to ear. Qabil turned his attention back to Leshru, only to see the thickset man ducking, dodging, punching, headbutting like a man half his age, grinning all the time. A bandit with an axe stepped up behind the bald brawler and raised his weapon to cave in Leshru's skull. Qabil opened his mouth to shout a warning, but before he got any words out, a stick appeared from the man's eye.

No, not a stick. An arrow. The man toppled backward, the weight of the axe outweighing the momentum of the missile. The bandit landed in a cloud of dust and blood, and Qabil saw Prynne standing atop a small house with her bow in hand. She nodded at him, then waved at the remaining ruffians as if to say "what are you waiting for?"

Qabil nodded and ran to the scrum surrounding his friend. A pair of bandits heard his approach and turned to face him. One was a boy younger than Qabil, with the barest hint of reddish peach fuzz on his chin and upper lip. He held a short sword like he wasn't sure which end of it to poke into someone, and sweat beaded his forehead. The other one was the threat. He was thin, not the whipcord lean of the leader, but scrawny, with a pointy nose and chin that gave him a rat-like appearance. He had a long thin sword and a dagger with a wide crosspiece, and he stood with a confidence that told Qabil he knew how to use them.

He knew he had to end as much of this fight fast as he could, so before either of the bandits could get themselves set, Qabil sprinted in, stopped suddenly, and lifted a foot right into the junction of the terrified boy's legs. His green eyes bulged out, and his face, already pale under a mass of freckles, went a sickly shade as he sank to his knees and toppled over, clutching his groin.

"There. Now we can dance," Qabil said, his heels pounding a beat into the dirt.

The rat-faced man smiled at him, a slow creeping grin full of menace and the promise of pain. He turned slightly to one side, presenting a narrow target and holding his long blade out in front of his body. Qabil took a step forward, but his opponent dashed toward him with a flurry of cuts and slashed that left Qabil scurrying to deflect the flashing blade. The clatter of their blades drowned out the sound of his feet, and Qabil lost the rhythm. Suddenly floundering, he barely knocked aside a thrust that would have skewered a lung but wasn't fast enough to stop the man's dagger from scoring a deep cut along the outside of his right thigh.

"Fuck!" Qabil hissed, spinning to the left to try and keep his leg clear of the man's flashing sword. He skipped backward, testing his leg and finding that it was just a flesh wound. A deep flesh wound, though, and one that would kill him if left untreated. If the man with the rapier didn't do the job first.

The man came at him hard, pressing his advantage, and with every strike, he came closer and closer to penetrating Qabil's defenses again. The more the man attacked, the more frantic Qabil's defense became, until his heel caught a stone and his foot went out from under him. Qabil went down, his sword flew from his hand, and the grin on the bandit's face became downright hungry.

"Time to die, little hero," the man said as he raised his sword to skewer Qabil to the earth. Then his eyes went wide and he froze at the top of his downward stroke. Qabil watched as the man coughed once, a trickle of blood running down the corner of his mouth, then collapsed to his knees and over on one side. Then Qabil saw the grim face of Thallis standing behind the dead bandit, a bloody dagger in each hand.

"You dropped your sword," the young thief said.

"I tripped on a rock," replied Qabil.

"Shouldn't do that."

"I'll try not to do it again."

"See that you don't." Then with a nod, Thallis turned and engaged another bandit as Qabil rolled over and scooped up his sword.

He took a moment to look around the impromptu battlefield and saw Nipural freeing the innkeeper's family and ushering them off to presumed safety. Prynne overlooked the fight from her rooftop perch, arrow nocked in case one of the bandits got the drop on another of their party. Leshru squared off against three men, two heavyset bruiser types and the whip-wielding leader, who had regained his feet. The bigger men were thick-bodied, ham-fisted types, the kind of men who go into taverns just looking for an excuse to start fights they almost always win. They were of a type, dark hair pulled back in loose ponytails, lots of rings in their ears and more on their fingers, wearing their fortune in jewelry as many mercenaries did. Qabil could see from their ornamentation that they were very prosperous ruffians indeed.

For his part, Leshru looked more like a blacksmith than a legendary hero, with his rough-hewn pants, homespun shirt, and scuffed boots. His fists were clad in the metal bands he'd worn earlier, and that was all that passed for a weapon. But more frightening than his bare-handed confidence was the look on his face. The brawler wore a broad grin, his brown skin smeared red with a rivulet of blood running down from his scalp, and a slightly mad look in his eye.

The pair of fighters came at Leshru simultaneously, and before Qabil could limp forward with his sword, he saw that his friend had just been toying with the thugs this whole time. As the first man reached him, just half a step ahead of what looked like his brother, Leshru dropped to one knee and buried his fist in the big man's expansive gut. The massive bandit doubled over, and Leshru stood into an uppercut, and from ten feet away, Qabil could hear the man's jaw crack. There was another crack as the man's skull slammed into the earth, and he lay still at Leshru's feet.

The bald brawler spun around, clapping his hands together, one on either side of the onrushing bandit's sword, and stood frozen, smiling at the bigger man. The bandit jerked on his sword once, twice, three times, to no avail. Leshru's grip would not be broken. Qabil watched in awe as the big man twisted his arms first to the right, then the left, then back again until finally he wrenched the sword from his opponent's grasp and sent it tumbling end over end into the dirt. Leshru balled up his fist and punched the man right between the eyes. The bandit slumped to the ground, unconscious.

Leshru looked at the bandit leader, who had regained his feet, then glanced around the square. "See? Outnumbered."

The lean man smiled. "You think you're smart now, but just wait until —" He fell back to the dirt as Leshru punched him in the face. He sat on his arse in the middle of the square for a few seconds before scrambling to his feet and running away as fast as his unsteady feet would carry him.

"Well now we may never know what we're waiting until," Nipural said as he walked up beside his friend.

"I don't really care. Wasn't planning on waiting on anything," Leshru replied. He looked around the square at the scattered bodies and the still-blazing inn. "Guess we're sleeping outside again tonight."

Qabil limped over to the pair, looking down at the bandit. "You think he's the boss?"

"Nah," Leshru replied. "He said something about some Lord Some-thing-or-other. Probably means there's more of them in the hills not too far from here. We'll probably be long gone before he hears about this mess."

"Wouldn't count on that," Thallis said as he walked up cleaning his daggers on a torn piece of what looked like a shirt. "Saw dust coming up on the road west of here as I finished my conversation with one of the fellows over yonder." He jerked his thumb behind him, where a pair of corpses lay bleeding their last onto the ground. "Musta been a lookout. If this Untrek, that's what Skinny here said his boss's name was, is anywhere close, he'll be here by nightfall."

"What have you done?!?" shouted a fat man with a red face, who came storming out of a home across the square from the inn. "Are you mad? Untrek will burn us all to the ground now!"

"What we've done is saved the lives of three people you lot were going to let be flayed alive while they watched their home and livelihood go up in smoke," Prynne said, her tone dripping acid.

The fat man whirled on her. "What you've done, girl, is to sign all our death warrants. You idiots—" The man's words cut off with a loud *crack* as Prynne slapped him hard across one cheek. He spun completely around and raised a fist to her, then froze as he looked down at the sword she held leveled at his crotch.

"Don't call me girl, you fat shit," Prynne said. "If you're too much a coward to protect your home from bandits, then you don't deserve a home. So either take up a blade or a bow, or shut the fuck up." She turned to Qabil. "You lost the beat," she said, her tone accusing.

"Aye," he replied.

"Almost lost more than that."

"Aye."

"Come with me, then. Let's get that leg bandaged. And try not to be stupid next time." She turned and stalked off to sit by the well in the center of the village, motioning Qabil over to her.

He looked at Thallis, who shrugged. "I'm not going to be the one to tell her no," he said. "Best get over there."

Qabil looked at his friends, then at the scowling ranger currently laying out water, needles, and fine thread on the stone lip of the well. "What is she going to do to me?" he asked.

"Well," Leshru replied. "She's either going to stitch up that gash on your thigh so it can heal, or she's decided you talk too much and she's going to sew your mouth shut. Although I'd figure Thallis for that second treatment, so she's probably just going to play surgeon a little. Go on, boy. Skin out of them pants and let her stitch you up. She's almost never killed anyone with her treatments."

Qabil limped over to Prynne with one word ringing through his head. "Almost?"

CHAPTER TWENTY

Qabil hissed with pain as Prynne slapped him on the thigh, directly over the newly sewn gash in his leg. "There you go, boy. That'll leave a lovely scar to impress the ladies with. Although I suppose by the time they get to see that much of your leg, you'll either be impressing them with something else, or not at all." She grinned up at him, then rose from where she knelt on the ground beside him.

Qabil stood and pulled up his trousers, tying his belt back around his waist. "Thank you," he said.

"Don't mention it," the ranger replied. "Just try not to let it happen again. I don't mind sewing up idiots, but it's a long road from my favorite thing to do after a scrap." She gave him that same lascivious grin, then laughed at his blush. "Gods, boy! I like to drink after a fight, not fuck! I want a bath and a bed for that, and those are rare enough on the road at all, much less after a battle. Case in point." She gestured at the rubble of the inn, now just bare timbers smoldering in the late afternoon sun.

The villagers had gotten the bucket line going as soon as the last bandit fell, and while Prynne and Nipural tended to Qabil's leg and a few other minor injuries suffered before their arrival, they got the fire out in short order. Now a fat man in fine clothing stood before Leshru, gesticulating wildly and cursing with an expansive tongue and impressive imagination.

"I don't know what you idiots thought you were doing, but now we're going to have to pay even more in penance to Untrek and his men, *if* they don't decide to punish us all for your stupidity! I should—"

"You should what?" Leshru asked, one eyebrow climbing toward his bald pate, dotted with sweat and the blood of his fallen opponents. He stood before the fat man, his mighty arms folded over his chest and storm clouds on his brow, an implacable wall as the merchant, or mayor, or whatever he was to the village raged in front of him like a hurricane against a cliff face.

The man stopped talking. His eyes widened and he looked around the square for the first time since beginning his tirade. The smoking remnants of the inn stood behind Leshru, and all around the village square pairs of people were dragging corpses into a rough line, stripping them of any weapons, purses, jewelry, or armor, and covering them with sheets. The gear they deposited in a pile before Thallis, who rifled through it all before pitching it into one of three piles off to his right side.

The innkeeper and his family just stood before the wreckage of their home and livelihood, now nothing but ash and pain. The boy who had been strapped to the wooden whipping posts alongside his parents sobbed unashamedly, tears pouring down his soot-stained face. His mother stood with one arm around his shoulders, her face stoic but the tracks of tears running down her cheeks as well.

"He saved our lives, Barth," the innkeeper said. All eyes turned to the round man, who looked at Leshru with gratitude. "Untrek's men weren't going to just flog me, they were going to flay me alive. I heard that whip-slinging bastard say as much as his toadies lashed my hands to the posts. This stranger saved my life, and likely the lives of my wife and boy, too. While you hid under your bed, if you could fit under there after all of my beer you've drank, these people who have never seen us before in their lives rode in and rescued us from death, or worse."

"Worse?" the man called Barth asked with a smirk. "What's worse than death, you idiot?"

"What they would have done to your daughter is worse, Barth," said the innkeeper's wife. "What they wanted to do to me, to your wife Mellie, to young Melissande, and all the other women and girls of this village. I heard them talking, too. They weren't planning to stop with us. Once they murdered Stephan, Everette, and I, they figured the rest of you would be too cowed to even look at a sword, so they could just have all the women, and some of the boys."

"Who's the idiot now, asshole?" Thallis called from where he sat sorting loot.

"Quiet, boy," Nipural said.

"No, I don't think so," Thallis replied, getting up and walking over to stand next to Leshru. "I've seen shit like this before. A gang moves in, and maybe there's already a gang in that neighborhood, or maybe there's not. But either way they have to show everybody who's the new boss. So they make an example out of somebody. Usually the person they think could most threaten them." He turned to the innkeeper, a heavy man with broad shoulders and thick arms.

"Let me guess," Thallis said. "You was in the army when you was young, saw some fighting, know your way around a blade. Maybe there was even a sword hanging over the back of the bar, or maybe you had a bunch of souvenirs you took off men on the battlefield all over the walls."

"There were a few trophies from my younger days," the man admitted.

"Figured. I've seen my fair share of taverns," Thallis said. "So this bunch, maybe they work for the lord, maybe they don't. But either way, they decide this town is theirs, and they're going to make you suffer to show the rest of everybody what happens if you don't fall in line. So they pick a fight. One of them probably grabs your wife's ass, or maybe he tries to pull a serving girl into the back for a little roll around. Whatever. Doesn't matter exactly what it was, it had the desired effect—it pissed you off enough to intervene."

The innkeeper's son laughed. "Damn, it's like you was sitting in the corner watching. That's exactly it. One of these assholes—" He pointed to a body under a sheet. "I think it was that one, but his face didn't look like ground meat when I saw him last."

"My fault," Leshru said, without an ounce of regret in his voice.

"Whatever. He was a prick. So the prick tried to feel Ma up. And not just a slap on the arse, either. That happens once in a while with a traveler, or a merchant. Usually Ma just slaps him across the face and rings his bell right good, and the whole thing is over in a second. Not this one. He was running his hands all over her, and when she told him to stop and hit him, he knocked her to the floor and told her that Untrek owned her and everything in this land and if she didn't like it, she should just..." His voice trailed off.

"It's okay, mate," Thallis said. "I can guess the kinds of things he said to her. Might have mentioned, I've seen this play before. So your da comes out, beats the thug's ass for him, tosses him into the street, and a day or two later, this whole big bag of assholes spills out onto your doorstep and burns your home to the ground."

"Pretty much," the innkeeper said with pride. "But it wasn't me knocked the bastard on his ass."

"Yeah, that was me," said the younger man. "I knocked him to the ground and spent a couple minutes kicking his balls into new places before I hauled him to his feet and tossed him out the front door. His buddies were laughing it up until I told them all to get out, too. That didn't make them any too happy."

"And a lot less when you told them they weren't allowed back in until their friend apologized to your ma in front of the whole tavern." The fat innkeeper beamed with pride at his son, a sturdy lad, but young, maybe fifteen summers.

The young man had the kind of thick muscle that only comes from hauling kegs of beer and firewood for many years, so Qabil could see how he tossed the slovenly guard out without any real trouble. The men he'd faced had been mostly bullies, accustomed to getting their way because there were a lot of them and they had swords. When faced with skilled opponents who also had swords, it had gone badly for them. His thigh throbbed, and Qabil was abruptly reminded of how close it came to going very badly for him as well, and promised silently to redouble his training efforts. Just as soon as he could walk without opening up his wound.

Qabil felt for the innkeeper and his family. They were putting a brave face on things, and their gratitude at not being dead or maimed with flesh hanging in ribbons from their backs was genuine, but he knew from growing up in a village not much larger than this one that everything they owned had either been in that building, or had *been* that building. People like this were unlikely to have much in the way of money set aside, and anything they had hidden away was likely to be nothing more than melted slag now.

"So that's how we left it, and that was six days ago. Then today Untrek's Sergeant-At-Arms, at least that's what he calls himself, Guenther, showed up with more of his thugs and a whip. They said we could take a ten lashes each, and twenty for me, while we watched our home burn for my insolence, or they could cut our throats and make the inn our funeral pyre." Fury warred with shame in the young man's eyes, and Qabil knew what he was feeling. He was angry at the men who destroyed his home, but he was ashamed and angry at himself for choosing not to fight.

"You made the right choice," he said to the young man, stepping forward and putting one hand on his shoulder. "They would have done exactly what they threatened to do—kill you all and burn the inn down around you for good measure. Even if you took the flogging, you could rebuild. But dead men don't build inns. Sometimes the cost of revenge is greater than the satisfaction it brings."

He heard his own words, and they rang hollow in his ears. Because what was he doing but dragging his friends along on his quest for revenge? Knowing it was almost certainly going to cost him his life, and might leave more bodies than that behind, but he knew he wouldn't stop. Couldn't. And Hells, at this point, he might as well stay the course, because Prynne was going to put an arrow in Walfert's eye if given the chance, so Qabil's mother would get justice, whether he was skilled enough to bring it about or not.

Thallis coughed beside him, and Qabil could swear it sounded like the other boy said "hypocrite" under his breath, then the young thief stepped to the right and pointed back at three piles of items he'd taken off the bandit's corpses. "I split up everything they had on them. Arrows and spare bowstrings and sharpening stones and the like we're taking with us. You got no need for that kind of stuff here. Same for a few throwing knives one of them had. There's a couple of purses there, and I put all their money into those. Ain't much, but ought to get you a start on some wood and nails. Then there's a bunch of swords, scabbards, boots, and heavy jerkins. Most of it isn't worth the name armor, but if you can find a merchant passing through on their way to someplace bigger, you can sell all that crap for enough to pay some men to help you rebuild, and should be able to get enough for new furnishings and booze."

The innkeeper's eyes widened, and his face split open with a broad grin. "Thank you! I thought you'd be taking all that stuff. Spoils and all."

"We're all pretty well kitted out already," Leshru said. "And you need it more than we do."

"I don't know how to thank you," the big man's wife said, a tear welling up in her eye. "If you hadn't come along, I don't know what we would have done."

"I'll tell you!" the well-dressed fat man interjected. "You would have taken a beating, and the whole village would have come together to help you rebuild. And we wouldn't have to fear every hoofbeat on the road until Untrek brings his retribution down on all of us. It won't take long for word to reach Tyndale about this, and when it does, he'll be riding here with his entire guard company."

"You mean his whole gang of bandits and murderers," the innkeeper said, then spat in the dirt at the other man's feet. "Let them come. I'll not stand aside any longer and let Untrek rule this place worse than even his mad father did."

"Did you say...Tyndale?" Nipural asked.

"And did you say Untrek's father was...mad?" Prynne's words followed tight on the heels of her brother's.

"Aye," said the well-dressed rude man. "Lord Untrek's grandfather, Lord Trekkage, ruled this land well for many years until he caught brain fever and died. His son, Lord Bartrek, was nothing like the ruler his father had been. He was mean, and petty, and within a few years of taking the throne, it was evident he was stark raving mad. Untrek succeeded his father some two dozen years ago when—"

"When a group of mercenaries was hired by the merchants of Tyndale to rid the region of their oppressive and insane ruler," Leshru said.

Qabil looked at his friend and saw a grim look on his face. Suspicion grew, and he asked, "How do you know about that, Lesh?"

The battle-scarred brawler turned to Qabil with a dire expression on his face. "Because we're the ones that killed the mad son of a bitch. We put Untrek on the throne."

"Well, shit," Qabil said.

"Pretty well sums it up, lad," Prynne said, putting an arm around Nipural's shoulders. "Come on, brother. Let's get ready to storm a petty lordling's castle."

Nipural gave his sister a long-suffering look and said, "Again."

CHAPTER TWENTY-ONE

W hat do you mean, we have to assault a castle and overthrow the rightful lord of the region?" Torgan demanded. He stood facing Leshru, his mustache quivering with indignation. "I show up late to one fight and you lot turn us into revolutionaries? Leshru, we *cannot* just go around the countryside randomly taking down the lawful rulers." He glanced over at Celia, who sat on the ground playing with a couple of the village children. "A little help, wife?"

"I'm just here to write songs about your grand adventures, husband. I'm not one to get involved in policy decisions." Qabil could tell by the frost dripping from her words that there was more left unsaid than said in her statement.

The pair had ridden into the village moments after everyone had made the decision to go after Lord Untrek, with a panting horse that looked as if it would fall dead in its tracks if asked to move another foot. Torgan seemed a little disappointed to have missed the fray, but he quickly got to work saying prayers for the dead to ease their passage into the next world. His priestly duties completed, he asked Leshru what happened, and that's when everything went sideways.

"We don't really have a choice, Torg," Nipural said. "We're the one that put the asshole in power in the first place, so it's on us to take him out."

"That's not true at all," Torgan shot back. "He was the heir. He was always going to inherit the throne, assuming his madman of a father didn't murder him in his sleep. We simply removed a terrible ruler from power, which is what we were hired to do. Now you want to do it again? *For free?*"

Qabil wasn't sure which part of the problem bothered Torgan more, the idea of killing a lord they had put into power in the first place, or the fact they weren't getting paid for it.

"We could loot the keep after we kill Untrek," Thallis said. "Ain't like he's going to have any need for money where he's going."

"That would be a poor decision," Celia said, cutting off her husband, who turned his sputtering attention to the young thief. "If we rob the manor blind, whoever takes over as lord will not have funds to pay his troops, or pay his taxes to the crown, or hire builders to help these people reconstruct their inn. There may be some potential for pillage, but it would be severely limited, unless we wish to make this area an annual visit to take down one bandit warlord or another."

"See? Even a *bard* knows better than to steal every penny you can wrap your fingers around, boy," Torgan growled.

"Even. A. Bard?" Celia's tone was positively frost rimed as she turned her attention to her husband. She handed the baby she was holding back to its mother and stood, walking over to tower over the enraged dwarf. "I am *sure* it was not your intention to cast aspersions on the intellect of the person who not only shares your bed but carries the tent you sleep in and is responsible for returning you to where you left your pony. Unless, of course, you relish the idea of walking to Lennox."

Torgan's red face paled behind his beard, and he took a step back from his angry wife. "Of course, dear. I misspoke. I would never deign to… whatever you said I did that I shouldn't do."

"Good," Celia said, then turned to Leshru. "Now let me see if I understand the situation. A long time ago, a nearby town hired you lot to kill the lord, because he was a barking mad asshole. You did and went on your merry way. Now the son is all grown up, and while not mad, is still at least as much a raging asshole as his father."

"Seems about right," Leshru replied. "From what I understand after talking with the innkeeper and his family, Untrek's band of drinking buddies has grown into a barely veiled bandit crew that does what they want to whoever they want. With Untrek's approval, either spoken or not."

"Okay, then. So who do we put in his place when we kill him?" Qabil was stunned at the cold tone in Celia's voice. Until now, she'd been the kind, motherly figure among the party. She was the one who made sure everyone had enough to eat, arranged the chores so everyone took a turn cleaning up and everyone but Nipural took a turn cooking (a decision everyone agreed was not only wise but necessary after his first attempt at rabbit stew), and generally took care of them all. Now she was discussing murdering a sovereign lord with no more emotion than she showed when discussing whether carrots or potatoes were better in vegetable soup.

"He's got a cousin in Tyndale. A cobbler. Good man. Not a good enough cobbler for a big city, but he's a fair hand at repairing a sole and doesn't cheat anyone," the innkeeper said.

"Can't ask for much more than that in a country lord," Leshru said. "Can you get a message to this cousin and tell him he's about to change jobs?"

"I can."

"Good. Do that. We'll go deal with the dictator problem."

"Again," Prynne said.

"Again," Leshru agreed.

卌 ||

"That's...not much of a keep," Qabil said from where the group stood clustered in a small copse of trees a few hundred yards from what could generously be called a "manor."

"It wasn't any bigger the last time we rode through here, although it was a little better kept," Torgan replied.

"Or it was when we first arrived. There were a few doors missing and a fair amount of blood on the floors by the time we left," Lehru added.

Untrek Manor was basically a large country house, about the size the inn had likely been before it was put to the torch. It looked to be two stories tall, with a portico large enough to drive a carriage under at the front door. The building stretched quite a distance from the road, and there were several individual tendrils of smoke rising from the back edge of the house, indicating a sizable kitchen with multiple ovens going at once. There were small, shuttered windows along the front, with arrow slits left open for defense, but anyone trying to storm this building was going to have to go through the front door or make their way around back and hope for easier access.

There were several outbuildings scattered across the grounds nearby, a pair of low-slung barracks, a windowless storage shed big enough to keep two dozen men fed for a winter, a massive barn that spoke of many horses, and even a small chapel on the far side of the house. A pair of guards patrolled narrow parapets along the roof of the main house, and another pair walked regular routes around the outer edge of the grounds. There was a log fence around the perimeter of the compound, but nothing that couldn't be leapt over with little effort.

"What's the plan?" Leshru asked.

"Who do you think is coming up with a plan, exactly?" Nipural replied, giving his friend a curious look. "You're the one who set our feet on this mad path, so you should be the one to come up with a plan."

"We've seen what happens when Leshru comes up with the plan, brother," Prynne said. "Why not let someone with a better head for planning and strategy work on it?"

"You mean you, Prynne?" Nipural countered. "As I recall, your idea of a complex strategy was shooting everyone you don't like in the leg as opposed to the throat."

"That was a good plan," Prynne said, "But no. I mean her. She's obviously the smart one among us, so let her do the thinking. Not like she's going to do much fighting. I mean, she's a bard, after all." She pointed to where Celia sat at the base of a slender oak tuning her lute.

"I'm a lover, not a fighter," the bard said.

"Please, can we not think or speak of your love life? Ever?" Prynne asked, her face stretched into a grimace.

Celia's head snapped up. "What's wrong, Prynne? You don't think a half-orc can find love?" There was a snarl to the half-orc's voice that Qabil hadn't heard before, and everyone took an involuntary step back from the massive woman.

"No. I just don't want to think of Torgan having sex. It must look like a beaver humping a log. Or maybe a really obese fox, since he's got red hair. See? Now I'm picturing it, and I can't get drunk enough to unsee it before we ride into a fight."

The half-orc chuckled. "Okay, let me take a look at the place. Well, any idea of surprise is right out."

"Why's that?" Thallis asked.

"The sentry on the roof has a spyglass. If he's not a complete moron, he knows we're here. So we can either go in the front door and fight our way through everyone there, or we can walk up and knock. Maybe we can have a friendly conversation with Lord Untrek and convince him that his subjects will produce more for him if he treats them like human beings rather than cattle."

"You think there's any chance of that?" Qabil asked. The idea of making it through without killing anyone else was very appealing.

"Oh, not a chance in all the Hells," Celia replied. "We'll probably have to gut every bastard in the place, and the stubborn ones twice. But it's worth a try."

"Let's at least divide our forces so that we aren't all in one clump, making ourselves an easy target for those sentries," Qabil said.

"What sentries?" Prynne asked.

"The two walking along the...where are they?" He looked to his right and saw Prynne standing there, bow in hand and a smirk on her face.

"Won't need to gut that pair, Celia," the ranger said.

"I like the way you work, dear, but a little warning next time would be good. Now we have to run for the door, and Torgy doesn't like to run." The bard carefully leaned her lute against a tree, set her pack next to it, and checked the pair of short swords at her belt. Then she looked around at everyone else, who were all similarly checking weapons and dropping gear. "Are you all coming, or is the bard going to lead the charge?"

"When the bard is seven feet tall and has arms bigger than my thighs, I'm content to follow along behind her," Nipural said.

"Old man, I have arms bigger around than those twigs you call thighs," Thallis said. "Let's go."

Qabil fell into step with the young thief, a pace or two behind Celia. Prynne angled out to the left, heading for cover in another stand of trees. Leshru jogged a few steps behind, while Nipural and Torgan followed at a walk. Qabil's heart pounded fast in his chest, rushing faster than his feet. He'd seen plenty of fights since embarking on this journey, but this was the first one he had enough warning to be frightened of. Would he be able to fight well enough to stand next to these legends? Would his training fail and he lose the rhythm of the fight again? Would his leg hold up this soon after being injured?

With that last thought, as if he had called it upon himself, a jolt of pain issued from his thigh, and he looked down to see a small dark stain beginning to grow on his pants. He slowed until his pace matched Nipural and Torgan, limping heavily.

"What's wrong, lad?" Torgan asked.

"My leg. Got cut in the last fight. Prynne sewed it up, but I think I tore it open trying to run like an idiot."

"You aren't running *like* an idiot. You happen to be an idiot who was running. Stand still and let me look at it," the dwarf said.

"It's fine," Qabil protested.

"I'll be the judge of that."

"Prynne said—"

"I don't give a damn what that string bean said. I may be the one that taught her everything she knows about patching up a wounded warrior, but I sure as Hells didn't teach her everything *I* know."

Qabil stopped walking and stood still, staring after Thallis and the others. He fidgeted as Torgan pulled the tear in his pants apart to look at the cut.

"Be still, boy," Torgan snapped.

"We need to be up there," Qabil protested.

"You'll do no one any good trying to fight on one leg," Nipural said. "I'll go after them and keep everyone alive. Well, everyone we care about, at any rate." The old wizard turned, his face taking on a slightly green cast as he hurried after the others.

Torgan chuckled, a deep-throated sound that made his shoulders shake. "Nip's a funny old bastard. Doesn't mind the stench of the battle-field, and I've seen him covered in enough of our enemies' blood to make you think he bathed in the stuff, but one look at his own blood, or even that of a companion, and he's trying to decide whether to faint or revisit his lunch."

The dwarf pressed his hands to either side of Qabil's thigh and closed his eyes. He began whispering a rhythmic chant, and after a few seconds Qabil recognized as a prayer to Felrand, the dwarvish god of battle and warriors. His hands began to glow, and Qabil felt the flesh beneath them growing hot. Torgan's voice rose and his chanting came faster and faster as his hands glowed brighter and hotter by the second. Finally, with a shouted string of syllables in a dwarven tongue Qabil had never heard before, the dwarf took his hands off his leg and stepped back. Qabil looked down, and the gash in his leg was fully healed, with only a slight scar and the remnants of black thread to show where it had been.

"There you go. Now let's go catch up to the others. If I know them, and gods forgive me I do, it's pretty likely somebody else is going to need the goddess's favor before they is through." He looked after the others, let out a huge sigh, and began to jog toward the manor.

Qabil tested his leg, bending it once or twice to make sure everything felt in working order, then gave it one more look. "Torgan?" he called after the retreating dwarf. "What am I supposed to do about the stitches?"

CHAPTER TWENTY-TWO

O ne of the front double doors lay on the ground to the side of the entrance, smoke curling up from the grass beneath it. An arm and a leg stuck out from under the door, unmoving and scorched blacker than the wood itself. A second guardsman sat slumped against the left-hand door, the lower half of his face covered in blood. His nose was flattened and split, and both his eyes were already blacked and swollen shut. It looked like someone had taken both hands and slammed a frying pan into his face with all their might. Or like Leshru of the Broken Blade punched him.

Qabil knelt by the sitting man and felt his neck. There was a heartbeat there, so depending on the disposition of the man under the door, it was possible that these two both survived their meeting with The Seven. If they walked away from this scrap with a shattered face and crisped flesh, it would still mean walking away, which was more than they should have expected.

Qabil drew his sword and stepped into the entryway, blinking to speed up his eyes' adjustment to the darkened interior. Sounds of fighting came from farther inside the house, and a slight groan came from an interior doorway to his left. He went toward the groaning and found a third guardsman holding clumps of fabric to a pair of wounds in his left shoulder. Seeing Qabil, the man tried to stand, but gave up after a feeble effort.

"I'm not going to kill you. Not if you don't make me," Qabil said.

"I ain't gonna make you do shit," the man said.

"Can you walk?"

"Not yet. Maybe in a bit."

"Well, as soon as you're able, you should get up and work very diligently at being elsewhere. Permanently. Lord Untrek will no longer torment the people of this region with his taxes and his bullyboys, and any who stood with him or took his coin will find themselves very unpopular soon."

"Pretty words, boy. But you have no fucking idea the mess you're walking into. You think Untrek's been running this operation? Untrek's been dead five years! So don't mind me if I ain't too confident in your lot taking out the boss. He's put down a lot of assholes since he killed Untrek at the dinner table and drank his life's blood out of a soup bowl. I think I'll just sit here and try to stop bleeding. If you make it back, we'll discuss me leaving."

"When I come back," Qabil replied, putting emphasis on the word "when," "you really want to be long gone." Then he turned and hurried to catch up with Torgan, who was well down the main hallway ahead of him.

"You have a nice chat, boy?" the dwarf asked as he caught up.

"We don't have to kill them all," Qabil replied, a trifle defensively.

"I expect you'll find that to be demonstrably incorrect."

"You speak a lot finer the farther you get from home," Qabil observed.

"When I'm out here, I'm supposed to be the wise dwarven war priest. When I'm home, I'm just Torgan, the man who runs the mines. Not much call for deep philosophy when you make your living carving gemstones out of the ground. Now did he say anything useful, or shall we continue to chat about my vocabulary?"

"He said Lord Untrek has been dead for five years and that we're walking into something much more dangerous than a simple bandit lair," Qabil said.

"Didn't want to start with that bit, eh?" Torgan glowered up at him and picked up his pace. "Looks like the Great Hall is just down this hall. If there's a boss, it'll be there. Come on!" The dwarf began to run, his armor jangling loudly through the empty halls. Qabil followed close behind, wincing at the racket. There was no hope of them surprising anyone, unless they were stone deaf. Admittedly, stealth had probably been off the menu from the moment they blasted the front door off its hinges.

The doors to the Great Hall looked much like the front of the house, except they were still hanging, albeit barely. There was a huge black scorch mark at the center where the doors met, and a section of wood was simply missing, turned to splinters, or maybe dust, by what Qabil assumed was Nipural's magic. There were no corpses or wounded men on the floor beside the doors, but it was still very apparent this was the path his friends had taken.

"Stand behind me, lad," Torgan said, then barreled through the double doors into the room and stopped cold.

Qabil, running behind him, slammed into the dwarf's back and barely resisted tumbling them both to the floor. He righted himself, glaring down at the dwarf and opening his mouth to speak, then stopping himself as he saw the look of awe on Torgan's face. The dwarf stood frozen, staring dead ahead into a room that easily dwarfed anything Untrek Manor should have been able to hold. The Great Hall wasn't just the dominant feature of the house, it was *larger* than the house.

The floor, polished wood with rugs throughout the rest of the house, was gleaming white marble here. The walls, ordinary wooden paneling in every room and hallway they had passed through, were now made of hewn stone, fitted together and rising thirty feet to a huge, vaulted ceiling worthy of a grand cathedral, not a manor lordling's home a week's ride from anywhere significant. Huge tapestries hung on the wall, all depicting battles between men and huge dragons breathing fire and lightning and tearing knights into pieces. Qabil noticed a theme—in every image, the dragon was winning.

"Oh, fuck me," Torgan said under his breath. "Not again."

"What?" Qabil asked. There was no reply from the dwarf. Qabil poked Torgan in the shoulder. "Not again, what?"

The dwarf didn't say anything, just lifted his hammer and pointed to the far end of the hall, to the dais that was, like everything in the building, more suited to a throne room than a country lord's home. It was massive, some forty feet wide at least, with four steps leading up to a carpeted platform on which rested a creature that so confounded Qabil's perception of the world that for a moment he failed to realize exactly what he was looking at.

The creature sat on its haunches, on four legs, with its long neck craned high near the ceiling of the room. It was enormous, at least the size of the fishing boat his father had gone out on, with a body twenty feet wide and wings, even tightly folded against its sides, that were obviously far too long to ever stretch out in the confines of the building. Qabil idly wondered how the beast ever got a good stretch in before he gave himself a shake, trying to focus his addled mind on the crimson-scaled behemoth in front of him. The monster's legs were as wide as a big man's shoulders, and curved claws measuring at least a foot in length tipped each one. Its head was a massive thing, with huge bony ridges running back over its forehead and extending into wicked spikes that gave the impression of a crown. The glittering black eyes sparkled with intelligence, and Qabil was certain that he saw a smile stretched across the creature's face, exposing two rows of massive, pointed teeth that looked as though they could chop a man in half quicker than an axe.

"Fuck me, that's a dragon."

"Aye, lad, that's a dragon. And don't worry, we're already fucked." Torgan slipped his hammer back through a loop in his belt and walked forward to where the others stood before the dais. The four of them—Leshru, Nipural, Thallis, and Celia—stood in a rough line before the beast, hands on their weapons, but no one had drawn steel yet. Torgan stepped to one end of the line by his wife while Qabil stepped into a space between Leshru and Thallis. The young thief looked over at him, and Qabil saw the slightest tremor in the other boy's jaw. He was a hair's breadth from bolting, and there was no way that ended well.

"So..." Qabil said without taking his eyes off the monster before them. "A dragon, eh?"

"Yep." Leshru's typically laconic tone was even drier than normal.

"Was it a dragon when you opened the door?" Qabil asked. "Because, you know, I'm just wondering why we didn't see you running for all you're worth back out the way you came."

"He was not a dragon when we entered the hall," Nipural said, sounding even more testy than his usual. Qabil decided that people were right—everyone becomes more themselves in times of great stress, and if there was a time of greater stress than standing twenty feet from a giant red dragon, he didn't want to live through it.

"So...what's the plan?" he asked, no one in particular.

"Let the orc do the talking," Leshru said.

Qabil turned to Celia, who leaned down to kiss her husband on the top of his head. "If I get burned to cinders, spread my ashes somewhere warm. If you bury me in that goddamned icebox you call a home, I swear I'll haunt you until the end of time."

She turned back to the dragon, who stood watching all of this with a bemused expression, and stepped forward. "Um...hello."

"Greetings, little ones," the dragon said, and his voice was so deep as to make a rumble that Qabil felt all the way to his bones.

"To whom do I have the pleasure of speaking?" Celia asked.

"I am K'niss the Magnificent, Ruler of All I Survey, Lord of the Skies, Desecrator of Mine Enemies' Graves, Decapitator of Multitudes, Devourer of Armies, Lord of Death and Fire!" His pronouncements grew in volume until he let out a mighty roar with the last and lifted his head to spew forth a great stream of fire over their heads. Qabil clapped his hands over his ears and shut his eyes against the incredible heat.

Celia stood her ground, never flinching until the flame died down, then looked up at the dragon. "That's impressive. Can I call you K'niss for short?"

The dragon let out a surprised chuckle, a thin tendril of flame shooting from one nostril. "You may. Why have you trespassed on my domain, little ones? Do you come seeking my treasure? Do you come seeking the glory that would accompany vanquishing K'niss the Magnificent, Ruler of—"

Celia took her life in her hands even more at that moment because she held up a hand and interrupted the dragon. "No, Your Magnificence. We…we didn't know you were here."

The dragon reared its head back, eyes widening in shock, and Qabil reached out to his right and gripped the back of Thallis's belt. "No. Sudden. Movements." He felt the thief trembling under his hand, but the other boy didn't try to break free.

The dragon lowered his head to look Celia in the eye, turning so that the yellow-and-black orb hung less than a foot from the half-orc's face. "You're telling the truth."

"It's much easier than a lie, most of the time," she replied.

"Then why are you here?" The dragon raised its head and looked down at all of them. "You're clearly warriors, so you must be here to steal from me."

"Not at all, K'niss," Celia said, and for the first time Qabil noticed that she had a tiny finger harp in her left hand and was plucking out a light, soothing melody. "We came here to overthrow a foul beast, but not one of your magnificence. We are here to cast down the evil Lord Untrek and free the surrounding lands from his oppressive rule."

"Untrek? That festering pimple? I bit his head off years ago."

"Then who's been running the thugs all over the countryside making life miserable for the people 'round here?" Thallis shouted, and Celia threw him a black look.

"I have no idea. I care nothing for the people of this region, so long as they provide me with my reasonable tribute. One full-grown cow every cycle of the moon, and a sheep in between cows."

"All you ask is one cow and one sheep each month?" Celia asked. "You do not impose any other taxes on the population?"

"No. I have gold, what do I need with their grain or their vegetables? I have rubies and sapphires, why would I want their eggs or their meager copper pennies? Untrek cared about that garbage, and he bled the countryside dry with his taxes. I told him it would come back to haunt him, but I never expected that he would be the one doing the haunting by the time it did." The air around the dragon shimmered, and with a flash of white light that made Qabil look away, the creature transformed into a man of middle years, ostensibly human, with longish brown hair and a strong jaw. "There. That should make it easier to talk. It seems that my minions have been taking initiative, and that never ends well."

The dragon, now man, waved a hand, and with another flash of light, a table with eight chairs appeared between them. K'niss stepped forward and sat at the head of the table, gesturing for the others to join him. "Come, we have much to discuss. Fear not," he said with a chuckle as they all eyed the seats closest to him with suspicion. "I won't bite. Not in this form, any road."

No one moved. K'niss looked from one to the other and after a long moment, said, this time with more force behind his words, "Sit. We have much to talk about."

Qabil hurried forward to take one of the seats farthest from K'niss, and so The Seven parlayed with a dragon.

CHAPTER TWENTY-THREE

H mm..." The dragon leaned back in his chair and laced his fingers behind his head, a contemplative expression on his unlined face. He looked to be a hearty man of no more than thirty summers, with reddish-blond hair and a trimmed beard to match. Qabil idly wondered who the dragon patterned its human form after, or if it had no more choice in the matter than he had in his own dark brown hair and golden-hued skin. "It seems that we have a problem, you lot and I," K'niss said.

"What problem is that, Your Magnificence?" Celia asked. No one in the group wanted to challenge the half-orc bard for her role as the spokesperson, mostly because if she put her foot wrong in conversation, the rest of them might have half a second to prepare while the dragon was searing the flesh from her bones. Also because none of the other options were in the least bit suitable. Qabil almost chuckled at the thought of Thallis and his smart mouth negotiating with a dragon, then shuddered at the thought of his friend a steaming pile of ash on the marble floor.

"My minions are acting without direction," K'niss replied. "It sounds as though they have decided that I am not compensating them to the full extent of their worth, so they have turned bandit, only pretending to act in my name."

"Actually, they're pretending to act in Lord Untrek's name," Prynne said. Every head at the table whipped around to the ranger, who leaned back in her chair and was peeling an apple with one of the throwing daggers she kept tucked into her bracers. "What? They are."

"That does provide us with some opportunities, Your Magnificence," Celia said. "You have kept your true nature hidden from the citizens, haven't you?"

K'niss inclined his head. "I have indeed. They have not yet earned the right to gaze upon my true glory."

"And you didn't want to scare them into shitting themselves all over your nice floors," Prynne said, proving that she either had no idea how her words landed to others or that she had the most active death wish Qabil had ever seen.

But the dragon in man's form just laughed. "You are correct, of course. After each and every minion soiled themselves upon learning of my true self, I felt it not only safer but easier for the cleaning if I remained in human form much of the time." He cocked his head to the side. "But you lot seemed unaffected by my appearance. Do you not fear dragons?" There was an edge to his voice that threatened mayhem, and Qabil let his hand drift to the hilt of his sword. Not that he had any illusions of being able to stand against a dragon, but if he was going to die, he at least wanted to die on his feet with a weapon in his hand.

"Not like you're the first dragon we've run across," Leshru said, his voice a deep rumble.

"Honestly, not the biggest, either," Nipural added. "Might be the most well-spoken, though."

"But definitely not the most frightening thing we've encountered," Torgan added. "That probably goes to the banshee we fought that one time."

"Oh, the banshee wasn't that bad," Prynne said. "She was just misunderstood."

"And insane," Leshru shot back.

"Wouldn't you be, if some man treated you so badly in life that you came back from the grave for vengeance?" Celia asked.

"You weren't even there!" Torgan protested, earning himself a slap on the back of the head for his troubles. The stout dwarf rocked forward with the blow from his massive half-orc wife, but stopped himself before his face hit the table.

"Well don't worry, Your Dragonness," Thallis chimed in. "You're definitely the scariest thing I've ever seen. And I ride with this lot now, so seems like every day is something else terrifying. Right, Ears?"

Qabil groaned a little, seeing all his work at not getting involved in the conversation evaporating before his eyes. "I think if I'd walked in here alone and seen you in your...larger form, I probably would have pissed myself, too, your...sir."

K'niss laughed, and at the end of it there was a tiny little hiccup of flame that belched forth from his mouth. "Sorry," he said. "The human form sometimes cannot contain the force of a dragon's magic."

"And it makes you burp fire?" Thallis asked, leaning forward and turning his head to the side as if trying to see down the dragon's throat or up his nose.

"Sometimes," K'niss said, leaning back and shifting in his seat to hide his nostrils from the young thief's prying gaze. "But to the point—I have minions who have developed an unhealthy habit of thinking for themselves, and you lot have a burning desire to see the countryside put to rights. I think we may be able to work together to achieve all our goals."

"What are your goals exactly, Your Magnificence?" Celia asked, waving the others to silence.

"I want to be left alone to count my gold, admire my gems, and tinker with my magical artifacts," the dragon replied. "I want to be well-fed and not attacked by every idiot adventurer with a death wish and a lust for treasure. No offense."

"We're not offended," Prynne said. "We're not idiots, and we have more gold than we can ever spend."

"And most of us don't have a death wish," Leshru added, with a look at Qabil. "Most of us."

"I propose a brief but strategic alliance," K'niss said. "You bring my minions to heel, and perhaps find someone willing to serve as my seneschal to keep my mundane affairs in order, and I will aid you in your quest for vengeance."

Qabil couldn't hide his astonishment. "How did you know we were on a quest for vengeance?"

"And it's justice, by the way," Thallis said. "Not vengeance."

"That is almost always a matter of perspective, little elflet," the dragon replied. "To the one doing the questing, it's justice. The one at the end of the quest, it always looks like vengeance." He held up both hands as Qabil and Thallis opened their mouths to argue. "I don't care which it is. The matters of mortals sometimes intersect with those of dragons, but they are almost always so fleeting as to be beneath notice for one who lives as long as we."

"So we kick the piss out of your hired thugs, find you someone to serve as a new tax collector, majordomo, or whatever else you need, and you give us some kind of trinket to aid us in getting close to Walfert and carving out his tripes? Sounds good to me," Thallis said. "Where do we find the minions?"

IIII III

Two hours later, Prynne walked back to where she had left the others waiting outside a small village to the east. "Looks like there's nobody there but assholes and cling-ons," she said, keeping her voice slightly lowered. "I counted about twenty, including your friend with the whip from earlier. He seems to have made it here on foot to rally his troops. They're all strapping on arms and armor and readying the horses. It looks like we have about five minutes before they ride out and probably burn down the rest of that little town."

Qabil and Thallis both sprang up from where they knelt on the moss-covered ground and took a couple steps in the direction of the village before realizing that no one followed them. They turned back to the others, who stood in a loose circle, checking weapons and tightening buckles on their armor. "Well?" asked Thallis. "Ain't you coming?"

"Why, lad?" Nipural asked. "So we can rush in there against an armed force three times our size and face them on their home territory?"

"I think I'm going to pass on that one," Celia said, stringing a short bow that Thallis had never seen her fire.

"Aye," Torgan said, nodding in agreement. "Let's wait until they ride out of the gates, all hell-bent for leather, let Celia and Prynne thin them down a little bit, and then pick up the pieces after the odds are a little more in our favor."

"Don't that seem like...I don't know, cheating?" Thallis asked.

Prynne let out a little chuckle. "There's only one rule in fighting, little thief. Don't get dead. I'm a big fan of that rule, personally. So I think I'm going to stick with it a little longer. Now, you follow Lesh and Celia, while your bloody-minded friend and I go with my idiot brother to the other side of the one road out of here so we can flank these morons and cut them to ribbons. Once we're done shooting holes in the worst of them, you can run in and stab anyone that's left. I promise."

Thallis nodded. "A'ight. That sounds like a smarter way to go 'bout it,

I'll give you that. I'm still not used to sneaking around in the woods like this, but I reckon you know what you're doing."

"We ain't dead, boy," Nipural said, then shot a regretful look at Qabil. "Sorry, lad."

"Don't worry about it," Qabil said, his eyes nearly as cold as his tone. "It was no fault of my mother's she wasn't expecting attack in her own home from someone working for a man she once considered a friend."

"Aye, that's true enough," said the wizard. "Now come with my harpy sister and I, and you can see what my magic will do to an unsuspecting rider."

"Oh, this one's good," Leshru said. "I've seen Nip use this trick before."

The party split and moved forward, settling on either side of an east-bound road that the bandits would have to take to seek their revenge on the rebellious townsfolk. Qabil knelt in front of Prynne and Nipural, who watched the road intently. Thallis could just make out his shape in the brush from his spot beside Leshru across the road.

Moments after the party settled in to wait, hoofbeats thundered toward them Nipural's hands glowed, and the old wizard's brow furrowed in concentration as he stepped forward to the very edge of the woods. He raised both hands over his head, staring intently toward the village. The hoofbeats grew louder, and Thallis looked on in concern as the old man just stood there as the bandits rounded a bend in the road.

There were nearly two dozen of the rough-hewn men and women riding in their direction with grins on their faces and blood on their minds. Nipural stepped out into the road and spread his hands wide over his head. A narrow band of energy stretched from palm to palm, and he bent forward at the waist, seeming to hurl the energy at the oncoming riders. The strand of power stretched as it flew, until it reached from one edge of the dirt path to the other, strung at neck height on a mounted rider. The first pair of bandits riding shoulder to shoulder hit the magical rope, and they flew backward like a fish on a line, crashing into the pair of bandits behind them and tumbling all four of them into the dirt at the feet of the horses behind them.

The front mounts ran under the glowing band of power with no effect and kept running several yards past Nipural before they realized they no longer carried a burden and wandered off to the side of the road to graze. The rest of the bandits and horses all tangled together in a spill of legs, hooves, and swearing that shattered the stillness of the forest and tumbled all but three of the bandits from their saddles. The three who kept their saddles may have considered themselves the lucky ones at first, but the feathered shafts that suddenly sprouted from their throats put the lie to that immediately.

Thallis looked across at his old mentor, who now limped back to the scant cover of the trees lining the road, clearly exhausted from his working, then glanced up at Leshru. "Fuck me, he really is a wizard," the boy breathed.

"Best I ever rode with," the grinning archer replied. "Now let's go clean up this mess. They didn't all crack their skulls or their legs in the tumble, and they're a lot harder to shoot with all those horses milling around."

"Aye, don't want to hurt the horses," Celia said. "I like horses more than most people, and certainly more than this lot."

With a shouted challenge, Leshru plunged out of the woods and sprinted toward the bandits, a grin painting his face and a slightly mad look in his eyes.

Thallis watched him go, then looked up at the wizard leaning against a tree and panting. "He's barking mad, isn't he?"

"Oh, child. If you weren't barking mad, you would have stayed home. This is The Seven. We're all mad."

CHAPTER TWENTY-FOUR

The two men who first encountered Nipural's glowing line lay on their backs in the dirt, unseeing eyes staring up at the canopy of leaves overhead. Three corpses with arrows sprouting from their throats lay several yards behind them. In the middle teemed a mass of angry shouting, curses, and men scrambling to gain their footing and draw steel. One large bandit with an axe in each hand slapped a horse with the flat of his weapon, spurring the whole clump of milling animals to flee into the relative safety of the woods. He saw the party of adventurers hurrying down the open road toward them and smiled, then spit in the dirt by his feet.

"Come on, you cowards!" he bellowed, slamming the heads of his axes together with a thunderous clang. His rugged face was split by a long scar running from his pate down along the side of his nose to twist up one corner of his mouth is a cruel smile. "I'll chop pieces off every thrice-damned one of you and feed it to my dogs!"

Torgan charged straight at the man, who towered over the stocky dwarf. "The mouthy one's mine. You all handle the rest."

"Leave it to Torg to claim one and leave the dozen for the rest of us," Prynne said, sprinting past the stubby-legged battle priest with her sword in her hand. She veered off to the left of the milling throng of bandits and skewered one who was still trying to find his feet, then squared off against a skeletal man with greasy black hair slicked back from his forehead to gather in a long tail that ran halfway down his back.

Thallis hesitated at the edge of the fray as Celia caught up to him. "What's the matter, child?" the bard asked, her brow knit in concern. "Surely you've been in a fight before."

"More than I care to," Thallis replied. "But not many against a pack of thugs, and never fighting alongside people I gave a rat's arse about. I don't want to step wrong and get in the way, or get somebody hurt."

Celia looked down on him with a kind smile splitting her frightening features. "Dear boy, if they can't manage to keep from getting distracted by a boy who stumbles in a scrap, they would have been carved up long before they got here. Now get in there and help your friends."

Thallis nodded and set his jaw, then darted in behind a bandit who was running at Prynne's back with a studded mace raised high. With two quick slices across the man's hamstrings a fountain of blood sprayed across the road, and the mace thudded to the dirt as the bandit collapsed in a screaming, writhing mass. Then everything became a blur of dust and blood and screaming as the bandits quickly realized exactly how big a mistake they'd made.

Qabil ducked under a wild strike from a fat bandit whose armor gaped open under his arms. The young man rose as the broadsword whistled past his head and drove his sword into one of the gaps. The man's eyes went wide, then blank as he toppled to the road, his weight ripping the sword from Qabil's grasp. He bent down to retrieve his weapon, only for his not-quite healed leg to buckle under the strain. He threw his weight forward, turning his stumble into a roll, and heard a muttered curse behind him as he struggled to his feet. Still swordless, he spun around as he regained his footing, drawing his dagger with his left hand and tossing it over to his right as he assessed his foe.

He froze for just an instant, but it was long enough for the bandit to step forward and plant a foot squarely between his legs. Flashes of light exploded behind Qabil's eyes and his breakfast threatened to bolt for freedom as he sank to his knees. He looked up as the bandit, a girl no older than Thallis, stepped forward with her sword ready to chop off his head.

All Qabil could do was fall to one side, avoiding the blade but not improving his position in the slightest. His mind whirled, trying to reconcile the smooth cheeks of the girl who stood over him with the rage and bloodlust in her eyes. She reversed grip on her sword and stepped in close, raising her blade to stab down into Qabil's middle. He had other plans, so he rolled over onto his other side, flinging a handful of dirt and pebbles into her face as he did. She staggered back, spitting and wiping at her face, and Qabil sprang to his feet, stabbing the girl just above her belt and gutting her as he stood.

Her eyes went wide with shock and pain, and she opened her mouth as if to speak. Qabil drove his dagger into her left eye, leaving her last words unspoken as she collapsed in a puddle of blood and viscera. He picked up his sword and looked around, but there was no one left to fight. His band of...heroes, for lack of a better word, had dispatched nearly two dozen bandits in barely more than a minute.

Looking around the field, he heard groans from several of the robbers trying to drag themselves off into the woods to some kind of safety, and the thudding hoofbeats of a galloping horse echoed from the direction of the town. Prynne stepped into the middle of the ribbon of dirt and blood that passed for a road, drew her bow, and let fly an arrow that arced high into the air, disappearing over a small hill dozens of yards distant. She slung her bow across her chest and began collecting salvageable arrows from the corpses, stopping now and then to inspect a bow or quiver one of the bandits carried.

"Ain't you gonna go see if you hit him?" Thallis asked. Qabil appreciated his friend asking the question he didn't, but he was the tiniest bit concerned for the young thief's health as he questioned Prynne's marksmanship.

"You can if you like," Prynne said, never wavering in her quest for plunder.

The sound of hoofs and jingling tack drew Qabil's attention to the direction the bandit had fled, only to see a riderless horse coming over the hill, one boot still hanging from a stirrup.

"Nah, I think I'm good," Thallis said with a shake of his head.

"Drag all the bodies to the middle of the road and lay them out in a row," Torgan said, raising his voice to be heard over the groans of the few criminals Celia had yet to dispatch with her mercy blade. "I'll call down the blessing of Felrand upon them after we've salvaged anything worth taking or selling."

"We looting corpses now?" Thallis asked. "Not that I'm complaining, mind you. I've robbed plenty of deaders in my day, just didn't think an upright lot such as you would be in for such as that."

"The people in the village can sell the armor and weapons this lot carried for money to rebuild, and the horses can either work a field or bring good money as well," Leshru said.

"Which isn't to say we're above snatching up a sparkly or two for ourselves, if these ragamuffin ruffians have anything worth taking," Celia added, holding up a jeweled bracelet. "Robbers and highwaymen like this often wear their entire life's savings on their arms, necks, and ears. Easier to pull a bracelet off and pawn it than to work a day at an honest job."

Qabil didn't say anything, just cleaned the blades of his dagger and sword, then sheathed both weapons. He grabbed the arms of the woman he'd killed and dragged her into a rough line the others had started.

Thallis looked up from the corpse he was looting when Qabil dropped the woman by his knees. "What's this? Girl bandit?" He shook his head. "Stands to reason. If we got woman heroes, oughta be woman robbers, eh? You kill her?"

"Yeah."

"That bother you?" the thief asked.

"Yeah."

"Good."

Qabil's eyes locked with his friend. "What's so bloody good about it?"

Thallis sat back on his heels, looking up at the other young man. "The minute killing don't bother you, that's when you turn into one of these." He gestured to the growing row of bodies. "A brigand, not a corpse. Although it probably don't do anything for your longevity, either. So maybe you turn into a robber first, then a corpse. But either way, you oughta be bothered by it. Taking a life ain't supposed to be easy. Did you have a choice?"

"I suppose I did," Qabil said after a pause. "I could kill her, or I could die myself."

"Well, I reckon I'm...what do you call it? Biased. I'm biased, but I think you made the right decision. I didn't know this girl, but I, for one, like having you around." He smiled up at Qabil, then gestured to the other bodies. "Now get on your knees and help me search for anything worth keeping before Torgan calls down heavenly fire to turn these assholes into ash-holes."

Qabil smiled at the stupid joke but knelt by his friend and began to strip off armor, weapons, boots, purses—anything that might have value to a decimated village.

CHAPTER TWENTY-FIVE

The crowd that gathered as the small band of blood-spattered warriors rode into town was a solemn one, led by the surly man called Barth. They were, to a person, sweat-stained and haggard, with soot smearing hands and faces. The ruins of the inn smoldered, but the work of removing the burned timbers and working to salvage what could be used in the reconstruction was already well underway.

"What now," the fat village headman called as a loose circle gathered around The Seven. "Decided you wanted our gold after all, so you came back to pick the bones clean?" He looked around at the assembled villagers. "I told you all this lot would end up worse than Untrek's parasites. They're just going to keep coming back asking for more tribute every time we turn our heads. I told you—"

"Oh, shut the fuck up," Prynne said, cutting off the fat man's bluster as she tossed a large sack that landed at his feet with a wet *thump*. "You won't have any more bandit trouble. That shit's sorted." She waved toward the burlap sack, which was stained along the bottom with something dark and damp.

Barth opened the bag, then stepped back in horror, dropping the sack as he did. It *thumped* to the ground again, this time gaping open and allowing the head of the whip-wielding bandit to roll out, his sightless eyes staring up at the clear blue sky. "What did you do?"

"We solved the problem. A problem we may have had an inadvertent hand in causing, so there will be no charge for our services," Celia said, stepping forward and gesturing for Qabil and Thallis to uncover a large rectangular shape that was covered in horse blankets.

The boys pulled back the quilts to reveal a pair of large wooden chests, which they then opened to reveal the armor, weapons, and purses they had stripped from the bodies of the bandits before Torgan called down heavenly flame to cremate the corpses. "We brought you some more plunder," Thallis said with a grin.

"And a proposition," Celia added. "Where is the innkeeper?"

"Everette?" the erstwhile mayor asked. "I think he's still somewhere digging through the wreckage of his inn."

"I'm here," the massive innkeeper said as he walked up, drying his hands on a towel that looked more like a handkerchief in his hands than anything else. Qabil realized upon a better look at the man how very large he was, nearly Leshru's match in width, but what he had mistaken for fat earlier was more a general tight thickness, the kind of build that comes from someone who is very large and very active, but then settles into a more sedentary life. Perhaps Thallis's guess that Everette had seen army service was more on the nose than he knew. "Sorry. Took a moment to scrub off the worst of the ash before greeting guests. Welcome back."

The big man peered down at the head lying in the dirt, then turned his gaze to the still-bulging sack and the chests. "Few of his friends still in the bag?"

"Aye," Leshru said, stepping forward. "We paid Lord Untrek a visit and had a discussion about the way his people have been collecting his tribute. Turns out he never approved of any increase in taxes, nor has he been filling a war chest for some far-off battles. This band of pricks was just acting on their own initiative. Untrek gave us leave to...persuade them that their services were no longer necessary."

"They objected," Prynne added.

"Looks like it," Everette said, nudging the sack with his foot. "This all of them?"

"No," Leshru replied. "Just a few keepsakes to show we're telling the truth. Most of them were burned to ash a ways back up the road."

The townsfolk looked at the party with concern, and maybe even a little fear, dancing across their faces, warring with relief and weariness. The fat mayor stepped up again, but Leshru held up a hand to the taller man.

146

"You need to think about how I'm going to like what you're thinking of saying. Preferably before you say it. I'm hungry, covered in blood that started the day inside someone else, and I have a long ride this afternoon before I'll get to bathe and eat. So my fuse is a little shorter than normal, and that leads to people getting punched a bit more readily. Now, you were saying?"

The big man shook his head and backed away. "Nothing. I'm just going to…"

"Go somewhere else," Prynne said, her voice wicked and her smile vicious. "Before you annoy the people with all the pointy things." She ran her fingers over the hilt of her sword as she spoke, just in case there was any doubt who she meant.

The village headman turned and stalked away, muttering under his breath about outsiders and mercenaries and interlopers. Celia chuckled and turned her attention back to the innkeeper. "Now that he's settled, we have a proposition for you, Everette."

The big innkeeper looked up at the half-orc, suspicion darkening his features. "The last person who offered me a proposition wanted to rape my children, flog my son, and beat all the flesh from my bones as my neighbors watched. I hope this is a bit less one-sided a proposal."

"Not much," Nipural muttered.

Celia shot him a dark look, and the wizard stepped back, his hands raised as he carefully positioned himself out of slapping range. After watching her bludgeon her husband, he didn't have any interest in exploring her strength firsthand. Or firsthead, as the case may be.

"Anyway," the bard continued, turning her attention back to the innkeeper. "Lord Untrek finds himself in need of a seneschal to manage his holdings, preferably someone with a family that could also see to the upkeep of his manor. You would have to leave the village here, but you would be well-compensated, provided with a place to live in Untrek's manor, and as the person responsible for collecting taxes, you could ensure that no other band of brigands try to duplicate what this lot did."

Everette's brow knit, and he wrung his hands as he spoke. "Can I think about it? I mean, *could* I say no, if I decided I wanted to just run my little inn and not mess with the life of lords and the like?"

"You could," Celia said. "Lord Untrek needs someone to serve in this capacity, and we felt you would be a natural fit, based on what we've seen and how your neighbors respect you."

"And it ain't like you got any place better to lay your head," Thallis said with his usual level of decorum. "I mean, um...sorry..."

"It's all right, lad, we know you weren't saying it to be cruel," Everette's wife said as she came to stand by her husband. "So we'd live in the manor, clean for the lord, cook his meals, and collect his taxes. In exchange, we... get what, exactly?" Everette relaxed as his wife took on the negotiation. It was obvious that while he was a very capable man in many ways, his wife was the shrewder of the two.

"A roof over your heads, the direct protection of your liege lord, a well-paid position, and the surety that no one like this bag of rabble gets to terrorize you or your neighbors again," Leshru said. "And like the boy said, albeit less politely than we may have liked, it's not as though you have a better option looming, unless you have a secret store of riches and a mansion tucked away in the woods?" He gestured to the still-smoking rubble behind the family.

"I...I think we should speak to Lord Untrek, dear," the innkeeper said. The relief on his face at the offer had calmed to an optimism tinged with reasonable suspicion.

Qabil would have been more surprised if they hadn't been suspicious. After all, here was a bunch of people they'd barely met coming into town with a sack full of heads, telling them that their liege lord wanted to pluck them out of the rubble of their former lives and turn them from mere vassals into employees. He could only imagine what was going through their minds, and was desperately glad that he would be long gone from this place before the topic of working for a giant creature of legend came to the fore.

"Then that's settled," Nipural said, clapping his hands together once and drawing everyone's attention to him. "Now, where's that ass-faced mayor of yours? I think he and his family are going to volunteer to take a brief camping trip while a group of weary—"

"And hungry," interjected Prynne.

"—and hungry heroes spends a comfortable night in his home instead of sleeping on the ground again. These old bones would definitely be better served by a goose-down mattress than a bedroll and rocks digging into my arse all night."

"Not to mention a bit of distance from Leshru's snoring," Torgan said with a smile. "I bet if we put enough walls between him and the rest of us, it will only sound like two grecks mating instead of an entire herd."

"I don't snore," Leshru grumbled, a slight smile creeping across his features at the gentle teasing.

"No, you don't," Prynne agreed, throwing an affectionate arm over the big man's shoulders. "To call what you do mere snoring would be an insult not only to the volume that you produce, but also to the near-infinite variety of sleeping noises that you make. I thought I'd heard every disgusting man-noise in the world after traveling with you lot for years, not to mention growing up alongside this one," she jerked a thumb at her brother, who was studiously ignoring her jibes, "but these past couple of weeks have taught me one thing, old friend."

"What's that?" Leshru asked, despite the look on his face telling all in sight that he very much didn't want to know the answer to his question.

"That men don't just get fatter as you get older. You also get louder, smellier, and grumpier, and I never thought that was even a possibility for some of you."

Everyone laughed, and some of the tension seemed to fall away from the innkeeper and his wife. The big man stepped forward and held out a hand to Leshru. "Thank you. For everything. If you hadn't come by, I'd probably be dead, with everything we've ever owned put to the torch, and most of our neighbors right alongside us. I don't know how I'll ever repay you, but I swear on my life I'll try."

The big brawler looked downright bashful at the other man's words and stammered out an unintelligible response before Prynne stepped up beside him. "That's Leshru for 'you're welcome.' Come along, big guy. Let's see what kind of expensive booze the mayor keeps hidden under the floorboards in his office." She dragged the flushing fighter off toward the largest home in the village, her arm threaded through his as Leshru looked back over one shoulder in a silent plea for help.

"Think we oughta rescue 'im?" Thallis asked from where he stood at Qabil's elbow.

"That would mean going against Prynne and possibly interrupting her search for a drink. Is that something you want to try?" Qabil asked without even turning to see his friend's face.

Silence fell over the town square for a long moment before Qabil finally answered his own question. "Yeah, I thought not. Come on, then. Might as well see what kind of shiny bits might be lying around the rich asshole's house, right?"

"I thought you weren't a thief?" Thallis asked as they started toward the mayor's house.

"I wasn't a fighter before I left home, either. This is the kind of trip that changes people."

"Aye, that's for sure," Thallis replied. "So far we've turned a good number from alive into dead. I reckon that number's gonna get nothing but higher before we're through."

"Yeah, I'm counting on it going up by a couple more, at least," Qabil said, his face grim. "But until then, might as well drink."

CHAPTER TWENTY-SIX

The sun was setting on a weary band of adventurers as they rode into the town of Bedtev, a middling place with no walls, no guards surrounding the town, no visible defenses of any sort.

Qabil slowed his horse to pull alongside Leshru. "This place seems awfully wide open. Shouldn't there be some way to keep bandits out?"

Leshru turned to the boy, a bright smile splitting his dark face. "What makes you think this isn't a town built just for bandits? For all you know, everyone you see on the street is thinking of a new way to relieve you of your coin, and whether or not they're going to have to slit your throat to do it."

Qabil looked around again, this time his eyes lingering on every man, woman, and child he spotted, from the grubby boy with pudgy cheeks playing jacks in the mouth of an alley to the stooped old woman sweeping the wooden walkway in front of what looked like a flower shop, her long gray braid hanging down nearly to her waist. Did she have a throwing knife hidden in her braid? Was the broom really a quarterstaff that she would use to crack his skull seconds after he rode past? Was the boy a lookout for a gang of bashers, lingering just out of sight in the shadows between buildings?

A low chuckle jolted him from his paranoid reverie, and he looked back to see Leshru grinning at him. "Gods, boy, if you're this skittish in a hamlet like Bedtev, I'm almost afraid to think about how jumpy you'll be when we roll into Lennox, where there are actually people who want to hurt us."

"You were messing with me?" Qabil asked.

"To a point," the big brawler replied. He turned into the saddle, looking Qabil in the eye. "There are dangers everywhere, even a sleepy little place like this. There's a pickpocket that's been following us since we first rode into town, probably acting as a lookout for a gang of thieves who want to see where we settle in for the night and help themselves to our belongings while we sleep."

"Where?" Qabil asked, whipping his head around. Nothing looked out of the ordinary, just people going about their business, walking, talking, shopping, looking in windows. The normal activity for a small town at the end of the day. He scanned the crowds in the streets, then peered down the nearest alleys, straining to see what Leshru was talking about.

Thallis rode up on his other side, then reached over and put a finger under Qabil's chin, lifting his head until he was staring at the long row of mostly connected rooftops making a highway of sorts alongside the main street. Every four or five buildings there was an alley, and as they rode past another of these, Qabil caught sight of a thin form leaping from one building to the next, keeping pace with them exactly.

"Thieves either gonna go high or low, depending on the city and the job," Thallis said. "You look at the street, you're never going to see the hand that lifts your purse. Gotta pay attention to the Thieves' Road, and watch out for people crawling out of the sewers to come at you, too."

"Does this place even have sewers?" Qabil asked.

"No idea," Leshru replied. "But since I don't see any grates in the street, it's likely you only have to watch for danger from above. And any little gifts that might be lingering in the gutters that weren't washed away by the last rain."

"I hate these pissant little towns," Prynne said from behind them. "At least in real cities most of the shit and piss runs off underneath your feet, rather than getting stuck to the bottom of your boots."

"This from the woman who's spent the last decade living in a tree," her brother grumbled under his breath. "I reckon you've spent more time in cities in the past month than you have in the past year."

"True enough, brother," the archer replied. "Plenty of time to remember the benefits bigger places have over these little waste dumps. And at least in the forest, everyone covers their shit. Except bears. Bears just leave their scat lying around wherever they like."

"And what do you do about that?" Thallis asked.

"What? Bear shit in the woods?" Prynne asked with a chuckle. "You cover it up yourself. No point arguing with a bear about it, and you still don't want to step in it. Unless it's really fresh bear scat. If it's really fresh, then you probably want to be somewhere else very quickly."

"Why?" Qabil asked.

Prynne looked at him as if he'd been hit in the head one too many times. "Well, townie, if the shit is still steaming, it means the bear's still close. And if I learned anything living in the woods for the better part of ten years, it's that if there's a bear in one patch of forest, you want to be in a different patch as fast as you can get there."

"Okay," Qabil said. "Watch roofs for thieves, the woman sweeping in front of the flower shop probably isn't going to try and murder me, and if I see bear shit, I should run. Any other lessons you'd like to impart?"

Leshru chuckled. "No, boy, that'll be plenty for one day." He reined in his horse and turned to look at the others. "Now, we're obviously staying here for the night—"

"And tomorrow, too," Prynne said, with Nipural nodding beside her. "I need arrows, a new bowstring, and we need to resupply. We're low on food for us, which isn't much of an issue, since I could just bring down a deer for us every few days, but we're almost out of feed for the horses, too. And I can't go into the woods and shoot oats."

"I could use a few more components for spells, and this place looks like it's large enough to have an apothecary where I can acquire those plus a few powders and medicines that I need for potions," Nipural added.

"But—" Qabil started to protest, but Leshru held up a hand.

"No, lad. Walfert will still be in Lennox when we get there, but if we ride our horses on insufficient food, it'll take us a lot longer to make the journey. Besides, I've learned it's usually better to just do what Prynne wants. She's going to anyway, and it's easier to just surrender than to fight her over it. Whatever it is."

Qabil looked back at the lean archer, sitting easy in her saddle in her green-and-brown mottled armor, her bow hanging from the saddle horn and a quiver in easy reach. She gave him a shrug and a little smile, taking the edge off her usually near-murderous expression.

"He's not wrong, lad," Nipural said. "I used to try to change her course. It usually ended up with me sporting new scars."

"Those little cuts wouldn't scar if you could keep your dirty fingernails off the scabs, brother," Prynne said.

153

"They also wouldn't scar if you didn't feel the need to punctuate every argument with a dagger," Nipural replied. Qabil noticed their bickering had a certain rhythm to it, something he hadn't picked up on when they first joined up with the prickly ranger, but the more they traveled together, the more apparent it became that the woman truly cared about her companions, she was just largely incapable of showing it.

"Okay, then we need to find an inn. This place has grown since the last time I was through here, so if anyone has any information, let's hear it," Leshru said.

Celia cleared her throat. "I believe this is exactly why you travel with a bard. I have heard quite a bit about Bedtev over the years, as it's but a few days' ride from one of the larger dwarves' encampments outside the Dragon Peaks."

"Well, we mostly travel with a bard because you came with Torgan, and nobody's daft enough to try and tell you to stay home," Thallis said, his familiar lopsided smirk stretching his features. "But you do prove useful now and then."

"Now and then? Boy, get down off that horse and let me show you exactly how 'useful' I can be," the half-orc growled.

"Don't murder the child, love," Torgan said, patting his wife on her massive forearm. "He's teasing. He's stupid enough to poke fun at you, but not stupid enough to risk actual insult."

"Not wittingly, at any rate," Thallis agreed. "So, oh fountain of all knowledge, what can you tell us about the bustling...metropolis of Bedtev?"

"I think the word you're looking for is 'font,'" Celia corrected. "Which is technically a fountain, so I suppose it is still accurate, if not as lyrical. As of the last news I heard, there are four inns that serve Bedtev, one in each corner of the town. The Drunken Ass on the west side is a working-man's pub with a small stable and cheap beer. By all reports, the food is safe to eat, and they rent out sleeping space in the common room for those passing through, or customers who are just too drunk to stagger home."

"Pass," Prynne said. "If I'm sleeping indoors, it's going to be in a bed, and I want a bath. Preferably at least a mostly private one, without too many peepholes cut into the walls."

"Then there's the Cat's Custard, on the eastern side. A small step up from the Ass, but still not much in the way of privacy. The menu is reportedly better, but I think I heard that they share a stable with the Watch."

"If there's an option that doesn't put me anywhere close to the law, I'd prefer it," Thallis said.

"I'm with the thief on this one," Leshru said. "I don't think there are any warrants still out for any of us, but there's no guarantee. We made more than a few enemies in our former life, and a couple of them are still alive. No point in tempting fate. Plus, Prynne has a tendency to punch any constable she encounters."

"One time," the archer argued.

"I remember at least three," Torgan argued.

"And those are just after we all started traveling together. There were half a dozen or more before we ever got more than an hour from home," Nipural added.

"Fine," Prynne said. "But I never punched one who didn't deserve it. Every constable I've ever met is an officious prick who can't keep his hands to himself."

"That bit of fact aside, let's not put ourselves on a path to make jail unavoidable, at least not right from the outset," Celia said. "That leaves two choices—north or south. North is farthest away from where we stand, and the most expensive option, if the nicest. The wealthiest merchants and residents live on that side of town, and the Mayor's Dinner Bell is the inn that services that sector. It's nothing to write home about as far as major cities goes, but the rooms are reportedly spacious, with luxurious beds and private baths."

"Sounds like heaven," Prynne said.

"For some of us," the bard replied.

"Oh, Hells," Nipural muttered. "What now?"

"They have a strict 'Humans Only' policy. They do provide lodgings for their non-human guests, but it's in the stables. Seems the mayor doesn't like anyone without round ears ringing his bell. Or short people, no matter the shape of their ears," she added with a glance at the glowering Torgan.

"So fuck them, then," Thallis said. "If my boy Ears can't go, I ain't going."

"Pretty sure your ears are just as pointy as mine, idiot," Qabil said to him.

"I'm making a stand on my principle, here. The least you could do is shut up and let me stand on it."

"That would indicate that you only have the one, lad," Nipural said with a slight smile.

"Couple months ago, you'd have said I don't have any principles at all, so this is an improvement, right?"

The old mage just shook his head as the thief grinned at him, then turned to Celia and motioned for her to proceed. "Go on with it, then, bard. Tell us the name of the inn on the southern side of town, and how to get there. You've obviously been building us up to where you want to go."

The large woman's face went wide, and she pressed a massive hand to her equally massive chest. "I am appalled! Appalled, I say, that you hold such a low opinion of me, Nipural, after all these months we've spent riding together. How could you think that I would manipulate my friends so shamelessly, much less my dear, sweet, Torgy?" To punctuate the affront, she thumped Torgan between his shoulder blades three times, almost knocking the dwarf off his pony. "But yes, I do think the Sleeping Duergar is the best option for us—a middling-sized tavern with a dozen or so rooms above the main floor, with separate or joint bathing chambers, a menu of food that is reputed to be safe for most systems, and a private stable attached. It's about three streets over from where we currently stand, and this early in the day, there should be no trouble booking a room for tonight."

As the group moved in the direction Celia indicated, Thallis leaned over in the saddle, pitching his voice low so that only Qabil could hear him. "So if she thought we oughta go to this place all along, why did she bother telling us about all them other joints?"

"She's a bard," Qabil replied. "They all seem to fear that if they don't listen to the sound of their own voice for at least an hour every day that they'll forget how to talk."

"Oh," Thallis said. "That makes sense. You think we could get her to maybe get her practice in when we ain't surrounded by pickpockets and eavesdroppers next time?"

"I think what we call eavesdroppers is what a bard calls an audience," his friend said. "Why should we care who's listening in on what we say? We're in town, after all. Not like some bunch of highwaymen are going to leap out of the bushes and attack us."

"No, but they might block off the streets and alleys and corner us between some run-down buildings," Thallis replied. He pointed to the ten men standing in a line across the street before them, then waved his hand around to indicate the rough-looking customers standing in the mouth of every all and clustered up behind them.

Qabil then took notice that there were no people on the street who weren't wearing steel, and all the shops had closed their shutters and doors, presenting a wall of brick and wood to the party. An older man with clothes cut finer than his cohorts stepped out into the middle of the street, a smile stretching his face, an almost-handsome thing punctuated by a silly waxed mustache and pointed goatee. "Welcome to Bedtev, Seven. I've missed you."

"Can't say the same, Lockbay," Leshru said, sliding down off his horse and motioning for the others to do the same.

"Well, shit," Qabil said under his breath.

"You know this guy?" Thallis asked.

"No, but has anything good come of us being recognized? Ever?"

The young thief appeared to ponder the question, then sighed. "Well, shit, indeed."

CHAPTER TWENTY-SEVEN

As the party dismounted, Thallis leaned close to Qabil's ear. "Who the fuck is Lockbay? I never heard of nobody by that name."

"Me neither. Maybe he's an old friend?" Qabil studied the man who was obviously the leader or employer of the goons surrounding them all. Four men flanked Lockbay, all wearing the mismatched scraps of armor and weapons that gave a hint at the success, or lack thereof, of their life as mercenaries. Six more held positions at the mouth of alleys or in a loose line behind them, cutting off any avenue of escape. Not that Leshru and company looked like they wanted to escape. The burly warrior wore a resigned expression, as though he knew how this encounter was going to play out, whether he liked it or not.

"Okay, you know how I know he's not a friend?" Thallis asked.

"No, how?"

"Because people like this don't have friends in random towns. They have people they did jobs for, and some of them they don't hate. Then they have people they fought because of a job, and there's probably a few of them they don't hate. But friends? I expect if you'd ask them while they were drunk enough to be honest about it, they'd all tell you that every friend they've got in this world is standing here right now."

Qabil considered this and decided that the other boy was probably right. Even his mother had made very few deep connections in the town where he grew up. Everyone was friendly, and almost everyone was happy to see Eltara whenever she walked to the market, or when she was just going about her business in town. But there was no one that she seemed particularly close to. No one that came over just to chat, or to check in on them on the rare occasions when one of them fell ill. Not even the town priest, since after his father's funeral they never darkened the door of the local church again. When he asked his mother about it once, she'd told him he was welcome to attend services, but she worshipped a different set of gods, in a different way, and nothing in her beliefs required her to drag herself from a comfortable bed on her one morning of each week and sit on a hard wooden pew listening to a man with three mistresses tell her how to live her life. Even at a young age, without completely understanding what she meant, he was old enough to grasp that she'd just given him permission to sleep in one day a week, and that was deity enough for him.

"What do you want, Lockbay? We've got shit to do and don't have time to waste with you," Prynne said, and Qabil could see Torgan wince as the waxed mustache on Lockbay's face quivered with outrage.

"I just wanted to take a moment to greet my old friends, The Seven," the man called Lockbay said, sweeping the plumed hat from his head and affecting a bow so deep the bright yellow feather atop his ridiculous headgear brushed the top of a pile of horse apples, earning a brown strip running its entire length.

"Watch who you're calling old, you chinless fop," Nipural growled. "I can still roast your guts from the inside out."

The men on either side of Lockbay stepped back at the mage's threat, but the man with the shit-stained hat simply smiled. "Now, Nip, is that any way to greet one of the most respected members of Bedtev's Merchant Guild?"

"Probably not, but it's a perfectly reasonable way to greet the cheapest fence to ever trade coppers for stolen merchandise," Leshru answered, cutting off Nipural's venomous reply. "Now what do you want? We're tired, dirty, and hungry, and I need to piss. So either get out of the way, or I'll paint your shoes yellow to match the feather in your ridiculous cap."

Lockbay's face darkened, and he took a step toward Leshru, his hand drifting down to the jewel-encrusted basket hilt of the rapier that hung from his belt. It was a ridiculous-looking weapon, matching the rest of the man's colorful ensemble of a purple cloak, brilliant white shirt, and blue pants, all tucked into crimson boots. The entire effect was almost painful in its clash, and Qabil wondered idly if the man chose that ensemble because he looked like an idiot, thus giving him an advantage in a fight, or if he was just an idiot who dressed with his eyes closed. Given the lack of respect Leshru and the others were showing him, his money would be on him actually being an idiot.

"You'll show me the respect I deserve or my men here will slice off your testicles, Broke-Blade. I'd heard you took up bartending, but I didn't know you'd spent all your time since we last saw each other sampling your wares. You got fat as well as bald, Leshru. And your friends got old. Except for Walfert and Eltara. I heard he got rich and she got dead. Too bad, she was a prime piece of—"

"You want to think very carefully about the next words that come out of your mouth, sir." Qabil looked down to see his sword held low by his side, with no memory of having drawn steel. The men around him hadn't missed it, however, as they were all now armed and positioned to attack. "Eltara was my mother, and she died in my arms, so if you have a disrespectful thought about her, I suggest with all strength that you let it remain but a thought. Because if anything other than praise of her passes your lips, I'll be forced to cut them off and sew them onto your left cheek, so you can spend the rest of your life kissing your own ass."

Lockbay's face flushed a crimson so rich Qabil thought the man was going to collapse right there in the street. He drew in a great breath, began to draw his sword as he took the first step toward Qabil, and opened his mouth to shout orders to his men.

Those orders never came, his blade never cleared leather, and he never made it more than a step in Qabil's direction. Because Leshru of the Broken Blade took a long step sideways, planted himself directly in the taller man's path, and punched him in the jaw. One punch, not even a particularly hard one by any observation, but either Lockbay had a glass jaw or Leshru landed his blow perfectly, because the strangely clad man just let out a short "*uh*" of breath and spun around to fall flat on his back.

"Oh, that's gonna leave a mark," Nipural said.

"Nah, I didn't hit him that hard," Leshru replied.

"No, not that," the wizard said, pointing. "He fell in that pile of horseshit. No way he gets that out of his cloak without a stain."

Leshru let out an amused grunt, then raised his voice loud enough for everyone in the nearby street to hear. "Here's the deal. Lockbay is a prick, and he's been a prick for a long time. I don't know any of the rest of you, and I don't have any quarrel with you. We just want to get a drink, a bath, and a meal, then we want to resupply and be on our way. If you want to make that a problem, then we can have all the problems you like. But if you don't want a problem, you don't have to have one. What would you prefer?"

The minions looked around from one to the other, obviously confused. Qabil had no idea what Lockbay had told them to expect from this impromptu reunion, but he was certain that this wasn't it. "What he's saying is that you all have a choice. Get the fuck out of the way, or get pummeled and dropped into piles of shit all your own. Now I'm going to assume none of you have any love for scrubbing horseshit out of your hair, so I'm getting back on my horse and leaving. If you really think you want to stop me, think back on all the stories you heard about Leshru of the Broken Blade. Because they're all true, and he's actually much, much worse than the tales paint him to be. So, to ask once more, plainly—who among you wants to die this afternoon?"

That had the desired effect. Four of the men came forward, each grabbing one of Lockbay's limbs, and they hauled him over to an alley. The rest simply melted back into the shadows they'd come out of, and suddenly every shop door around them was flung open and the street once again bustled to life. "A wise decision," Qabil said. "Celia, I believe you said the inn was this way?"

CHAPTER TWENTY-EIGHT

The Sleeping Duergar was a basic inn and tavern, similar to dozens Qabil had eaten or rested in since leaving his home months ago. A large common room, dominated by long trestle tables with a few smaller round tables nestled in the corners, and a half-circle of comfortable chairs arranged in front of the fireplace. A small stage took up one of the prime chunks of real estate, near both the fireplace and the swinging door to the kitchen, and a skinny bard with a shock of unruly blond hair sat on a wobbly three-legged stool tuning a lute. Qabil didn't know much more about music than he'd learned from watching Celia for the past few weeks, but even he could tell the boy was struggling more than seemed typical for anything approaching a professional.

Their appearance in the doorway cast a wave of silence over the room that started at them and radiated out until every mouth in the pub either hung open at the sight of them , or snapped shut in surprise. Celia gave no indication that she noticed, striding across the room to the bar and leaning across it, one thick pale green arm thumping to the wood.

"How many rooms do you have available? And how much for room, bath, dinner, and a night in the stables?"

A plain young woman with mousy brown hair, but a smock slightly cleaner and better-fitting than the rest of the serving girls, stepped up, pulling a tankard from under the bar and filling it from a wall of casks behind her. "Silver for a bath, silver for dinner, and two silvers for a room. We got four, so some of you lot will need to double up, but ain't nobody in none of them, so they're all yours."

"Sounds good," the bard said, reaching for the purse at her side and counting out coins. The barmaid pulled out a scale to weigh the coins and nodded that the weight was true. Then she took a small gray stone out of her pocket and touched it to each of the coins. When none of the silver stuck to her rock, she looked back up at the bard.

"'S'all real," she said. "Your coin will be good here from now on, long as I'm working. And since my pa owns the place, I expect that'll be about forever. Now, you want dinner down here, or you want me to have one of my cousins bring it up to you? And all she'll be bringing is the stew, bread, and cheese. We ain't the kind of inn where other things is on the menu."

Celia chuckled. "No worries there, dear child. None of us have the energy left for a tumble after the ride we've had. But we'll take our meal down here. I assume stabling our horses is included in the two silvers?"

"Aye," the girl said. "But if you could see fit to slide a coin or two to Hance, the young man out there who'll be tending your mounts, it would be appreciated."

Qabil saw the barest hint of a flush rise up the girl's throat when she mentioned the stableboy, and smiled to himself. He'd had a girl once, back before his world turned upside down, and they too were trying to put a nest egg together for when he was old enough to ask for her hand. He lost himself for a brief moment in those happy memories, before the darkness that followed crept in and cast a scowl across his face. A sharp elbow in his ribs brought his attention back to the present, where Thallis was grinning at him.

"Wow, mate," his friend said. "You was gone there for a minute. Was she pretty?"

Qabil paused before answering, almost long enough for Thallis to wave off the question, but he shook his head and spoke. "Yes. She was pretty. Not glamorous, like some of the women we've seen in our travels. She was small-village pretty, the kind of pretty that doesn't dazzle, but makes you feel warm from the inside."

"She gonna wait for you?"

"I hope not. I told her not to. It's not like there aren't plenty of men in town that were interested, and she doesn't need to be alone just because I..."

"Got yourself killed in a fight you can't possibly win against a more skilled, more experienced opponent totally lacking in honor or morals?" Thallis finished for him.

"Not exactly how I would have put it, but basically yes," Qabil replied.

"Well, if you're not interested in any of the girls around here, maybe you won't mind if I…"

"I'd really rather not have to listen to you getting friendly with a serving girl while I try to sleep," Qabil said.

"Don't worry," Thallis said. "Most of the girls here are missing too many teeth for me. That cook's helper taking the dirty dishes away, though…he's far too pretty to not at least enjoy the occasional stroll on the other side of the street."

Qabil tried to keep the surprise off his face, but by the peals of laughter that came from his friend, he obviously did a terrible job of it. "What's that, Ears?" Thallis asked. "You couldn't tell I'm not interested in girls? Where have you been all your life, a convent?"

Qabil chuckled. "Narim, but it may as well have been a convent. There were a couple of men who lived together there, but they weren't very… open about anything."

"Couldn't be, could they? Not way out there. Things are different in the city. More people means more people of all sorts, and that's a lot better for somebody like me. Somebody who ain't like everybody else." A shadow flickered across the young thief's face, banished in an instant, but just enough to make Qabil wonder what his friend had seen in his life on the streets.

"Well, I can honestly say that you aren't like *any*body else I've ever met, and that was before I had any thought about who you liked to share a bed with." He threw an arm over his friend's shoulder in a quick half-hug. "Now come on, someone mentioned dinner."

As the two young men followed their party over to a large table set off from the main room in a small alcove, neither one noticed a wiry little man with a long, pointed nose stand up from the end of one of the long benches and slip out the front door to the inn.

$$\text{卌} \text{||}$$

A bit more than an hour later, Qabil pushed back from the table, his chair thumping against the wall behind him. As one of the youngest and smallest of the group, he was wedged deep into a corner, hemmed in by the thick form of Leshru on one side and Celia and Torgan on the other.

Thallis took his time as they walked over to the table and strolled up when but one empty seat remained, with his back pointing directly at the door. When asked if he was worried about sitting where he couldn't see who came in, he laughed and pointed at Qabil.

"His face is as good as a mirror," Thallis said. "If his eyes get wide, I'll be diving for the floor in a quick hurry. Long as he looks calm as a pond at daybreak, I don't got nothing to worry about."

"Like you've ever seen a pond," Nipural said.

"Like you've ever seen *daybreak*," Qabil added.

"Hey!" Thallis protested. "I seen the sun come up plenty o' times. Mostly when I been up all night, but it still counts. Doesn't it?"

"That it does, little thiefling," Prynne said. "Now how about you head over to the bar and get us a couple mugs of ale?"

"I'd love to, my fine lady of the feathered shaft, but if the nervous look on Qabil's face is any indication, we're about to have unwelcome visitors." The thief lifted himself slightly out of his chair, reached beneath himself to grab the seat, and spun himself around, leaning back with his shoulders against the edge of the table as he faced whoever had his friend so concerned.

Qabil was concerned not on account of who he recognized walking across the tavern, but rather due to the people he *didn't* recognize. The shit-stained popinjay from earlier, Lockbay, Lesh had called him, stomped toward them with a scowl pulling the massive purple bruise on his jaw into an odd shape. More concerning were the half-dozen grizzled fighters behind him. They were an assortment of men and women clearly accustomed to taking care of themselves, of perhaps others, with violence. Mismatched weapons and armor spoke to mercenaries rather than any official Watch, but to a person, they all wore their armor like they were born in it, and their weapons, while not drawn, were near enough to hand that he had no doubt they could clear steel in half a breath.

"Hello, Lock," Leshru said. "You seem to have something on your chin."

The slender man's face turned red all the way up to his eyebrows, and he shoved his way past Thallis to lean on the table and glare at Leshru. "I will be satisfied for the insult you dealt me this afternoon. I hereby challenge you, Leshru of the Broken Blade, to a duel of honor!" He stripped off a bright yellow lambskin glove, stretched so far across the table that he almost squashed the few pieces of bread left over from their meal, and slapped Leshru across the face with it, twice, like he was painting a fence.

Leshru picked up the glove from where Lockbay had dropped it on the table, looked at it for a moment, then slipped it onto his hand. It didn't fit, and when the rugged brawler clenched his fist, the seams of the glove split, leaving just the fingers wrapped around Leshru's hand. He peeled the remnants of glove off and dropped it back to the table, standing up slowly. Lockbay took a hurried pair of steps back, bumping into one of his mercenaries in the process.

"No," Leshru said. He looked at all of the hired muscle arrayed behind the skinny man with the twisted taste in clothing, and settled on the largest of the bunch. "You in charge of this bunch?"

"No, that'd be me," said one of the two female goons. She wore dark leather armor that was designed for mobility rather than face-to-face conflict, and her dark hair was clipped short and out of her eyes. A rapier hung from her waist, but unlike the bauble Lockbay sported, this was a plain, unadorned weapon, obviously chosen as any craftsperson chooses their tools—for efficiency and function, with form a distant third. "And yes, we know who you are. No, we won't be leaving without Locky getting some form of satisfaction, on account of we don't get paid if he ain't happy with how things finish up here. You understand, right? It ain't personal, just business."

"I understand," Leshru replied, his tone disappointed. "You look capable, so this is probably going to hurt a bit. I know you're all just trying to earn a decent coin, so we'll try not to kill anyone."

"We'll afford you the same courtesy, then," the leader replied with a curt nod.

"Like there's a snowball's chance in all the Hells of them putting down one of The Seven," Thallis muttered to Prynne.

"You aren't The Seven," Lockbay said with a wicked smile. "You're what's left over when the smart one kills the pretty one and a couple of children try to fill their spots."

"We'll see who you call a child when I knock you flat on your ass, you pestilent cockwart," Thallis said, springing to his feet. Lockbay grinned at the brash young thief, but his grin vanished when Thallis did exactly as he promised and faked a kick at the older man's knee. Lockbay swatted his leg aside, which left him wide open to the roundhouse punch that landed just behind his left ear, dropping him to the floor in a heap.

"Well, I reckon that's any chance of talking our way out of this one shot right to shit," Torgan said, picking his helm up from the table and sliding it onto his head.

"Yeah, but we knew this was where we going to end up," Prynne said. "The little thiefling just hurried things along a bit." She stood and cracked her knuckles. "I suppose we should try not to kill them, unless they draw steel first."

"Okay, fuckers," the female mercenary leader said, pulling a short club from her belt. "Let's dance."

CHAPTER TWENTY-NINE

Thallis flung himself at the mercenary with the club before she could adjust to the whirling dervish of fists, feet, and swearing that sprang at her. He tackled her and the pair of them rolled around on the floor like schoolchildren, punching, biting, and pulling hair. Leshru stood up, looked at the scuffling pair, glanced at the prone Lockbay, then turned to the five guards who remained standing.

"Are we going to fight? Or are we going to roll around on the floor?" He waved a hand at Thallis and the young woman scrabbling about. "Personally, I'm too old to be doing all that nonsense."

"Then maybe you're too old for this business, Baldy," a tall man of medium build with a tooth missing from his wicked grin said, stepping up to Leshru. "You want to dance, Grandpa?"

"Not really," Leshru replied, slamming a fist into the taller man's gut, then clubbing him in the back of the head. The goon dropped to the floor, and Leshru looked at his companions. "Anyone else?"

The answer, made more with punches and shouts than words, was still an unmistakable "yes," as the rest of Lockbay's impromptu retinue launched themselves at The Seven. Qabil planted his hands on the table, vaulting atop the circular surface and then launching himself at the other female fighter. None of the thugs held blades, just clubs, blackjacks, staves, and fists. So Qabil left his sword sheathed and just tackled the woman to the rough wooden floor. He punched her in the face, all chivalrous thoughts about not hitting women vanishing as the woman he grappled tried to bite his nose off.

His opponent couldn't get leverage to make a full swing with her billy club, so she settled for pounding her elbows into the side of his head. It hurt, but he could tell no lasting harm was being done. What worried him more was that he couldn't tell how his friends were doing. A thumb in his eye drew his focus back to his own problems, and he drew himself up onto his knees.

"I don't want to hurt you," he said, panting a little.

"Well, you ain't my type, so if you don't wanna fight, get the fuck off me and go running back to your mommy's skirts, little boy. This is a game for the professionals, not some wet behind the ears pup who wants to see how sharp his teeth are. I'll give you a tip—they ain't that sharp."

"I said I didn't *want* to hurt you," Qabil said as he drew back a fist. He slammed a heavy punch into the woman's chin, knocking her head back into the stained planks beneath them. "I didn't say I *wouldn't.*"

His foe unconscious, he stood up just in time to see Thallis and the other female guard still rolling around, now moving dangerously close to the fireplace, where the never-ending pot of mystery stew that hung in every tavern in the world hung over the open flame. A moment of concern for his friends' safety vanished as he heard the clatter of tin plates and pewter mugs falling to the floor behind him. He whirled around to see Leshru holding the table above his head, pounding the largest of the mercenaries in the skull with the massive oaken disk.

His mouth gaped open at the sight. That table was big enough for all seven of them to sit around comfortably, with room for at least one more, and now Lesh was using it to bludgeon his opponent? How strong *was* this unassuming, brown-skinned man? His legends seemed to be more than true, they began to seem almost understated.

His friends seemed to have their fights well in hand, and a quick glance to the floor let him see that his own foe showed no interest in rejoining the fray, so he stepped aside to watch the show. And show it was. Besides Leshru's feat of ridiculous strength, he saw Nipural standing back in a shadowy corner weaving odd designs in the air with his fingers while a glowing simulacrum of himself ducked, dodged, and generally baffled a thickset goon with one eye covered by a black triangle of fabric. The one-eyed bandit swung wildly, nearly punching his own companions in his flailing after the false Nipural, but he never seemed to even consider that there might be something more than a preternaturally light-footed opponent. *Well, I don't suppose there's much of an intelligence test when you're hiring muscle,* he mused.

Prynne was having at least as much fun as her brother, but in a very different fashion. Her opponent swung a quarterstaff at her head, but her head never seemed to be in the right place when he struck. She ducked, dodged, bobbed, weaved, and never let the broad grin slip even an inch on her face. After a few seconds, it became brutally apparent that she was only keeping the fight going as a diversion, and as soon as she was no longer interested in sparring with the man, she would bring a hasty end to their "duel."

Torgan and Celia seemed to actually be fighting the pair of mercs they were matched up against, with the stout dwarf trading punches with a fat bald man with a scruffy growth of hair on his chin that could only be called a beard by the most generous of loved ones. The big man dropped clubbing blow after clubbing blow onto the dwarf's head and shoulders, but Torgan just stood there like the mountain he came down from, as implacable as stone, until the fat human seemed to run out of steam. Then Torgan simply stepped aside, and Celia punched the man, twice, right on the tip of his nose.

Qabil heard the *squish* of pulped cartilage even above the din of the fight, and the *thump* as the unconscious man fell straight backward was enough to rattle the tankards on a nearby table. Qabil mused about how many people it would take to haul the fat man out of the inn if he couldn't be roused. The other man squaring off against Torgan and Celia was lean almost to the point of emaciation, with his face looking like nothing so much as skin stretched over a too-large skull. His features were flattened out and seemed somehow mutable, like he could pull and push them into different shapes, and Qabil thought for a moment that he might see Torgan do exactly that, but the dwarf just repeated his approach with the other thug. He stood there and let the man punch himself out, not seeming even the slightest bit concerned. Then, when the skinny man took a step back and dropped his hands, panting, Celia stepped in and the punching started.

With his opponent unconscious, and his friends having their fights well in hand, Qabil just stood up and moved back into the crowd of onlookers, planning to rejoin the fracas if a companion needed him.

Which seemed unlikely, given the way things had gone so far. That distance from the body of the fight ended up being his saving grace, because he wasn't currently entangled with a mercenary when the door to the inn burst open and a dozen members of the City Watch trooped in, swords drawn and plate armor gleaming in the firelight.

"Stop this in the name of the Queen!" a short man with a gold braid across his shoulders and a gleaming golden triangle on his breastplate shouted. "You are all under arrest for public nuisance. If you resist, you will be dealt with harshly. If you draw steel on a member of the Watch, your life is forfeit. Now on your feet, you lot! It's to the jail with all of you."

Qabil stepped farther back into the shadows, picking up a tankard from the table beside him so he looked more like one of the crowd. The Watch strode into the fight, armor clanking with every step. Leshru set the table down, taking care to avoid planting the legs on any of the unconscious combatants. The rest of his party stepped back from their personal battles and stood with their hands raised, showing themselves to be unarmed. Thallis and the female fighter he'd been scrapping with stayed on the floor, but as the young thief threw his arms around her neck and kissed her, Qabil understood what his friend was trying. If he looked like he was just taking the opportunity for a quick romp, perhaps they wouldn't end up in jail with everyone else.

It worked, because mere moments later, The Seven, Lockbay, and all the hired muscle save one were carted off to jail, while Thallis, Qabil, and the mystery woman sat back down at the recently vacated table and watched their companions depart in custody.

"Well," Thallis said. "That sucked."

"I dunno," the girl said. "There were parts that weren't so bad."

Thallis blushed a bright crimson as the woman laughed. "What's your name, skinny boy? I like to at least have some idea of who I'm rolling around on a tavern floor with." She was pretty, with a dangerous glint in her eye and cords of lean muscle running down her arms. Dark red hair framed a pale face with a smattering of freckles dotting her cheeks and nose. She had angular features, made all the sharper by the way she wore her hair, pulled into a tight ponytail at the nape of her neck, accentuating her sharp cheekbones and slightly pointed nose. Her green eyes danced with amusement at Thallis's embarrassment, but Qabil decided the thief had suffered enough and held out his hand.

"I'm Qabil. My mute friend with the typically quick lips is Thallis. We ride with The Seven."

"Or you did, until they got arrested," the girl replied. She shook Qabil's hand. "Marin. I usually work out of the Cat's Custard, but Lockbay's coin bit true, so I signed on for this little party. Getting tossed in the clink wasn't part of the bargain, so when loverboy here decided he'd rather get frisky than fight, I thought that seemed like a fine idea. I've never known anyone with any elf in them, so I thought maybe getting a little elf in me might be fun. More fun than jail, at any rate."

Qabil gaped at this brash young woman. Before going on this journey, he'd never met a woman who talked as plainly as Marin. Or Prynne, for that matter. Come to think of it, no one he'd met since leaving home had been much of what he expected, with the possible exception of Torgan. He was, as described, short. But every other person he'd encountered seemed to have more depth, more layers to their life, their personality, than the simple fishermen and their families he'd grown up with. He wondered if it was that depth of personality that made people want to take to the road, or if living among the kind of variety of individuals one encounters traveling made folks somehow just...broader, somehow.

He shook himself out of his reverie as he noticed Thallis and Marin were looking at him with quizzical expressions. "Um...sorry. I was..."

"Were you thinking about getting a little elf in you, too?" the mercenary said, then slapped him on the shoulder with a laugh that echoed through the quiet bar. The entire place had fallen silent with the arrival of the Watch, but at Marin's laugh, the bard began picking out a lively and almost-recognizable tune on his lute, and conversation returned to the low rumble that it had been before Lockbay made his appearance.

"Um..." Qabil stammered, feeling his cheeks flush as bright at Thallis's.

"It's fine, boys. If I couldn't tell by this age when a man kisses me without meaning it, I'd have a lot more tear-stained pillowcases in my washing. Now, what are you going to do about your friends?" the young woman asked.

"Why should we talk to you about it?" Thallis asked, suspicion writ large across his face. "You came in here with Lockbay to attack us."

"I came in here because that trussed-up popinjay promised me more coin than I make in a month as a caravan guard to come over here with him and give some 'old friends' a little 'welcome back,' as he put it. I've got no love lost for that moron, and given that he already paid me, and the fight is over, I consider my duty to Mr. Shit-Stained Feather well and truly discharged. Now, do you want my help breaking them out of jail or not?"

"I think that sounds like a truly terrible idea, Marin," a man at a nearby table said, turning around and pulling back the hood of his cloak. As he stood, Qabil saw the badge of office hanging around his neck.

"Well, fuck," Thallis said.

"That is well put, young sir. I am Captain Reg Kirby, of the Bedtev Watch. And it seems that my decision to stand aside from most of my men and make sure we didn't miss anyone in our sweep was an excellent one." Qabil thought he looked like one of those men who assumed all their decisions were excellent, no matter how it seemed to anyone else.

He was a tall man, with broad shoulders and olive skin, with gleaming half plate peeking out from under his thick gray cloak. A broadsword hung within easy reach of his hand, and he stood with the loose, easy posture of someone accustomed to springing into action at the merest hint of trouble. "Now," he said. "Why don't the three of you go pay the innkeeper for your meal and for the damages you caused, and then I'll escort you to a nice warm bed where your friends are undoubtedly waiting with great concern for your welfare."

"Why do I get the feeling he's totally full of shit about that warm bed part?" Qabil asked Thallis as they walked over to the bar, feeling the captain's eyes burn into his shoulder blades.

"Because there's never been a jail built with comfortable beds," the thief replied. "It's like the apothecary making medicine taste bad so people don't want to stay sick. If they made jails nicer than the slums, nobody would ever want to leave."

Having already paid ahead for their rooms and food, all that was left was to slide a few silvers to the innkeeper for the broken chairs and dented tankards. Thallis murmured a few other words to the man that Qabil didn't hear, then passed him a trio of purses that he somehow made appear as if from thin air.

As the pair walked back to Marin and the captain, Qabil felt at his hip and realized something. "One of those purses was mine!"

"Of course it was," Thallis replied. "And the other was Marin's. I told the innkeeper we'd pay double for our rooms when we came back if he'd hold onto those for us."

"Won't he just steal them and then deny he ever had them?" Qabil asked.

"He might," Thallis said with a nod. "But he might not. And if there's a chance he won't rob us blind, it's better than we'll get turning our money over to Captain Shinypants here."

"Makes sense," Qabil said as they returned to the table where Captain Kirby waited. "Okay, Captain. Take us to prison."

"With pleasure."

CHAPTER THIRTY

As accommodations went, it wasn't the worst Qabil had seen since leaving home on his quest for justice. The jail was underground, only reached by a winding torch-lit staircase then a long stone corridor lined with oily soot. He estimated that they were at least twenty feet below the town when they finally stopped descending, and the corridor twisted and turned so that he had no idea where in the city he would be if he could somehow just dive up to the surface through solid earth. The cells were roomy enough for one person, but cramped for six. Leshru, Torgan, and Celia were in one cell, and Qabil was tossed into another with Thallis and Marin.

He sat on the floor, his back resting in a corner as far as he could get from the privy hole, which offered no real privacy, but was a simple hole in the floor with a grate over it to make washing out the cells easier. He'd seen something similar in a stable once, where instead of mucking out the stalls, the owner had constructed an elaborate sewer system beneath the building and the grooms had to remove all the straw and wash the waste down every day. He'd thought at the time it was probably more time-consuming than just shoveling horseshit like everyone else, but he'd learned long ago that the wealthy have different ideas about what is and is not a reasonable expense than he did.

"What's the plan?" he asked, turning his head to peer across the hall at the other cell containing his friends.

"Well, lad, if I had a plan, and I don't, I doubt I'd be shouting it through the entire jail," Celia replied.

"Oh, come on!" shouted a voice from farther into the dank hallway. "I want to hear the plan!" A chorus of other voices chimed in, all clamoring for an escape plan. Qabil thought it must have been a busy night for the Watch with all these people arrested. Then he began to think about how long some of them may have been there, locked away under the city, without even a sliver of sunlight to remind them that there is a sky above them. He shuddered and drew back into his corner, pulling his knees up to his chest and wrapping his arms around them. For the first time since he left home, he felt truly hopeless, like he had not only failed his mother, but dragged all her friends into this mess with him and managed to fail them as well.

"Buck up, Ears," Thallis said from where he knelt by the privy hole in the back of the cell. Qabil kept his head turned away, attempting to give his friend a modicum of privacy. "Nipural will bust us out of here. I'm sure he's got some kind of plan."

"Best hope it's not Prynne with the plan, lad," Leshru said from his cell.

"Aye," Torgan agreed. "If she's the one coming up with escape ideas, it's probably something similar to 'murder everyone in the city and wash them out of the dungeon on a tide of blood.'"

"Like that time in Mityn," Leshru said with a chuckle.

"I think they only stopped chasing us because someone finally asked what would happen if they caught us," Torgan said, laughing himself.

"I hate to think what Tara would have done if someone tried to pen her up again. One week in jail was more than the Fairy Princess could stand," Leshru added.

"My mother was in jail?" Qabil asked, incredulous.

"We all were, son," Leshru replied. "More often than not, it was something like this. Some rube in some shitheel city pays off a bunch of hired muscle and the Watch to arrest us on some fake charges because we either embarrassed them—"

"Or didn't pay their protection money," Torgan added.

"Or maybe held a grudge from a previous encounter," Leshru agreed. "But at any rate, we all saw the inside of a number of jail cells, and made our way out of all of them."

"Not without some outside intercession," Celia added. "Which in this instance is a homicidal archer and a crotchety wizard. The perfect allies for a seemingly impossible situation."

"Your enthusiasm is...encouraging," Qabil said, his spirits lifting slightly at the bard's words.

"I think you mean insane, lad," Torgan said. Qabil didn't have to look to know what the meaty *thwack* that came from across the hall meant—Torgan's wife was once again expressing her disagreement with his opinion.

"Well, that's one idea down the shitter. Literally," Thallis said, dropping down beside Marin on the bench bolted to the far wall of the cell.

"What?" Marin asked. "You forgot your plan while you were using the privy? You're not as bright as I thought, thief."

"I wasn't using the privy; I was trying to see if we could remove the grate. It's not attached to anything, but it's heavy as fuck, not to mention disgusting. But that's not the problem."

"No, I expect that what with us being locked in a dungeon yards below Vilad's tannery, not being able to take the lid off the toilet is not our biggest problem," Marin agreed.

"Tannery?" Qabil asked. "I thought the jail just stunk like this."

"It does," Leshru replied. "This is jail stink, not tannery stink. That's a very different aroma."

"A lot of the same elements," Marin said. "Especially the piss."

"That's all fascinating," Qabil said, hoping to cut off this deep analysis of the varying stenches of mid-sized cities. "But what was the new problem you found, Thallis?"

"Oh, yeah. We can't fit," the young thief said.

"Can't fit where?" Qabil asked.

"Down the sewer, of course. I told you, thieves never walk on the street if we can help it. We're either over it, or under it. And the only thing under the streets is the sewers. I figured if we could get the grate up and fit down the hole, like as not we could find our way out through the sewers. But it don't matter. The hole is too narrow. I couldn't come close to fitting through there, so there's no way any of them could." He pointed across the hall to the cell holding the beefy Leshru, the stocky Torgan, and the massive Celia.

"So now we're...what?" Qabil asked.

"We're going to trust in our crew and wait. If all goes well, Nip and Prynne will be breezing through here any minute and we'll all walk out the front door laughing," Leshru said.

"And if it goes badly?" Marin asked.

"Then we'll be most likely be running out a smoking hole in the wall pursued by a screaming horde of guardsmen, mercenaries, and towns-folk," Torgan replied.

"Can't wait," Marin said, leaning back against the wall with a resigned expression on her face. "I should have just stuck with Lockbay. He's a prick, but he's not in jail."

"Day's not over yet," Leshru said. "And Prynne holds a grudge. She finds Lockbay, he won't be in jail."

"No," Thallis said. "He'll be in the ground."

𝍷𝍷𝍷 𝍷𝍷

"Any minute" stretched into hours, then all day, then all night, as Qabil and the rest of The Seven languished in their cells. Torgan spent the time in prayer and meditation, although his meditation sounded a lot like snoring for most of the time. Leshru did a complex series of stretches and movements that Thallis watched from their cell and followed along. Marin attempted some of the poses to keep herself occupied, but after the bald man leaned forward and slowly balanced on his hands and began to press his body weight up and down with his feet straight up in the air, she laughed and walked over to sit by Qabil, who brooded in the corner.

"Why so glum, elflet?" she asked, a wry grin twisting up one corner of her mouth. "We're indoors, they've fed us twice since we've been here, and the privy hole doesn't even stink too bad. If I was getting paid, this would be one of the best jobs I've ever taken."

"It's taking too long," Qabil grumbled. He sat as he had from the moment they were deposited into the cell, with his back pressed against the stone wall, knees drawn up to his chest, and his arms wrapped around them. His chin rested on his kneecaps, but other than burying his head in his arms, he looked like the perfect picture of abject misery.

"Look, I don't know the two of you who got away. Hells, I don't know any of you, really. But I've seen you lot fight, and if the rest of your little band of idiots feels like your archer and her brother can get you out of here, who are we to question it?"

"I'm the one who got everyone swept up in my fight to begin with," the boy said, his voice as dark as the corner of the cell he sat in. "I'm the one who ripped them from the lives they led and dragged them off on my stupid quest for revenge. It's my fault we're down here, and my fault any of them are on this trip to begin with."

To his surprise, the young woman beside him just leaned back and laughed. Her peals of amusement felt incredibly out of place in the dank jail, and Qabil gaped at her. "What's so funny?" he asked, the defensive edge sharpening his tone.

She waved a hand in the direction of the others, who had all stopped what they were doing to stare at her. Even Torgan had ceased his "meditation" and stood wiping his eyes at the bars of his cell. "Look at that bunch! Aside from your little thief boy, those are some of the toughest sons of bitches I've ever seen throw a punch, and they were holding back on my mates. If they'd wanted to maim or kill, they wouldn't have needed live steel to do it. I have no doubt that your bald, brown-skinned goon over there could have used that table to squash Lockbay like a cockroach without batting an eye."

"The thought did cross one's mind," Leshru replied, his slow voice low and grumbling, like two boulders rubbing against each other.

"Yeah, they're good fighters, but what of it?" Qabil stuck his chin out in a belligerent, if childish, pose.

"What of it?" Marin scoffed. "What makes you think you could *make* any of them do anything? These aren't just grown people, idiot. They're the fucking *Seven*. No one makes them do anything they don't want to do. If they're riding with you into some idiotic question for vengeance, justice, glory, or coin, then it's not because you're so persuasive no one can resist your silver tongue. Look at me, after all. I been locked up in here with you for hours now and am somehow holding myself back from jumping you and riding you like a cheap mule. So it looks like everyone here is pretty much immune to your charms. Must be some other reason they're down here with you."

"Aye," Thallis chimed in from where he sat cross-legged on the bunk. "Like maybe we're doing something that needs to be done, and we're the only people that can do it."

"See?" Marin said, waving her hand in Thallis's direction. "Even the idiot thief thinks what you lot are doing is important, more important than any one person. Might have been you brought them all together, but it's a crew now, and a good crew rides together through sun and rain. Or...at least that's what I've heard. I live here, and never been with any bunch decent enough to stand by each other when the shit starts splashing around."

"But even if I'm just the catalyst, I'm still responsible for them," Qabil said, this time earning a laugh not just from Marin, but from everyone watching as well.

179

"Boy, if you want to be responsible for anything about us, be responsible for paying the bar tab," Torgan said. "Between Nip's taste in expensive wine and Lesh's tendency to break furniture over heads, our bill runs high at almost every tavern we set foot into. But if you want to be responsible for our decisions, then you're about a lifetime too late for that shit. I was making bad choices half a century before you came squalling into this world, and I expect I'll be making them a century or more after you're gone. Now get up off your ass, limber up your brain and your body, and let's figure a way out of this hole. The bed is too firm for good sleeping, and Leshru snores."

"Not that anyone could hear it over the din you make," the brawler replied.

"I supposed you're right," Qabil said, pushing himself to his feet. "I guess first we need to—"

His words cut off as a commotion erupted from one end of the hallway. Qabil pressed his face to the bars but couldn't get a good look at what was happening, just a crush of bodies pushing and shoving, and shrill, officious voice ordering everyone around in an aristocratic tone that brooked no argument.

"Do you know who I am?" asked the piercing voice. "Do you?"

Without waiting for a response, the sharp sound of fingers snapping echoed through the jail, and the tremulous voice of an old man said, "It is my honor, privilege, and pleasure to present you with The Duchess of the Nurani Sands, The Huntress of the Gaugrin Forest, The Glory of the Nations of Pilmarin and Toprey, Her Magnificence, The Light of—"

"Get on with it, you senile old shit," the haughty voice came again, but this time it was instantly recognizable. Qabil felt a grin split his face before the man spoke again.

"I present you Her Ladyship Prynne Marchexon."

Qabil stepped back from the bars to sit on the bench. Prynne was here to try and talk her way through the guards and get them all released. And against all reasoning, she had already managed to get into the dungeon with Nipural by her side. Now they just had to find a way to get back out again.

CHAPTER THIRTY-ONE

That's the one," Prynne said, her voice haughty and cold enough to make the damp underground jail feel like there might have been a frost coming outside. "That's the thug who robbed my carriage, violated my manservant, and frightened the horses!" She pointed straight at…not Leshru, the most intimidating member of the party, if not the largest. That title was held by Celia, the massive half-orc's bulk taking up an inordinate amount of cell real estate.

No, her finger was aimed straight at Torgan, the pious-looking dwarven cleric who could barely reach the withers on a carriage horse, much less frighten them. The dwarf looked affronted, his whiskers trembling with outrage as he vaulted to his feet.

"I never did any such thing! I might'a robbed this scrawny wench, but I never done nothin' to no man, servant or not. And I ain't never done nothin' to no horse, neither! What you think I'm doin', carryin' a stool around to every robbery so's I can climb up and slip one to a horse in the middle of taking some dizzy bitch's trinkets. All her jewels were naught but shiny paste, anyhow." The grumbling dwarf's voice was an octave lower than normal, and more gravelly than Qabil would have thought possible if he hadn't been standing there to hear it. And the affected accent certainly made him seem like nothing more than a common ruffian, in a way the cultured speech of a traveling priest of Felrand never would.

"I swear on my butler's life that this man, almost certainly aided by the rest of this disreputable lot, is who robbed me yesternight," Prynne argued. Her tone was that of a woman who brooked no argument, who was accustomed to having her every whim catered to, and who would not be leaving until she had accomplished everything she set out to do.

Which Qabil fervently hoped was talking their way out of the dungeon, not just breaking the locks on the cells somehow and expecting them to fight their way through the entire City Watch. Which he gave them a slightly better than even chance of doing, but not without almost certain injury to some of their less-experienced party members. Namely himself.

"We ain't robbed nobody!" Thallis yelled, throwing himself against the bars of his cell. "We was just having a nice, quiet drink when these goons come in and arrested us for a lot of nothin'! Now we got to stand here and listen when some woman with more jewelry than brains accuses us of more we didn't do? Why don't you come over here and say that crap?"

Prynne did just that, taking two long strides across the hall and slapping Thallis across his face, which was barely wedged between two bars. His head rocked to the side, slamming into the steel framing his skull. He staggered back, spitting blood into his hands.

"I'll get you for that, you—" His words cut off as two guards drew their short swords and took a step toward the cell. "Once we get outta here, I'm gonna come find you, lady. You just wait."

"I'll be looking forward to it," Prynne replied. "But you might want to have a meal or two first. I expect I'm more woman than you're used to."

The guards laughed as the young thief slunk back to stand between Qabil and Marin. Qabil glanced down as he felt something press into his palm, but a hiss from Thallis snapped his eyes front again. He took whatever was being passed to him and ran his fingers along the slender shape. Somehow in the act of slapping him, Prynne had passed Thallis a key. One that Qabil could only assume opened the door to his cell. His mind raced as he tried to come up with a plan for utilizing this new element of their possible escape, and he walked over to the bars where Prynne continued to harangue the guards.

Qabil said nothing, just leaned his hands out into the hall with the key palmed. He waited and watched as Prynne filleted their head captor, until finally the man's will broke under the constant barrage of Prynne's siege engine of insults and demands.

"Fine!" he said, his voice ringing through the cells and bringing an abrupt end to Prynne's latest diatribe. "If it will shut you up, and you promise to take these bastards well out of the city, I will happily turn them over to you. The whole stinking lot of them. Open the cell!" Guards hastened to do as he ordered, opening the cell containing Leshru, Torgan, and Celia and herding them out into the narrow hall. There was barely enough space between cells for Celia to turn around fully, and Leshru's broad shoulders almost touched the walls on either side of him. He looked Prynne up and down, and let out a grunt.

"What about them?" he asked, jerking a thumb at Qabil and the others.

"They weren't mentioned by your 'victim,' so they stay," said the lead guard, a wicked smile playing across his face as he looked Marin up and down. There was no question that his intentions toward the young mercenary were anything but innocent, and Qabil felt his blood boil in remembered anger at the way Walfert treated his mother; like she was his property to be claimed, rather than a human being.

That lecherous up-and-down appraisal was all he needed as motivation, and the key he'd used to unlock his cell while Prynne was gloating over the guard's concession was his opportunity. He flung the door to his cell open, caching the guard right across his cheekbone and flinging him backward, then the brawl was well and truly on.

Qabil sprang out of his cell and pounced on the head guard, driving him to the ground and slamming his head on the stone floor. He heard rather than saw Thallis and Marin bolt out behind him, and the sounds of struggle filled the small dungeon. Somehow they managed not to alert the rest of the Watch to the pitched battle taking place beneath their feet, and within moments, the guards were all stripped of weapons and armor, tossed in cells, and locked up with their keys tossed down the privy holes.

"Should be someone along to rescue you lot at shift change," Marin said. "Just hope they recognize you in your skivvies!" She sketched a mocking salute, raising her hand to her brow, and turned to go. "Can we get out of here?" she asked Qabil. "Your friends are very exciting, but I'd like to go back to my normal, boring life of cracking skulls and kicking asses. This 'legendary band of outlaw' life isn't for me."

"Not sure it's for me, either," Qabil said, following her to the stairs at the end of the narrow hall.

"Don't know as how you've got much choice now, Ears," Thallis said as he fell in behind his friend.

"Don't know that any of us ever did," Leshru said, his voice a low rumble that propelled them up the stairs, and to freedom.

||||| ||

Well, almost to freedom. To freedom's courtyard, at any rate. Qabil and company were paraded up the stairs, down the hall, and outside, heading toward the front gate of the jail, which seemed to be located underneath a building meant for all kinds of town business. Guards bustled about looking busy, although if they were actually busy or had just mastered the art of appearing so was beyond any reckoning. Men and women lined up along one side of the courtyard, some in bickering pairs, some silent and alone, in a queue that seemed to be for having their grievances heard by the mayor, or maybe a judge.

Carts rolled in through the double gates, under a massive portcullis with spikes the length of Qabil's thigh protruding from the bottom bar, then vanished into stables or other parts of the massive complex for unloading. A quartet of guards stood by the exit, giving people a quick glance as they left, more a cursory glance to make sure that if they'd stolen anything that they had the good sense to make a token effort at hiding it or bribing a guard, but they just waved everyone through without stopping.

Until their motley bunch tried to step through the portal to freedom, only to find a pike lowered across their path. "Hold," said a stern voice.

Qabil turned his full attention to the guard who stopped them, a man of medium height, medium build, brown hair, and a light scruff of beard. He was as nondescript as anyone Qabil had ever seen, which was why the rich baritone coming from the man was a little startling.

"What is the meaning of this?" Prynne stepped forward, the affront to her entourage demanding the personal attention of The Lady herself, or at least the lady that Prynne was pretending to be. Her tone was perfect, Qabil thought. Haughty, yet demanding, without being anything less than horrifically insulting at the same time, as though she was offended by having to speak to someone of a station so far beneath her own.

"These prisoners are under special detainment," the guard said, a tiny hesitation in his voice the only indication that something may be amiss with the situation. "They are not to be allowed to leave the premises for any reason until they have been seen by the magistrate or an equally authorized representative of the duke."

"There's a duke?" Thallis asked Marin.

"There's always a duke or a baron or some little princelet that needs to stick his nose in everything so they feel important," Nipural murmured.

He needn't have worried about his voice carrying because Prynne was working herself into a towering fury and unleashing that tornado of terror upon the guard, who somehow stood his ground despite the onslaught of entitlement, insults, and threats he received. Prynne's entire story seemed to be centered around asking "do you know who I am?" repeatedly, then threatening to utilize her nebulous "contacts" within the city government to make sure the guard's duties were limited to mucking stables and scrubbing chamber pots for the next year if he didn't get out of their way immediately and let her be about her business.

Qabil kept his eyes moving, trusting his ability to hear Prynne dressing down the guard and insulting not only his ancestry, but also his children, his dog, and the entirety of the Watch in a string of insults that were both rhythmic and spectacularly staccato at the same time. While she was shrieking, he noticed that all the civilians in the courtyard were gone, and the number of guards around them was steadily increasing. With no weapons or armor, he really didn't want to try and fight off an entire garrison's worth of trained soldiers, legendary band of heroes by his side or not. He'd already learned that traveling with legends doesn't make one impervious to harm, and he was in no hurry to experiment with his durability further.

Leshru stepped to the side, clearing space around himself to fight, as Torgan moved forward to take a position on Prynne's other side. Nipural drew himself deep within his hooded cloak and began to mutter strange words under his breath, weaving complicated patterns in the air with his fingers. Thallis stepped forward to try and cover Nipural's side, as Celia stepped out and positioned herself to catch anyone rushing the wizard from the left.

"I guess we take the back," Qabil whispered to Marin, who nodded.

"Aye," the girl replied. "I thought this was all too good to be true. I know that guard. He's Lockbay's pet watchman, making sure none of that mouthy prat's people spend any real time in jail. I've gone with Lockbay a time or two and met this prick at the entrance where they brought us in, or a couple other places scattered around the city."

"How many secret entrances are there to the prison?" Qabil asked.

"They ain't secret. They just let folks get brought in or out of jail without every idiot on the street seeing them come in or leave. Sometimes they bring in wives for visits to their husbands when they're locked up, if the husbands have been behaving and the crimes aren't too serious. Most of the time they use it to let some minor noble's bastard son out the

185

back way when he gets arrested at a pub. Keeps him from further embarrassing the family, and keeps the rabble from griping too much about justice being different for rich people than poor."

"So why didn't we go out that way?"

"I expect your friend didn't know about the tunnels, and since I don't know where they are from inside the jail, I didn't mention it. My first time being arrested. Kinda took me off my game a touch."

"So there's no chance this guy lets us go just because Prynne yelled at him?"

"Not a one. Matter of fact, I'm pretty sure I saw one of the street kids run off as soon as he stopped us. I bet we'll see Lockbay strutting up to the front door any time now."

And just then, the prissy adventurer rounded a corner and pranced into the courtyard like a preening rooster. "What's this, Armisto? Are our friends trying to leave before justice can be done? What kind of place would this be if we allowed travesties such as that to occur? We should have them hauled back downstairs, and this time perhaps our loud friend here would like to join her traveling companions?" His smile was oily, an unctuous thing that slithered across his face and settled on his lips more as a sneer than anything demonstrating happiness or pleasure.

Then his lips exploded into blood and shards of teeth as Leshru stepped forward and slammed a massive fist into Lockbay's mouth. "Fuck all this talking," he said. "If we're going to fight, let's fight."

And that's when things got festive.

CHAPTER THIRTY-TWO

Qabil was stunned by the speed at which his companions leapt into action. He'd seen them fight before, but that was mostly groups of untrained bandits or a village full of dwarves who just wanted a scrap to get warm. This was the legendary Seven against an entire courtyard filled with trained guards, each of them well-armed, well-armored, and at least somewhat trained.

They seemed to be unwilling to draw their swords, at least all the guards did. Lockbay and the two men he had flanking him pulled steel the second he got his bleeding nose under control. Qabil stepped up beside Leshru and faced off against one of the swordsmen, drawing a concerned glance from the big man.

"You sure you want this fight?" Leshru asked under his breath.

"Fuck no, I don't want it," Qabil said, ducking to avoid a wide, testing slash from his opponent. "But I'm probably better suited to it than most. Now shut up and let me listen."

He narrowed his eyes to slits, until all he could see was the big man with the broadsword before him. The man was barrel-chested, with the kind of big, round belly that you know is hard as granite before you ever make the mistake of punching it. He had a pair of small scars on his chin that gave him the appearance of fangs and a wicked smile that spoke of a true love of inflicting pain.

Qabil dodged, slipped aside, and barely managed to avoid the thrusts the big guard sent his way, all while sorting through the sounds of combat, trying to find the rhythm of the fight, the ringing of armored boots on stone, the jingle of mail, the swish of blades through air. He let himself slip into the pattern of *crash-thud-jingle-crash-swish-jingle-crash*, feeling his body adapt to the repetitive sounds around him, moving almost without his control, slipping past thrusts and sidestepping punches with barely a feather's-width of space to spare.

He added the staccato drumming of his heels on the courtyard to the song, using his own steps to pace the guard, whose face grew redder the longer he failed to connect with the lithe young man. After the same pattern of slash, stab, uppercut, slash failed to connect for the second time, Qabil went on the offensive, ducking under a wide slash that would have taken his head off had it connected, and drove the heel of his right hand into the side of the man's kneecap. There was a sickening *pop* as the ligaments around the knee tore, and the hard disk of bone slid around to the side of the guard's leg, dropping him with a scream.

Qabil stood and took the man's sword from his hands, freeing him up to clasp his injured leg with both hands and create entirely new languages of profanity, casting aspersions not only on Qabil and his lineage, but also on Lockbay, Lockbay's money, Lockbay's *sister*, and his dog. "Sorry," Qabil said. "But I didn't kill you. That's something, at least."

He stood and stepped around Leshru, who was alternating swatting aside strikes from Lockbay and the remaining guard, laying his purloined blade against the guard's throat with a dark look. The man took the hint and dropped his weapon, raising his hands in surrender.

"About time you finished warming up and joined the fight," Leshru growled. The big man took one step forward, positioning himself inside Lockbay's wide slashing strike, and punched the man with the manicured mustache. He hit him once, a solid strike to the solar plexus that dropped Lockbay like a stone. Leshru turned back to where his companions were battling a dozen guards to a standstill and let out a piercing whistle.

Nipural disengaged from the guard he was scuffling with, a grizzled man who looked more as if he were merely passing the time than actually trying to apprehend a criminal. The wizard raised both hands to the sky, muttered a few words Qabil couldn't hear across the courtyard, then brought his hands together over his head.

The sky split open, a bolt of lightning streaking to the ground, turning a circle of sand four feet across to polished glass. The thunderclap that followed was tremendous, enough to knock those nearby off their feet. There was no rain, not even visible cloud cover, just a bolt of lightning from a clear blue sky and thunder that left ears ringing for yards around.

"Now can we cut this shit out, or do we have to beat every goddamned one of you to a paste before you'll get the fuck out of our way and let us leave?" Prynne's shout filled the silence that fell over the courtyard. "We're not fucking criminals. Well, not much, and not lately. Lockbay had us arrested because he's a poncey twat with his underthings in a bunch because we beat him out on a bounty decades back."

"It was more than one bounty," Torgan corrected.

"Shut up," Prynne snapped. "If they can't speak, neither can you."

The dwarf held up both hands in surrender. The fire crackling Prynne's eyes brooked no argument from anyone. She walked over to where Lockbay knelt on the ground, hands clutched to his midsection. "Here's what's happening, you over-manicured prick. We've beaten your ass so many times I'm tired of counting, and Leshru has put you flat three times since we got to this fucking city yesterday. But now we're done. Done playing with you, done wasting time with you, done worrying about what kind of bullshit you're going to try next. Done. Do you fucking understand me, you stupid fucking fuck?"

Lockbay opened his mouth to respond, but Prynne slapped him so hard that he almost fell to the ground. "If I want you to speak, I'll ask something complicated. For everything else, just fucking nod. Do you understand me?"

Lockbay drew himself up to his knees, sucked in a breath, and looked in Prynne's eyes. Then he nodded.

Prynne straightened up, her time as a torturer of kneeling men apparently finished for the moment, and turned in a slow circle. "Does anyone object to us gathering our belongings from the gate guards and going on about our business? Or is there someone who would like to see just how godsdamned precisely my brother can aim those lightning bolts?"

No one spoke. Very few of the gathered guards and spectators were even willing to meet Prynne's gaze. "Good," she said. Turning to one of the still-standing guardsmen, she said, "Now bring us our shit and we'll be out of your hair. And if we're all lucky, we never see one another again."

"I think I have an objection," came a booming voice from the battlements. Qabil looked up to see a broad-chested man with a waterfall of snow-white hair spilling down over his shoulders, barely constrained by a silver circlet on his brow. Piercing blue eyes stared down at them from a face lined with years and sun. The man had a strong posture, with thick fingers curling over the stone before him. A trim beard matching his white hair obscured the lower half of his face, but Qabil could see enough to recognize a slight smile, even from this distance.

"I object," the man continued. "To guests of my home leaving without even having dinner. Please, allow my personal guard to escort you to rooms where your belongings will be returned and you will be given an opportunity to clean yourselves before dining with me in the Great Hall this evening."

"And if we decline your gracious invitation, your...grace?" Prynne asked.

"You may call me Lord Mayor Gwinnett Dalif. Sir will suffice. And I would highly recommend not declining my invitation. It wasn't a request." And with the air of man accustomed to his dictates being followed whether her was present to enforce them or not, the Lord Mayor turned and walked away.

"Okay, then," Prynne said, looking at her companions. "I suppose we're having dinner with the boss." She took a step toward where Nipural and Torgan stood with the others, paused, then turned and kicked Lockbay in the side of the face. His jaw dislocated with a loud *pop*, and Prynne turned to continue her walk into the keep. "That should shut his fucking mouth for a few days, at least."

𝍬𝍫

The Lord Mayor's home was large and well-appointed, but not ostentatious. It wasn't even the largest building in the compound containing the jail, the Watch barracks, the city stables, and the administration building. It was a nice residence, but not showy.

There were armed guards at the front door, but just a pair of them, and they weren't the gleaming show pony guards Qabil had seen at other rich men's houses on their travels. They were just regular soldiers, maybe members of the Watch, or mercenaries more likely, since they weren't sporting Watch uniforms. Thallis wondered a bit at that as they approached the house. If this was the mayor's house, why wasn't it guarded by the Watch?

190

These men were obviously experienced, and well-armed, if they weren't the type of guards one would expect to see at a joust or other frivolous mock battle. Their armor was fitted well, if none of it was exactly gleaming. Their weapons showed signs of use and were mismatched, seemingly chosen for familiarity and wielder's preference rather than a particular image they were meant to portray.

"These boys look like they know where to put the pointy ends of those swords," Thallis murmured as they passed through the heavy wooden doors. Even the doors were well-crafted without being overly ornate. The foyer was more of the same, and as a servant escorted them to the Lord Mayor's office, Thallis marked the furnishings and decorations through the home as nice, but not extravagant.

"What does his home tell you about His Mayorship?" Leshru asked.

"A quiz?" Thallis replied. "Fair enough, then. I don't know if it's an elected or inherited job, but he takes it serious. He's not putting on airs like your friend Locky. His guards are for real, experienced fighters with killer's eyes. They've seen some shit, and I wouldn't want to dance with them unless I had some way to cheat. I wouldn't tussle with them in a fair fight."

"Killer's eyes?" Marin asked with a smile. "What kind of eyes does a killer have?"

Her teasing tone vanished when Thallis pointed straight at Leshru. "Eyes like those," he said. "You can tell from a glance that Lesh's taken life, and will again if he has to. That shit changes a person. Unless they're a monster already. Then it seems like the first time their hands come away bloody they develop a taste for it. I seen it on the streets. That kind don't last long. But these fellows? They're professionals. They've got no appetite for killing, but they'll dance to whatever tune is called, long as it serves their master, or their conscience, or whatever they listen to."

"And these men, without exception, listen to me," the Lord Mayor said from behind a massive desk of dark, polished wood. The office was a cluttered room with a desk, a pair of chairs facing it, a large fireplace, a pair of diamond-paned doors that opened out onto a balcony, and a table that dominated the entire half of the room opposite the crackling fire. "Please make yourselves comfortable. I apologize for the mess. I didn't have time to put everything away before I heard about your...disagreement with Traven."

"Who's Traven?" Prynne asked, dropping bonelessly into a chair and immediately leaning back on two legs with her feet on the long table.

"Traven Lockbay," Mayor Dalif replied with a quizzical expression. "I thought you knew him."

"Oh, we do," Prynne replied with a chuckle. "But I always thought his first name was Fucking." At the mayor's puzzled expression, she delivered the punchline. "Because every time he walked into any tavern anywhere in Relhye, someone would say, 'There's Fucking Lockbay again. Make sure your daughters and sheep are locked up tight.' Now I have no direct knowledge of Lockbay having relations with any farm animals, but..." Her voice trailed off with a smile.

"But if anybody in the world looks like a sheep-fucker, he's it," Thallis finished for her, taking the seat by her side.

The rest of The Seven and Marin settled into seats around the table, with Leshru taking the foot of the long wooden expanse, directly opposite the mayor. "We're here," Leshru said. "I'm guessing you didn't bring us here just for a nice dinner and a reward for beating Lockbay up."

"Again," Celia added. When Leshru shot her a quizzical look, she shrugged. "For beating Lockbay up again. It's not the first time you've dropped him on his arse, is it?"

"First?" Torgan asked, laughing. "Shit, love, it's not even the fifth! There was a time when I swore Leshru was trying to beat that pompous prick's face in every month!"

"Did it for eight months running," Leshru said, his face impassive. "Broke my streak when we went across the Foundling Sea on that job in Tence."

"Oof," Torgan replied. "Well, that job wasn't worth the sacrifice, now was it?"

"As enjoyable as it is to watch retired heroes reminisce, that's not exactly why I brought you here," Mayor Dalif said.

"You mean you didn't just want to get drunk with The Seven and listen to us recount tales of our misspent youth?" Nipural asked.

"Speak for yourself, old man," Thallis said. "I'm still misspending mine."

"No," the Lord Mayor replied. "As thrilling as I'm sure tales of your exploits must be, I would like to hire you for a small job. It's very simple, more an investigation than anything I expect to lead to any real trouble."

"You ever notice how they always say how simple a job is going to be right before they tell you exactly how little they want to pay?" Prynne asked.

"Or right before they describe in great detail how absolutely fucked the situation is, to the degree that only a band with our legendary skills could attempt the job and survive," Nipural said with a nod. "So, Lord Mayor, what's it to be? Are we slaying another dragon? Routing an invading army? Overtaking a sovereign nation? It's been a while since we've done that last one, and I'm not sure you have the resources to hold it even if we took a country for you."

"Nothing like that," the mayor replied. "And...have you actually slain a dragon?"

Leshru held his fingers about a thumbs-width apart. "A little one. Now what's the job?"

"And where's that dinner?" Thallis asked. Everyone turned to look at the young thief. "What?" he asked, a note of protest in his voice. "I'm a growing boy."

"You'll be growing in all the wrong directions, you keep eating like you do," Celia said.

"Dinner will be served momentarily," Mayor Dalif said. "And as for the job, I need you to check on a nearby dwarven village. Oakrune is about two day's ride northwest of here, and we typically do a brisk trade with them. But no one from Oakrune has shown up at the past two market days, and some of our vendors are becoming concerned."

"Concerned because of their lost revenue, not because there might be something wrong with a bunch of dwarves," Celia said, her voice a disapproving rumble. "Why is it that we're never asked to look in on someone because a person actually cares about another's well-being? Why is money always—"

"We'll do it," Torgan said, his voice cutting off his wife's diatribe in mid-sentence. "I know the place. We'll go find out what's happened."

"How do you know this village, love?" Celia asked. "You told me you weren't very familiar with this part of the land."

"I'm not, but Oakrune is a name I've...heard recently," Torgan replied, his cheeks reddening beneath his beard.

"Heard where?" Nipural asked. "We've been with you ever since we left Steelhammer and none of us have heard anything."

"That's because I heard in a dream," the dwarf replied.

"A...dream?" Prynne asked, laughter bubbling up and beginning to escape in her voice.

"A vision, more like," Torgan said, cutting off the archer's mirth like turning off a faucet. "I've seen it in dreams the last two nights. A village full of dwarves, all going about their business, but there's a darkness coming, maybe already there by now. But the name of the town in my dreams...was Oakrune."

"A...vision?" Marin asked, her eyebrows climbing.

"From Felrand. I have to go save this village. My god demands it."

"Okay, then," Leshru said, clapping his hands together with a booming *thud*. "Looks like we're on a mission from god. Now where's that dinner?"

CHAPTER THIRTY-THREE

It was a well-fed, well-rested, well-outfitted Seven that rode out of Bedtev the next morning. Lord Mayor Dalif had their horses brought over from the inn, along with all of their belongings confiscated when they were arrested.

"How will we get word back to you when it's done?" Thallis asked.

"That would be my part of the job," Marin said as she entered the courtyard right outside the stables. She looked as well-rested as The Seven and was now outfitted in armor emblazoned with the city seal, just like all of Dalif's personal guards.

"You working for the city now?" Thallis asked with a mocking lilt to his voice.

"Well, it's about time she put aside this ridiculous life as a pretend sellsword and joined the family business," Lord Mayor Dalif said from beside her.

The young thief raised an eyebrow but said nothing. Silence hung over the courtyard like the morning fog, only thicker and less malleable. After a long breath, Marin said, "The Lord Mayor here is my uncle. He's raised me since my father died on a caravan guard gig. My mother died giving birth to me, so Uncle Gwinnett is the only family I have left. He's 'suggesting' that my recent arrest and involvement with Lockbay is proof that I should no longer work freelance jobs."

"Yes," Dalif agreed. "I'm 'suggesting' that very thing."

Thallis watched the unspoken communication between uncle and niece, and shook his head. "There ain't many times I'm happy not to have a family. But about every time I watch somebody deal with their family, it crosses my mind."

Nipural stepped over and put a gnarled hand on Thallis's slender shoulder. "Tell me about it, lad." He glanced over at Prynne. "Tell me about it."

"So you're going to ride with us and report back to your uncle when we've handled whatever is bothering this village," Leshru said, bringing everyone's attention back to the task at hand.

"Aye, that's the plan," Marin said. "Uncle says if I manage to do this without getting myself killed, he'll let me skip out on the apprenticeship part of joining his guards."

"That's...nice of him, I suppose," Thallis said.

"Not really," Marin replied with a dark look at her uncle. "I've already seen more action than half his guards, and I'm a better archer and swordswoman than two out of three."

"Then I suppose you can ride with us and probably not skewer yourself with your own sword," Prynne said. She threw an arm over the younger woman's shoulders. "Maybe somewhere along this little adventure you can give Qabil here a few lessons."

"I know how to wield a sword, Prynne," Qabil protested.

"Not the sword, or the lessons, I'm talking about," Prynne shot back, then broke into a loud, braying laugh that startled her horse. "And the look on your faces tells me that you both certainly need those lessons!"

With no response at the ready, Qabil turned, face flaming, to check the straps on his horse's tack, arrange his packs and weapons on the beast, and climb onto its back. "Are we ready to go, or are we going to spend all morning talking about my love life?"

"Let's ride," Thallis said, springing into the saddle. "Cause it'll only take about ten more seconds to cover your love life, and I don't need you lot taking any kind of look at mine."

"Or your lack thereof," Prynne added with a smirk.

"If your old friend Lockbay hadn't ruined our night of relaxation, I think I had a decent play with the bard at that inn," Thallis argued.

"Ronak?" Marin asked. "He's happily and faithfully married, to a woman, I believe. So I don't think you had as much chance with him as you thought. Now Nicklas the bartender, on the other hand..."

"Oh, he was a fine-looking man," Qabil said.

"Good hands, too," Marin replied. She caught the puzzled look Qabil gave her and shrugged. "What? Just because Nicky likes boys doesn't mean he *only* likes boys. And who's to say I *only* like boys myself?" She gave Prynne an overstated, leering up-and-down look as though evaluating a haunch of beef in the butcher shop window.

"Well, lovey," Prynne said, patting the girl on the head. "You can bunk down between Qabil and me tonight, and either decide which one you want to play with later…"

"Or not decide at all," Marin agreed with a saucy smile matching the smirk Prynne wore. Both women turned their gazes to Qabil and erupted into more laughter at the wide-eyed expression on his face. "We should stop teasing him," Marin said. "Or he won't be able to ride comfortably for the next hour."

Prynne gave the flummoxed young man a smile. "Don't worry, lad. I'm not one for ladies. I just talk a good game."

"Too bad," Marin said.

"And I don't fuck people I have to fight beside," the archer continued. "It never ends well."

"And sometimes ends far too abruptly," Leshru said. "Now can we ride before this turns further to the maudlin?"

They mounted up and headed out into the early morning light, water-skins hanging from their saddle horns and meat pies in hand, breaking their fast as they rode off to see what kind of trouble would be plaguing a remote dwarven village enough to require a literal message from a god.

$$\text{卅}\text{II}$$

$$\text{卅}\text{II}$$

$$\text{卅}\text{II}$$

The village was most of a day's ride from Bedtev, and Torgan barely spoke for the entire trip, responding with the barest of mumbles whenever someone asked him a direct question. As they turned off the main road onto a smaller wagon track that wound through deeper woods, Leshru dropped his horse back from the head of the party to keep pace with the taciturn dwarf.

"What's going on?" he asked.

"Nothing," Torgan replied, his tone curt and his expression dark.

"Don't bullshit me, Torg. We've ridden together far too long for that. Your god sends you a vision of a bunch of dwarves in trouble, and you're lagging behind everyone on the journey to rescue them? That's not like you, old friend. Normally you'd be whipping that pony into a lather and damning all of us for slowpokes."

"This is different."

"Want to explain it to me?"

"No."

"Wasn't really a request."

Torgan glared up at his friend, anger flashing in his eyes, barely visible beneath his helm and bushy eyebrows. "You giving me orders now, Lesh? Thought you were the one always said you didn't want to be in charge. 'Let Nip run things, he's got the head for it.' Wasn't that you? Or do I have you confused with another Black human who isn't smart enough to figure out which end of a sword to point at the enemy, so he fights with his fists instead?"

"No, I'm not giving orders. Or maybe I am. Fuck, Torg, I don't know. I know I don't want to be out here with blisters on my ass from this saddle, I don't want Tara to be dead, I don't want to be leading her kid and maybe everybody else I give a shit about to their certain deaths, and I sure as water is wet and grass is green don't want to ride into a fucking dwarven village that's in such deep shit that a fucking god is calling for help without a single godsdamned idea what kind of trouble I'm heading into. So if you could, in the deepest corners of your heart, find an ounce of fucking charity, I'd certainly appreciate you sharing anything you know about whatever the fuck we're heading into. Please." The big man folded his arms and glared down at the dwarf.

Torgan returned his glare with equal fire for a moment, then another, then finally he let his hands fall back to his saddle horn and he let out a long sigh. "They're forest dwarves. I'm a mountain dwarf. We...don't get along so well most of the time."

"There are different kinds of dwarf?" Leshru asked.

"Are you a bigot, or just a moron?" his friend shot back. "Of course there are different kinds of dwarves. There's more than one kind of human, isn't there? Or did you just stand too close to the fire to get your skin scorched that color?"

"Alright," Leshru replied, holding his hands up in supplication. "I deserve that. So what's the problem between forest dwarves and mountain dwarves? Is it likely to cause bloodshed?"

"No, it's nothing like that. We worship the same gods, and we're all mostly the same. It's just a matter of where we're from and thinking that one group is inherently better because they live in the mountains or the forest."

"So it's just about looking down on someone else because of where they live?" Leshru asked. "Just when I think humans have cornered the market on any flavor of stupidity, I'm reminded that every species has their own distinct brand of idiocy."

"Pretty much," Torgan said. "It's not likely to cause any real problems, but there may be some who don't want my help because I'm a mountain dwarf, or because I worship Felrand as opposed to Relmond, the god of the lowlands. But if the situation is as dire as it appeared in my dream, they aren't likely to turn away any help that presents itself, even if it comes from someone they deem an unbeliever, like me."

"So you're moping around and being a grouch because you're afraid the dwarves in the woods won't like you? Is that basically it?" Leshru asked.

Torgan's cheeks flushed, and he took a long moment before responding. "I suppose if you wanted to put it in the most insulting manner possible, yes."

"I doubt that was the most insulting way I could have said it, but if you'd like to hear exactly how insulting someone can be when their friend is determined to examine their own asshole by sticking their head up it and talking through the godsdamned thing, I can have Prynne come back here and ask you why you're being such an idiot."

"Let's not and say we did," Torgan replied. "Maybe I can be satisfied with second-rate insults for the time being."

"Glad I could oblige," Leshru said. "Now, are you good, or are we going to have to beat the hell out of these people before we can help them?"

"I'm good. And if this place is anything like what I've seen in my visions, they won't be in any shape to argue with us too much."

"Yeah, what about that, anyway? Have you seen anything that tells you what we're walking into?"

Torgan's eyes dropped, and he took another long breath before looking back up at Leshru and replying. "Aye, there have been some things I've seen. And a lot I wish I hadn't."

"So what is it, Torg? What are we dealing with here?"

Torgan made a sign of supplication and touched the holy symbol he wore around his neck, an anvil with two swords crossed over it. "If my visions are true, and they wouldn't be very good visions if they aren't, the village has been beset by a plague of the undead. From all I was able to discern from the somewhat cryptic images Felrand sent me, the church-yards have emptied all their graves, and the town is overrun by zombies."

"Well, fuck," Leshru said. "I might have been better off not knowing. Next time, I'm just going to let you sulk."

CHAPTER THIRTY-FOUR

I t was about an hour later when the trees cleared and the party began to see farms along the side of the road, well-tended plots of corn and cabbage in neat rows, with well-maintained fences surrounding them to keep the wildlife out.

"That's odd," Prynne said as they rode.

"What is?" Thallis asked.

"There's no one working."

"Maybe they're all taking a day off?" the boy replied.

Prynne turned to him, her face clearly indicating her readiness to ridicule the young thief for his ignorance, but she stopped before she spoke. "You're serious, aren't you?"

"Why wouldn't I be? People got to rest, don't they?"

"Not farmers," the archer replied, her natural instinct to sarcasm somewhat muted by the city boy's obvious ignorance. "When you live on a farm, you work. Every day, without fail. If the sun is up, you're working. It might be nothing more than feeding the chickens and milking cows, but you're doing something from the moment it's light enough to see, sometimes until it's far past dark and you're walking home from the fields with a lantern hanging from your plow horse's saddle, so tired you can barely see your feet, but you know you've still got to brush down the horse and make sure she's got food and water before you go in for supper. But I don't see anyone here. No one. No children playing hide-and-seek in the corn, no one walking behind a plow, or even checking on crops. This isn't natural."

Thallis leaned back a little in his saddle and stared at the woman. "I never woulda thought you to be one for the country life, Prynne."

"I was living in a treehouse when you found me, idiot. I've always loathed cities. They're too confining. Any time I'm stuck in all those buildings, it makes the back of my neck itch. I'd much rather be out in the wide world where I can see for a hundred yards in all directions. Besides, farmers and most small-town people are more honest and less likely to try and cut your throat while you sleep than most city folk."

"Hey!" Thallis protested. "I'll have you know I've never cut anyone's throat while they slept."

"But how many people have woken up from their night's rest to find their most prized possessions missing after a late-night visit from you or one of your friends?" she asked.

"Yeah, but I still never cut no throats," Thallis grumbled.

Prynne just laughed and rode ahead. "I'm going to see if the town is as quiet as these farms, or if the undead have got everybody huddled together for safety." She nudged her horse forward with her heels, pulling her bow and nocking an arrow as she drew away from the others.

Thallis looked at Nipural. "Should I go with her?"

"Why? Do you think she's suddenly incapable of defending herself?" the wizard asked.

Thallis spluttered a little before he spat out, "No, of course not. I just…"

"Son, I promise you, out of everyone here, my sister is the least likely to get herself into a mess she can't get out of. If she sees one undead, she'll shoot it. She sees two, she'll shoot them both. But if there's more than a pair, or they seem to be particularly strong, you'll hear hoofbeats and cursing a full minute before she rides back into view. Prynne is not burdened by any false sense of honor that is only sated by staring down impossible odds in the service of a god or nation. No, she's perfectly content to help people, but never at the expense of her own well-being."

"Makes sense," Thallis said. "If she ends up dead trying to help one person, then the bunch of people she coulda helped later ain't gonna get help. So it's better for her to stay in one piece so she can do more good in the future."

Nipural cast a long-suffering gaze up at the sky and let out a long sigh.

"Gods, why did you do it? Why did you burden me with another one? I'm too old for this shit."

"What do you mean, Nip?" Thallis asked. "Did I say something wrong?"

"No," the old magic-user said with another sigh. "You said nothing wrong. It's just that you sounded so much like Prynne that it made my blood run a little cold. She said that exact thing to me many times over our years riding together, usually when we were trying to decide whether to stick our noses into an unpleasant situation or not."

"Well, it's easier this time, right?" Thallis asked. "On account of Torgan's god told him to get his arse over here, and we ain't got a choice in the matter. So you ain't gotta convince nobody to help out. You win!"

Nipural fixed the slender young man with a piercing gaze. "You only put on the stupid street urchin accent when you want someone to take you less seriously, don't you?"

"I dunno what you're talkin' 'bout, mate," Thallis said with a twinkle in his eyes.

"Of course you don't," Nipural replied. "Well, here comes my sister, and she isn't riding like the hounds of hell are nipping at her horse's rump, so it must not be that bad."

Everyone stopped as Prynne reined in her horse before them. She looked from one to the other before pronouncing, "It's fucked. It's all fucked."

An eerie silence hung over the village as The Seven rode in, the only sound the jingling of their horses' tack. The village was laid out, as so many are, around a central well with buildings radiating out based on their need to be close to water. The inn and tavern was the focal point of the main square, with a large building beside it that Qabil took to be the town hall. A general store sat on the other side of the inn, and a smithy, stable, and small schoolhouse rounded out the central buildings. Houses ringed the center of town, with the largest and most affluent homes being afforded the better proximity to the well, while the working-class homes were farther out.

It never failed, Qabil mused as he rode, no matter how small a town, there would always be a hierarchy, and the need to feel superior to someone, anyone, apparently was universal across all species, and not limited to humans. He thought back on the small village he grew up in that was all centered around proximity to the docks and the water. The more important your business or the wealthier your family, the closer to the dock you built. The less influence you had, the farther inland you lived.

Qabil and his mother had lived in a house fashioned in the front half of a cave cut into a nearby cliffside. Their home actually overlooked the sea and had a long, narrow staircase leading from their front porch down to a small private dock where his father had moored his boat. But they were near the town, not of the town, and being close to the water wasn't enough to round off the tips of his mother's ears or stop the sidelong glances cast at her by the other women in town every time she went shopping. It seemed that in his case, geography could not outweigh prejudice.

"Where is everybody?" Thallis asked, sliding off his horse and looping the reins over a hitching post by the well. The others did likewise, and Celia drew up a bucket and began to fill a trough with water for the animals. Nipural waved his staff over the bucket before she poured the water out, then nodded his approval that it was safe. Qabil had no idea if the old man used magic to detect poisons and impurities in the water, but he did the same thing over their food every night, and as no one had gotten sick on the journey so far, Qabil was content not to ask questions and just allow the wizard to go about his business.

After a moment of everyone standing around looking at each other, Leshru clapped his hands and began handing out tasks. "Okay, split up into pairs. Nip, you wait here at the well. Thallis and Prynne, you two go east. Celia, you and Qabil go west, and Torgan and I will head north. See if you can find any people, or any indication of where they might be. Meet back here in an hour. Nip, scry each pair and fire off some of your sparklers if anybody gets in trouble."

"Good plan," the wizard said, settling onto a bench on the general store's front porch. "Try not to need help. I could stand a nap."

Qabil nodded to Celia and went to his horse, pulling a waterskin and his scabbard from the saddle. He belted on his sword and took a long drink of water, then hung the skin from his belt. He turned to Celia, who had carefully packed her lute in among her belonging and pulled a massive two-handed mace from her saddle.

"Ummm…Celia, do you know something I don't?" he asked, staring at the massive weapon.

"No, but Torg has been griping about me hiding how strong I am. He says to be good at this life, I have to use every asset I have, even if I don't think they're assets. And while I don't think being a half-orc, half-dwarf freak is much of an asset, I do think he's probably right that I should use the tools nature gave me. And one of those tools is strength. So I added a little melee to my arsenal, as it were."

She slapped the mace into one palm with a meaty *thwack*, and Qabil shuddered a little at the thought of her hitting someone with that thing. It was easily half as long as he was tall, with a haft the width of his leg at the knee and a spiked head bigger than the one on his shoulders. He had no doubt that Celia could unleash significant pain and suffering upon anyone who got in her way. He just really hoped he never ended up in her way.

"Come on, let's go see what happened to all these folk," Celia said. "And maybe we'll get to hit something along the way." Qabil hung back a few steps from his suddenly bloodthirsty friend as they started off to investigate the western quadrant of the village.

CHAPTER THIRTY-FIVE

Well that was a waste of fucking time," Prynne said as she dropped onto the bench beside her brother. "Two hours looking through tiny houses trying to find a clue, and all I ended up with for my troubles was a sore back."

Qabil knelt down in front of the horse trough and gave his head a good soak, letting the cool water slough off the sweat and road dirt he could feel caking on his skin like armor. The day had started off mild, pleasant even, but after bending and stooping to search homes that were never designed for someone his size, he felt much the same as the vocal archer.

"Not our fault you're too tall," Torgan said, dropping down onto a bench with a clatter of armor. None of the others had gotten into their full kit to search the town, but Torgan insisted on not only his full suit of chain and helm, but also his clerical robes over it. Qabil thought privately that he was wearing his vestments to make sure the local dwarves looked upon him as someone there in an official capacity, and not just a nosy interloper. It made sense, but Qabil was still very happy he wasn't the one tromping around in full armor.

"Did anybody find anything to give us a hint as to what happened here?" Leshru asked. A chorus of shaking heads answered him from the dispirited adventurers. "Okay, what *did* we find?"

"A bunch of empty houses, a bunch of chairs with short legs, and nothing that looked like this town had been attacked by undead. Or anything else, for that matter," said Thallis.

"The boy is right," Celia said. "Every building we searched was the same—it looked like the occupants either vanished into thin air or were never there in the first place."

"Aye," Torgan agreed. "Some places looked like no one had lived there for years, if ever. A few houses didn't even have any furniture."

"It seems this village, even before their recent troubles, was well into its decline," Nipural said.

"What could make a village die like this?" Thallis asked. "It ain't like they were making their money through trade, so seems like as long as there were crops, this place should do just fine."

"There was something I noticed on the east side, just between the two outermost rings of houses," Prynne said. "It looked like a dried-up streambed, but not one that's been dry for decades. This one still had sharp edges where the water flowed, and not all the river rocks had been pillaged for gardens or paving. I'd guess it might have dried up two harvests ago, if that."

"So the village lost its water source?" Leshru asked. "That would certainly hurt, but would it empty the whole place like this? Doesn't seem right."

"I don't think it's the whole story, but it's likely part of it," Prynne said. "There's still water here, obviously, because the well works, but if there were businesses or farms that depended on that creek, they'd have a serious problem once it dried up."

"Everything in a village depends on water," Qabil said. All faces turned to him, and he shrugged. "The town I grew up in wasn't much larger than this, and even though we were right by the sea, we still had to have fresh water for drinking, bathing, and our crops. Not to mention the mill needed running water to grind wheat and corn, the smithy had to have a steady supply of fresh water for its work, and the stables were built right by a stream. I bet if we walked over behind those buildings," he pointed to a string of businesses not far from where they stood, "we'd find either a running creek, or the same dry streambed that you saw on the east side of town. Water is as important to a small community as people and churches."

"That's it!" Thallis said, springing to his feet. He flushed, slightly embarrassed at pulling all the focus from Qabil's explanation. "Sorry, go on."

Qabil chuckled at his friend's discomfort. For all the thief's bravado, he got terribly upset at the thought of being rude to one of the few people he actually cared about. "No, please. I can't wait to hear what kind of inspiration my mention of churches brought you leaping to your feet."

"Well, there aren't any," Thallis replied. He smiled and shook his head at the confused looks everyone gave him. "Not inspiration or feet, I got those. But there are no churches. I didn't see one anywhere in town, and usually it would either be right here in the town square so they can guilt everybody who passes by to drop something in the offering box, or they're outside of town on a wide path. You can't miss them most of the time, but here there's not a pew to be found. Nor money-grubbing priest, neither."

"Is that a dwarf thing, Torgan?" Marin asked from where she sat on a bench beside Nipural. Qabil wasn't quite sure what he thought of the pretty young mercenary. She'd been fun and flirty back in the tavern, and certainly seemed to enjoy his company, but having her appointed as their escort by the Lord Mayor made him somewhat distrustful. He just wasn't sure where her loyalties would lie if trouble arose, but he shoved those concerns to the side. It wasn't like they were going to get into much trouble in an abandoned village, after all.

"Is what a dwarf thing?" Torgan asked, his voice a low grumble.

"Do you do churches, or are you like elves and just wander around talking to trees?" Marin continued, oblivious to the fire in the dwarf's eyes.

"We. Are. Nothing. Like. Elves." Torgan stood up and moved right in front of the girl, speaking very slowly and very clearly. "Do you understand that, lass? We have churches, but we usually don't set them in the middle of the town square and draw attention to them like humans do. We prefer to worship apart from our homes and workplaces, away from the mundane daily concerns so we can focus on our relationship with our gods. The wood dwarves might have a *few* similarities with elves in their choice of homesites, but there should still be a good, sturdy church here somewhere."

"So maybe if we find it, it would give us a clue to where everyone went? Or that could be where everyone is?" Marin mused.

Torgan paused for a moment, scratching his chin through the thick red beard. "Aye, could be. It should be in a clearing where worshippers could touch the bare earth and see the sun. It would also be near a water source. Some of our gods require fresh or running water for certain rituals, so our places of worship tend to be near streams."

"So we go follow the dried-up creek and maybe we find the church?" Leshru asked.

"Most likely," Torgan said. "I might not be a woods dweller, but our people aren't really all that different from one another when you get right down to it. But don't tell none of them tree-hugging dwarves I said so."

"If we don't find any of them alive, that won't be much of an issue, little buddy," Prynne said, patting the surly dwarf on top of his head and getting a dark look for her troubles. "Come on, let's go wander through the woods looking for a church full of dwarves," she said. "There's a joke in there somewhere, I just can't find it."

The streambed led them right to a large, cleared patch of woods with a squat, solid-looking building inside. It reminded Qabil quite a bit of the buildings he'd seen outside the mountain in Steelhammer, only made from wood instead of stone. The rest of the buildings in town had looked like human construction, just scaled down for shorter occupants, but this had a sense of…difference about it. The slightly obtuse corners of the building's front, the inward slant to the walls leading up to a pitched roof, everything about it looked like foreign design to him, but he couldn't quite put his finger on what it was.

"It's mountain dwarf design," Celia said as she walked beside him. "That's why it looks odd. You probably didn't notice back at Steelhammer because all the buildings were built the same way, but here, with it being the only building, and so different from the ones we saw in town, it stands out."

"Why do they build like that?" Qabil asked. "With the walls leaning in like that? I think it would make me crazy to sit in a place where it looked like the walls were about to fall on my head."

"That's exactly what the construction is meant to stop. It's a bit overkill for out here, since I doubt there's more than a foot or two of snow in a year, but up in the mountains, the tipped walls and interlocking roofs make for a stronger building. It spreads the weight of the ceiling out across a broader base and keeps the roof up when the weight increases dramatically."

"What would make a roof heavier?" Qabil asked. His mind whirled through scenarios, but most of them hearkened back to Thallis talking about thieves running across the rooftops, and not having giant thief festivals on church roofs.

"Do you know what snow is, Qabil?" the big half-orc asked.

"Of course I do," he replied. "White stuff, cold, makes your tongue tingle when you catch flakes on it. Don't eat the yellow snow."

"But what is it?"

"Huh? It's frozen rain, everyone knows that."

"And what is rain?"

Qabil was certain there was a point, but he had no idea if he was anywhere near it. "Water?"

"Exactly. You've carried enough water just for our campsites to know that water is heavy, right?"

"Yeah, but...oh, I get it. Snow is frozen water, rain that doesn't roll off the roof, so it just piles up there and gets heavier and heavier. Unless..." He looked at the building again, how it all fit together to make the building into a ramp. "Unless the building is built to let the snow slide off."

"Exactly. This church is designed for a much colder climate than this one and was probably built by a mountain dwarf who came down into the forests for whatever reason. Now we just need to find out what happened to him, and to everyone else in this town."

As they dismounted and hitched their horses, Leshru looked over the front door to the church. "I hear something inside," he said in a loud whisper.

"You know that carries farther than just speaking in a low voice," Nipural told him.

"I know that the more you fucking yap out here, the more likely it is that whoever is in there is going to hear us," Leshru hissed back. "Now Celia, you take Prynne and Thallis around to the back and come in that way, quietly. If you hear something that sounds like fighting, run."

Celia nodded and started off around the church, the other two following close behind with weapons in hand. Qabil thought privately that it might be a little much to plan an all-out assault on a small church in the woods, but since he wasn't the legendary adventurer who had battled all types of monsters in all types of places, he let the experts lead the way.

"I'm going in first, and I'll turn to the right once I'm in the door. Qabil, you stand behind me and peel left. That leaves Torgan to charge right up the middle and Nip to stand back and blast lightning at anything bad we might encounter."

"Why is it always lightning?" Qabil asked, trying to lighten the mood.

"Because fire catches, and very few things are intimidated by a furious blast of pansies streaming from a wizard's hands," Nipural replied in a dry monotone.

"Let's go," Leshru said, and yanked the door nearly off his hinges pulling it open. The group stepped into the church and moved just as planned, but then froze a few steps inside the door.

"What the..." Qabil's voice trailed off as he took in the sight before him. The church was packed, with a body in every seat, but no one was moving or making even the slightest noise.

Celia, Prynne, and Thallis came into the church from the back of the sanctuary and skidded to a stop, looks of abject horror in their faces. "Holy shit," Thallis said. "Ears, are you seeing this shit, or am I hallucinating? Please say I'm hallucinating."

"I..." Qabil's mouth opened and closed a few times, like a fish on the dock gasping for air, but no words came out.

"What the hell is wrong with you—" Nipural, frustrated, strode into the church from where he had hung back just outside the front doors. The moment he crossed the threshold, the outer doors slammed shut on their own and a sickly green light blanketed the sanctuary.

"That can't be good," Qabil muttered.

"Pretty much never is," Leshru agreed.

"I...think we found the villagers..." Prynne said, her normally sardonic voice laced with a hint of fear, the tiniest quaver that frightened Qabil more than if she had let out an ear-piercing scream. If something had rattled Prynne so badly that she couldn't even make some smart remark about her brother triggering a trap that locked them in the church, whatever they were seeing at the front of the church must be truly terrible indeed.

Then he saw it. Rising from the pews in jerky, disjointed movements, were two score of dwarves, all silent as stone. Then the first one turned toward the back of the church, and another, and another, until all the dwarves were on their feet, some facing Qabil and company at the back of the church, some settling their baleful gaze up Thallis and the ones up front.

But every dwarf, without exception, had one thing in common. They all had the blank stares and pallid expressions of the very, *very* dead. They were locked in a church with a congregation full of zombie dwarves, and it looked an awful lot like they were hungry.

"Well, shit," Leshru said.

"I think we found the villagers," Nipural added.

"Aye," the big brawler agreed. "Problem is, it looks like they found us right back."

Then the first dwarf zombie lunged at Torgan, and the melee was well and truly on.

CHAPTER THIRTY-SIX

W hat the hell are those?" Thallis cried, whipping his sword from its scabbard.

"Zombies," Torgan said, smashing the nearest walking corpse in its right knee, then crushing its skull as the creature collapsed in a heap. "They're dead, so they don't feel pain. So you got to do a lot more damage than normal, and you can't count on the rest of them getting scared and running off when you splatter one's brains all over its friends." Celia reached over her husband's head with her massive mace, knocking one's head clean off its shoulders.

"Yeah," Torgan said with an approving nod. "Like that."

Qabil pulled his own blade and whirled around to watch their rear, noticing that Prynne had moved past her brother and was loosing arrows into the knot of undead lumbering toward them from the back of the church. The creatures moved in a jerky, disjointed gait that was somehow both slower and faster than a normal person's walk. They were all dwarves, most barely four feet tall, and thickly muscled, dressed in the rough homespun clothing suitable for residents of a small village.

The scuff of a boot on wood was the only warning he got before a meaty hand with stubby sausage fingers clawed at his cloak, pulling him nearly off his feet with unnatural strength. He hammered down on the zombie's head with the hilt of his sword, then reversed his grip and stabbed down into the thing's shoulder, using both hands on the hilt in a sawing motion, trying to decapitate the creature with no room to swing his blade. It took several long moments of struggle, but he managed to slice and saw his way through enough important parts of the monster, and it fell, wrenching his sword from his hands as it went down in a lifeless pile of flesh.

"Shit," he said.

"What?" Prynne asked without turning to look at him.

"Lost my sword," Qabil grunted, pressing the heel of his palm into a dwarf's head to keep the creature from reaching him, glad that the space between pews was too narrow for more than one to approach from each side.

"Use your dagger," the archer replied. "And try not to drop that." She had her sword out and was using it like a painter wielding a brush, a slash here, and stroke there, and zombies fell with every move.

Qabil gave the dwarf in front of him a two-handed shove, then yanked the dagger from his belt and jammed it through the monster's eye before it could close on him again. He spun to his right and stabbed another zombie upward under its chin, pinning its mouth shut and piercing its brain. The creature dropped, nearly pulling his blade from his grip.

"I told you not to drop that one," Prynne growled as a zombie latched onto her sword arm for half a second before a tiny glowing spark flew from behind them and streaked right through the side of the dwarf's skull. The creature fell sideways with smoke pouring from its eyes and ears as Nipural's spell roasted it from the inside out.

"I didn't...never mind," Qabil turned back to the side, slamming an elbow into a dwarf that was scrabbling at his belt, trying to drag him to the floor. The zombie staggered back, and Qabil took the brief window of opportunity to reach down and yank his sword free from the neck of the first zombie he'd killed. He stood, swinging his blade up to run the nearest undead through, but lost his grip as it toppled backward.

"Gods damn it!" he swore, switching his dagger back to his right hand.

"Again?" Prynne asked, a mocking lilt to her voice. "We're going to have to get you a leash for that thing."

"Shut up, Prynne," Qabil growled. He kicked an oncoming zombie in the chest, shoving it into a pair that shambled into the narrow space between pews. The trio of undead went down in a heap of twisted arms and legs, then turned on each other, biting and snapping in a mindless tangle of rage and teeth. Pulling his sword from the corpse in front of him, Qabil leaned forward and stabbed, piercing one zombie's skull right below its left eye. He then stepped forward, barely able to wedge himself between the pews and still fight, but with two quick slashes, a pair of decapitated dwarves crumpled to the floor.

With no more undead approaching from between the pews, he turned his attention to the mass of zombies clogging the aisle between them and the main entrance. He stepped up in the tight space next to Prynne, then felt a pressure between his shoulder blades.

"Down!" the ranger yelled in his ear, dragging him to the rough wood floor. Qabil felt a massive rush of heat sear the air above him, singeing the tiny hairs along the back of his neck. He sprang to his feet, ready to continue the fight, but the zombies that had been clamoring for their flesh were reduced to piles of ash. As were the pews, the floor for a good ten feet in front of him, and the inner doors of the sanctuary. Qabil turned to gape at Nipural, just in time to see the old mage's eyes roll up into the back of his head.

He tried to step forward to catch the old man, but Prynne was faster. She wrapped one arm around Nipural's narrow shoulders and the other around his waist, and dragged him over to a nearby pew, bunching his cloak up underneath his head as a pillow. She patted him on the cheek, then turned to look at Qabil.

"Not a word, youngling," she said with a snarl, then picked up her sword and vaulted the pew in front of her, sprinting around the left side of the church to fall upon the remaining zombies from behind. Qabil followed her lead, but by the time he reached the remaining fray, Celia had caved in the last dwarven skull with her mighty mace and sagged into a nearby pew, panting heavily.

"This is not the life I became a bard to lead," she said between gasps and long draws on her waterskin. "It was supposed to be all singing in taverns for my supper and writing fanciful tunes for wealthy patrons. It was *not* supposed to be dwarf zombies in creepy deserted villages. I was promised wealthy patrons, and I want my damned patronage." She looked around, a slight flush coloring her green-tinged cheeks. "Sorry."

Torgan walked to the front of the church, climbed the three steps to the pulpit, and turned. "My brothers and sisters, children of the stone and the earth, I commend your souls to Felrand. May the light of his forge call you home from this place so you can live forever in the warmth of our ancestors. Know that I, Torgan Steelhammer, first of my name, son of Tragan Stonefist and Alisa Smallforge, cleric of Felrand and warrior of The Seven, shall hunt down those who have subjected my people, sons and daughters of Linnair the All-Mother one and all, to this treatment. I swear upon the graves of my ancestors that this shall not stand, not so long as I walk upon this earth."

Tears rolled down the dwarf's scarred and gore-spattered face as he called upon his god to grant the dead safe passage to the afterlife, and to infest the people who caused this horrific suffering with boils upon their genitals. When he finished, Celia wrapped him in a smothering hug and led him off to sit by him in the front pew, talking in a low, reassuring voice.

Prynne watched the couple for a few seconds, then gave a sharp nod and threaded her way past the corpses and pews to where Nipural sat up with a groan. "What happened?" the old wizard asked, looking around with the bleary eyes of someone waking up from an involuntary nap.

"You sent a river of fire washing over the zombies, then passed out," Qabil said.

"Aye," Thallis said with a nod. "That was amazing, old man!"

"Amazingly stupid," Prynne said, leaning over the pew behind Nipural and giving him a swat to the back of the head. "How long has it been since you cast a spell with that kind of power? Two decades? Three?"

"It worked, didn't it?" Nipural shot back, rubbing his head. "And don't do that. I have a headache."

"That seems to happen whenever you cast a spell," Thallis observed. "Does that happen to every wizard, or are you just special?"

"It happens to everyone, to some degree. It depends on the spell, really. Tiny things, like lighting a candle of campfire, take so little energy as to be almost free to cast. But anything more significant takes energy, and that energy must come from somewhere. Most practitioners use their own personal stores of energy, and some even use stones or staves to focus and store their energy. I haven't been a fan of that method since I saw an unattended staff explode and destroy an entire tavern in Palkanuk, a small city on the southern coast of Kroy. The staff's owner was a student, a friend of mine, and he left his focus leaning in the corner of the room when he left one night, a little too much in his cups to remember it. Some idiot from our school thought it would be funny to enchant the staff so that once Tam, the boy that owned the staff, picked it up, the thing would bond to his flesh so tightly that only a spell to remove curses would do anything. And there was no one in town with the knowledge to cast a spell of that sort."

"What happened?" Qabil asked.

"I don't know for certain because I wasn't in the building when it happened. You can tell, because I'm not dead and no one had to use a blade to scrape pieces of me off the ceiling. But apparently Tam had cast some defensive magics upon his staff, and when the boys from school tried to curse the staff, it...responded. With extreme displeasure."

"You make it sound like this guy's walking stick could think on its own," Thallis scoffed. "I hate to be the one to break this to you, but weapons can't talk, and they can't think."

"Oh, well now that Thallis, expert on all things magical and possible, has deemed my story too incredible, then it must all be false. I mean, after all, it's not like we've parlayed with a dragon then fought a horde of undead dwarves, or like I just *threw fucking fire from my bare hands*. But obviously you are the final authority on what is and isn't possible, so I should just forget everything I've learned in decades of study and practice, because a street rat and half-skilled pickpocket doesn't believe me."

"Hey!" Thallis protested. "I'm a very good pickpocket!"

"Not really," Leshru said, his gravelly voice amused. "I caught you, after all."

"He's right, you know. He did catch you without even trying hard," Qabil added.

Thalls shot him a betrayed look. "Whose side are you on, Ears?"

"Yours? Ours? Look, I'm not on a side, but maybe we should listen to Nipural on all matters magical. I don't know anything about intelligent staffs, but I didn't believe in dragons when I left home, much less zombies. So who knows?"

Thallis sighed. "Okay, fine. Maybe his walking stick could think on its own. Hells, maybe it could sing an aria and dance the Mirandelle for all I know. Finish the tale, Nip, I'll keep my mouth shut."

"That'll be a blessing," the old wizard said, then gave Thallis a kindly wink. "Anyway, Tam had stored enough power in his staff that when the boys tampered with it, the entire tavern was blown to matchsticks, along with everyone in it. But that's not the point. The point is that magic has a cost. Usually in personal energy, be it stored beforehand or called forth at will. Most spellcasters use their own energy, or take very small amounts from their surroundings. Evil wizards use energy drawn from other people, often leaving very little of them once they've harvested all the life force in them."

"That's...disgusting," Qabil said.

"Yes," Nipural agreed. "Using an unwilling person as a power source is one of the greatest sins a magic user can commit. But if you only pull power from within, larger spells take a massive toll."

"And you aren't as young as you used to be," Prynne reminded him.

"Neither are you," he snapped back.

"True, but the worst thing that happens to me if my reach exceeds my grasp is I miss a shot. If you try to call on more power than you have…"

"I'll drop dead," Nipural said. "There are worse ways to die, sister."

"Worse ways to un-die, too," Leshru said, waving a hand at the piles of ash and corpses. "Now if you're done lecturing the children on the rules of magic, can we find out who did this to the village?"

"And kill them," Torgan said, standing up and wiping his eyes before turning back to face his companions. "We find them, and we kill them."

CHAPTER THIRTY-SEVEN

Qabil collapsed into a pew, sweat streaming down his face. It had been the work of a solid hour to drag all the remaining corpses out of the church, search the bodies for any useful clues, or in Thallis's case, money, and build a funeral pyre large enough to consume most of the village's citizens. Torgan said a somber prayer to Desanir, the Dwarven god of the dead, and Celia sang a funeral dirge that she said came down from her mother's people. It was a low, mournful song that spoke of love and loss, and despite not understanding the words, Qabil felt the sentiment deep in his soul. There was an emptiness, a sense of something missing in the world, that the music and the intonations Celia gave the words, that made Qabil reflect on everyone he'd loved and lost, and he found himself wiping away tears as he stood by the blazing pyre.

When the ceremony, such as it was, concluded, Torgan and Celia walked off into the forest to perform a final ritual to safely shepherd the souls of the deceased off into the afterlife, and Qabil went back into the church where he found Thallis sitting on the front pew with his head bent and his elbows on his knees.

"Why are you in here all by yourself?" he asked as he sat. He drew a handkerchief from a pocket and mopped his brow, noting the prodigious amount of soot on the cloth.

"It's not right," the thief said, staring off into space.

"No, it isn't," Qabil agreed. "But we're going to find out who's responsible and set it right. Because that's what these people have always done."

"That ain't what I mean," Thallis said. "You're right, somebody needs to answer for this shit, but I mean the whole thing isn't right. This isn't how criminals operate. There's nothing to gain here, so what's the point in killing all these people?"

"You're thinking that evil needs a purpose to do bad things?" Qabil asked, the corner of his mouth quirking up.

"I know, it's not supposed to work like that, with reasons behind everything somebody does, but the fact of it is that there usually is a logic to the shit things people do to one another. It's usually one of three things —money, power, or sex. Or some combination of those. Like my ma—she slapped a guard captain, and he couldn't look like his power was in question, so he had to beat the shit out of her. He didn't mean to kill her, but it doesn't make her any less dead. But there's a reason. Same thing with your mother—Walfert wanted to...be with her, and from what you said, she wasn't having none of it. So if he couldn't have her, nobody could. That's power and sex, all mixed up in a weird, disgusting blend of asshole."

"Okay, that all makes sense," Qabil replied.

"Yeah, but this doesn't. There's no money here, and it ain't like there's power to be had by massacring a village of peaceful people in the middle of the woods. It ain't even like there was any relics or shit to steal from the church. I know, because I looked around pretty good and couldn't find any place in here that looked like something special used to be there. If there was some kind of super holy thing it woulda been in a special spot, probably right up there near the altar, and we'd notice that something was supposed to be there, even if it was gone. But there's nothing, not even a place for anything important. So what's the point?"

"You had it at the first, lad," Nipural's creaky voice came from between two pews a few rows back, and both boys started and whirled around as the old wizard heaved himself up from where he had lay resting. "It's about power. This took a necromancer of no small skill and significant power, but the only reason to unleash this kind of suffering on a small village such as this is if you're planning on a much larger, more lucrative target in the near future."

"So this was a rehearsal?" Qabil asked. "For what?"

"I expect to find the answer to that, we're going to need to find the necromancer who caused all this," Nipural said, waving his hand around the interior of the church. "And by 'all this' I mean the undead, not the spectacular conflagration that burned half the building to ash. We know who did that." It seemed like he tried not to look proud of the devastation he'd wrought, but if so, he failed mightily.

"How do we find this necromancer?" Qabil asked. "We searched the town top to bottom, and there was nothing."

"And there wasn't anything here in the church, either," Thallis added.

"Really?" Nipural asked, one bushy gray eyebrow climbing.

Qabil had ridden with the mage long enough by then to know when Nipural had something up his sleeve and was just waiting for the right moment to spring it on them. "I can see you're practically bursting to tell us what you've figured out, so why not just skip the parts where we ask dumb questions and get straight to the part where you tell us the stuff that makes you look really smart so we can all be impressed."

Nipural's expression was that of someone who had unexpectedly bitten into a lemon when they were expecting candy. "You've spent entirely too much time around Leshru. It's made you cynical. But fine, go get the others and meet me behind the church. It's better if I just show you."

"And better if you have an audience, right?" Thallis asked as he got up and headed toward the door to fetch the rest of the party.

A few minutes later The Seven, with Marin their escort, were gathered around a well behind the church. It was a normal well, perhaps a little larger than one would expect for it to just serve the church and the parsonage, but nothing to rouse suspicion. It was covered with a large wooden lid, which made sense to Qabil, since you wouldn't want things randomly falling into your drinking water, and there was a heavy canopy of tree overhead.

"Okay, old man, what's so damned interesting about a well?" Prynne asked, leaning against a nearby tree.

"Nothing at all," Nipural replied, shoving the lid off to *thunk* to the ground. "Unless it isn't a well." He fished a copper coin from his purse and dropped it in. "Listen."

"You gonna make a wish, Nip?" Leshru said with a grin. His grin faded when the sound that floated back up the well wasn't a soft splash, but a faint clatter of the coin hitting wood. "What the hells? Did the water dry up?"

"I might think so, if there weren't a ladder running down the inside of the well," Prynne said, looking over the edge. "This isn't a well. I don't

221

know what the hell it is, but I don't see or hear any water, and I've never seen a well with a ladder in it."

"Although it wouldn't be a bad idea, given some of the stories I've heard of adventurers falling into them," Celia said. "There was one about a half-elf who was so convinced that there was a secret at the bottom of a town well that he almost drowned trying to investigate. But that's probably just a tale. No one could really be that stupid, could they?"

"Never underestimate people's stupidity," Thallis replied. He looked over the edge. "I guess the next step is to go down and look around." He swung a leg over the edge, but Leshru reached out and snatched him back onto solid ground before his foot touched the top rung.

"Let's see if there are traps first," the big man said.

"That's what I was going to do," Thallis said. "Unless you think you're better at disarming them than me."

"Not a bit," Leshru said. "But I do think Nip can send a fireball or something down there to trigger anything before we get close enough to get hurt. So why not try that first?"

"I'd love to," Nipural replied, then stepped over to the edge of the well and held his hands out over the yawning portal. He closed his eyes, took several deep breaths, and then opened his eyes again. "That...isn't going to work. I've exhausted too much power. I'll have to rest before I can do anything more strenuous than lighting a match. Sorry."

"Not to worry, old man," Thallis said, hopping back up onto the rim of the well. "That's why you fill your crew with people who are good at different stuff. If everybody on a job is a high-walker or a basher, who's gonna pick the locks, right?"

"Okay, fine," Leshru said with a sigh. "Go on."

The young thief smiled and spun around, hopping down onto the ladder and scampering down the rungs at a speed that felt to Qabil like there was no way he could find any traps, unless he sprung them himself.

Thallis moved quickly for the first ten rungs or so, then slowed considerably. He looked up at the cluster of faces looking down at him. "I don't suppose you've got anything that I could hang around my neck to make light, do you?"

Nipural held a hand over the mouth of the well. "That I can do." He dropped a stone on a cord down into the blackness, barely able to see Thallis in the gloom. The boy's hand flashed out and snatched the bauble out of midair, then he turned his face up to the sky.

"How do I turn it on?"

"Squeeze it."

Thallis wrapped his fist tight around the stone, and in a few seconds, light began to seep out in the cracks between his fingers. He opened his hand and put the cord over his head, letting the amulet fall against his chest. A dim light illuminated the diameter of the well along with about ten rungs above and below him. "That's great, Nip. Now I'll probably be able to see anything that's going to cut my nuts off. Hopefully before the cutting."

"Hopefully," Nipural said with a small smile.

"Give a shout when you hit bottom and let us know if it's clear to come down," Leshru said.

"Don't worry," Thallis replied, grinning up at his companions. "If it ain't, you'll hear me loud and clear." He turned his attention back to the ladder and continued his descent.

The trip down the ladder took several long minutes, and Thallis's arms were trembling with effort by the time he made it to the bottom. He discovered no traps, either through examination or accident, but there were several missing rungs that made his descent more difficult, and one section of ladder that threatened to pull away from the well under his weight.

"I'm down," he called up. "But I don't know if all of you can come down this way. That ladder's pretty rickety, and there's a few spots where the missing rungs make for a big step to get across. I'd be worried about Leshru or Celia yanking the whole thing down on our heads."

"Probably better if I stay up here, anyway," Nipural said. "Without some rest, I'm not going to be good for much in a fight. Swordplay isn't exactly my strong suit, and underground caverns are usually bad places to swing a big stick around."

"I'll head down," Qabil said, stepping over to the edge and slipping into the darkness. "How far to the parts where the rungs are missing?"

"Count twenty-three rungs down, the twenty-fourth is missing. So is the fortieth and sixty-seventh. The big gap is between eighty and eighty-three, though. Two rungs are missing there, so it's a bit stretch unless you just grab the sides of the ladder and slide a bit. Oh, and the section between fifty and sixty is the loose part, so go slow and easy down that bit," Thallis called.

"How many rungs are there?" Qabil asked.

"One hundred ten. The ladder is bolted into the wall every ten rungs, so every ten feet, and there's a brace at the midpoint of each section.

Except that fifth one—the brace there is missing, and that's what makes the whole thing so shaky."

"Got it," Qabil said as his head disappeared below the rim of the well.

"Torg, you should probably stay up here, too," Prynne said as she watched Qabil descend. She held up a hand to cut off the dwarf's protests. "You heard the boy. There's a gap between the rungs down there that's half your height. You try to climb down that, you're likely to end up in a dive that leaves naught but a smear of grease on the bottom of the well. Not to mention your armor is heavy as hell. You probably weigh as much as Lesh, and don't talk about trying to unwrap yourself, either. It takes too damned long, and doesn't make you any more nimble, just squishier."

The dwarf grumbled, but eventually nodded. Prynne looked down into the well, saw that Qabil was almost at the bottom, and slipped over the side like a fish diving into a pond. A remarkably short time later, her voice echoed back up from the bottom, thin and echoing off the stone.

"Fuck me, boys. What the shit is that?"

CHAPTER THIRTY-EIGHT

C ries of dismay and alarm fell down the well like coins, only without the good wishes attached. Qabil looked up and shouted, "It's okay, there's nothing attacking us. Just...a strange room. Really strange. Like a shrine or a secret church or something. We're going to check it out. But stay up there. Thallis wasn't joking about how rickety that ladder is. Honestly, I'd feel a bit better about getting out if someone would drop a rope or three down here and maybe tie them off to horses. That way if we do need to get out in a hurry, we can use the ropes."

"Or we could use the ropes to get down there ourselves," Leshru muttered as he turned and stomped off to where the horses were tied. "Not like we're famous adventurers who've investigated dungeons, caves, and all sorts of ruins. Seems like one of us could have thought about a rope before now. Gods, we really are rusty..."

Thallis stood at the entrance to a large underground chamber, obviously carved out of the rock underneath the church and turned into a place of worship, but unlike any church he'd ever set foot in, or any he'd want to. Black candles stood in holders lining the walls, burning with no smoke or dripping wax, obviously magic.

The candles illuminated a room perhaps forty feet across, with a rough wooden floor, heavy black velvet curtains lining the walls, and a glassy black stone altar as the centerpiece of the shrine. It was rectangular, roughly four feet long by three feet wide, with a bowl-shaped impression centered at one end. Long grooves formed a cross in the top of the altar, about a third of the way down from the bowl and running across, then another groove bisecting the bowl and running down the center of the altar lengthwise. The grooves were an inch or two deep, but the bowl at the head of the altar was deeper, several inches at its deepest point. More candles burned in ornate holders at each corner of the table, each with five tapers flickering merrily away as if oblivious to the sensations of darkness that permeated the room.

As Thallis drew closer to the front of the room, checking for tripwires and pressure plates as he went, he began to notice dark brown stains in the grooves of the altar, and as he stepped up beside the thing, he saw carved stone bowls sitting on the floor under each end of the cross, including the depression at the top. He leaned over, breathing deeply as his nose almost brushed the glossy black surface, then he let out a long breath.

"Well, that's fucking awful," he said, turning to the others. "This thing's made for sacrifices."

"Well, lots of gods require sacrifices from their worshippers," Qabil said, his tone and posture saying that he knew exactly what kind of sacrifice Thallis meant, but didn't want to face it.

"And no small number of those gods require their followers to sacrifice each other," Thallis replied. "Which is, exactly what we've got here. See the size of this altar? It looks pretty much dwarf-sized, doesn't it?"

Qabil nodded. "Okay, you called it. That's terrible."

"But if they're sacrificing dwarves, who's raising them and sticking them in church pews?" Prynne asked, looking around. She pointed to a section of curtain. "Look behind that drape."

Thallis walked to the panel she indicated. "Why this one?" he asked as he began to check for booby traps.

"There's some fraying at the right edge, and the bottom edge is dirtier on that side, like someone has moved it aside to get to something behind it," she replied.

"You can see that from there?" Thallis asked, incredulous. "No wonder you can shoot the nuts off a squirrel at a hundred yards."

He pulled the wall covering back to expose a polished wooden door with ornately scrolled hinges and hardware. "I bet whatever we're looking for, it's behind this door." He turned the knob, but the door didn't budge. He pulled again, but there was no give. "A little help?"

Qabil came over and grabbed the handle, then pulled away. "Something's not right," he said.

"What do you mean?" Thallis asked, taking his hands off the knob. "I didn't see any tripwires or anything."

"I didn't either," Qabil said, shaking his head. "It's probably nothing."

"Trust your instincts, boy," Prynne's voice was sharp, more an order than encouragement. "You're not a complete idiot, so if you felt something amiss, there's probably something odd about the door. You're part elf and a sword dancer. Magic is a part of you, so trust the warnings it gives."

"I don't know if it was a warning," Qabil said. "It's just... I think it's nothing." He wrapped his hands around the doorknob again and gave a massive pull. The wood creaked in protest, but held for a long beat, then another, then, finally, a loud *SNAP* split the air, and the door flew open in a flash of red light.

The door opened to reveal another candlelit passage, and a voice echoed from around a corner in the part of the hallway that was visible. "No! No! Oh, no..." The voice dissolved into sobs, then as the trio stood staring into the darkness, it morphed into sniffles, then...laughter. A cackling, piercing laugh filled the room, then a high-pitched voice that sounded like rusty nails being pulled from old, twisted wood came floating out of the hall.

"Thank you for my freedom," it said, a sibilance to its words that made it seem even more otherworldly than just the laughter alone. "As a token of my appreciation, I shall grant you a swift death."

"Well, shit," Prynne said. She turned back to the hall they entered through and yelled, "Might want to hurry up with those ropes!"

Moments later, the entire party stood by the shattered door, with the exception of the exhausted Nipural and Marin, who flatly refused to, in her words, "scamper down some ropes like a spider just to chase certain death under an abandoned dwarf village."

No sounds issued from the space behind the door, which led to another dark corridor, this one with no candles providing their flickering illumination. They all stared into the blackness, silent as the grave, until Prynne picked up her bow from the pile of weapons Nipural had lowered down to them, wound the glowing amulet around the shaft of an arrow, and sent the shining missile down into the maw of gloom. Barely a second later, the sound of an arrow *plinking* off stone walls echoed back up the tunnel to them.

"Damn," she said, gently placing her bow back next to their packs. "I hoped I'd at least hear a scream. Anybody see anything as the arrow flew?"

"No," Leshru said. "Looked like there was a bend in the passage about fifty yards in. I think that's what your arrow smacked into, but it ricocheted deeper into the passage because there's no light coming from that direction."

"So now what?" Qabil asked. "With no light, and something really nasty sounding down there, do we haul ass back to Bedtev and rally the Watch or something?"

Thallis snorted. "Yeah, like a bunch of fat town guards are even going to climb down here. More like they'd just put the lid back on the well and hope nobody ever moved it again."

"So cynical for one so young," Celia said with a shake of her head. "I don't disagree, mind you. I just think it's a little sad that you have no faith in people."

"I have faith in people," Thallis said. "I just have faith in them to look after themselves and screw anybody they can to get an extra coin or scrap of food."

"We can't run," Qabil said. "At least, one of us can't." He gestured to Torgan, who knelt by the opening, head bowed in prayer. "And we can't leave him behind. So we should get ready for a fight."

"He's right," Leshru said. "His god wouldn't let him leave even if Torg wanted to, and the rest of us won't leave Torg. So gear up, but only what's going to be good for close-quarters fighting. Probably not going to be much call for bows down here."

"You'd be surprised how effective an arrow to the face from two yards away can be," Prynne said with a smirk. "But I suppose I have other tools at my disposal."

"Do we know anything about what we're walking into?" Qabil asked. "Other than it can live underground, apparently without food or water, for quite a long time."

"Its voice is scary as hell," Thallis added.

"It's a demon," Torgan said, his mail clinking as he rose from his prayers. "Felrand told me that we face a great evil, of a kind that would gladly devour all it encounters and bend them to its will unless it is stopped."

"And that means demon?" Prynne asked.

"Or something close enough that the name fits," Torgan said. "Whatever it is, we cannot let it get out of this cave. If it makes its way back to Bedtev, it will unleash carnage like this world has seldom seen before."

"But not too different from some of the shit we've seen time and again," Leshru said.

"Aye," Torgan agreed.

"Did Felrand give you any special help to fight this thing?" Thallis asked. "Sounds like we'll need every edge we can get."

"That's not how he does things," the stout dwarf said. "The gods count on us to handle our own problems. They only get involved if one of the other gods is meddling around this plane."

"And a demon turning a whole village of dwarves into zombies isn't meddling?" Thallis asked.

"It might be meddling, but I doubt it's god-level meddling," Celia answered. "This doesn't feel like the machinations of a deity. More like a mortal playing with power beyond their understanding and unleashing something they couldn't control."

"Are you going to come play?" That voice screeched down the tunnel again, a piercing, undulating sound that rose and fell in a dissonant rhythm. "Or must I come out there?" There were grunts and muffled cursing from the darkness, as if someone was grappling the demon.

"Shit," Qabil said, drawing his sword. "Somebody's down there. We've got to help them!" Without another thought, he sprinted off into the blackness.

"Well, balls," Thallis said as his friend ran headlong into danger. "I guess it's time to go to work." Then he took off down the tunnel himself, at a much more considered pace than Qabil.

Torgan looked at the rest of the party, then grunted. "I guess we should go after them. Wouldn't do for the puppies to take care of all the fighting while the legendary adventurers stood around scratching their balls, would it?" He followed the boys into the tunnel, Celia close behind.

Leshru and Prynne exchanged a look, and the big man shrugged. "Might as well go fight," he said. "You don't have balls to scratch, and mine don't itch, so that's off the table for the moment."

"So let's rush headlong into almost certain death just because we don't have anything better to do?" Prynne asked with one corner of her mouth twitching upward.

"Not the worst reason we've ever gotten into a fight," Leshru replied. "Come on, before we miss all the fun." He took off down the corridor in a brisk walk, quickly vanishing into the blackness.

Prynne stared up at the small sliver of daylight she could see up the well shaft. "It was so much easier just being a bandit. Rob from the rich, give a little to the poor, keep most of it for myself, and the worst thing I had to worry about was some guard getting lucky and putting an arrow in my ass. Now here I am, following these morons into almost certain death again. I'm such an idiot." Then she took off down the tunnel at a jog. "Wait for me, assholes! If you kill it before I get there, I'm going to make you eat Nip's cooking for a week!"

CHAPTER THIRTY-NINE

Qabil stumbled through the darkness, dropping to a knee once as something under his foot rolled and almost sent him headfirst to the ground. He put a hand down to steady himself and found the tube or pipe that he'd stepped on. Drawing it up to his eyes, he could just make out a rough shape in the gloom, but as he realized what he held, he threw it away with a gasp.

"Careful!" He shouted back to the others. "Footing's bad up here."

"Traps?" Thallis called back.

"No, bones," Qabil replied.

"What? I don't think I heard you right," Leshru said.

"There's a fuckload of bones scattered all along the hall. I stepped on a leg bone and almost broke my neck."

"Okay, then I heard you right," the big man said.

Qabil moved forward, his steps slower and more cautious now after his near fall, stopping when he came to the bend in the tunnel where Prynne's arrow stuck in the dirt wall. He pulled the shaft free and pulled the glowing amulet off it. He dropped the shining stone around his neck, then turned to look down the tunnel to see if the others were approaching. "The light is me, not a monster," he called. "So don't shoot the glowing thing."

"Good call on the warning," Thallis said, emerging from the gloom. "You know how quick Prynne is to let fly. See anything farther in?"

"Not yet," Qabil said. "I stopped here to wait for you lot."

"Oh, so you decided now that running off alone into dark tunnels with terrifying disembodied voices emanating from them is a bad idea?" Leshru asked. He walked into the light with Torgan, Celia, and Prynne in tow.

"Well, I thought since all of you were kind enough to follow my lead, it would be rude to just leave you in the dark," Qabil said.

"That's truly awful," Celia said. "Any hopes you had of being a court jester can be put to rest right now."

"Come play with meeee," said the sing-song voice that sounded like someone running a dagger along the length of a longsword, a piercing screech that penetrated deep into the skulls of everyone present. "Come play with me before I go up to the light and destroy everyone that's ever dared to walk in the sunlight. Come play, mortals, and I will grant you a reward for freeing meeeeee."

"Yeah, a quick death," Thallis shouted back. "Going to have to pass on that, creepy voice guy. How about we come down there and cut you up into little pieces, instead?"

"You are welcome to try, Thalesien, son of Gert the Tavern Whore. You are welcome to bring all your little friends, Qabil the Motherless, Prynne the Fatherslayer, Leshru the Traitor, Celia the Halfbreed Abomination, and please don't forget Torgan the Faithless. I expect his doubt and self-loathing will make for a particularly pungent sauce as I slurp the marrow from his bones."

"Traitor?" Qabil said, raising an eyebrow at Leshru.

"Long story," the big man said, frowning.

"Fatherslayer?" Thallis asked a myriad of questions with one glance at Prynne.

"He was a prick," she said. "I put an arrow in his eye from a hundred yards away as Nip and I rode away from home for the last time. Was the only way I could make sure he wouldn't put hands on our baby sister."

"Seems reasonable," Thallis said. "Although maybe I'm not the best choice for moral compass. You know, sneaky thief and all."

Qabil looked at his companions' faces, seeing the doubt and fear carved there by this creature. This thing had done what an actual *dragon* hadn't managed—it had rattled The Seven. Leshru looked downright shaken, and Torgan wouldn't meet anyone's gaze. Celia and Thallis just looked angry, but the proclamations aimed at them were mere insults, not dark revelations.

"Shake it off," he said, pleased to see all eyes snap to him. "It's trying to rattle us, shake our confidence in ourselves and each other, make us easier to slaughter. I don't know how this thing knows who we are, and I don't care what it means when it talks about all that shit. All I care about is that whatever is in there, it murdered a whole village, it wants to get loose and murder a lot more people, and we're the only things standing in its way. Now are we going to stand here in the dark scared of a faceless monster we've never even laid eyes on, or are we going to find our fucking balls and go fight like the goddamned Seven?"

Silence reigned in the tunnel for a long moment before Prynne let out a breath. "Good speech, kid. Might have worked better if we all had balls to find, but the point was solid. We're the heroes, time we sucked it up and acted like it. Now let's go kick this thing's ass."

Everyone nodded, and with a final look around the party, Qabil turned and headed toward the faint glow at the end of the tunnel. When he finally saw what they faced down there, he wished they'd lost all nerve and run for the hills.

The chamber was massive and seemed as though a natural cavern had been enlarged and reinforced for some purpose or another. It was at least twenty feet high at the center, with the roof sloping down to maybe fifteen feet at the edges. The room was roughly circular, with a massive creature occupying the central part.

The...thing was unlike anything Qabil had ever seen, or even heard tales about around a campfire. It dominated the interior of the space, its bulbous head wobbling on its narrow neck. Three faces blended together on that massive skull, each more twisted and warped than the last. One looked like a dwarven male, with a thick black beard and bushy eyebrows, but when its mouth opened, the jaw stretched until it seemed almost unhinged, and row upon row of needlelike teeth glistened in its gaping maw. The dwarf-face roared, and disjointed syllables from an unknown language echoed off the stony walls. The creature turned, and a second face came into view, this one even more horrific. This looked as though it was modeled on a human, or perhaps was intended to be a cruel mockery of humanity, with its two eyes, one mouth, and narrow nose. The illusion of any semblance of normalcy was shattered by the red tinge to its flesh, and the yellow glow emanating from its eyes fixed Qabil with a stare that sent shivers running down his spine and threatened to loosen his bladder on the spot. The creature's gaze was *hungry*.

But it was the final face that truly horrified the young warrior. The last face that the creature turned to him was the worst image by far, the one that would haunt his nightmares for many years to come. Because when the creature rotated its head on its preternaturally long neck, showing its third visage to the party, Qabil saw the true depth of the creature's depravity. The third face, the one that sent Thallis to retching in a corner, was that of a newborn dwarven child.

It had all the typical features of a baby dwarf—round, red face, chubby cheeks, and the barest hint of a blond beard. But that's where the similarities ended. Its beady eyes, nestled in rolls of baby fat, glowed a sickly greenish-yellow, and its mouth was nothing more than a round hole rimmed with pointed triangular teeth. Strings of yellow drool hung from its lips, and each drop hissed and bubbled as it struck the floor.

All this sat upon a neck far too long and undulating to support the weight of a triple-faced head as it writhed back and forth in the air over the massive gelatinous body. The body was just as wrong as the head, with four overlong, spindly arms that resembled spider's legs as much as a person's arms, each arm tipped with four long multi-jointed claws that ended in wicked hooks designed to rend and tear flesh. No legs were visible as corpulent rolls of flesh hung down off the creature's nude torso, brushing across the floor in a horrible swishing sound as the monster turned from side to side.

"What the unholy fuck is that?" Thallis gasped.

"I have no idea, other than the thing that's going to haunt my nightmares for the rest of my days," Qabil replied.

"That is a gorge, a gluttony demon," Torgan said. "They're nothing but hunger and rage and will consume everything in their path until they are destroyed or until they grow too massive to move, eventually starving when no more prey wanders within their grasp."

"So...all we need to do is run away and leave it here?" Thallis asked.

"Oh, you can't leave now," the gorge said, its shrill sing-song voice boring straight into their brains. "We haven't even started to play."

With that, the creature drew in on itself, like a snake coiling to strike, and sprang forward, its rolls of fat rippling like waves on the shore as it flew through the air at the party, who scattered lest they be crushed beneath the demon's monstrous bulk. They spun around, weapons in hand, then dove for the floor as the gorge's arms slashed the air where their heads had been. The creature cackled as the adventurers rolled to the side and clambered to their feet, Celia reaching down to help her heavily armored husband to stand.

"Oh, what's wrong, fleshbags? I just want to dance with somebody, where's the harm in that?" Two more arms shot forth from the demon's midsection, oozing, wobbling ropes of flesh and fat that grew straight out of the monster's flabby rolls and shot toward Thallis and Prynne a spider's webs, only much more deadly.

The thief and the ranger dove in opposite directions, Prynne rolling to her feet with bow in hand, loosing three shots at the gorge in an instant. Thallis also hopped up and immediately went for weapons, throwing knives in his case, that flew from his fingertips to sink unerringly into the demon's midsection. Neither attack had any visible effect, as the creature swept its original four arms through the air, scattering the party and sending several of them diving to the floor again.

"How the fuck do we kill this thing?" Thallis cried as his blades vanished into the demon's blubber with no effect.

"I have no godsdamned idea," Leshru said. "This is more Nip's realm than mine."

"You can't," Torgan said, reaching underneath his breastplate to draw out the amulet of Felrand, his god. "Only the power of a god can combat the power of the dark realms."

"Dark realms?" the gorge repeated, its piercing voice ululating in laughter. It turned the dwarf-like face to them. "We are not of the dark, any more than you are of the light, Torgan the Faithless. You and your hypocrisy, wandering the world with your holy symbol and your half-breed whore wife, letting the world think you are such a pious little dwarf, all the while not believing a word of what you preach. Come to me, Apostate, and learn to revel in the truth of the world. Come to me and be filled with power that the puny gods you repudiate can only dream of!"

"How about...no?" Qabil said, stepping back to stand at Torgan's left elbow. "How about we chop you up into little bits of demon lard and use your carcass to season our meat like pig fat?"

"You are welcome to—" The creature's voice cut off as its beady black eyes went wide. It screamed, a fantastic shriek of agony that shook dirt loose from the cave's ceiling. The gorge reached up behind its head and snatched Thallis from its back. The thief came away with a grunt, but as he was drawn into view by the demon's sticklike arms, Qabil could see the viscous fluid dripping from the end of his short sword, and a small round object pierced through with the tip of his dagger.

"Fuck me, he cut its eye out," Leshru whispered.

"I will rip out your throat and bathe my wounds in your blood!" the demon screamed, flecks of yellow spittle covering Thallis's face and chest as the creature held him high above the cavern floor.

"Not today," Torgan said, pulling a war hammer from his belt and slamming it into his shield. The dwarf glowed with a faint orange light that seemed to emanate from everywhere and nowhere all at once, and as he slammed his hammer into his shield again and again, in a steady rhythm that reminded Qabil of the sounds of the smithy in his village, the dwarf began to swell, and as the glow brightened around him and suffused the chamber with orange-yellow light, the dwarf began...to *grow*.

"Not today," Torgan repeated, now the height of a human man, his armor and weapons growing with him as the magic flowing through his body increased his size more and more.

"Not...*TODAY!*" The words ripped from Torgan's throat, a battle cry infused with the power of Felrand, a howl of righteous fury that made Qabil clap his hands over his ears as it came from the now-giant Torgan, who had grown to the same height as the gorge, with his hammer glowing red as new-forged steel in his right hand. The dwarf's voice was different, deeper, with an ethereal echo to it, as though his words came from somewhere else, somewhere not of this world.

"Now, demon," he said, towering over his party and looking the monster right in the eye. "Now I show you the true strength of my faith."

With a bellow of rage, Torgan charged.

CHAPTER FORTY

The massive Torgan, the glowing nimbus around him flickering like fire, rumbled forth, slamming his shield into the demon's mass and shoving it back against the far wall of the cavern. The creature's arms scrabbled against his breastplate, shredding his tabard as it tried to find a crack or seam that it could wedge those razor-sharp claws into, sending wicked shrieks of tortured metal echoing through the cavern. Torgan never wavered, just stood like a bulwark holding back a tempest, and raised his hammer.

"Not today!" he cried, bringing the head down upon the demon's skull.

"Well, what are you waiting for?" Celia asked, looking at the others. "He needs our help!" The half-orc drew her massive club and ran headlong into the fray.

Qabil stood back beside Thallis, both looking down at their swords, which seemed far less dangerous against a creature the size of a small caravan than when aimed at a human. "Ummm...what are we supposed to do with these?" he asked.

"At least you use a sword," Leshru said as he stood by the young men. "In times like this, I've learned that it's sometimes better just to stand off to one side and drag the bodies out if somebody goes down. And someone always goes down."

"Some of us still have options," Prynne said, nocking an arrow and letting it fly through the air, only to have it *twang* off Torgan's plated shoulder. "Okay, maybe moving to a better vantage point is also an option." She skirted along the cavern wall, studiously avoiding the dark look the dwarf fired in her direction. Thallis took the hint and traded his sword for a bow and moved off toward the other side, trying to create a pincer attack that would allow them to riddle the demon with arrows.

Torgan, however, just stood there, implacable, resolute, and *massive*. He rained down heavy strikes upon the demon, and everywhere his hammer struck, orange light danced like fire along the monster's flesh. The demon's counterattacks were vicious but ultimately useless, as whatever magic increased his size also raised the durability of his armor by several degrees. No matter where the demon struck, the worst it did was raise a few sparks. It couldn't find purchase in the armor's chinks, and it couldn't penetrate the magically enhanced metal.

Seconds after Prynne and Thallis moved to the sides, arrows began peppering the demon from both right and left, piercing the creature's flesh with tiny darts, no bigger than toothpicks on the thing's massive body, but it howled in pain and rage with every strike nonetheless. Then Celia stepped up and began to slam her spiked club into the monster's quivering flesh again and again, sending ripples through its corpulent torso as she tried to find anything vital that she could reach through the flab.

And all the while, Torgan hammered. After his initial charge and slam into the demon, he developed a rhythm to his attacks that felt familiar to Qabil as he watched the struggle unfold. It looked like Torgan was working a forge as his hammer rose and fell, rose and fell, rose and fell, the *swoosh-slam* of the hammer into the demon's body, then a tap to reset, and withdraw. Tap-swing-*slam*, tap-swing-*slam*, tap-swing-*slam*, over and over, again and again, the dwarf's hammer struck true time after time. Finally, in a move born out of agony and desperation, the demon wrapped itself in a cocoon of flame, pushing its attackers back as it whirled in place, a dervish of blazing red and yellow that shrank down until it was the size of a normal human.

Then the demon stood before them in a totally different form, this one more human in scale but equally horrific. It was a thin to the point of gauntness, with an elongated skull that curved at the top and bottom to create a crescent moon effect out of the demon's face, with a pointed chin and a single long horn protruding from its forehead. It had the same spindly claw-tipped arms, but now they were merely long and skeletal instead of horrifying appendages that could stretch from one side of the cavern to the other. Four skinny legs protruded from the bottom of the monster's torso, and they were all hinged strangely, like the demon had seen pictures of legs but didn't really know how they were supposed to work.

But the legs worked well enough that the demon skittered out of the path of Torgan's next blow, knocked an arrow out of midair, and slashed one of those wicked claws down of Celia's bicep, sending the bard to the ground screaming as she dropped her war club. She fell to her knees clutching her arm, but quickly scrambleds to her feet and moved back to where Qabil and Leshru stood.

"Here," Qabil said, kneeling on the ground and opening his pack. He pulled out supplies and started binding the wound, understanding at a glance that the damage was far beyond what he could hope to patch up, but also that if the bleeding weren't stopped quickly, she could lose the arm or worse. Celia staggered over to him and knelt, then collapsed to a sitting position on the ground.

"I'll just...sit for a moment," she said, her eyes rolling back in her head. She fell to the ground and began to twitch, foam beginning to form on her lips.

"Leshru!" Qabil cried. "What the hells is this?"

"Looks like the thing's claws have some sort of venom on them," he said. Leshru cupped his hands around his mouth and shouted, "'Ware the claws! They're poisoned!" Without waiting for acknowledgement, he knelt by Celia and began helping Qabil bind her wounds.

Torgan, in the meantime, had shrunk down to his normal size, but he still glowed like a midnight forge, flickers of orange, yellow, and red dancing along his armor and shield like flame itself. He pursued the demon, swinging his hammer in vicious strikes. But the demon was much more nimble in its smaller form and only one blow in three landed. Add to that the now much smaller target for Thallis and Prynne, and the monster was taking far less damage now that it had shrunk to less massive proportions.

"Prynne, switch off!" Leshru bellowed, getting to his feet and charging toward the fight. The ranger saw him begin to move and nodded, loosing a final pair of arrows before she dashed to her fallen comrade's side. She began pulling various herbs and powders from her pack as she barked instructions at Qabil and brushed Celia's hair back from her face.

Leshru, now freed from first aid duty and in the presence of a foe he could physically match up to, grinned as he lumbered forward, his stride more a hopping walk than a run. He steadily picked up speed, though, and by the time he neared where Torgan stood toe-to-toe with the demon, he was moving like a runaway cart through a market square, steady and nearly unstoppable. He crashed into the monstrous thing with his arms wide, hugging the creature to his chest and throwing his momentum into a spin, lifting the demon off the ground and slamming it down with his entire body weight atop it. The sound of snapping ribs echoed through the cavern, and the monster let out a howl that sounded like it came from the very depths of all the hells.

Leshru rolled off the demon and shouted, "Now!"

Torgan nodded and took three quick steps forward, flinging his shield aside and wrapping both hands around the haft of his hammer. He raised the glowing weapon over his head, and as he brought it crashing down on the demon's skull, it seemed to change into a construct of pure fire, an extension of the dwarf's righteous fury, designed for nothing more than the wholesale destruction of his foes. The flaming hammer passed into the demon's head like it was sharper than a razor, carving a path of fire and agony through the demon until finally his momentum ran out with his hammer buried in the middle of the thing's chest, and the demon's scream withered away to a last, dying wheeze.

Torgan stood over the fallen abomination, his chest heaving with exertion and fire still licking the outline of his armor, the light around him slowly dimming. "Not today," he said, his voice barely above a whisper. Then he turned to look at his companions, and when his eyes fell upon the form of his wife, writhing in agony on the cavern floor, he sprinted to her side.

"Celia!" he cried, dropping to his knees beside her. He dropped his hammer and stripped off his gauntlets, pressing his bare hands to her arm. "Hold on, my love." The flame that seemed to wreath his body enveloped Celia's, and Qabil drew back as the arm he was bandaging grew unbearably hot in an instant. He watched as the cloth wrapping burst into flames, burning to ash in an instant, and the torn flesh beneath it knit closed before his eyes. Celia's entire body seemed to be wrapped in flame, glowing around her injured arm, but the orange and yellow light suffused her flesh, turning her into the brightest light source in the small cave. Torgan knelt by her side praying softly as energy flowed from his god, through him, and into the body of his fallen wife. After long moments of stillness, the half-orc's eyes flickered once, twice, then she drew in a shuddering gasp and sat bolt upright.

"Sweet fucking mother what was that?!?" she cried, her head whipping from side to side.

Torgan looked at her, smiled, said, "You have been healed by the grace of Felrand" in a thready croak, and collapsed, his eyes rolling back in his head as he clattered to the cavern floor, the glow around him fading to nothing as the exhausted dwarf passed out.

"Um...does this mean we won?" Thallis asked. He stood looking down at what remained of the demon, now dissolving into a bubbling yellow slime that burned an outline of the creature's form into the floor.

"We're all still alive, and it isn't," Prynne said. "In our world, that's the very definition of winning. Now let's see if there's anything in here that can tell us how this shit happened, and if there's anything we need to do to make sure it doesn't happen again."

"Shouldn't we...?" Qabil waved a hand at Celia and Torgan, one very confused half-orc and one very unconscious dwarf.

"Leave them be," Leshru said. "It'll take Celia a bit to get back enough strength to stand, and Torg will be out for a few hours. That level of healing takes a lot out of both parties. Trust me."

"I...I...that was...wow..." Celia slid around so her back was pressed up against the cave wall and leaned her head back, staring up at the ceiling. "Yeah, I'm going to need a moment. That was a lot."

"In the meantime, you pair can get your asses over here and help me search this place," Prynne said. She was standing over a shrine against the far wall, a horrific collection of bones, desiccated organs, and other vile offerings intermingled with jewelry and other trinkets offered up to the vile being that sent the demon, or perhaps to the demon itself. Words were scrawled into the walls behind it, incomprehensible glyphs from various languages, none ones that Qabil could read, but the dark brown stains that splattered those walls were unmistakable as anything but blood.

"Yeah, might as well," Leshru said. "Not like I'm carrying Torg's snoring arse up a ladder. Not now. My back can't take that shit like it used to, and he's a little thicker through the middle than he used to be."

"Aren't we all?" Prynne asked, slapping at her own thigh. She was by no means a heavyset woman, but she also wasn't the rail-thin archer described in the tales, either.

Leshru grinned at her and rubbed his round belly. "I'm the exact same size I was thirty years ago. Of course, I'm guessing, since my eyes have gone too bad to read a measuring tape." With a chuckle, he walked over to the shrine and began searching it with Prynne.

Thallis and Qabil began to search the rest of the cavern for clues to the creature's origin, and as they did, Thallis leaned in close and whispered, "Do you think they've always been crazy, or is it something that came on with age?"

"What makes you think they're crazy? That they're joking about getting old? Most everybody does that."

"Yeah, but not everybody does it moments after fighting a demon for their very lives."

"Most people never fight a demon. Maybe if they did, they'd be cracking wise, too."

"Kind of a defense mechanism, you mean? Like they laugh so they don't go insane?"

"Oh, no chance of that," Qabil said. "The insanity armada left the harbor a long time ago, and we were on the first boat out. Sane people don't put themselves in positions to *have* to fight demons. But it takes a very special kind of crazy to not just fight one, but to win. That's the kind of crazy we're riding with."

"I thought you wanted to ride with heroes?" Thallis asked.

"There's not much difference between a hero and a lunatic," Qabil replied. "Heroes just win a little more often."

CHAPTER FORTY-ONE

It was a dirty, sweat-stained, and exhausted bunch of adventurers who gathered in the rectory as night fell around the now-abandoned church. Marin had a fire going in the parlor, and Nipural had helped her move furniture to the walls and spread out their bedrolls on the floor. The flickering orange light reminded Qabil of the light that wreathed Torgan during his battle with the demon, and it made him feel just the slightest bit uneasy, as though he was looking at his traveling companion with new eyes.

Until now, Torgan had seemed the most even-keeled and possibly even "normal" member of their little band. He wasn't a snarky bandit leader hiding her talents as one the realm's best archers by poking small holes in tax collectors from treetops. He wasn't one of the world's most famed spellcasters hiding his light under a pawnbroker's sign. He wasn't even the mighty brawler, still wading into battle with nothing but his fists and his skill to protect him against armed opponents. No, he was a dwarven priest and smith, pulled from his forge and his village by circumstance. He had always seemed the most reluctant hero of the bunch, but now that he'd seen a hint of the true power coursing through the stocky cleric, Qabil would never look at Torgan the same way. It truly drove home the fact that he traveled with legends, when the most unassuming of them could grow to massive height and not only face a demon in single combat, but emerge alive and victorious.

"Here's what we found in the demon's lair," Prynne said, pointing at a small stack of items they'd carried up from underground. There was a journal, a holy symbol of the dwarves' goddess Siramis, two golden rings, and a pair of wire-rimmed spectacles. That was all they'd found after an exhaustive search of the cavern—just those few items and a horrifying number of bones, some animal, but most belonging to dwarves or men. "We couldn't read the book. It seemed to be enchanted to keep away unwanted readers."

"I recognized some of the symbols, but there's a heavy pull of blood magic wound around the pages, and I could feel it beginning to affect me just looking at the first page," Torgan said. "One thing I can tell you, though. That's no symbol of Siramis. It's close, but it looks like someone took an icon of the goddess and created a mockery of it. There is something very wrong with this place, and that book is the worst of it."

"I read every language Torg does, and I couldn't decipher a single word. Everything just looked like worms crawling across the page to me," Celia said.

They were clustered around a long table in the rectory's dining room, with Torgan and Celia both seated as the rest of the party stood examining the items. A chandelier glowed above them with soft candlelight, casting light across the table and throughout the room as darkness fell outside. It had been decided that they should try to secure the building and rest before returning to Bedtev the next morning. Not only would they be better rested, it would also give them an opportunity to make sure nothing rose from the cavern under the cover of darkness.

"It may be specifically attuned to dwarves," Nipural said. "It's difficult, but possible, to set a discerning curse upon an object that will only affect certain people. If you have something that belongs to your target, you can fine-tune a spell to such a degree that it only harms the target and is inert to anyone else. It might be fooled by a close family member, but it's a very useful style of ritual. Difficult though, and very time-consuming."

"So this curse only affects dwarves?" Qabil asked. "Why would someone do that?"

"There are those that would prefer not to live near my people," Torgan said. "Prejudice and stupidity are two of the only constants in the universe, but they abound."

Nipural reached out and pulled the book to him, then sat with it flat on the table, both hands pressing on the cover. He closed his eyes, his lips moving as he called up magic and wreathed the book in a bright blue-white light that gained intensity until it was painful to look at, then faded away as quickly as it had come. "This is old magic, powerful stuff. This wasn't some bigot in a nearby town who just doesn't like dwarves. This was cast by the demon itself."

"The demon that was trapped underground?" Leshru asked.

"The demon that wanted to *not* be trapped underground," Nipural corrected. "The book has several types of spells layered upon it. First there is a beacon, a spell made to draw the intended target near and find the book. Then there is a masking spell to make it seem as though it is a holy text of Siramis."

"Goddess of the harvest," Torgan said with a nod. "Makes sense. A rural community makes most of its way through farming, so she would be worshipped strongly here."

"Then there are spells designed to burrow deep into the reader's mind, slowly taking them over until they are completely in the thrall of the demon," Nipural continued. "The victim will descend further and further into bloodshed and depravity until it has murdered everyone they care about, then the final master stroke was to drive the victim to suicide, becoming themselves the blood sacrifice required to open the pathways between planes and allow the demon free reign upon our world."

"So if all that was supposed to happen whenever a dwarf read the book, why was the demon still stuck down there?" Marin asked.

"Because the person that found the book was a priest of Siramis," Celia said. "His piety afforded him some limited defense against the book's influence, enough so that when he finally fell victim to the book's commands and took his own life, he used the last of his breath to seal the chamber."

"The chamber that we opened," Thallis said dryly.

"Yep," Prynne said. "That's us. Big damn heroes, letting demons loose then having to kill them before they go tearing off through the countryside."

"Could be worse," Leshru said. "Remember the time we summoned that dragon on accident? It burned up four villages before we brought it down."

"Oh, and the time Nip accidentally put on a cursed amulet and every corpse within a dozen miles clawed its way out of its grave and came after him?" Prynne said with a laugh.

"That wasn't funny," Nipural said, scowling. "Not nearly as funny as the time a gorgon fell in love with you and you had to figure out how to tell her you weren't into snakes without getting turned into a statue."

"So you're saying this is normal for you people?" Marin asked. The city girl looked stunned at this idea, as though everyone around her had gone stark raving mad.

"I wouldn't call it normal," Thallis said. "Ears and me been riding with this lot for a couple months now, and we ain't seen nothing weird like that."

"Except for the dragon," Qabil said.

"Oh yeah. Well, there was a dragon, but he wasn't too bad. Didn't eat nobody, and only threatened to chomp us a couple times. So outside of a dragon—"

"And a church full of undead," Qabil added.

"And several groups of bandits," Prynne said.

"And a blood feud and quest for vengeance," Leshru said.

"Yeah," Thallis finished, his voice far less resolute than it had been seconds earlier. "Except for those things, this bunch is pretty normal, I'd say."

"You have a strange definition of normal," Marin replied.

"Oh, you have no idea."

"So what now?" Qabil asked. "The demon's dead, but so is the village. Do we tell someone? Do something?"

"What's to be done?" Leshru asked. "We can't raise the dead. Besides, that's already been tried, so if the citizens were brought back to life now, they'd mostly be twitching parts on the ground."

"What's now is you lot get some rest while Torgan and I dispose of this book. The demon under the town may have been destroyed, but there are plenty of other creatures lurking around the abyss that would love to come feel the warm sunshine and blood spatter on their faces. Come on, old friend. Our work isn't finished yet."

Torgan and Nipural headed for the door but froze at the sound of a chair scraping across the floor. Celia stood, using the table for balance, but moving under her own power. A marked improvement from her entry into the house, which had been on an improvised litter borne by Leshru, Qabil, and Thallis. She was unsteady, but vertical, and the look on her green-tinged face was resolute. "I'm coming with you."

"No," Torgan said, holding out a hand to his wife. "Your wounds were severe, and the healing needs time."

"I wasn't asking permission, Torg," Celia said. "You, girl, come here."

She beckoned to Marin, who stepped over to her side. "Closer." Marin took another step toward her, and Celia reached out, grabbing the young woman and pressing her against her side with one arm slung over her shoulders.

"There," Celia said, a satisfied look on her face. "I'll use this youngling as a crutch. Now I can go anywhere. So where are we headed?"

"The church," Torgan replied. It was apparent from the look on his face that he was not pleased with this turn of events, but it was just as obvious that nothing he said would dissuade his bride from her planned course of action, and no one in the room felt like challenging a seven-foot-tall bard. That kind of confrontation only ends in fisticuffs or bagpipes, equally painful for all involved.

"Let's go," Celia said, nudging Marin with her hip to prod the young woman into motion. The four of them headed out the back door of the rectory, Nipural carrying the book.

After they were gone, Thallis asked, "Why did Celia want to go? Is she scared they'll get killed, or that Torgan will go insane from the book's magic?"

"That's part of it," Prynne said. "But there's another piece to consider. Celia's a bard, but half-orc, half-dwarf bards aren't afforded much respect in the world. At best, she's looked on as an outsider, and at worst, she's thought to be a stupid monster who learned a few tricks, like a circus bear taught to dance. If she can learn enough watching them dispose of this book, she could write a poem or song about it, and if it becomes famous, then she won't be Celia the Abomination anymore, she'll just be Celia the Bard. She wants to be known for what she's done, not what she is, and this is a chance to make that happen. Very few people outside church leadership have ever seen a ritual like this because it is very dangerous. For her to be able to describe it in verse would be a huge feather in her cap."

"Huh," Qabil said, looking up at the ceiling as he contemplated Prynne's words. "I never thought of—what the hells?"

A thunderous *boom* came from the church, powerful enough to rattle the dishes in the cupboard. They ran out through the kitchen toward the church, or more accurately toward where the church had been.

Because there was no church there now. There was just a massive pile of wood and slate roof tiles, splattered with the gore of the dozens of undead they'd left to their rest in the church. The party stood, dumbfounded, for a long, breathless moment until, like a phoenix rising from the ashes, a section of roof buckled upward, then flew off to one side as Celia stood, throwing debris in all directions as she freed herself from the rubble.

As she tossed boards and tiles in all directions, the others sprang into action, picking their way across the devastation as they fought to get to their friends. Celia reached down to her left side and flipped a large section of wall up and over. Nipural, Torgan, and Marin stood up, seemingly sheltered from the destruction by that chunk of wall, and looked around at the destruction.

"I told you there'd be wards," Nipural said.

"Shut up," Torgan grumbled.

"What the actual fuck was that?" Leshru bellowed.

"Wards," Nipural replied. "The second Torg called down the blessings of Bothun upon us to protect us from the evil we faced, safeguards in the book triggered, destroying it and everything nearby."

"How did you...?" Qabil's voice trailed off as he gestured toward the wreckage.

"I called to Siramis. She answered. We were protected," Torgan said, clambering out of the hole he was in and stomping back toward the rectory.

"Didn't think to ask her not to let the building fall on you?" Leshru asked with a slight smirk.

"Not my god, not my request," Nipural said.

"I'm not a dwarf," Marin said. "Don't think dwarf gods listen to me much. But I know one thing. I'm going back to Bedtev and hoping to all the gods, dwarf or otherwise, that I never see you lunatics again. I'll give my report to the boss, but then I'm going to find some nice, safe line of work, like manning a siege engine."

"I sing. He prays," Celia said as they all watched Marin drag herself free of the wreckage and stomp off back toward her horse. "I don't ask gods for favors, Torg doesn't sing. That's our deal."

"Good call," Prynne said. "I've been drunk with Torgan many times. Trust me, I'd rather have a building dropped on my head than listen to him sing."

CHAPTER FORTY-TWO

The fog was just burning off the grass as they recreated a hill and looked down at the walled city of Lennox, home of Walfert and the final destination for Qabil's months-long quest for justice, or vengeance. He was no longer certain that there was much difference in the two things, at least not in this case. It was by far the largest city they'd yet visited, a far cry from the prosaic fishing village where he grew up. Qabil glanced down at his threadbare traveling clothes, the frayed hem of his cloak, the layers of road dirt on his boots and his tack, and marveled at the glittering metropolis that lay before them.

"Afraid we're going to stick out like a sore thumb, as dirty and poor as we look?" Thallis asked as he pulled his horse up alongside Qabil and his mount.

"Yeah," the other boy said, never taking his eyes off their destination.

"Don't be," Thallis replied. "It looks all pretty and shiny from here, but I promise you as soon as we get close enough to see color of the gate guard's mustaches, you'll be able to smell the shit and the rotting garbage and the tanneries and all the other kinds of stink you get when you cram a lot of people together and then put walls up around them. People are like animals, only they don't keep their cages nearly as clean."

"Aren't you a ray of sunshine?" Qabil asked, chuckling.

"Not even a little bit," the young thief replied. "But I know cities. Even Talberg looked pretty from the outside, but it had as rotten a heart as any other place. There'll be shiny spots, like the market square and the temple row, and wherever your friend Walfert lives will be smack in the middle of the poshest part of town. But for every big fine house, there's got to be somebody somewhere doing the laundry and mucking out the stables. This pretty sparkly shit, that's just for the tourists. Like us. It makes us think everything's lovely and safe, so we don't even feel the fingers dipping into our purses."

"Wow, you are a cynic," Prynne said from behind them. "You're not wrong, just a cynic. Come on," she said, pointing ahead of them on the road. "We need to get in line to get into the city. We've missed the worst of it, but it'll still take a while to pass through the gate."

They joined a long line of wagons, caravans, riders, and pedestrians heading into the city. Some were obviously farmers bringing their wares to sell, while some were from outlying towns, driving empty carts they hoped to fill with goods they could sell back home. There were a few groups like theirs, obviously armed people who looked like they could handle themselves in a fight, but most of the folk they saw as they rode into the city were dressed plainly and carried the air of weary workers rather than travelers.

The sun was moving high overhead, they reached the gate some two hours later, and Prynne stepped forward, waving Qabil and Thallis back. She slid down off her horse and spoke quietly to a guard with a pair of golden chevrons on his breastplate, then Qabil saw her pass a few coins to the man, obviously some type of supervisor, and he waved them through without even a cursory search.

When they were through the gates and out of earshot of the guards, Qabil turned to the woman. "What did you give him?"

"Enough silver to get him and all of the men he had working this morning very, very drunk. In a place like Lennox, where you know the head of the city is a corrupt piece of shit, you can assume that everyone working for him is a corrupt piece of shit. Or anyone in a position of authority, at the very least. So when I saw there was a full guard captain overseeing this entrance, I assumed he could be bought. I didn't expect the price to be so cheap, though."

"Must have been your winning personality, sister," Nipural said.

"I don't care why. I just care that he only wanted half as much as I was prepared to pay," Prynne shot back. She turned to look at Qabil. "Now what's the plan? Are we just going to ride up to Walfert's door and announce that you're here to murder him? My name is Qabil

Pointy Ears. You murdered my mother. Prepare to die. That kind of thing?"

Qabil stared straight ahead, not meeting anyone's gaze. "I...I don't really have a plan. I guess if I was alone, I'd do just that, and probably end up with an arrow through my eye. But when you all actually came with me, I..."

"Thought we'd plan the attack on our old companion for you? Thought we'd take care of all the planning and the heavy lifting so you could just roll into town, poke Walfert with your sword, and go home whistling a merry tune?"

Prynne's words hit like daggers, burrowing deep into Qabil's chest. He opened his mouth to speak, but nothing came out. Qabil sat his horse in silence for a long moment before finally turning to look at his friends, only to see them fighting to hide grins. "What?"

"She's fucking with you, lad," Leshru said, reaching out to clap the flustered boy on the shoulder. "Prynne knows good and well that you don't know the first godsdamned thing about assassinating a city's mayor, or anyone else for that matter. She just wanted to see if you had a plan because mocking your plan would be more fun than making up her own."

"I'm not wrong," Prynne interjected. "It would be funny."

Leshru nodded. "She does have a point. But as amusing as I find her witty dismantling of your ego, we should move on to the first part of *our* plan before too many people recognize us on the street. I'd prefer it if we had a few hours in Lennox to scout around before word got to Walfert that we were here."

"You think anyone would still recognize us?" Torgan asked, sitting up a little straighter on his pony and smoothing his beard.

"Several of us used to ride with the man who now rules this city," Nipural said. "It stands to reason that there's a bard or two around that would know us on sight. We were pretty famous at one point, remember?"

"At one point," Leshru agreed. "I'm more concerned that the slimy little fuck gave our descriptions to the city guards after he murdered Tara. He'd have to know we'd be coming after him, so it's not out of the question that there could be eyes upon us right now."

"Three sets, at least," Thallis said, his voice pitched low. "There's a man standing in front of a fruit vendor thirty yards behind us, and I can see his mail poking out from under the homespun shirt he's wearing. One of the urchins playing jacks at the mouth of that alley off to the left scampered off as soon as she caught sight of us, probably to report us to the local thieves' guild. And there's a person in brown robes with a deep hood up ahead of us keeping an eye out. I noticed them when we first came through the gate, and they've been leapfrogging us ever since. They'll pop up half a block ahead of us, then when we pass them, they slip off down a side street, only to reappear half a block ahead a few minutes later."

"Are you sure it's the same person?" Qabil asked.

Thallis gave him a withering look that held for an uncomfortable moment, then said, "I'm sure. They move the same way, and I've gotten a glimpse of their boots a couple of times. Polished riding boots, expensive from what I can see, and not what someone wears to wander a city."

"How many boots do you think most people own?" Qabil said. "I have two pair, and we were considered quite well off in my village."

"I've got the pair on my feet and that's it," Thallis replied. "But the soles I saw were very ill-suited to walking long distances, and the boots had the high arch that fits well into a stirrup. Anyone who can afford custom boots of that quality has more shoes than you or I have ever seen outside a cobbler's shop."

"Who do you think that is?" Prynne asked.

"No idea. Could be someone else from the thieves' guild, could be someone that works for Walfert, could be someone he hired to murder us before we get a chance to murder him."

"Could be another old friend like Lockbay," Celia added.

"Doubtful," Leshru said. "Most of our old friends like Lockbay are dead."

"Usually at my hand," Prynne added. "Your husband is the only reason Lockbay didn't wake up to an arrow through his ear more than once."

"You can't just slaughter people while they sleep, Prynne," Torgan said. "We talked about this. Felrand doesn't condone murder. Certainly not for snoring."

"Lucky thing for you, my love," Celia said.

"So we've got at least three people keeping tabs on us and we're still standing around in the middle of the street yapping?" Prynne asked. "Come on, let's at least find some place I can get a beer. If I have to listen to you old women natter on, I'd prefer not to do it sober."

She turned her horse off to the right, leading them down a narrow side street to a tavern tucked back between two buildings, with the only sign a beer keg hanging from chains over the door, its sides caved in by what looked like a massive fist.

"Do we have to go here?" Torgan asked, his voice turning into a bit of a whine.

"What's wrong with this place?" Thallis asked.

"Torg's just embarrassed because he's the reason it's called the Splintered Keg," Leshru said with a grin. "He got in a...discussion once with a table full of men who had strong opinions about dwarves and mixing of species. They were being purposefully loud enough for us all to hear, and Torg had just met Celia a few months before, so he had...strong opinions on the matter."

"Opinions which he expressed by smashing a beer keg over one man's head. Then he slammed another man's face into the table so hard that a tooth ended up embedded into the wood," Prynne said. "That was the... second time we were in Lennox?"

"Third," Nipural corrected. "The second time was when Xethe burned the brothel down trying to breath fire."

"I think technically he did breathe fire," Leshru said. "If he hadn't, the brothel would have still been standing."

"And I wouldn't have lost one of my favorite cloaks in the blaze," Prynne said with a rueful nod.

"You were..." Thallis's question trailed off, not sure how to continue the question, if he even should.

"I was getting laid, boy," Prynne said. "There was a lovely young woman with long red curls and a delicate touch. I enjoyed her quite a bit. Until Xethe tried to impress some girl in the other room. Fucking idiot. You don't need to impress a working girl. It's their job to impress you. Just spend your coin and hope you both have fun. He could have saved the seduction for the farmers' daughters."

"If we could maybe waltz down memory lane somewhere that we won't have quite as many eyes upon us," Qabil said, motioning toward the door of the tavern.

"Good plan," Nipural said, sliding down off his horse and walking over to an unmarked door. He banged on the smooth wood, and seconds later, a bleary-eyed stable boy came out.

"What?" he asked, more a grunt than a question.

"Need lodging for the horses," Leshru said, stepping forward and reaching into his purse. "Here's a silver per mount. Have them fed, rubbed down, and watered, and check their hooves for stones. If they're still here with all our belongings when we come back for them, I'll give you

253

another silver per mount. If anything is missing or damaged..." The big man let his words trail off, the ominous tone unmistakable.

The boy wiped sleep from his eyes, despite it approaching midday, then he looked more closely at Leshru and his companions. Recognition dawned on his face, and he straightened up, the color draining from his cheeks. "Yes, sir! I'll take perfect care of them. And I guarantee no one will touch any of your things."

The Seven slid from their saddles and slung bows, swords, and purses onto their belts and over shoulders, taking anything they might need with them as the horses were led off into the stables.

"I think he recognized you, Lesh," Nipural said with a grin.

"Yeah, could be," Leshru replied. "Or maybe he recognized the dwarf traveling with an archer, an old man in robes, a bald fighter with no sword, and a half-orc carrying a lute. We're a fairly recognizable lot, you know."

"Fair point," Nipural replied, pulling open the door to the tavern. "Let's see if there's still breakfast to be had. I hate planning an assassination on an empty stomach."

CHAPTER FORTY-THREE

The Splintered Keg looked like every tavern anyone had ever set foot in, with its dark corners, bar polished to a high gloss by a thick-necked scowling bartender, half a dozen round tables scattered around the floor, a tiny stage in a corner near the fireplace, a pot of never-ending stew bubbling over the flames, and a middle-aged woman bustling around serving drinks and platters of food. This early in the day the crowd was sparse, maybe a dozen people total in the place, between customers and staff, but when Qabil and his friends walked through the door, it was as though someone cast a spell of silence over the place. Every tongue stilled, knives froze in the air above trenchers of bread and cheese, and tankards were placed silently atop tables.

"I think they noticed us," Prynne said with a smirk. She walked over to the bar, leaned over it and spoke quietly to the bartender, who looked as though she was the very last person he had ever wanted to speak with. She waved a hand back at Leshru and the others, then pointed to a large unoccupied table near the fire. The bartender nodded and waved the waitress over as Prynne walked back to the group.

"What was that about?" Leshru asked.

"I told him who we were, that we were here to slit Walfert's fucking throat, and that we'd like some breakfast before we get on with our murdering. He thought that the best way not to end up as a little light exercise before our main course of slaughter was to snap to and get us fed as quickly as possible."

"You didn't say that," Thallis said, laughing. His chuckle died in the air as she fixed him with a steady stare, pinning him in place until all signs of mirth faded away. "You said exactly that, didn't you?"

"Of course. There's probably half a dozen runners on their way to whatever Walfert uses as a manor house or office or wherever he plays at being ruler. If he doesn't already know we're here, he will within minutes."

"And he'll know why we're here," Leshru said. "Especially since *someone* told him that the next time she laid eyes on him she'd put an arrow through his dick."

Thallis and Qabil looked at Prynne, who shrugged. "It was early, and he woke me up. I was grumpy."

"Sister, you're always grumpy. That particular morning you were downright irate," Nipural corrected.

"He woke me up, and I was *warm*. I don't like being woken up, and I certainly don't like being woken up when I'm sleeping in a bed, under clean, warm blankets for the first time in weeks."

"With a very pretty barmaid. Or was it the tavern owner that time?" Nipural asked.

"Both. They were married. And *very* warm. Thus my annoyance."

"And threatening to murder Walfert," Leshru said.

"Is it really murder if he deserves it?" Prynne asked. No one replied, or was given an opportunity to reply, because she turned and walked over to the table in the corner, where a young barmaid stood looking nervous. "Don't worry, lass," Prynne said, taking a seat where she could lean her bow and quiver in a corner within arm's reach and see the door. "They're mostly harmless. Now seven ales, and a platter of meat, bread, and cheese, if you don't mind."

The girl scurried off and the others settled in. "Do you think we'll even have time to eat breakfast?" Torgan asked.

"Almost certainly," Leshru said. "It'll take Walfert a while to gather enough men with the balls to even come speak to The Seven. I wouldn't be surprised if it was after lunch when they made an appearance."

"You underestimate the fear Walfert puts into his men," said a hooded man at a neighboring table. He sat with his back to a wall, nestled half in shadow with a tankard and an empty platter in front of him. Qabil thought he'd been sleeping when they first walked over but realized he'd likely been observing them from the moment they set foot in the tavern.

"About time you decided to speak, Songbird," Prynne said to the man. "You going to keep pretending we don't all know who you are, or you going to drag a chair over here and join us?"

"Didn't know if I was welcome," the man said, pulling back the hood of his cloak to reveal a handsome face of perhaps sixty years.

"I'm not sure about that, either," Leshru said, his voice low and dangerous. Qabil looked over at the man and was startled to see a threatening glower on the big fighter's face. "Wasn't the best of times when we parted."

"That was all a misunderstanding, Lesh," the hooded man said, a brilliant smile splitting his features. He was stunningly handsome, with high cheekbones and full, almost feminine lips. Blue eyes sparkled under neatly trimmed brows, and an equally perfect thin beard and narrow mustache completed his look. A long blond ponytail hung artfully down over one shoulder with the kind of careless placement that spoke of much time spent arranging it to look like it fell there accidentally. Qabil marked this man as someone whose deepest personal relationship was with his mirror, and decided he likely saw other people as mere objects to be seduced or influenced in some way. Feelings us distrust and suspicion bubbled up within him, much as they had the first time he'd met Walfert.

"Keep it off your face," Thallis whispered.

Qabil turned to his friend, confused. "What?"

"You hate this guy's guts. And everyone from three bars around can read it on your face. So tamp that shit down. If Prynne hasn't stuck an arrow through his eyeball, it's probably because we're going to need him."

"Or she's playing with her food again," Qabil suggested.

"Or that."

"Why are you here, Songbird?" Torgan asked, waving the newcomer over to their table.

"Same as you, I expect. Walfert murdered the Princess, and I intend to see him gutted and hung up by his jewels for it."

"You knew my mother, too?" The words burst from Qabil before he could claw them back. He thought he knew who this was, since there was only one person his friends had referred to as "Songbird," but he wanted to hear it straight from the man himself.

"I rode with her, and this sorry lot, for years. I'm surprised she didn't tell you about me. We were...close at one time." The smirk and the pause made the innuendo clear, and Qabil flushed red and started to rise, his hand drifting toward his blade. He stopped as Leshru's hand fell upon his shoulder and shoved him back into his seat, then he watched in amazement as a meaty light-green hand reached out and slapped Xethe across his face.

The handsome stranger's head whipped around as the sound of the slap echoed through the tavern, dropping a veil of silence back over the customers. "Do not presume to insult the boy's mother, bard," Celia said, her voice dark. The half-orc leaned one elbow on the table and put a thick index finger in Xethe's face. "I've heard the tales, and Torgy has told me about your love for stirring the pot, but this is one that is not to be stirred. Are we clear?"

The man sat back in his chair, the shock slowly fading from his face, replaced by a mien of affable agreement. "Of course," Xethe said. "My apologies, young sir. I was not aware Eltara had a son, much less that he had grown into such a strapping young man." He looked at Celia. "Does this mean that you're my replacement? Has The Seven, most feared band of heroes on Watalin, replaced their longtime chronicler and boon companion with a...new bard?"

"Upgrade, I'd say," Torgan said, reaching out to pat Celia's hand.

"I heard you married, Torgan," Xethe said. "I'm afraid my wedding gift was lost en route."

"Your absence was gift enough, Xethe," Torgan said.

"Well, now that we're all together again, let's have some breakfast and catch up on what everyone's been doing," Xethe said, a huge smile stretching across his face. "Torg, I hear you got married and live in a cave now, just like you always wanted. Lesh, you finally got around to opening that pub in your little nowhere town, right? Prynne, last I heard you were living in the woods shooting soldiers for sport. And Nipural Wyrmrider? What of you? I heard you died."

"Nipural Wyrmrider was dead for a while," the old mage replied. "I got better."

"And who are you?" Xethe said, gesturing to Thallis. "It's pretty obvious who the terrifying woman with the lute is, she's Torgan's half-orc bride. And the one so offended by the idea of Tara sleeping with me must be her son. But who's the skinny one? Is he supposed to take Walfert's place? He doesn't look like he could pick the lock on a chastity belt, much less a treasure chest."

"If you can steal the girl right out of the belt, no need to unlock it,"

Thallis replied, holding out his fist, palm down, over the table. Xethe gave him a suspicious look, then held his own hand under Thallis's. A slight jingle of coins echoed across the tavern as a small coin purse fell into the bard's outstretched palm. "And I figure a bard's purse is likely to be more fiercely defended than most girls' virtues."

Xethe leaned back and laughed, but Qabil noticed him pat all the other pouches hanging from his belt as he secured the purse again. "Well done, young man! Tammin, where's that breakfast? These legendary heroes can be hard on the furniture when they get hungry!" He lowered his voice so that only those at the table could hear. "Or they used to, back when we rode together. I can't say what they'll do now. Maybe Nipural will barter you to death if you don't hurry up. Or maybe Torgan will pray over you until you give in and feed him."

"I'll still put an arrow through your eye from a hundred yards," Prynne said.

"Probably," Xethe replied. "But back in the day it would have been two hundred."

The waitress came over with a huge tray and deposited a tankard of ale in front of everyone but Xethe, setting down a jug of wine and a tall glass with a stem. She placed trenchers of cheese and sliced meats in the center of the table, with a basket of still-steaming buttered rolls.

"Thank you," Nipural said. "Now, if you could make sure no one sits at those two nearest tables, I would very much appreciate it."

"What he means is, if anyone sits there, he'll turn them into a toad," Prynne said. "He's a mighty wizard, and a bit of an asshole."

Every drop of color faded from the serving girl's face, and she stammered out an affirmative as she backed away, never taking her eyes off Nipural.

Xethe poured a healthy amount of wine into his glass and leaned forward, elbows on the table, as everyone started to dive into the breakfast. "So, now that we're all together, would someone like to tell me what's the plan for assassinating that slimy fuck Walfert?"

CHAPTER FORTY-FOUR

I don't trust him," Thallis said later that night as he and Qabil settled into their room.

"You don't trust anybody," Qabil replied.

"Okay, that's mostly true. But I *really* don't trust this guy. He just seems a little too...everything for me."

"He's a bard. They're like that."

"Celia isn't."

"I don't know if you noticed, but Celia isn't like most bards."

"And were there many bards in your fishing village?"

"Probably about as many as in the back alleys of Talberg," Qabil shot back.

"I'll have you know I tripped over many a bard passed out in the gutters of Talberg, thank you very much."

Qabil threw a pillow at his friend's head, then realized the folly of his assault when Thallis caught it, shoved it under his head, and rolled over, thunderous fake snores erupting from him almost immediately. Qabil stomped across the room, snatched his pillow back, and went to sit on his bed. "I know what you mean, though. Everything about him seems a little too... I don't know, is convenient the right word?"

He closed his eyes and leaned back against the wall, thinking about everything they'd gone over with the newcomer, who was only really a newcomer to some of them, since he was one of the original Seven, the ones who really did ride off into the mists of legend. The group that included his mother... He gave himself a mental shake and brought his attention back to the problem at hand, or tried to. When he opened his eyes, he found Thallis staring at him.

"Thoughts of your mum?" the thief asked.

"Yeah."

"Hurts like a bitch, doesn't it?"

"Yeah."

"It gets better. Not much, and not fast, but eventually you'll be able to remember her without the grief and rage feeling like a wave knocking you ass over teakettle and throwing you onto a rocky beach."

"Maybe you should have been a bard," Qabil said with a grin.

"I'd probably get laid more. It's been a while, you know?"

"I know," the young fighter replied. "It feels like a year since I was..."

"Playing grab-ass with your blacksmith's daughter in a hay loft?" Thallis teased.

"It was a storage shed for fishing nets, thank you very much. Piles of rope and nets are much more comfortable than straw, and less likely to end up stuck in uncomfortable places."

Thallis chuckled. "And the ropes have all those other uses, too."

Qabil blushed as his mind wandered back to the blue-eyed girl he'd left behind. He was sure she wouldn't wait for him, even if he survived this trip. Hells, he wasn't sure he'd be able to go back to Narim if he was alive when this was all over. He wasn't the same awkward boy he'd been when he left, and he wasn't yet sure who this new Qabil was. He'd killed people, but was he a killer? He was seeking revenge, but did that make him a warrior? Apparently he had some kind of magical sword dancing ability, but did that make him a hero? He was only sure of one thing: if he survived this adventure, he would never be able to go back to being a small-town boy. He'd seen too much of the world now, and too many of the people in it.

"Those must be some deep thoughts," Thallis said.

"Yeah."

"Burdens are usually lighter when shared."

"Just wondering who I'll be when this is all over. I'm not a kid from a remote fishing village anymore. I've been places, done things—"

"Fought the walking dead, talked with dragons, killed bandits... You're not wrong. Life changes you. Or it kills you. I saw it a lot with new boys in the city. Either they ran away to Talberg and ended up on the streets when they realized there was no honest work for them, or they ran away from the first 'honest' work they found when they realized they didn't want to rent out their bodies for coin.

"Sometimes it was kids who grew up there, but circumstances changed. Parents died and left them with no family, rent got too high and they didn't have a roof over their heads anymore… Whatever the cause, they thought they knew what they were getting into. Until they were in it and paddling frantically to keep their heads above water that was much deeper than they expected.

"They either adapted, or went home to their mommies and daddies, or they died. You don't have a mommy and daddy, so you can either change, or we can find a nice sunny patch of grass to plant you in, so the sun can warm your bones as you rot."

"Well that's fucking cheerful," Qabil said, his voice barely a grumble.

"I'm not here to be your fucking herald, Ears. I'm your friend, and a real friend will give you the straight shit, especially when you don't want to hear it. Now get some sleep. We've got a murdering prick to slaughter tomorrow. You can have your existential crisis once you've slit Walfert's throat."

Thallis lay down, punched his pillow a few times to fluff it up, then settled in, his face to the wall. Qabil sat crossways on his bed with his back pressed to the opposite wall for a long time before sleep finally claimed him.

Qabil looked at the bundle of cloth in his hands, then back up at Xethe. "This is supposed to get us inside? Just…guard uniforms?"

"Sometimes the simplest plans are the best," the bard replied, flicking his long ponytail so that it fell artfully over one shoulder. Qabil wondered how often he practiced that flick in the mirror so that it looked effortless, but held his tongue. Despite his misgivings, the others seemed to trust the man. He couldn't shake the sense that there was more to Xethe than met the eye, but without any proof, he couldn't just accuse the bard of being a traitor. Besides, if he did betray them, Qabil felt certain that any punishment he dealt out would pale in comparison to what Prynne did to the slender man.

"So it's The Prisoner?" Torgan said with a sigh.

"Oldie but a goodie," Xethe said. "And look at it this way—you don't have to dress up."

Celia looked confused. "Why doesn't Torg need to... Oh, he's the prisoner. I get it."

"You both are," Xethe replied. "If you two are prisoners, then I don't have to try to steal guard uniforms that would fit you, and there are very few half-orc or dwarf guards in Lennox. But there is a picture of each of you hanging at every guard post in the city, so it makes perfect sense that a patrol would have spotted you two and hauled you in to meet Walfert's justice."

"And get their reward money," Torg said.

"Of course," Xethe replied. "Without a reward, how would anyone expect to make a fat city guardsman get off his lazy, bribe-collecting ass? This way we can waltz right through the front door of the keep and likely end up in Walfert's throne room before anyone's the wiser about who we really are. Nobody notices guards."

"I do," Prynne said. This was the first time she'd spoken since she saw the disguises and heard Xethe's plan.

"Of course you do," the bard replied without missing a beat. "That's because you expect to be shooting arrows at everyone you meet."

"I usually do end up shooting arrows at most people that I meet."

"I...think that's indicative of deeper issues than we will be able to resolve here," Xethe said, bathing Prynne in one of his glowing smiles. The archer seemed completely immune to his charms. Qabil made a note to ask Prynne about the bard sometime when he was sure no one could overhear.

Everyone split up and headed to their rooms to change, and moments later, a group of guards in ill-fitting uniforms gathered in the tavern's common room. "I look stupid," Thallis griped, plucking at the hem of his tunic. "How is anyone supposed to fight in this shit?"

"They aren't," Leshru said. The burly man's uniform fit significantly better, stretching tight across his broad chest and shoulders. Qabil noted that he did have to roll his pants legs up twice, since he was built more like a tree stump than a mighty oak. "Your rank-and-file guards don't do much real fighting, if any. They walk around and 'keep the peace' through intimidation, numbers, and cracking the occasional skull. There's not much running or actual combat in the job description for most city guards."

"Well, I sure won't be doing any climbing or scampering across rooftops in this getup," Thallis said. "The pants are too short and too tight for any real jumping or rolling, the boots are slick-bottomed and too thick to find purchase on a slippery rooftop, and I jingle like a tinker's wagon with every step. I couldn't sneak up on a deaf beggar."

"Probably because all the 'deaf' and 'blind' beggars on the streets are no more deaf or blind than you are," Nipural said. "Now quit your bitching and let's go. I don't like these disguises any more than any of you, but the sooner we place Walfert's head on a pike outside the city gates, the sooner I can go back to my comfortable robes."

No one had anything more to add, so Xethe produced two sets of shackles and bound Celia and Torg hand and foot. He left enough chain between their ankles that they could shuffle along unaided, but they were hobbled too well to be able to run. He passed each of them a small key, which they tucked into their boots so they could unlock themselves when it came time to fight, and led the party out into the street.

Qabil blinked against the bright sunlight, the cheery blue sky a stark contrast to the storm clouds brewing in his mind. He fell in beside Leshru at the front of their procession, with Torgan and Celia behind them flanked by Thallis and Nipural. Prynne took up the rear guard with Xethe, as much to keep an eye on the bard as anything else, Qabil figured.

"Can we trust him?" Qabil whispered to Leshru, trusting the noise of the busy streets to muffle his words.

"No farther than I can throw Celia overhand," Leshru replied. "He's a slimy little fuck who'll switch allegiances with the shifting breeze. But he was never very fond of Walfert, and he always wanted to get into Prynne's knickers, so if he treats us square, this might be his chance to both fuck up Walfert's life and impress her."

"So he's motivated to help," Qabil said.

"Unless he gets a better offer," the brawler replied. "But she's not walking back there with him so he can chat her up. She's back there to put an arrow through his skull if she gets even a whiff of betrayal."

"Okay, so I don't have to trust Xethe, as long as I trust Prynne to keep him in check."

"Pretty much. Now look grumpy. We're underpaid, undertrained, underfed, and underfucked. We're just a bunch of city guards who managed to apprehend a pair of dangerous fugitives and now we're going to turn them over to the captain and hope he doesn't shit us out of our reward money. Keep all that on your face and quit worrying about things you can't do anything about. If Xethe is leading us into a trap, the only thing we can do is spring it."

"And kill his ass," Qabil added.

"Yeah, that," Leshru agreed.

The two walked in silence, Qabil trying to school his face to appear like a bored guard only in it for the money, rather than looking like someone walking into a lion's den with a pound of beef in his underpants. He felt a pressure in his chest, a mix of anticipation, fear, and grief all tangled up in his quest for vengeance, or justice, or whatever it was. He thought of his mother the last time he saw her, laid out in a funeral dress with her face painted to hide the bruises left by Walfert's men. He thought of the laughing face of Walfert's man as he stood over her dying body, and the rage within him burned cold as ice.

It was time to end this. It was time for Walfert to pay.

CHAPTER FORTY-FIVE

After a nervous walk through the city, the group came to the gates of Lennox Keep, a massive structure carved out of a cliff face that the entire city backed up to. The keep was unapproachable from two sides because of the sheer stone face, and a fifteen-foot wall encircled the rest of the building that rose at least four floors higher than the walls, with a pair of narrow towers at the corners leading up to shooting platforms. The thick walls had ramparts above where more archers lounged, keeping a lazy eye on the comings and goings below.

The Seven, now Eight with Xethe in their company, walked under a massive iron portcullis that rose behind a pair of enormous wooden doors that looked to be at least a foot thick. Eight guards stood flanking the doors, with two checking papers and packages while the other half-dozen leaned on their pikes or sharpened their swords. All seemed to be in a posture of near boredom, exactly the right mindset for a group of burglars and assassins.

"Papers," said a bored guard with a golden cloth braid over his left shoulder. "What is your purpose for visiting Lennox Keep?"

"We ain't got no papers, but we gots a couple prisoners that the boss-man'll want to see," Xethe said, his voice rough and gravelly. Qabil looked askance at the bard, who was nearly unrecognizable as the same man who sat at their table the night before. He was dressed in the same clothing as the night before, but where he looked neat and clean in the tavern, now he looked remarkably disheveled. His shirt hung loose around his waist, his pants sagged at the knee, and his long blond hair had escaped the tight ponytail he wore in the tavern and now hung around his face in lank, greasy, clumps. He had a pronounced lean in his stance, and one shoulder rode at least three inches higher than the other, giving him an odd, twisted appearance. He spoke in a thick lowbrow accent, sounding more at home around thieves and prostitutes than soldiers and nobility, no matter how false their lineage.

"We'll be the judge of that," said the guard. "Who is this supposed to be."

"'At's Torgan Steelhammer and his half-orc cow," Prynne said, affecting the same accent as Xethe. "Ain't you seen none of the signs your own men been puttin' up all over the city? Says they worth ten gold apiece, and we wants our reward."

The guard turned his attention to Prynne, looking her up and down with a leer. "Well now, pretty lady, maybe I need to search you and make sure you aren't trying to smuggle any contraband into the keep."

"Search all you want, Cap'n," Prynne said, smirking. "'Cause I can see from the fit of your trousers you ain't got nothing for me to find if I go lookin'."

The guard flushed red and stepped forward, raising his hand as though he meant to strike Prynne, but froze as every one of the Seven except for Torgan and Celia pulled their cloaks back and rested hands on hilts. "You sure you wanna do that?" Xethe asked. "'Specially when you could just wave us past, and call for the seneschal. Then we're outta your hair and you can maybe get a bribe out of that fat-assed merchant behind us with a stash of widow's pride hidden under the bananas in his wagon."

"Widow's pride" was a powder derived from crushing the roots of a water oak and mixing the paste with wyvern blood, then letting the concoction dry into a powder. It had become very popular with older men for its restorative properties on certain aspects of their stamina, and popular with older women for its restorative properties on certain aspects of men's stamina. Its sale was highly regulated and heavily taxed, so smugglers were always trying to find new and innovative ways to avoid paying tax on it, but the pungent smell of the wyvern's acidic blood made it very difficult to hide without an equally strong-smelling cargo. Like bananas or other fruit.

"Widow's pride, huh?" the guard said, a thoughtful expression on his face as he looked past them to a large wagon loaded down with bananas and other fruits. "Go on in, then, but don't go far. Just wait in the courtyard by the fountain. Grandil here will run ahead for Master Terisack, the head of Lord Walfert's private security detail." He gestured at one of the guards loafing about, and the young man stepped forward with a rough salute.

"Grandil, go to Master Terisack and tell him there's a bunch out here with what they claim is two of the fugitives Lord Walfert has been posting signs about."

"Perhaps I should go with—" Xethe started, but a sharp look from the captain cut him off.

"No. Gran knows the way, and you stink. Go over to the fountain and wash off. If these two are who you claim, you'll find yourselves in the presence of His Lordship today, so you better not go in there smelling like a fishmonger." He waved them through and let a greedy smile slip over his face as he waved the produce wagon through.

"That guy's going to end up either paying a huge bribe or getting everything in his wagon unloaded and searched," Thallis said as they gathered by the fountain.

"I'm counting on that second thing," Xethe replied, sitting on the stone lip of the large fountain. "Oughta keep that captain and at least four other guards occupied for a good hour or more. That's five we don't have to worry about noticing something off about our prisoners, or more likely, our mercenaries." Qabil and the others were dressed in mismatched armor and clothing, all of a rougher cut and lower quality than the gear they left hidden in the hayloft at the tavern. They'd each smeared dirt on their cheeks, and all wore some type of hat or hood to obscure their features as much as possible. For Qabil, that included a knit cap that he pulled down over his ears to hide the pointed tips. He was fairly certain that Celia in chains would draw most of the onlookers' attention, but he wanted to leave nothing to chance. They'd come too far to get tripped up by a minor detail now.

The group gathered by the fountain and made a show of scrubbing the dirt and grime off their faces, hands, and arms. It sloughed off easily, having been applied earlier that morning to hide their features, but bending over the running water allowed Qabil to speak with Leshru unheard by any of the guards milling about. "Does this seem strange to you?"

"You'll need to be more specific, lad. Most everything we do could be called odd by someone, and if I'm being honest, I'd be one of those calling us strange."

"There's almost no one in the courtyard that isn't a guard. Even some of the people dressed as peasants carry themselves like soldiers and have weapons peeking out from inside their cloaks. Did we follow Xethe into a trap?"

"Probably," Leshru said, splashing water on his face. "That's why Prynne rigged the cuffs Torg and Celia are wearing after Xethe gave them the keys. None of us trusts the little bastard, except maybe Torg, and he's so damned good-hearted he still thinks Prynne is joking about shooting Nip. Xethe was a rat when we traveled together, and rumors of him meddling in some nasty shit since those days traveled all over the continent, even to my little backwater pub."

"So, is there a plan?" Qabil asked, looking around.

"After a fashion. We let him spring his trap, then try to figure out if it's better to run away or fight our way out of here."

"That...seems like a terrible plan."

"It's not my best, I'll admit. But it was what I could come up with on short notice that had a hope of not alerting Xethe to our suspicions."

"So...we just wait, and hope those archers up on the ramparts don't just shoot us full of holes and leave us to bleed out on the ground?"

"And murder the songbird if he does in fact turn coat on us. Don't forget that part, because Prynne sure as fuck won't."

"Is there something to why she hates him, or is it just her normal loathing of, well, everyone?"

"Just the normal," Leshru said. "I've found that, with very few exceptions, the more time Prynne spends around someone, the more she wants to cut their throat while they sleep."

"I hope I'm one of the exceptions."

"You'll know you aren't when you wake up dead one morning. Now look sharp, the archers just drew arrows and all moved to the inside of the battlements."

They turned to see the guard Grandil approaching with an older man in more ornate armor approaching. Where most of the guards wore a tabard over a chain shirt and regular wool or cloth trousers, this man was clad in half plate, with a gleaming breastplate, fully armored arms and legs, with just a hint of chain at his shoulders and other joints. He walked with a slight limp, but nothing in his gait suggested infirmity. He strode through the courtyard like a man who was accustomed to respect, and unaccustomed to asking for it. This was a man who had been through the fires, and survived to tell the tales.

"Master Terisack?" Xethe asked, his tone confused.

"The lord seneschal is occupied with important matters. I am Andres Bartalone, Commander of Lord Walfert's personal retinue. I am here to examine the prisoners."

"And pay our reward?" the bard asked, his smile verging on the obsequious.

"Oh, don't worry, you'll get everything you deserve," Commander Bartalone said, raising his right hand to the sky.

"Gods damn it all," Prynne muttered. "I fucking hate it when I'm right."

As she spoke, the archers along the ramparts stepped forward with arrows nocked, and all the "civilians" in the courtyard threw off their disguises and drew steel. "Lord Walfert thanks you for your loyalty and wishes to reward you for your service," the commander said, before drawing his own sword and advancing on the bard, who at least had the good grace to look surprised at the betrayal.

"What are you doing? This is not how it was supposed to go!" Xethe cried, drawing his rapier. The slender blade looked remarkably out of place set against the broadsword Bartalone wielded, but Qabil could hardly be bothered to care, given Xethe's actions.

"It seems Lord Walfert has altered the terms of your arrangement," Prynne said, her voice dry as a desert. She stepped forward with her left foot, leaned forward, and extended her own longsword through the bard's side, skewering the traitor. She drew her blade back and watched in complete and utter calm as the bard dropped straight down to his knees, clutching his middle. "I told you what would happen if you betrayed me again, Songbird. Might have been a couple decades since I made that promise, but I never forgot."

Xethe never spoke, just looked up at Prynne in shock and agony as his lifeblood flowed out of matching holes on either side of his belly. Silence reigned throughout the courtyard for a long moment until finally the bard let out a long sigh and fell over sideways, dead before his head hit the stones.

"Now," Prynne said, raising her blade toward Commander Bartalone. "Shall we dance?"

CHAPTER FORTY-SIX

The guard captain looked stunned, as though he'd never watched anyone stick a sword through one of his companions' guts before. As that thought ran through Qabil's head, he realized that Prynne's pragmatic approach to killing, even those close to her, probably wasn't what anyone would consider "normal." He quickly shoved that thought to the back of his mind, one of the many things he'd encountered on this trek that would be entertaining to ponder over a boring evening, preferably in his warm house with a roaring fire and a full stomach. It was not, however, anything he needed to be contemplating when surrounded by an armed contingent of men and women ordered to kill him.

"Kill them!" Bartalone shouted, raising his sword arm and bringing it down in a chopping motion.

The Seven moved almost as one, making a loose semicircle with Nipural in the middle and the fountain behind them. The white-haired old man cast off any hint of infirmity as he raised his staff overhead in both hands. A string of unintelligible words sprang from his lips as an arc of flame sprang from the wizard, making a canopy of fire that floated several feet over their heads, incinerating the first wave of arrows as the archers let fly with their initial barrage.

Qabil gaped at the magic flowing from the old man, more impressive than anything he'd seen out of the wizard to this point, but his attention was dragged back to the situation at hand as a jingle of mail warned him of an attack. He got his blade up in time to swat aside the thrust of a guard who stabbed at his unguarded back.

"That's not very nice," Qabil said, stepping forward and kicking the man between the legs. He clubbed the guard behind his right ear with the pommel of his sword, and the man's eyes rolled back in his head as he fell to the ground. Qabil turned his attention to the next guard in line, deciding that he had to count on Nipural to do his part while he and the others did theirs. They'd spent an hour the night prior discussing what they would do if Xethe betrayed them, and archers were always one of the main threats. The courtyard was essentially a killing field unless Nip could keep his shield up, and he could only keep his shield up if they stopped anyone from sticking a blade in his guts.

A burly man with a two-handed axe charged forward with a vicious grin on his face and a scar stretching from the point of his chin up to his scalp, bisecting his face with a ropy pink line of puckered flesh. He was thick, almost as broad across the shoulders as Leshru, but nowhere near as fast, and nowhere near as nimble. Qabil easily spun out of the way of the lumbering charge, and as he slid sideways, he lashed out with his sword and felt the man's hamstring part beneath his blade.

The man fell to the ground screaming, his axe forgotten in his pain. He rolled around on the stone floor of the courtyard clutching his leg and cursing for long seconds before Prynne stepped out of her place in the circle, stabbed him through an eye, and went back to defending her brother.

"He was out of the fight!" Qabil protested.

"No," Prynne shot back. "Now he's out of the fight. And you need to watch your back." Her left hand dipped to her belt, then flicked out toward him. He barely saw the flash as a throwing knife whirled past his face. Qabil spun around to see another guard staggering back with the blade buried in his throat. Qabil ran him through, pulled the knife from his neck, and pitched it underhand at the nearest guard.

The knife bounced off the man's helmet and clattered to the ground, doing no real damage but causing a moment's distraction, which was all Thallis needed to step forward with a pair of long knives and open the man's throat. The flesh on the back of Qabil's neck tingled, and he dropped straight down, landing on his knees and spinning around as a sword whistled through the space where his throat had been. A surprised guard looked down at him, eyes wide, then he let out a shrill scream as

Qabil reversed grip on his sword and stabbed the man through his left foot.

The guard dropped his sword and hopped back out of reach, smacking into one of his compatriots and tumbling to the ground in a tangle of arms and legs and cursing. Qabil stepped forward to engage another foe, but a firm grip on his sword belt hauled him back.

"Don't break the line," Leshru said, the big man's voice gruff in his ear. "Let them come to you."

Qabil nodded and planted his feet as another guard stepped up to fill the hole in their ranks. Qabil spared a glance for his friends as he parried the man's clumsy strikes. Everyone was engaged in close combat except Nipural, whose face was drenched with sweat just as though he'd been dodging cuts and thrusts himself. Maintaining the spell was taking an obvious toll, and Qabil wasn't sure how much longer the old wizard could manage.

"Fill in my spot," he said to Leshru. Qabil darted across their semi-circle of blades and stepped in beside Prynne, skewering the guard she was toying with. "Nip looks like he's fading. Can you give the archers something else to think about?"

Prynne glanced back at her brother and nodded. "Cover me," she said, withdrawing from her spot in the line.

Qabil slid into her place, batting aside a young guardsman's weak slash and punching the man between the eyes. The guard was barely more than a boy, even younger than himself, and as his nose fountained blood, Qabil leaned forward and spoke in a low voice. "Run, boy. Make your injury seem worse than it is and get the fuck out of here. This is The Seven, and you are not in their league. Hells, I ride with them and I'm not in their league, so what chance do you have?"

The terrified guard nodded and scrambled to his feet, throwing his sword to the ground and running to the keep, blood pouring from his face as he staggered to make himself seem more injured.

"That was a good thing," Celia said from beside him. The half-orc's manacles lay in the dirt, discarded when the charade fell apart. She and Torgan had replaced the chains Xethe bound them in with ones Leshru provided, complete with false cuffs that broke away with a twist of her wrist.

"Make a beat," Qabil said, swatting a sword aside. Celia nodded, and barely a second later, the sound of bells came from her left ankle. Qabil glanced down and saw that the bard wore a band of small bells fastened just below her pants on that leg, so every time she thumped her heel, they jingled. She started with a simple rhythm, almost like a metallic heartbeat, but it was enough.

Enough for the magic within Qabil to rise up, to wrap itself around him and bathe him in music. His vision seemed to be overlaid with a ghostly image of the man before him, a blue-tinged illusory guard whose slashes and strikes came half a heartbeat before the real man moved, giving Qabil just enough warning to parry every attack, to block every cut, and to make one dazzling riposte that opened the guard's throat and sent him staggering off into the path of a big, looping cut from another axe-wielding brute. The axe bit deep into his companion's neck and buried itself in the bone, yanking the weapon free of its owner's hands as the dead man collapsed. Celia took one step forward and skewered the shocked guard, who fell on top of his own axe.

For what seemed like hours but was probably barely moments, Qabil lost himself in the rhythm of battle and Celia's jingling steps. He parried, cut slashed, and stabbed, all without missing a beat as he stepped to the rhythm. The music swelled within him, and he was lost in the block-block-cut-block-cut-block-stab pattern, his whole world narrowing to the field of battle and the song running through his veins, a triumphant pounding battle hymn that wrapped him in its gleeful dance of blood and agony.

The rapid-fire *twang* of Prynne's bow provided a counter-beat to Celia's bells, and Qabil spared a quick glance to the ranger, just to make sure she was safely apart from the melee. She caught him looking, glared at him, and spun, firing an arrow past his ear that buried itself in a guard's eye. "Pay attention. You still need to make it inside to murder Walfert. Can't do that if some prick puts three feet of steel through your liver."

Qabil ducked without looking, letting another guard's blade *swish* through the air over his head. He flopped flat onto his back and stabbed upward, opening up the artery in the man's thigh, then rolling back to his feet and stabbing another guard through the throat. "Got it," he said over his shoulder to Prynne, a saucy grin splitting his features.

That grin shattered as an arrow streaked in from the side of the court-yard, coming in low and catching Prynne in the meat of her thigh. Her bow clattered to the ground, and she fell, clutching her leg. "Fuck!" she yelled.

Nipural turned to look at his sister, and the moment his concentration wavered, the shield exploded in a shower of flame and sparks. "Prynne!" the wizard shouted, kneeling by her.

"Time to go," Leshru said as he saw Prynne fall and Nipural tending to her. "Come on, let's get the fuck out of here!" he shouted, then charged forward, bowling over four guards in front of him and creating a big hole right through the center of their mass. Celia and Torgan followed right behind, each behind and slightly to the side, opening a wedge-shaped path through their attackers. Thallis left his sword buried in a guard's gut and picked up Prynne's discarded bow, sending shafts to the ramparts as fast as he could draw and release.

Qabil bent down and helped Nipural haul a screaming Prynne to her feet. With one arm over each of their shoulders, she managed to move forward, albeit far more slowly than was at all comfortable. Nipural threw a handful of dust into the air above them and muttered some words in another language Qabil didn't recognize, and suddenly a dense fog hovered over the entire courtyard at head height, giving them some respite from the archers, at least.

They punched, slashed, stabbed, and hacked their way to the front gate, only to find the massive portcullis down and blocking their way. Leshru didn't even break stride, just bent at the knees, wedged his hands under the bottom of the enormous gate, and began to lift. Celia stepped up beside him and lent her considerable strength to the task as Torgan and Thallis struggled to keep their attackers from overwhelming them. It took long seconds, but finally, to Qabil's abject amazement, the pair lifted the iron gate high enough for them to make their escape. Thallis went through first, firing arrows back through the openings in the portcullis to keep the guards at bay while Nipural and Thallis hauled Prynne through, leaving a streak of inventive profanity in her wake. Torgan and Celia followed, with the half-orc spinning under the gate and turning back to Leshru.

"Come on, Lesh, let's go!" Nipural shouted.

"I'll hold them off," the big man said, then planted a foot in Celia's midsection, shoving her back off the gate as he stepped back, empty hands raised. The portcullis crashed to the ground, with Leshru on the wrong side of it.

"Go. They won't kill me. Walfert hates me too much," Leshru said as he turned to the oncoming guards. "I am Leshru of the Broken Blade, and I'd bet a month's wages that your slimy little taint-licking boss Walfert would much rather you take me alive than dead. But if you want to kill me, you're fucking welcome to try."

Qabil knelt by the portcullis, yanking uselessly at the huge gate. "Come on!" he shouted at his party. "Help me."

"No." The voice was firm and came from the one mouth Qabil had expected to be right beside him trying to get back in there. "No," Torgan repeated, his face solemn. "Leshru gave himself up for us. Now let's get out of here and put his sacrifice to some use."

"But—"

"But nothing, mate," Thallis said. "He ain't dead, and that's more than we'll be able to say for the rest of us if we're still standing here when those morons remember that they have the winch on their side. Now come on."

"Part of the fight is realizing when retreat is the only option," Nipural said. "Now please help me carry my sister. She's not as thin as she once was."

Prynne stirred, her speech slurred from pain and blood loss, but her words unmistakable as she looked at her brother. "Fuck you, Nip."

CHAPTER FORTY-SEVEN

I t was a disheartened group that crowded into a room on the second floor of a shady inn nestled in the heart of the poorest section of Lennox. This was a part of town that Walfert's guards never ventured too far into because they knew that walking out again with their hides intact was far from guaranteed. This was the home of the thieves, the prostitutes, the fences, the cutthroats, the brokers who dealt in all forms of lethal and addictive substances, the men who rented out their fists for any job as long as the money was good and the body count was high. In short, it was where people who didn't want to be found by the authorities went when they needed to go to ground. It was perfect for a crew of once-famous heroes that had fallen on hard times.

A nervous little man knelt beside the lone narrow bed in the room, wrapping bandages around Prynne's thigh and very studiously not touching her anywhere that wasn't covered in blood. For her part, the foul-mouthed archer just lay back on the bed, really just a wooden frame with rope stretched across and a thin straw-filled pallet added for dubious comfort. Every once in a while, she hissed in pain as the chirurgeon cleaned and sewed up the wound. Torgan put a thick hand on her ankle, murmuring soft prayer to Felrand to aid her healing, and the thick sensation of magic being used hung over the room.

"That's the best I can do in this kind of setting," the pale, reed-thin man said as he rose, holding out a hand to Nipural. "If she stays quiet for a few days, it's likely she will regain full use of the leg. But there are some very important ligaments that have been partially cut by the arrow, so if she tears them further, it will be a long and painful recovery, and likely not a full one."

"Why are you talking to him?" Prynne growled. "I'm right fucking here."

The chirurgeon turned to her with a glare. "I'm talking to him because you're obviously an idiot and cannot be trusted to manage your own recovery."

"What?" Prynne said, trying to shove herself up to a sitting position, only to be held back by Celia's massive hands on her shoulders.

"Only a fucking moron would try to waltz into Lord Walfert's courtyard and take on an entire garrison of guards. And the arrow I pulled out of your leg was marked as coming from his personal security, so that's obviously what you did. Ergo, you're an idiot. This one at least has gray hair, so he might be expected to be slightly less idiotic. Now give me my money before Gert downstairs decides that you might be worth more to her in barter with Walfert than charging you her exorbitant rates for a room. Did she give you the extra charge for no rats?"

"Yeah," Thallis said.

"Don't believe her. There are always rats. Best you can do is leave some food on the floor when you sleep. If you give the rats something to eat that's easier to get at than your eyeballs, they're less likely to chew off any bits in the middle of the night."

"Hurrah," Thallis replied.

Nipural slipped a few gems into the slight man's hand and let him out of the room, taking a second to look up and down the hall for eavesdroppers. "I didn't see anyone," he reported as he closed the door.

"You got some kind of spell to keep us unheard?" Qabil asked.

"They exist," the old wizard replied. "But I have very little in reserve after my fire shield spell, and those kinds of workings are easily overwhelmed by anyone serious enough about snooping."

"We should be good," Thallis said. "I had a word with one of the kitchen boys. He sent a runner to the Shadow Lord. Should be someone here before too long to bring us to an audience."

"The Shadow Lord?" Qabil asked, barely holding back laughter. "What the hells is that?"

"Every city of any size has Shadows," Thallis said, the emphasis on "Shadows" clear. The Shadows are your professionals—teams of pickpockets, burglars, hired muscle, assassins, fences, information brokers, even a few of your ladies of the night who have other, more specialized skills."

"Like blackmail," Prynne said.

"Among other things," Thallis agreed. "And everywhere there are Shadows, there's a Shadow Lord. It's a bit pretentious, true enough, but if you want to get anywhere without being seen, kill anyone in a city without raising the ire of the local criminals, or buy or sell anything of… questionable provenance, you need the blessing of the Shadow Lord. There's a certain engraving on the door outside that marks this as a business under the protection of the Shadows, so I made some discreet inquiries."

Qabil marveled at his friend's transformation. Gone was the affable, smart-mouthed street kid with his thick patois and devil-may-care attitude. In his place was a competent young man with sharp eyes and a keen sense of the world. This Thallis was seemingly very different from the young man he'd ridden beside for months, but there was still the same mischievous twinkle in his eyes.

"So we just wait for a knock on the door?" Celia asked. "If we were going to be stuck sitting around waiting, we should have gotten more rooms." They were crammed into a small corner room as far away from the stairs as possible, but the one bed was taken up by the wounded Prynne, Nipural sat in the lone chair, and the others were left to find what space to stand and lean as they could. Thallis perched on the open windowsill with his feet on the foot of the bed, his shoulders pressed against the upper pane of glass to keep him from slipping out of the third-floor window.

"We could talk about a plan," Qabil said, frustration creeping into his voice. "We need to go get Leshru. Now."

"We *need* to make a good plan, not a hasty one." Torgan's voice was a low grumble. "Lesh has been my friend for a long time, and we've been in many truly dangerous situations. This is just another one of those. He's right, Walfert won't kill him, not so long as he's useful, and right now he's very useful."

"As bait," Qabil snapped.

"Aye, as bait, lad," the dwarf replied, his voice remaining placed as a lake on a windless day. "Walfert knows we'll come get Lesh. That means the big man is mostly safe, at least for a while. The slimy bastard also knows Prynne was hurt, so he won't be expecting us to come for him tonight."

"Exactly why we should attack again tonight," Qabil replied.

"There's some logic to that," Nipural said. "But if we go in tonight, we go without Prynne, and with me not at my full strength. I need rest and food to refuel my spells, and if we wait a day or two, Torg can get my sister healed up back to a semblance of usefulness."

"Your concern is immensely touching, brother dear," Prynne said from her bed. She was half-sitting up, pillows and cloaks piled up behind her. One leg of her pants was cut completely away, with a thick white bandage wrapped around that thigh. Two small dots of red could be seen seeping through the fabric, one for the entry wound, and one from where the doctor had shoved the arrow through her leg to remove it.

She looked pale, and for the first time since traveling with her, Qabil thought she looked vulnerable, like she was actually capable of injury. The air of self-assured invincibility that she wore like a suit of mail was gone, leaving an injured woman with gray-streaked hair and crow's feet spreading from the corners of both eyes.

"He's right, though," Prynne continued, pulling Qabil from his reverie. "We can't go after Walfert tonight. We're too weak, and we have neither a plan nor our gear, and without our two strongest fighters, trying to get Leshru out would be suicide."

"So we just wait?" Qabil asked. He couldn't believe what he was hearing. This was *The Seven*. They weren't supposed to get hurt, or captured, or fall for crass betrayal from the likes of Xethe. He gave himself a mental shake and brought his thoughts more in line with reality. His mother had been one of these legends, and she wasn't enough to stand before Walfert's man. He decided to put his impatience aside as best he could and listen to the people who had more experience in battling impossible odds.

"Aye," Torgan said. "We wait. Well, *you* wait. You and Celia and Thallis wait. Nip rests and studies up to make sure he's got the right spells. Prynne is going to lay still and concentrate on healing. I'm going to pray over her leg, pray for guidance from Felrand, and pray for Leshru's continued health. I might offer up a prayer for Walfert to suddenly develop oozing sores on his ballsack, just to be petty. I doubt she'll answer that one, as Felrand isn't a particularly petty god, but if anyone deserves a pus-riddled scrotum, it's Walfert."

"Well, when you phrase it like that..." Qabil said. He walked over to a corner of the room and slid down to sit on the floor with his back to the wall, leaning his head into the corner and closing his eyes. "Wake me when the Shadows come to take us to our meeting. If Leshru taught me anything, it's to sleep when I get the opportunity, because I might not get the chance again for a long time."

"Sounds fair, lad," Torgan said, kneeling by Prynne's bedside and pressing both hands to her bandaged thigh. The archer let out a hiss of pain but clenched her jaw and said nothing. Torgan bowed his head and began muttering softly in Dwarvish, imploring his god to help speed the healing in Prynne's leg. His hands glowed with a warm yellow light that suffused the room, prompting Thallis to hop to the floor and turn around to close the window.

"No need in telling everyone on the street there's magic going on," he said as he leaned out to reach for the shutters. The room fell to a shocked silence as the young thief immediately drew back into the room and stepped away from the window, his hands raised in surrender.

A slender form dressed in black and holding a hand crossbow popped into view over the sill. The person slid through the open window like black water in human form, all fluid movements and implied threat. They never took the crossbow off Thallis, but their eyes scanned the room. "You're the thief Darik told us about? The one asking about Shadows?" The shrouded intruder spoke in a hissing whisper that masked any hints as to their gender, and their slender frame could have been a thin woman, a skinny man, or even a teen. It was impossible to know much about them from their shape.

"Aye," Thallis said. "I ran with some Shadows in Talberg. They gave me a badge." He reached into his shirt with one hand, the other remaining high in the air, and drew out a medallion on a leather thong. It was a round metal disk with an intricate design of interlocking rings and triangles on both sides, and as he held it up, the intruder lowered their weapon, removed the bolt, and folded the crossbow into something unrecognizable as a weapon.

"I know that medal. Mr. Night gave it to you, didn't he?" There was a hint of challenge in their voice, just enough that Qabil could tell this was some kind of test.

"I don't know any Mr. Night, but my uncle Istvan gave me this necklace," Thallis replied.

That must have satisfied their visitor's curiosity because they reached up and pulled off their hood, revealing a young woman with light brown skin and long, wavy black hair. She had high cheekbones and had features just a hair over the line to "striking" rather than "beautiful."

"Huh," Thallis said.

"Didn't expect a girl?" the young woman asked.

"Not that," Thallis replied. "Didn't expect a pretty one."

The female thief blushed slightly, then almost immediately composed herself. "Thanks, but we'll have to wait a bit to explore that. Deacon wants to see you all, and he's not inclined to wait long."

"Deacon?" Thallis asked. "He's the Shadow Lord here?"

"Yeah," the girl replied. "But he thinks that name's pretentious as fuck. Does the king where you're from actually call himself that?"

"Nah," Thallis replied. "Aryel said that shit was pretentious, too. We just called them Boss."

"You all ready to go?" she asked, looking around the room. "Huh. Guess not, huh?"

"No," Qabil replied. "Just me and Thallis."

"And me," Celia added. They all looked at her and she shrugged. "What do you want? I'm a bard, and a deacon who calls himself a king but doesn't want to be called a lord means there's got to be a story in here somewhere. Besides, it'll be better than sitting here watching Torg pray and Nip and Prynne sleep."

"Yeah, you say that now," the female thief replied. "Come on then, let's go meet Deacon and see if he's going to help you murder Lord Fuckwit or turn you over to him for the reward. Meet me in the stables." She pulled her hood back on and melted over the windowsill like flowing water, disappearing into the night.

Thallis let out a sigh, and Qabil reached out and thumped him on the shoulder. "Put that away, Thal. We've got work to do."

"I know," Thallis replied. "But I've got to tell you, if there's ever been a woman that I might be interested in, she's it."

"Well, as interesting as I find young love, I think shadowy underworld crime bosses are even more interesting, so if you're done mooning after the girl, let's go meet the Shadow Lord," Celia said, putting a heavy hand on Thallis's shoulder and steering him toward the door. "Then if we're not dead when this is over, you can ask the Shadow Lord for his permission to court her."

"Celia, you're missing the point. Most of the fun of being a thief is in *not* asking permission for anything," Thallis said as he left the room with the big half-orc.

Qabil stood in the doorway for a moment, looking at his companions. "I hate splitting up, especially when Prynne's hurt."

"Get the fuck out of here, boy," the archer growled. "Last thing I need is you staring at me while I try to heal. Go. Follow the girl, get this Shadow Lord to agree to help us, then we can go show Walfert what his guts look like."

Qabil nodded. "Yeah, let's do that. Try not to get shot while I'm gone."

"Try not to die without me to look after you," Prynne replied.

Qabil chuckled he closed the door behind him, then his smile faded as her realized that there was likely very little jest in her directive. He was about to walk into the lair of a crime boss with only a half-orc bard and a brash thief by his side. If he put a foot wrong in this meeting, staying alive would likely take all his skill. He only hoped he had enough.

CHAPTER FORTY-EIGHT

Qabil froze as their guide shoveled a pile of straw to the side and opened a trapdoor set into the stone floor of the stable. The thickly muscled plow horse that had occupied that stall until moments before leaned its head over the closed door, sticking its nose back into its feed bag but otherwise completely ignoring the quartet of armed humans staring at a hole in the ground.

"You want us to go down there?" Qabil asked. Staring into the hole he could see nothing but inky black, shadows so thick they seemed almost sentient, like the darkness would swallow them hole if they put their feet too close to the edge.

"I want to be back in my warm bed with a companion safe in my warm bedroom," the thief replied. "But if you want to meet Deacon, you'll get your ass in the hole."

"I really don't like traveling the Thieves' Highway sometimes," Thallis grumbled as he sat down on the edge of the hole, then gripped the edge and lowered himself down. He let go, and Qabil heard a soft splash from below. "Come on down," Thallis called back up. "It's just a foot or two if you lower yourself the way I did. Hells, Celia might not have a drop at all, tall as she is. But that means watch your noggin."

"Got it," Celia said, her feet already dangling through the hole. She reached under her shirt and pulled out a small stone on a silver chain. The half-orc wrapped her left hand around the jewel, closed her eyes for a moment, then opened her palm. The gem now glowed with a soft yellow light, barely discernible in the lantern-lit stable.

"Where did you get that?" Qabil asked.

"It was a wedding gift from Torg's mentor in the church, Mattias," Celia said. "He told us that no matter how dark things got, we would always have Felrand's light to show us the way." She slithered down through the hole, carefully threading her broad shoulders through the narrow opening. It took long moments of squeezing and twisting, but finally she slid through. Qabil looked down to see the pendant illuminating a circle a couple yards wide around Celia and Thallis as they stood in a dark tunnel with water flowing around their legs.

"Is this a…sewer?" Qabil asked.

"The smell didn't give it away?" their guide replied.

"I thought it was just a hole where they dumped the horseshit."

"Nobody throws out valuable horseshit," the woman said. "The stable master probably makes as much selling turds to rich idiots for their flower gardens as he does brushing down travelers' horses. Now are you going to get your ass down there, or are we just going to call this whole trip off and let me go back to bed?"

"Oh, quit your bitching," Thallis called from below. "This isn't sleeping time for us. This is prime time. You wouldn't be asleep; you'd be crawling through some asshole's office window hoping his guards were as lazy as you thought they were."

The young woman shrugged and looked at Qabil. "He's not entirely wrong. But no matter where I would be if I weren't standing over a shit river with a bunch of strangers who make more noise than an entire platoon of Walfert's guards, I either want to get on with this or get back to my life. So would you please either get in the godsdamned sewer or go back to your room until the Watch comes by and arrests you and all your friends?"

"You think the Watch knows where we are?" Qabil asked.

"I found you less than four hours after you got away from them," she replied. "Why the actual fuck would you expect the Watch to be any less informed than a burglar?"

"Because guards are idiots." Thallis's voice came from below. "But they're not so stupid that a guy standing in a stable in the middle of the night talking into a hole in the ground won't be suspicious. Now come on, Ears. It stinks down here. Soonest begun is soonest done and all that shite."

Qabil let out a sigh and slipped down through the hole, adding another item to the "Things I never thought I'd do but now have somehow done" list he kept running in his head. As his head cleared the lip of the hole, the stench hit him full in the face, almost causing him to lose his grip and tumble into the water, which would have been very bad. Even though he managed to only drop the couple of feet into the flowing river of sewage, his tiny splash still stirred up enough funk to make his eyes water.

Celia caught him just as he moved to scratch them, shaking her head in the dim light. "You probably don't want to touch your eyes down here. Think about what might be on them."

Qabil shuddered and put his hands in his pockets. "I'd rather not, thanks. Not that I could possibly forget."

Their guide slipped through the hole last, dangling from one hand by a hook none of them had noticed on their descent, then reaching up behind her to tug on a rope attached to the trapdoor. It dropped into place with a dull *thump*, and she let herself fall the last few feet into the muck.

"Come on, then," she said, setting off down the tunnel. "Good idea on the light. Saves me digging one out of the cache I left here." She pointed to the wall, where a cloth bundle was barely visible in a jagged hole. "There's little stashes of stuff every couple hundred yards. Usually a light, a knife, and some clothes that are meant to fit about anybody." She looked over at Celia. "Not you, of course. Or me, neither." She gestured toward her slight frame.

"How many of these caches are we going to pass on the way to your boss?" Thallis asked.

The guide laughed. "Nah, you ain't getting it that easy, Talberg boy. You want to figure out anything about where the headquarters is, you're gonna have to do it without my help."

Thallis lapsed into a grudging silence as the young woman started off down the tunnel. He and the others fell into step behind her, not needing to be told to tread carefully. No one wanted to take a tumble down there, whether for dislike of filth, fear of disease, or not wanting the ridicule such a mishap would earn from their companions. No one spoke as they followed the slight thief through the sewer for what felt like hours.

Finally, as they passed through an intersection, Qabil stopped walking and said, "That's it. I'm done. You've walked us around in circles one time too many. Now either lead us to this Deacon, or take us back to an exit, because I'm not slogging through one more foot of nastiness without some clear destination."

The woman turned to Qabil, challenge writ large upon the small sliver of face he could see, now that she had her hood on once again. "What makes you think we're walking around in circles?"

Qabil pointed to the wall by his right hand. "The two marks on this wall. I made the first one after I became suspicious you were purposefully hiding our path so we wouldn't know where we were in relation to the city above. I made the second one when I was certain. Now I've just been following along waiting for you to bring us back through here, because I know I can get us out of the sewers from here if you decide to abandon us."

The young woman let out a sharp bark of laughter. "You *know* you can get out of the sewers? Pretty confident for a fisherboy, aren't you?"

Qabil's face went very cold. "I never said I was from a fishing village. I never told you anything about myself, save that I'm here to kill Walfert. Who are you, and what do you know about us?"

"Oh, bollocks," she said, pulling her hood off once again. "I always screw up that part. The pretending to be ignorant thing. I'm not good at it. Come on, I'll take you to the boss." She pulled a stone out of a pouch on her belt, clasped it in her hand for a moment, then dropped it around her neck. It put off a glow that eclipsed Celia's, sending brilliant white light some twenty yards into the blackness. In the bright glow of the stone, the outline of a door was clearly visible in the tunnel wall about ten feet from where they stood. The woman walked over to it, rapped three times, paused, then knocked five more times in rapid succession.

"What's the password?" came a gruff voice from the other side of the door.

"Open this goat-fucking door right fucking now or I'm going to sneak into your room while you sleep, cut off your manhood, chop that pitiful wiener up into even tinier pieces, and scramble it into my eggs tomorrow morning. How's that for your godsdamned password?"

"Works for me, Tarisa," the voice replied. A second later, the sound of stone grinding on stone filled the tunnel, and warm yellow light spilled out into the sewer. "Why you got your light on? You forget the way home?" the voice asked, chuckling.

"No, but your wife must have, since she was in my bed this morning when I left," the woman said, gesturing to the open door. "These are the people Deacon wants to see."

287

"Well, why didn't you say so?" said the voice, which Qabil could now see belonged to a heavyset man perched on a stool by the entrance. He was a grizzled older man, whose body showed the marks of a life lived outside the law. His left hand was missing at the wrist, the cauterized stump speaking to him being caught stealing one more than one occasion. A long scar ran from one corner of his mouth to his left ear, giving his face the look of someone pulling a wicked grin. He didn't rise as they walked past, and as Qabil looked down, he saw that the man only had one leg, the other ending in a wooden peg.

"What's your name, friend?" Thallis asked him.

"Lucky, and we ain't friends," the man replied, his face showing the degree to which he did not appreciate the ironic nickname. "Now fuck off."

"So they call you Tarisa," Qabil said, pitching his voice low as he walked beside their guide.

"Among other things. What you need to keep in mind isn't what people call me. You worry more about what they call you."

"What do you mean?"

"If they call you friend, you're probably good. If they call you Meal Ticket, then you're going to get to meet Walfert much sooner than you'd like." She gave him a wicked grin, then said, "Dunno what you did to the slimy prick, but the reward for your delivery to the keep, alive but not necessarily unharmed, is enough to keep a body in food and warm clothes for years."

"It's not about what I did to him," Qabil said. "It's about what he did to me. He murdered my mother."

"And that's why you lot are here? To kill Walfert because he murdered somebody's mum?" Her eyes were huge as she looked over the trio. "I knew you were nuts, but that's just...*crazy*."

"Do you have a mother?" Qabil asked.

"Not since I can remember," the thief replied.

"Then it wouldn't make any sense to you. But I had one, and I loved her, and Walfert killed her as sure as if he'd wielded the sword himself. So now I intend to kill him right back."

"But that has proven more difficult than you expected, Qabil, son of Eltara." This voice was new, coming from ahead of them in the tunnel. As they rounded a slight bend, they saw a good-looking man with dark hair and a long brown mustache waxed into elaborate points leaning against the wall. "My name is Deacon. Welcome to our humble abode. Please, come in, make yourselves at home. Once you divest yourselves of all weapons, including the throwing knives I know your young pickpocket has strapped to both arms and both ankles."

"Only the one ankle, but good eye otherwise," Thallis said.

"Only one ankle?" Deacon asked.

"If I can't kill somebody or wound them enough to get away with a sword, a dagger, knuckle dusters, and ten throwing knives, two more aren't going to matter. I'm pretty well fucked regardless."

The man nodded. "That makes sense. Either way, leave your weapons in the box with Tarisa and follow me. Let's see if we can work together to cut Walfert's pecker off and feed it to him." He turned and walked off, not looking to see if they would follow.

Thallis leaned over to Qabil and whispered at a level that hid exactly nothing of what he said, "They've got a real fascination with men eating their own Johnsons here. Let's keep an eye out that nobody tries to feed us ours."

"Yet another reason I'm very happy to not be blessed with that particular appendage. Those things seem to always cause more trouble than they're worth," Celia said as she handed her mace to Tarisa, placed her dagger in the box at the young woman's feet, and started off down the hallway after Deacon.

Thallis looked at Qabil and started to divest himself of all the knives, garrotes, swords, and other nasty pieces of hardware he carried. "She ain't wrong, you know," he said. "Men's willies have caused more wars than anything except religion, and that always seems to come down to gods measuring the size of their dicks, just on a larger scale."

"And now I can't get the image of gods standing around with a ruler and their pants around their ankles, each trying to outshine the other," Qabil said. "Thanks."

"Happy to help," Thallis replied, depositing the last sheath of two throwing knives into the box. "Now let's go see a man about a murder."

CHAPTER FORTY-NINE

Deacon's "office," for lack of a better word, was down a tunnel, through another hidden door, down another tunnel, up a long ladder, and through a trapdoor into a well-appointed room with large windows looking out over the city of Lennox. Qabil walked over to peer through the glass, hoping to orient himself somehow to the keep or the entrance they came through, but he wasn't familiar enough with the town to have any real idea of where they were. The keep wasn't visible, so Qabil knew he was looking in a southerly direction, but he couldn't figure out anything more about it.

"Trying to find Walfert's little toy castle?" Deacon asked as he sidled up beside Qabil.

"Wouldn't hurt my feelings to be able to get a good look at his defenses," the boy replied.

"I thought you got an up-close view of those defenses when Xethe and his friends ambushed you."

Qabil turned to the man, now clearly visible in the well-lit room. He was fit, tall and trim with cords of lean muscles visible along his forearms. He wasn't bulky like Torgan or Leshru, not the kind of strong that intimidated. No, he was leaner, more wiry like Thallis or Prynne. The kind of power that came out of nowhere and took an opponent by surprise. Qabil thought his slender frame, coupled with his almost feminine good looks, likely put the Shadow Lord in a lot of situations where he got the upper hand on an opponent who underestimated him.

"We saw something of the castle and the grounds, yes, but not enough to have an idea how to get in without causing another pitched battle in the courtyard. Which we'd like to avoid, if at all possible."

"What resources do you have at your disposal?" Deacon asked, leading Qabil over to a long table set with six chairs. The mysterious young woman who had served as their guide sat on one side of the table, with a muscular man who wore a dark cap pulled down low over his eyes. Deacon took a seat at the head of the table, leaving Qabil and his companions to take the open seats.

"Not much in the way of resources," Qabil said. "We have a mage, a bard, a priest, a thief, the best archer I've ever seen, and me. I'm decent with a blade, but not a master by a long stretch."

"I know who you are, boy," the thief-king replied. "I know what most of you can do, except you and the thief here. They're pretty much legends, especially in Lennox."

"Why? Because they used to ride with Walfert?" Celia asked, almost spitting the name.

"No," Deacon replied. "Because everybody around here thinks one day The Almighty Seven will come riding in and overthrow Walfert, then it'll be nothing but sunshine and roses from now until the end of time."

"But you don't think that's what will happen?" Thallis asked.

"I know better, boy. Your friends are old. They aren't at the top of their game anymore, if they were ever as good as the tales make them out to be. And Walfert's a piece of shit, but we know where we stand with him. Can't say the same about whoever takes his place, so I'm going to need some convincing if you want any help from the Shadows."

"What do you want to be convinced of?" Celia asked. "That Walfert is a piece of shit the town would be well rid of? Seems like you all know that already."

"Aye, we do. But what we don't know is who will step up and take his chair if we shove his narrow ass off the throne. And that matters more to me than revenge for your dear old mum, lad. Sorry."

"You got somebody in mind for the throne?" Thallis asked. "Maybe somebody with an overtrumped mustache and a rakish smile?"

Deacon grinned at him. "Rakish, huh? I like that. But no, lad. I want Walfert's spot about as much as I want a bleeding ulcer. I just want to make sure we either kill off enough of the Privy Council that a decent choice comes to the fore, or we murder all of them and give people a real choice in their leadership for a change."

"If we assassinate the entire council, who would run the city?" Celia asked.

"The guild leaders, for a while at least. Eventually some noble would likely be appointed mayor or governor or whatever the fuck Walfert calls himself. But there would be a period of chaos while things are settling down, and chaos isn't good for business. If a city is unsure about who they'll be paying taxes to next year, the people don't spend as much, and shopkeepers don't have as much buried under the floorboards of their bedrooms. That makes life harder on my second-story boys, and it hurts the profits at the whorehouses, too. So why should I put that kind of dent in my revenue to help you kill a mayor who's as much a thief as any of my Shadows?"

"Because we're going to kill him whether you help us or not," Qabil said, his voice resolute. "If you help us, then we'll be in your debt and would look kindly on anyone you put forth as a replacement for Walfert. If you don't help us, then we won't look nearly as kindly on government suggestions from the King of Thieves."

"So it's in my best interests to help you overthrow the almost lawful ruler of the city? Because that will make things more stable and make my life easier and better? Is that what I'm supposed to take from this meeting?" Deacon asked, leaning back in his chair and reaching for a glass of wine that rested on the corner of his desk.

Qabil's head whirled. There was a game being played, but he wasn't sure the rules, the objective, or even what the board looked like. And he wasn't entirely sure if he was a player or a game piece. What did he need to do to convince this man to help them? Was it money? Was it respect? Was it altruism? He wracked his brain trying to figure out Deacon's motivations, when Thallis came to the rescue.

"How much?" the brash young man asked, leaning back in his chair so it rocked up onto two feet.

"Excuse me?" Deacon replied.

"How much do you want to help us? We can dance around this shit the rest of the night, or you can tell us a number, we either agree or we don't, and everybody can get a little sleep. Not everyone lives on a Shadow's schedule, so my friends are going to start getting cranky if we keep them up too much longer. And nobody wants to be stuck in a room with a cranky half-orc."

"Or a half-dwarf," Celia added. "And I'm both, so I get twice as annoyed." She grimaced, making a point to show the small tusks that sometimes protruded from the corners of her mouth. She normally took pains to hide them, not wanting to terrify everyone she encountered, but there were certainly times when it was more beneficial to look scary, and Qabil had to agree that this was one of those times.

Deacon laughed, hold up both hands, palms toward the trio. "Okay, okay," he said. "Let's not drag this out any further. We don't like Walfert any more than you do." He looked at Qabil. "Okay, maybe we like a little more than *you*, but for those of you with merely an abstract loathing of the man, we're probably even. He's bad for business because he *knows* our business, so he knows our tricks and can put roadblocks in place that make smuggling nearly impossible, and then he raises taxes on goods to the point where he's making all the money we used to make off contraband. It ain't natural, I tell you. We're supposed to be the crooks, but now this prick sits up in his throne room raking in the coin from what should be *our* plunder, *and* now he's started up his own 'official' brothels!"

"Sounds like he's really put a wrench in your gears," Thallis said.

"Fucking right he is," Deacon replied, his voice laced with venom.

"So you're in?" Qabil asked.

"Boy, if we weren't in, you'd be floating face-down out to sea by now. Tarisa would have slit all three of your throats in the sewer and let you just flow on out of Lennox like the rest of the turds." Deacon took another sip of wine and waved to their escort for another bottle.

She uncorked it expertly and poured a sip out for him to taste. Deacon swirled the wine around in his mouth before smacking his lips and letting out a loud "Ahhh."

"I don't even know what I'm supposed to be tasting when I do that shit," the Shadow Lord said. "But it's what one is expected to do with wine, so I do it. Much of this job is about keeping up appearances. That's one reason I played coy about whether or not we'd help you. It's expected that the leader of a band of thieves will be money-grubbing prick, so I behaved like a money-grubbing prick. If I'd been a solicitous host and immediately pledged myself to your service to overthrow the evil Walfert, you never would have trusted me."

"Don't worry," Thallis said. "I still don't trust you."

"Good," Deacon replied. "You shouldn't. I'm a thief, a forger, a pick-pocket, and an assassin. I'm three of the least trustworthy people I've ever

met. But when I make a deal, I stand by it until the dregs, as they say here."
He stood up and held out a hand to Qabil.

Qabil looked at Thallis, then Celia, then stood and clasped the robber king's hand with a nod.

"Excellent. When do you want to move on him? Again, I mean. I've received reports on your attempt this morning. Not bad, trying The Prisoner. Not like you could have snuck her and her sawed-off husband in unnoticed any other way. Only problem was trusting Xethe. What the fuck was that about?"

"Leshru has a soft heart," Celia replied.

"Aye, and today a soft head to go with it," Thallis said with a snort. "Lumpy bald bastard should have trusted Prynne. She hates Xethe."

"Prynne hates almost everybody," Qabil replied. "You can't use that as a judge of character. You'd never trust anyone."

"And never be betrayed," Thallis said. A shadow flickered across his face, and Qabil wondered what that meant. He knew the other young man hadn't had an easy time of it. Mother gone, living on the street until he fell in with Nipural, then called Stinno, and pretending to be a fence for stolen goods. Now he was riding to almost certain death with people he had just met. Thallis was a good friend, one of the best Qabil had ever had, but there was a lot bubbling under the surface of the smart-mouthed rogue, and apparently this wasn't the first time someone had betrayed him.

"True enough, lad," Deacon said. "But that's a lonely life. Take it from the man who rules a kingdom of sewer rats, murderers, thieves, and whores. Friends are a rare commodity in this world, and when you find one, or a group of them, you better hold onto them tight as you can."

"Then let's quit jacking our jaws and figure out a plan to get into that castle, because Walfert has one of my very few friends in his clutches, and I'd really rather he be in one grumpy, bald piece when we get him loose," Thallis said.

Qabil stood up and held his hand out over the table, palm down, fingers spread. "If we're in this, we're in it. No half measures, no running away when things get bad, no mercy for Walfert and his men. We're in it to the dregs, as you say."

Deacon put his hand atop Qabil's. "To the dregs."

Celia and Thallis did the same, the bard's massive pale green hand dwarfing the rest. Then Qabil's eyes widened as the thief Tarisa stood and followed suit, kicking the other man in the ankle as she did so. He stood up and put his hand, almost as massive as Celia's, atop the pile. "To the dregs," he said, his voice a low rumble like distant thunder.

"Well, that's nice," Thallis said, taking his seat. "Everyone is friends, and the world is full of puppies and fluffy bunnies. But does anyone have the slightest clue *how* we're going to break into a fortified castle, fight our way through a small army of guards, and kill a world-class assassin?"

Deacon sat down and pulled his chair closer to the table, then leaned forward with his elbow on the polished wood surface. "Oh, my boy, do I have a plan? I have *the* plan, and it is a doozy. Gather round, my ducklings, and let's plot us some treason."

CHAPTER FIFTY

How exactly is this better than the last plan?" Qabil kept his voice to a whisper as he leaned down to ask his question directly in Thallis's ear.

"It's better because there's a bigger distraction, and we're not counting on guards being stupid for success," Thallis replied. "All we want them to do is their job. Chase pickpockets, break up fights, maybe put down a massive brawl at the docks. That kind of thing. We don't need to fool them, just direct their attention to somewhere we aren't. Then we slip in the back door while they're all watching the front, and we've gutted Walfert's forces at the same time."

"Do you trust this Deacon?" Qabil asked.

"Only the slightest bit more than I trusted Xethe, which is to say practically not at all," Thallis said. "He's a liar, a thief, a cutpurse, and almost certainly the type of man who would sell his own mother for a sticky bun and a mug of good ale. But his reasons for helping us are sound. Walfert's type of rule is bad for business. If people are giving all their money to a corrupt mayor for bribes and protection, there's nothing left to steal or to spend on shiny baubles."

"That can then be stolen from houses far more easily than from well-guarded jewelry stores."

"Exactly," the young thief replied. "Now you're getting the picture! Deacon will help us honestly so long as helping us has more potential benefit than turning us over to Walfert. And I think he's a little smitten with Prynne, so that doesn't hurt."

Qabil smiled. The Shadow Lord had certainly seemed struck by the foul-mouthed ranger when she'd limped into his lair. Even her tendency to threaten everyone she met had seemed to interest the man known as Deacon more than it intimidated him. Could it be that simple? Could the man be willing to put his entire world in jeopardy just because he found Prynne intriguing? He pondered that for a moment, thinking back to his walks with Linnea in Narim. Would he risk everything to win her heart? Probably not, if he was being honest, but Linnea was nothing like Prynne. No one in Narim was anything like any of the people he traveled with now, and that made him adjust his thinking.

These people lived in a different world than the prosaic fishing village he'd grown up in. A world of heroes and villains, of magic and monsters, of dragons and evil rulers. They lived in a bigger world, with huge personalities, where every decision came with potentially world-altering consequences. He wondered, not for the first time, if he'd be able to return to Narim after this was all over, assuming he survived, which was anything but a foregone conclusion.

"Penny for them," Thallis said.

Pulled from his reverie, Qabil felt his cheeks color. "Nothing, really. Just thinking about where we all go after this, if there even is an after this."

"There will be," Thallis said. "Not for everybody, and maybe not even for any of us, but the world will keep turning. No harm in daydreaming about it, so long as you don't let your daydreams interfere with getting the job done."

"I know," Qabil said. "I'm just anxious. We've traveled so far, dealt with so much, just to...sit here."

"Well, if we've got to sit somewhere, next time let's pick someplace that smells better," Thallis said, gesturing at the sewers around them. After hearing Deacon's plan in his cozy, clean office, they were led through the sewers to a network of natural underground caves carved over the centuries by rivers and streams. Apparently when Walfert took over, he rerouted one of those streams up to the surface to build a moat, not only disrupting villages that counted on that river for water, but also leaving empty tunnels threading the countryside, with one leading right under the castle.

They followed Tarisa through the mud and the damp for what felt like hours, the soggy group passing through a secret door hidden by a pile of rubble into a dry cavern with a trapdoor set in the ceiling. A ladder was suspended under the door on hinges, and Tarisa gestured for Celia to reach up and unfasten the clasp holding it in the up position.

"What do you do if you aren't traveling with someone who's seven feet tall?" Thallis asked.

"I let the people I'm navigating for talk at the ladder until it's so annoyed it gives up and fall to the ground," Tarisa replied.

Nipural reached out and tousled Thallis's hair. "If you're going to engage in a battle of wits, make sure you're actually armed, lad." Then the old mage pulled a small bowl out of his pack and sat cross-legged on the floor. He poured water into the bowl, then leaned forward with both hands placed on the sides of the container.

"What are you doing?" Qabil asked, but Nipural had already slipped into a trance and did not respond.

"He's scrying," Torgan said. "Using magic to see across great distances. Your Shadow Lord gave him talismans matching ones worn by several of Deacon's people all around the city, so he can keep tabs on the havoc taking place topside." Torgan looked tired, but fit, and Prynne walked with just the barest limp since Deacon's people had fetched them from the inn.

"So we can watch the shit storm Deacon's people are making through this bowl?" Thallis asked. "I love it. When does the show start?"

"Now," Nipural replied, looking up from the bowl. "Just stare into the water and it will show you what one of the amulet bearers is doing to sow discord among the citizenry."

The party gathered around the bowl, except for Celia and Qabil. He sat apart from the others with his back against a wall and his eyes closed. He let out a small grunt of greeting when Celia slid down the wall beside him, but otherwise did nothing to acknowledge her presence.

The sat for several silent moments before the bard opened her mouth to speak. "Let's not," Qabil said before she uttered the first word. "I know you're just checking in, or giving me some words of sage advice, but let's just not waste time figuring out what's running through my mind right now. I'm shit-scared that I'm never walking out of this castle, shit-scared that I've led my friends into a slaughter, and even more shit-scared of failing, of breaking the promise I made to my mother as she lay dying in my arms. But I don't really want to think about that right now. I just want to sit here and try to remember all the songs and war chants you and Prynne have taught me so I can sword dance my way right through Walfert's door and open up his guts like a zipper."

"Okay," Celia said, holding out a waterskin. "I was just going to ask if you were thirsty. Too late for any of that navel-gazing bullshit, anyway. We've moved past the thinking now. Nothing left but the doing."

"And the bleeding."

"Aye, lad. A lot of bleeding."

Nipural's voice cut through the low drone of conversation that filled the room. "Shut your holes! It's starting." Everyone gathered around the bowl to see what could be seen.

The first image was one of chaos in a market, with an enraged ox charging through the plaza, knocking over pedestrians, shopkeepers, and stalls full of produce, cloth, and other merchandise. A harried drover ran along behind the terrified animal as it dragged its tack and bindings along behind in a rattling clamor, frightening the animal more with every step, creating more and more noise and destruction with every passing second. Nipural kept the image on that scene until a cadre of guards appeared, six heavily armored men all running around tripping over themselves and each other as they tried to subdue the ox.

Nipural tapped the side of the bowl, causing the water to ripple and the image to shift, this time revealing another unit of six guards, these chasing a pack of street urchins through a maze of narrow streets, back alleys, and vacant buildings. The nimble youths had to slow down every so often to make sure the guards were able to follow them, but every time the seemed to have shaken their pursuers, they managed to send someone back just far enough to keep the fish on the line. The guards followed the children on a massive chase, picking up other pursuers along the way—other guards, shopkeepers chasing the guards for destroying their wares, street rats trying to hinder the guards' pursuit, and a couple of drunken onlookers who thought such a merry chase must surely lead to some place interesting.

Nipural struck the bowl again, sending soft ripples across the image and refocusing their attention to the inside of a tavern where a massive brawl was underway. There were ruffians of all sorts throwing chairs and punches, from humans to half-orcs to dwarves to one being Qabil was fairly certain was a rakshasa, a creature he'd only heard about in tales, but here was a man with the head of a tiger merrily winging plates across the room to smash into the wall above a guardsman's head. A dozen or more guards were making a futile attempt to quell the scrap, but the air of the whole gathering was more of a festival than a fight, as gleeful dwarves buried fists in men's bellies and huge half-orcs thumped skulls and left unconscious bodies with every punch.

Another shake, and the image reformed to a view from on high, as the bearer of this watch stone seemed to be nestled in a vantage point far above the city. Looking out over all of Lennox, smoke from a dozen separate fires wafted into the air, while a massive commotion occupied all attention near the main city gate. By twirling his fingers across the surface of the water, Nipural rotated the image and zoomed in, bringing the gate into sharp focus. A huge caravan, barely short enough to fit through the gate on its own, was wedged tightly into the opening, the baggage strapped to the top of the wagon blocking all progress. And to make matters worse, the team of four horses drawing the caravan had all lain down in the area immediately in front of the gate, blocking any access to attempt to pull the wagon through by force. A crowd had gathered behind the caravan, choking the walkway and preventing any access to the rear of the wagon or the roof, further complicating the process of taking anything off the top of the caravan to allow it to squeak through the opening into the city. At least a dozen guards from both sides of the gate were walking around scratching their heads and yelling back and forth with the driver about the stuck wagon, with a crowd of spectators and hecklers that grew by the moment.

One more tap, and when the ripples settled this time, the surface of the bowl split into four quarters, each showing a chase, near-riot, or a conflagration threatening to engulf an entire block of warehouses and tenements. More and more guards poured into view as Nipural scried the chaos Deacon had managed to create with just a few hours of planning and fistful of Nipural's gems spread liberally among the Shadows.

"Well, I think that looks like about enough of a distraction," the wizard said, setting the bowl aside and struggling to his feet with the aid of his staff and Thallis. "Shall we go rescue Leshru and beat Walfert into a bloody pulp?"

"Best idea I've heard all day," Prynne replied, reaching up to pop the latch on the trap door and give them access into the castle. "Let's go save our friend."

"And avenge another," Torgan's voice was low and dark, a far cry from the placid tone the dwarf typically used. "It's time to finish this."

CHAPTER FIFTY-ONE

The trap door opened into a dusty supply closet, filled to the rafters with cold-weather supplies—heavy horse blankets, shutters for windows, extra cloaks for guards, and a massive stack of firewood taking up fully a third of the room. By the time everyone clambered up the ladder and squeezed into the tiny bit of open floor space, they were elbow to elbow in the pitch black. Tarisa, last to ascend, swung the door back into place with just the barest squeak of well-oiled hinges.

Thallis opened the door to the castle and knelt with a small sliver of mirror in his hand. He extended the mirror out into the hall, looking right and left before declaring the coast to be clear. The group filed out into the halls, leaving behind a collection of filthy shoe coverings and baggy coveralls that kept the muck and dirt of their entry from marking them as intruders. Thallis took point, with Qabil directly behind him. Nipural and Prynne followed, with Tarisa and Torgan behind them. Celia brought up the rear because, as she put it, she could see to shoot over the rest of them, and it would take quite the ambush to sneak around her in the narrow corridors of the keep.

The keep bustled with the noise of the day, the day-to-day jumble of voices, dishes clattering, footsteps on stone floors, and sounds of people going about their normal jobs, completely unaware that a team of mercenaries had entered their midst with an eye toward assassination. As the passed the open door to a massive kitchen. The sound of humming

302

reached their ears. Qabil saw a fat man with a tremendous mustache kneading dough to the rhythm of the song he hummed, his thick fore-arms moving back and forth, back and forth. It was a homey sight that took him back to memories of his mother making bread in the kitchen of their small home, the comforting smell of baking one of the few things that could mask the scent of fish that permeated their lives in Narim.

"You coming, or you want to go ask for a job?" Thallis hissed. Qabil snapped out of his reverie and followed his crew.

They walked through the keep like they owned the place, Nipural's confident bearing and Prynne's haughty glare silencing the questions of a pair of maids before they could even draw breath to ask them. They passed the kitchens and took a set of stairs up one floor, bringing them back to ground level and opening up into a massive Great Hall filled with long banquet tables. One table sat apart from the rest on a dais at the near end of the room, turned perpendicular to the rest of the room so that whoever sat at the head table could look out over the rest of the room.

"Posh," Thallis said, running a finger over the heavy velvet wall cover-ings. The entire room was ornately furnished, with carvings on every heavy oak chair, filigree adorning every piece of drapery, and an embroi-dered silk runner on the head table.

"No silverware for you to steal, so let's keep going," Prynne said, crossing the room and opening the heavy double doors. "This should lead into the main foyer, and we can make our way to the stairs from there. If I know Walfert, and much to my regret I do, his quarters will be on the topmost floor, with an army of cannon fodder to fight through before we get to him."

The keep's main entryway was at least as ornate as the dining hall, with marble tiling the floor, a pair of swooping curved staircases leading to an upper hallway, and a massive chandelier flickering above it all. That wasn't what made Qabil gasp and draw his sword as soon as he stepped into the room. That reaction was due to the man lounging on the bottom step of the far staircase.

He was slender and tall, with a neatly trimmed mustache and close-cropped hair. He wore no armor save a pair of leather bracers and a light breastplate, but it was his sword that drew all attention. A basket-hilt rapier with glittering black opals set into the base of the blade, it seemed to flicker with a light all its own, independent of the light from the chan-delier or the tall, narrow windows set into the wall on either side of the huge double doors.

"Hello, Qabil," the man said. "I see you decided to return my knife. I wondered where I'd left it."

"No, you didn't, Bothun," Qabil said, moving apart from his friends and swinging his blade in a low arc, as if testing the weight. He needed no testing. This was the blade he'd practiced with every night since meeting up with Leshru, and trained seriously with ever since Prynne began teaching him about sword dancing and his strange ability to merge music and battle. "You knew exactly where you left it, buried in my mother's back as you rode away laughing, back to your master who was too much of a coward to do his own dirty work."

Bothun threw his head back and laughed, a harsh, bitter sound that made bile rise in Qabil's throat. "He wasn't being a coward, you fool. He was simply not wasting time on dealing with lesser creatures. Like your half-breed cow of a mother."

Qabil's face flushed and he took a step forward but paused as a hand landed on his shoulder. It wasn't heavy, not restraining him in any way, more a request than a demand. He turned to see Prynne standing there with a strange look on her face.

The ranger's eyes flickered back and forth between a familiar anger and a deep, abiding hurt the likes of which Qabil had never seen before. "He's mine, lad," Prynne said, her voice trembling as she seemed to have to force the words out. "Your Bothun and I have unfinished business."

"You have no business with Bothun, woman," the lean swordsman said as he rose from his seat on the staircase, his movements fluid to the point of being catlike.

"No, but I knew a man name Gartine who looked a lot like you and carried a sword with three black opals set into the hilt. A man who couldn't keep his other sword in the right sheath, as it were."

"A man who betrayed someone I care about quite a lot, and who I promised to turn into a toad if I ever saw him again," Nipural said, his voice dark. The old mage stood arrow-straight with his staff slightly off the floor. Nipural's eyes and the crystal embedded in the top of his staff both glowed with a sickly green light.

"Ah, so we have a little reunion!" Bothun/Gartine said, his face splitting into a huge grin. "I have missed you, Prynne. And Nipural, you know I have no magic, so it would be hardly fair to start throwing fireballs around, or wise, especially in an enclosed space."

Nipural looked around at the expansive foyer and its enormous high ceilings. "I think there's plenty of room. But if not, it won't be the first time I've come out of a fight singed."

Qabil looked from the siblings to the assassin and back again. "You know this man?"

It was Prynne's turn to flush, her ears turning slightly pink as she spoke. "Oh, I knew him, alright. He's the one I shot Nip over. The asshole that was going to sell me to Baron Dusen for barely enough coin to buy a decent horse. This is Gartine, my former lover."

"And *also* Bothun, right hand of Lord Mayor Walfert," the man said, smoothing out the front of his shirt under his breastplate. "Who would very much like to remind you all that you are trespassing and the guard will be charging through that door in a few seconds to haul you all off to the dungeon where you can watch him torture your friend until he's known as Leshru of the Broken Spirit. Then you, young Qabil, can watch him slit the throats of every remaining person on this world that you care about before he finally grants you the sweet release of death. That is the penalty for refusing my Lord Mayor's largesse, and you will pay for your mother's refusal to marry."

He turned his attention back to Prynne. "Except you, my dear. The Lord Mayor has promised you will be mine, body and mind, for as long as you have either of those things." His smile as wicked and cold, as cruel as any expression Qabil had ever seen on a person's face. "Which I don't expect to be very long, if I'm being honest."

"That would be a first," Prynne said. "You being honest. But you forgot one thing, Gartine."

"What's that, my dear?" His smile shifted from cold to oily, the kind of leering smirk that made Qabil desperately wish for a scalding hot bath just to wash the stench of the man off him.

"That we're the fucking Seven, you prick. We're the most legendary band of heroes, outlaws, cutthroats, avengers, and mercenaries the nation of Relhye has ever seen. If you think a bunch of undertrained and under-armed castle guards can take us down, you really should have paid closer attention the months we were together. Now draw that fucking pigsticker and let's dance, you son of a motherless goat." She handed her bow and quiver to Celia and drew her sword.

She stepped to the center of the room and faced the black-clad man. He watched her move, then drew his sword with such speed that Qabil never saw his hand move. One instant he was unarmed, the next he had his rapier in hand and was lunging for Prynne's unarmored chest.

She slapped the thrust away with a sneer. "Really, Gart? That's the best you've got? You've gotten fat and slow sitting around licking Walfert's boots. Eltara was out of the game for years before you murdered her. Let's see how you fare against someone whose skills are still sharp." She tossed a glance back at the rest of the party. "Go. Find Leshru and start cutting pieces off Walfert. Don't do anything permanent to him until I get there. This shouldn't take long."

"No, it shouldn't," Bothun said, advancing on the ranger, his blade a blur of silver slicing through the air. Prynne dodged and parried with seemingly no effort at all, a master of the blade showing her true skill for the first time since Qabil met her. She moved no more than was required to knock aside or block Bothun's strikes, wasting no energy with flourishes or flashy footwork.

"Come on," Thallis said, tugging on Qabil's sleeve. "Prynne's got at least as much reason to gut this prick as you do, and she's actually got a chance to do something other than find out exactly how much blood her body holds, which is more than I can say for you."

Qabil knew his friend was right. He'd known from the moment he strapped his mother's sword around his waist that he was running headlong into a fight he hadn't the skill to win, or even necessarily survive. But he hadn't cared, because with his mother gone and his life in Narim in ruins, he'd had nothing to live for. But now, with this strange assemblage of people, he'd found something he never even knew he was missing—a family. In that moment, watching Prynne step up and shoulder the burden he thought was his alone to bear, he understood what his mother meant when she spoke of the family she'd found.

"I can't leave her," he said. "I can't just—"

"Fucking go!" Prynne shouted, turning to the side to dodge a sword thrust, then knocking Bothun's dagger aside as he tried to skewer her with his other hand. "If I can't kill this prick, you can avenge me. But get Lesh first, then kill Walfert. If you're still alive after all that, worry about me."

"Go on, lad," Nipural said. "I'll stay with her. I have just enough healing magic that if Gart gets a lucky strike in, I should be able to keep her from bleeding out. As long as she asks nicely."

"Never gonna happen, you impotent old fuck," Prynne said.

"Shut up and fight, you withered old bag," Nipural shot back.

"Let's go," Torgan said. "If they're bickering, they're happy. And nobody's more dangerous than Prynne when she's enjoying herself." He looked around for Tarisa and saw her walking back in their direction from the front doors.

"Spiked them shut," she said. "That way at least our pair will get a little warning if they're going to have company. Now can we please get back to the back hallways and dark hidden corridors? All this light and open space is making me queasy."

"You know, I'm really starting to like her," Thallis said to Qabil as they passed through an open doorway into a long hallway decorated with ornate tapestries and thick rugs.

"Could we please wait until no one is trying to murder us or our friends to worry about your love life?" Qabil asked. He sheathed his sword and followed Celia's lead as she turned right into the hallway.

Thallis smirked at him. "If we wait for that, I'm never going to get laid."

CHAPTER FIFTY-TWO

Bothun grinned as he raised his rapier in a mocking salute. "You did promise to cut off bits of me that I would miss if you ever saw me again."

"And I'm a woman who keeps her promises," Prynne said. She stepped forward and slashed at Bothun's legs, no salute, no showmanship, just a cold-eyed hunter looking to carve her name in her enemy's flesh.

The grinning man hopped nimbly backward to avoid her cut, not trying to block the heavier longsword with his slender blade, just moving out of the way then lunging over the top of her reach. Prynne turned her head to the side as the blade streaked past, barely missing her right ear. She charged, trying to close with the nimble swordsman, but he dodged out of the way and swatted her on the rump with his blade.

"Too slow, darling," he called in a sing-song voice. "You never were fast enough to keep up with me." He swung his sword in great looping circles, the opals at the base of the blade catching the light in peculiar ways as the light reflected of the gold and iridescent flakes buried within the stones.

"Get the sword away from him," Nipural called from where he stood at the door. He couldn't get a clear shot to fire a spell at Bothun, but something in his brain tickled about that sword. He'd seen it many times over the years, first in a hoard of treasure they collected after slaying the dragon that gave him the name of Wyrmrider, then many times in

Walfert's hand as the rogue failed time and again to talk their way out of whatever trouble Xethe's tongue had gotten them into. Who would have ever imagined that traveling with a half-orc, half-dwarf bard would be safer and less prone to violence than traveling with a god-touched human? Perhaps Xethe hadn't been touched as firmly by the gods as he claimed. There was certainly nothing divine about the way he died, clutching his gut in the middle of the courtyard.

"I'll get right on that," Prynne yelled back. "Right after he stops trying to skewer me!" She knocked aside an obvious thrust at her midsection, then spun to the left to avoid the dagger driving at her throat. She dropped to one knee and lashed out with her sword, slashing at the back of her opponent's legs. He nimbly hopped over her strike, and she grinned.

That was the moment she'd been waiting for, for him to try something too flashy, something designed as much to humiliate his opponent as to gain a tactical advantage. This was something she and Bothun had argued about many times after sparring, with her always maintaining that flashy moves had no place in a fight for one's life. Now she finally had the chance to prove her point, preferably by burying it in his belly.

As he hopped up, she pounced, launching herself at Bothun at the apex of his leap, aiming to drive a shoulder into his gut and bearing him to the floor where she could pin his hands and beat him bloody before she finally excised all the bad memories of their time together by nailing his mouth closed, permanently.

Except there was no gut to slam her shoulder into. Bothun wasn't there when she pounced. He hadn't simply hopped up away from her slash, he'd launched himself several feet into the air and into a back handspring, bounding across the room to land on both feet and swoop down into a grandiloquent bow.

"What the fuck?" Prynne asked, then dove out of the way as a trio of daggers flew in her directions almost as though the weapons had a mind of their own. Bothun's hands moved so fast all she saw was a blur of movement and a glint of metal in the air, then she was barely moving out of the path of the whirling knives. One caught on her shoulder before it tumbled away, leaving a small wound and a trickle of blood running down her arm.

"What the fuck is he doing, Nip?" she called, never taking her eyes off her laughing opponent.

"I have no idea," shouted her brother. "But stay down!" Prynne had been up on her knees but dove back flat at Nipural's warning. She felt a blast of heat sear the air over her back as Nipural sent a wave of fire from his fingertips slicing across the room right at waist height. It was a little too low to easily duck under, and a bit too high for a normal person to vault over. It should have caught Bothun in the midsection and turned his innards to ash.

But Bothun was apparently no longer a normal person because as the fire neared, he crouched slightly, bunching his legs up, then launching himself straight up into the air. The line of fire passed harmlessly underneath him, leaving scorch marks along the wall and catching one of the tapestries ablaze.

"Good thing the keep is made of stone," Bothun said, a lopsided grin making his sharp features softer, almost attractive. Prynne remembered what she'd seen in him—a handsome, witty man who could hold his own against her in a fight. They'd been good together. At least she thought so, but apparently Bothun's affections had a price tag attached, and it wasn't even terribly expensive. She remembered the figure his old employer had quoted her right before she ran him through, and she wasn't sure what hurt more, being betrayed or being betrayed for barely enough coin to buy a decent pair of boots.

"Too bad you aren't the one made of stone," Prynne said, reaching down to the top of her left boot and flicking three throwing knives in Bothun's direction. *Zip, zip, zip,* the knives flew through the air, connecting with nothing but the far wall of the room as Bothun twirled and danced out of the way, his movements almost like Qabil's when he was sword dancing, but different somehow. Bothun had no magic, that she was sure of. So what was giving him this kind of speed?

"Is that fucking sword magic, Nip?" she yelled as she closed on Bothun again.

"Of course the fucking sword is magic," her brother replied. "I told you all that when Walfert took it from the dragon's hoard. It was the most powerful artifact in the room, and you all let it go to the least trustworthy member of the party. Which I objected to, if you'll recall."

"I promise to recall anything you want if you tell me what the fucking thing does!" Prynne yelled, furiously beating back a volley of slashes and lunges from the ponytailed swordsman. Her mind raced as her body fought almost by reflex, her months of sparring with this same man giving her muscles the memory of his fighting style, his preferred parries and ripostes, the cheap shots he liked best—all the things she needed to beat him, except he was too godsdamned fast to lay a finger on.

"It seems to absorb kinetic energy and channel it back through the wielder, enhancing their speed and strength. Be careful, he probably hits harder than you'll expect."

"I'm always careful when someone is trying to put three feet of steel through my gut!" Prynne yelled. She turned to the side to present a smaller target and batted away Bothun's next series of blows. He feinted low, then slashed with his dagger at her eyes, only to have Prynne lean back out of the range of his cut with barely an inch to spare.

"You always were better than me, Prynne," Bothun said with a tinge of regret in his voice. "It's why I hated to betray you. I learned a lot about fighting from our sparring sessions. Learned a few other things from you, too."

"While you taught me all about turning on the people who care for you, and then I learned that for some worthless bastards, it doesn't even take much coin to get them to throw away all the good things in their life." Prynne was sweating heavily, and she stepped back to wipe the sweat from her eyes.

"I don't know," Bothun replied, dashing sweat droplets from his own forehead. "I think I've done pretty well for myself since joining up with the Lord Mayor."

"I can't tell," Nipural called. "You look like the same spineless bag of dicks I warned my sister not to let within a mile of her bed. But she never listens to me. Unless I'm yelling for her to *MOVE*!" The mage shouted the last word, and Prynne did as she was told, diving to the left as a volley of lightning crafted arrows materialized and flew unerringly at Bothun's chest. He knocked three aside, but one slammed into his left shoulder. Sparks danced across the man's upper body, sending his hair up into jagged spikes all over his head.

He let out a scream that rose in pitch until he seemed to run out of oxygen, then he collapsed to his knees, bent forward with his elbows on the ground and his chest heaving in silent screams or sobs, Prynne couldn't tell which.

She regained her footing and took a step forward, but froze when Nipural shouted, "Don't go near him!"

Bothun raised his head, revealing a wicked grin that did nothing to melt the ice in his eyes. "Oh, no. Please come near. I promise, it won't hurt. For long." He flung another throwing knife in Prynne's direction, but then he sprang to his feet, slashing the empty air with his rapier. The dagger stopped its flight, then the opals on the blade flashed golden light, and the knife *changed direction* in midair, flying straight for Nipural's chest, where it landed with a wet *thunk*.

"Nip!" Prynne shouted. She dropped her sword and sprinted to her brother's side, but it was obvious before she got there that nothing she did would matter. She slid the last couple of feet on her knees, pulling the wizard's limp body to her chest, her tears cascading down into his tangled gray hair. "Don't you die on me, you gimpy old fuck. Don't you dare die. If I've said it once, I've said it a thousand times. Nobody kills my gods-damned brother but me, and I'm not ready to cut your throat yet."

"I'm sorry, Prynthalisse," Nipural whispered, using the name their parents gave her, a name she hadn't allowed to be uttered in her presence since the day they left home with their father passed out drunk on the floor of the kitchen again. She stopped being the sweet, innocent Prynthalisse that day, and that simple farm girl had been locked away for decades behind the rugged exterior of the finest archer in all of Relhye, the gruff and foul-mouthed hunter who never let anything touch her, who wasn't afraid to battle hordes of monsters or armies of trained soldiers as long as she had her friends, and her brother, by her side.

Her brother, who she tormented all throughout their childhood. Her brother, who she beat up at every opportunity, but defended with a stunning ferocity against any outsider who dared even look cross in his direction. Her brother, who grew from a sickly boy into one of the greatest wizards the world had ever known. Her brother, who lay in her arms with a bloody froth bubbling up from his lips as he struggled to speak.

"What is it, Nip? What are you trying to say?" She leaned forward, Bothun forgotten, Walfert forgotten, Qabil and his thrice-fucked quest forgotten. Everything vanished but her brother, his blood as it streamed from the wound in his chest, and the darkness reaching for her, stretching out for her, promising her comport in oblivion, promising an escape from pain, from betrayal, from loss. That darkness crashed against her soul as the last light left her brother's eyes in a long, rattling sigh.

As his last breath drifted out, Nipural locked eyes with his sister, and he whispered one word. "Dispel." His eyes flared purple, and a nimbus of lavender light expanded out from where Prynne knelt holding the one man who she knew had never and would never betray her. She heard that raspy whisper in a voice too old and fragile to belong to the powerful mage she'd ridden with for years, and she knew what it meant. As she gently lay her brother's body on the cold stone floor, she stood and turned to face Bothun.

She turned slowly, knowing he wouldn't stab her while her back was turned. That would be no fun for him, give him no opportunity to revel in her pain, in her loss. But as she turned back to face the rapier-wielding assassin, he stepped back at what he saw.

The expression on Prynne's face was nothing like he expected after she lost her oldest friend at the hands of the man she loathed the most in all the world. She didn't weep, although her cheeks were wet with tears. She didn't even frown, although her eyes carried a sadness that would live there forever. No, what made Bothun step back and raise his blade was far more frightening.

Because Prynthalisse the Keen-Eyed, daughter of Bryson the Miller, sister of Nipural Wyrmrider, the greatest wizard to ever walk the continent of Watalin, ranger, outlaw, and member of the legendary party of heroes known as The Seven...was *smiling*.

Prynne smiled at Bothun, and as he felt the magic drain from his blade, he understood what Nipural spent the last shreds of his life force on. The final spell of Nipural Wyrmrider came to him then, and he knew that for the next several moments, no magic would work within the boundaries of his casting. And while Bothun didn't know how far that magic reached, he did know one thing.

He wasn't going to live long enough to find out.

And he didn't.

CHAPTER FIFTY-THREE

Qabil forced himself to focus on the path ahead, trusting Nipural and Prynne to take care of themselves. They were the experienced heroes, after all. He was just some wet-behind-the-pointy-ears kid with a grudge who wanted to get justice for his mother's murder. Nonetheless, the more times the party split and broke apart into smaller and smaller groups, the less comfortable he was about his chances at walking out of this keep alive. He'd meant to rouse The Seven to ride again, but now it was more like The Four and a Guide running through the halls of Lennox's central home and administration building.

"Stairs up are that way," Tarisa said, pointing straight ahead. "If Walfert thinks there's even a chance you'll get through his guards and come for him directly, he'll be up in his chambers with the door barricaded. That way," she pointed off to the right down a long corridor, "leads to the stairs going down to the dungeon. There's a chance he's down there playing with your friend, but not much of one. Walfert likes to have people flayed alive, but he doesn't have the stomach to actually watch his orders carried out."

"So we need to split up," Thallis said.

"Again," Qabil grumbled.

"We'll head down to free Leshru," Celia said. "Torgan and I fight better in close quarters than either of you, and I'll lay good money that some healing will be in order when we get him free."

"Somebody's going to need a god's blessings, whether it's Lesh or those idiots holding him," Torgan said.

"So that leaves the three of us to go upstairs and challenge Walfert," Qabil said. "Assuming you're still with us." He aimed a pointed look at Tarisa.

The girl raised her hands in front of her chest. "I wouldn't miss this for the world. You lot are the most interesting thing that's happened in Lennox since we fed laxatives to a flock of geese and set them loose to fly over Walfert's marshaling yard while he was reviewing the Guard."

"Then let's go," Qabil said, drawing his sword.

"You safe to run with that thing?" Tarisa asked him with a smirk.

"Did you see how fast Bothun drew his blade? And he wasn't even one of The Seven. He was a second-rate mercenary at best, and I never saw his hand move. So I'll take my chances falling on the blade if it means I have my weapon in my hand when I need it."

She nodded. "Makes sense. Well, if we're doing this, let's do it." With that she turned and sprinted forward, turning right at the end of a short hallway.

Torgan clasped hands with Qabil. "Good luck, lad."

"Thanks."

Celia gave Thallis a stern look. "Try not to die before we get there with Leshru."

"I'll do my best," the young thief said, grinning. "We'll try to save some Walfert for you." Then he and Qabil turned and followed Tarisa up the hall.

Celia looked down at her husband and sighed. "Come on, my love. Let's go down the stairs to the dungeon, crack a few skulls, and rescue our friend."

Torgan smiled, an expression barely visible under his mass of facial fair, and held out his hand. "Well, with such a romantic invitation, how could anyone decline?"

The door at the bottom of the stairs was thick wood with bands of iron across to add solidity to it. Torgan pushed, but it was either locked or barred from the other side. He gave it a firmer shove, with no success.

Stepping back, he looked up at Celia, who waited on the bottom step. "Would you like to try?"

"Yes, but you probably want to go back up a few steps. Maybe all the way to the main floor."

"What are you going to do?"

"I have an idea that will likely get through the door, barring any magical interference, but it will also be hazardous for anyone standing too close to me."

"A spell?" Torgan asked, backing away and starting up the stairs. He moved about four steps up and halted, his face worried. "Are you sure?"

Celia sighed. "I know, Torg. I'm not much of a caster. But this is one I've been working on, a spell to amplify my voice so I can be heard in noisy taverns and the meeting halls back home. I think with a slight modification, I can use the same spell to knock the door down."

"I'm not even going to try to understand that," the dwarf said. "Go ahead, my love. I'm right here."

"Yes, you need to be a little less *right* here, if you get my meaning. Back up more, Torg. If you can hear me, you're in range of the spell. And if this does blast the door open, I'm going to need you once the people in that room understand what's happened to them."

Torgan grumbled, but stomped back up the stairs, his armor clanking with every step. Celia thought that sometimes her husband only objected to things because it gave him a chance to stomp around and make noise when he didn't get his way. Once he cleared the top of the stairwell and moved out of sight, she turned her attention back to the door.

Drawing a lute from its case on her back, Celia took a moment to tune, plucking each string with a dexterity that belied the thickness of her fingers. After testing each string and turning the pegs so the sound was just right, she nodded to herself and closed her eyes. She focused her attention inward, diving deep down within herself to the place where the music, and her magic, lived.

Nothing had ever come easy for Celia. As a half-orc, she was shunned by humans and orcs alike. As a crossbreed between an orc and a dwarf, she was even more alone, as other half-orcs wanted nothing to do with her. As a product of an actual marriage between two species typically at war with each other, and not known for their peaceful cohabitation, her entire childhood had been a series of unplanned relocations as one town or another became unwelcoming to one or both of her parents, or dangerous for her, as she grew older and boys wanted to prove they weren't afraid to touch the "weird girl."

As an adult, things had not been much better. Her dwarven heritage didn't show too much on her features, but enough that she never really fit in anywhere she went, and her love for music and performance was so atypical for both orcs and dwarves that finding a mentor was almost an impossibility. It was only after she became lost in the wilderness and stumbled upon Torgan's campsite that she found someone who accepted her for who she was as a person, not what she appeared to be. He had plucked her from a life as a bard who could barely find places to play that would keep her out of the rain and snow, and deposited her into a community that accepted her simply because Torgan did. For the first time, she felt what it was like to be part of a group, and to establish actual connections with people other than her parents.

Then Qabil came along, and Celia learned about something completely different. The Seven weren't a town, or a city. They weren't just a band of mercenaries, or heroes, depending on perspective. They were a *family*. A squabbling, sniping, joking, laughing, loving family. Not bound by blood, most of them at any rate, but they were a closer-knit group than she had ever known, and again she was welcomed not because of who she was or what she could do, but because Torgan loved her, and they loved him. So if he said she could be trusted, she was trusted. Now a member of her new-found family was trapped on the other side of this door, probably being tortured to within an inch of his life. That could not stand. Celia had gone her entire life without feeling a part of anything larger than herself, and anyone who threatened that now would learn that bards were more than just songbirds and pranksters, that the wide breadth of knowledge she possessed was good for much more than just telling stories around a campfire.

No, she knew about more than singing and telling tales. She was also somewhat versed in the arcane arts, with a much more limited selection of spells than someone like Nipural, a master wizard, but the few she did know, she could use to great effect. So Celia dug down inside herself, into the well of power that rests within all beings, and stirred that power. She stirred the power, brought it to a boil, and when she felt that she had focused all the energy she could possibly contain, she opened her mouth and let out a scream the likes of which she had never screamed before. Sound emanated from her in waves, battering everything within earshot, making the very bones of the keep rattle in their mortar.

Had Torgan been nearby, he likely would have been turned to paste inside his armor. But he was clear of the worst of the sonic assault. There was nothing near her except the stairs and the walls. And one very thick, very sturdy, very unfortunate door. After unleashing her massive scream, Celia closed her mouth, and her eyes, as she sagged against the wall to her right. She took several deep breaths, letting the power flow out of her back into the world around her, and opened her eyes to see how much she'd done to loosen the door on its hinges.

"I'd say that was pretty effective," Torgan said as he drew to a stop several steps upon from where she leaned.

Celia looked at the damage she had wrought and let out a weary chuckle through her strained throat. "Yes, love. I think it worked."

The door was simply *gone*. There was a lone board still hanging in the doorway, hinges still fastened into the stonework, but the rest of the door had been blasted into oblivion. They looked through the opening into the dungeon, wondering what kind of resistance they would have to face now, only to see Leshru hanging by his wrists from chains, covered in blood, and shaking his head as though to clear a ringing from his ears.

Lying between the splinters of the door and Leshru were three corpses, all...human. It was hard to tell their species because the entire front of their bodies had been turned to lumps of battered red meat by the shrapnel Celia's spell turned the door into. Blood dripped from Leshru's face and body, but the grin splitting his face gave testimony that little if any of it came from him.

"They were standing just on the other side of the door," the brawler said. "I think they expected you to break it down, then they planned to ambush you."

"I don't think that worked out according to plan," Torgan said, looking at the remains. "Last time I saw somebody this thoroughly dead was Remuta, wasn't it? That smuggler 'prince' the king hired us to hunt down. First time I ever saw somebody get really keelhauled. Barnacles can do a number on a body."

"I think this might be worse," Leshru said.

"You just think that because you got them all over you this time," Torgan replied, clomping over to his friend. "You always were the prissy one of the group."

"Not everyone can live in the woods without bathing for months on end like Prynne and not smell like the inside of a stable. Now would you like to get me down from here? There's a winch on the wall to my left."

Seconds later, Leshru was free, Celia having found manacle keys on one of the corpses. As he mopped the blood from his face and strapped on his gauntlets, he looked at the couple. "Where is everyone else?"

"The children are hunting Walfert, and Prynne found out that Walfert's right-hand man Bothun is also Gartine, a man she has...history with," Celia said.

"Gartine the man who betrayed her confidence by sleeping with other women then tried to turn her over for the bounty on her head?"

"That's the one," Torgan replied.

"Oh, that's going to get messy," Leshru replied.

Celia looked around the room at the devastation she had caused. "Messy seems to be our milieu."

CHAPTER FIFTY-FOUR

Qabil, Thallis, and Tarisa were headed for the stairs up when a piercing whistle caught their attention. Qabil's head whirled about to see Walfert leaning against a doorframe with a bored expression on his face.

"Hello, Qabil," said the Lord Mayor. "So good of you to come. And you brought friends. How quaint. It seems a few of your party have been...delayed?"

"They're busy taking care of the few of your guards who can still draw breath, Walfert," Qabil said, turning from his path to the tower and stepping into the narrow hallway overlooking the grand foyer. Walfert pushed off from the doorjamb with his shoulder, setting his feet and resting his hand on the dagger hanging from his belt.

"Looks like something's missing from your belt," Qabil said. He reached down and drew the dagger he'd found in his mother's body, holding it up for Walfert's inspection. "Did your errand boy forget to bring it home?"

Walfert's grin stretched almost unnaturally wide, then he whistled again. The weapon vanished from Qabil's hand and reappeared an instant later in one of the empty sheaths on Walfert's belt. "I had them enchanted ten years ago or so. Got tired of sticking them in annoying people and having to go fetch them myself."

"That's impressive," Thallis said. "I've heard some lazy shit before, but that takes the cake. No wonder you got fat when you took the throne. Or was he always fat?"

Qabil spoke up before Walfert could reply. "No, he's definitely gotten fat over the last few years. When he first came to our village, he still looked like an adventurer, all dashing and trim. Now...well, if it weren't for the gold embroidery, I'd think he was a pudgy bureaucrat."

"You little shit, why don't you come a little closer and I'll show you how fat I am?" Walfert growled. In fact, he wasn't fat. Not skinny, either, just...average. He was middling height, middling brown hair, middling features. All in all, he was as unremarkable a man as Qabil had ever seen. He remembered back to the first time Walfert came to visit his mother. She'd called him "an old traveling companion," but had said nothing else about the man. He had none of Prynne's swagger, Nipural's gravitas, or even Leshru's quiet confidence. He didn't look like he could fight his way out of a cloth sack, much less travel with the most famous band of heroes the world had ever seen.

Which probably made him very effective at going unnoticed, since the rest of The Seven could draw a lot of eyeballs. His mother included, now that he thought about it. She always turned heads, even decades removed from the life. She was beautiful, yes. But the attention she drew was more than just the roving eyes of men and women as beauty enters their presence. It was a sense when she entered a room that something important had just happened, that she was someone you should pay attention to.

Walfert had none of that. It came to Qabil then, as he stood in this ornate hallway, thick carpet under his feet and golden sconces lining the walls. *That* was what Walfert was after. It wasn't Eltara he wanted; it was the notice that came along with Eltara. He'd been unseen for so long that all he craved was the kind of attention his companions had always received.

"You're jealous," he said, almost before the thought had fully formed.

"What?" Three voices spoke in unison as three faces turned toward him.

"It's not that he's not the prettiest, or the smartest, or the most skilled," Qabil said after taking a breath to line his thoughts up in something that could be expressed logically. "He was just the easiest to overlook. That was the problem, wasn't it, Your Lord Mayorship? You were the one who wasn't supposed to be seen, who did your work in the shadows, without the accolades the others received. Because if a thief gets noticed, it means they did something very wrong."

"And are probably about to die," Thallis chimed in.

"But you were a *legend*. You were one of *The Seven*. You were supposed to be famous. Except no one could ever remember you. And who could, in that company? Leshru of the Broken Blade, the most feared bare-handed warrior the world had ever seen. Eltara the Fairy Princess, as deadly as she was beautiful. Prynne the Archer, who could knock a fly off your nose at a hundred yards. Her brother, Nipural Wyrmrider. How can anyone else hope to draw attention when the wizard rides in on a dragon? Torgan Steelhammer, the devout strong arm of righteousness. Xethe the Songbird, god-touched bard who's nearly as talented as he is attractive.

"Then there's you. Walfert the Nimble. Walfert the Quick. Walfert who everyone forgets ever existed. And that was the problem, wasn't it? You got tired of never hearing your name mentioned when they told the tales of The Seven, didn't you? It was always 'Leshru, Eltara, and those other people.' Or 'Nipural Wyrmrider and his retinue.' Walfert was never a name on anyone's lips. But if you had Eltara by your side? Then you would be *known*. Then everyone would be able to see that you were important. And wealthy, because all the gods know that a man of such... averageness would never be able to attract a woman like my mother without money, status, or both. Preferably both.

"So you sent your lap dog Bothun to make my mother an offer. An offer she rejected, then laughed at. And that was what you couldn't allow. No, the days of Walfert the Thief being laughed at and mocked were long gone. No one mocked *Lord Mayor* Walfert. No one, not even the woman he...loved? No, that's not the right word. You never loved my mother. You've never loved anyone but yourself. You *coveted* her. You *wanted* her. And if you couldn't have her, no one would."

Walfert took his hands off the hilts of his daggers and clapped, slowly, then building up speed. He clapped louder and louder, a broad smile splitting his face as he walked toward Qabil. He walked slowly, his steps measured as his boots clicked across the marble floor. He stopped walking, then he stopped clapping, a little more than five feet from Qabil, just outside the range of an easy sword thrust. "Well done, lad. You've figured out all my motivations from just a glance and few brief words. No wonder Tara was so very proud of you. But no, I didn't want your mother by my side because she would make me look important. I *am* important, lad. I don't have to prove anything to anyone."

"The gold door handles kinda put the lie to that one," Thallis muttered, earning himself a dark look from Walfert.

"Speak without permission again, little pickpocket, and we'll see how loyal Deacon's little bitch really is. I bet if I offer her your head's weight in gold, she'll cut it off an bring it to me."

"Not his head's weight," Tarisa replied. "That thing's empty. Wouldn't earn me much. You want to pay me for his ass, we can talk. That's where he talks out of most of the time, anyway."

Walfert smiled, a cold, oily thing that crept across his face but never reached his glacial eyes. "No, Qabil. I didn't want your mother with me because I needed her to make me look good. I simply felt that families should be together. So I sent Bothun to retrieve mine."

Confusion flickered over Qabil's face for an instant, as looks of shock and horror fell across Thallis and Tarisa. Then rage boiled up inside the young sword dancer and he flushed red all the way to the tops of his slightly pointed ears. "You lying motherfucker!" he screamed, drawing his blade and charging the man he'd traveled so far to find, to fight, to kill.

Blood rushed in his ears. Red tinged his vision. His heart pounded in his chest like a drum as he ran at Walfert, his sword swinging wildly. The thief dodged his clumsy slash with a smile, barely moving before he slapped the blade aside with his knife. He flicked out a hand, suddenly filled with another dagger, and a red line appeared on the sleeve of Qabil's left arm.

"Careful, lad. Got to watch both hands when you fight a real opponent. And trust me, I am very, *very* real." Walfert stepped forward, spinning his knives through the air in a whirling dervish of death and blood. Qabil barely stepped aside in time to avoid getting carved up like a turkey, and struck out with a clumsy, looping strike overhead. Walfert just slid to the right, opening up another long, shallow cut, this one along Qabil's ribcage.

"I would have thought Tara would have trained you better. But maybe she didn't want you growing up in the family business."

"My family business was fishing, you traitorous prick," Qabil growled, stepping forward into a lunge so telegraphed he might as well have actually send a rider ahead to tell Walfert where he intended to strike. The thief obliged by crossing his daggers under the sword and shoving it up, letting the blade run harmlessly by his ear and binding the hilts of his knives around the crosspiece of the sword. With his face so close to Qabil's they could tell what the other had for breakfast, Walfert grinned.

"Is that the best you can do, boy? I'm almost insulted. How the fuck did you think you were going to live through this fight? Did you learn *anything* from your mother?"

"Yes, you backstabbing fuck," Qabil said. "I learned to *dance*." With that, Qabil released the hilt of his sword, suddenly removing all resistance from Walfert's brace of daggers. The thief staggered forward as Qabil dropped to one knee and spun left, hopping nimbly to his feet and snatching up his sword before it even touched the ground. He hooked one foot in front of Walfert's and drove an elbow into the man's spine, sending him sprawling across the floor.

Walfert rolled over and over to avoid any strikes, but there were none coming. He got to his feet, glaring over at where Thallis and Tarisa stood with their own daggers drawn, beating out a rhythm on the banisters leading up to the landing where they stood. The metal hilts resonated with the hardwood, sending a repetitive *boom-boom-boomboomboomboom* to echo throughout the keep.

"Really?" Walfert said, his eyes wide. "'Tara birthed another Dancer? Well, that certainly changes things. But no matter. You two can pound on the walls all you like, but it won't matter. I'm still going to carve out your guts, boy. Such a shame, too. We could have been one big happy, wealthy family. But your mother couldn't see it. She couldn't get over—"

His words cut off as Qabil mounted a fresh attack, but this time without the pretense of ineptitude. He came in high, then struck low, forcing Walfert to adjust to save his leg. He managed to knock the blow aside, but only just, as Qabil moved with the grace of someone taken by the music, someone lost in the magic of rhythm.

All mirth faded from Walfert's face. Suddenly he wasn't the only "real" opponent. Suddenly he wasn't facing Eltara's rage-filled, vengeance-starved son. Now he was facing a Sword Dancer who had traveled and trained with The Seven for half a year, and he understood that one wrong move would end with his liver on the tip of the boy's sword.

Qabil thrust, Walfert parried. Walfert lunged, Qabil dodged. Qabil charged, Walfert spun out of the way. They moved in unison for long moments, far longer than any fight Qabil had actually been part of. Most fights are over in seconds, but this dragged on and on, the combatants too evenly matched, Qabil's magic negating the advantage of Walfert's experience, and Walfert's strength overcoming any lack of speed his age may have brought about.

In the end, it came down to experience. Experience, and treachery, and deceit, all hallmarks of Walfert's time with and after The Seven. He stepped backward, dropping to one knee as his leg appeared to buckle. One of his daggers skittered across the floor and slid between the railings to clatter all the way down to the grand foyer below. Qabil thrust for the downed man's throat, but Walfert threw himself full-length on his side across the floor.

Qabil stalked his downed prey, his face a mask of stone. After so many months, the rage within him had cooled, had transformed under the pressure of time and training into a crystallized core deep within him, a singular purpose that now took over the forefront of his mind. He was now an instrument of justice, and as Walfert flung his last remaining dagger at him, Qabil swatted it out of the air with a sneer.

He stood over Walfert, his sword poised to end the man. It felt like a moment where he should say something, where there should be words to commemorate the occasion, but nothing came to him. He raised his blade, and as he brought it down, Walfert...whistled?

The downed thief let out a shrill whistle, and both daggers reappeared at his belt, then he drew them with blinding speed, trapped Qabil's sword between them, and with a twist, wrenched the weapon away from the younger man. Walfert sprang to his feet, delivering a vicious uppercut to Qabil's chin with the hilt of one dagger as he stood. Qabil's eyes crossed for an instant as he staggered back, clawing for his own dagger as Walfert stalked toward him, the smirk returning to his face.

"Learning the truth about yourself, your abilities...it hurts, doesn't it, lad? Not as much as bleeding out all over my floor, but it still hurts. Come to think of it, I've never bled to death, so for all I know it just feels like going to sleep. But truth? I'm well acquainted with how painful that can be."

"I'll cut your fucking guts out. You never...she never...not in a million years!"

"Not in a million years, no. But on one rainy night huddled together in a small tent in a forest outside Tir'sud..."

Qabil flung his dagger at the oncoming thief. It tumbled wildly off to one side, his aim fouled by the stars in his vision.

"Come on, lad, is that any way to say goodbye to your—"

"You finish that sentence and I'll crush your fucking skull. Come to think of it, I'm probably going to crush your fucking skull anyway, so say whatever you like. Won't change the fact that Tara would rather eat pig droppings than lie with a swine like you." The voice that came from the top of the stairs was gravelly, as though the owner had spent much of the past day screaming at the top of their lungs. All eyes widened as Leshru stalked his way up onto the landing. Torgan and Celia followed, but no one was paying attention to the armored dwarf or the massive half-orc.

All attention was focused solely on the massively muscled shirtless man whose torso was crisscrossed with scars and scabs and burns and scrapes. He looked like someone had dragged him behind a galloping horse across a field of broken glass, there were so many small cuts on his upper body. His face was bruised a deep purple, turning his brown skin nearly midnight black, and he limped slightly every time he put his right foot down. But it was the look in his eyes that held the tongues of everyone gathered.

Leshru looked as though he could murder everyone in the building with just a glance, and as he topped the stairs, he gently pushed Qabil aside and stepped up right in front of Walfert. "I was going to let the boy kill you. It's his place, after all. Tara was his mother, and you took her from him. But now you've insulted my friend, and that's something no one is allowed to do."

"Insulted her?" Walfert asked, taking a few tentative steps back. "How have I insulted Eltara? I simply—"

"You implied that she had the poor taste to lay with you, Walfert, and I think that may be one of the most disgusting things I could think of. Tara wouldn't touch you with Nip's dick. She'd have lain with Xethe before she'd bed down in your arms, and you know how she felt about that flea-encrusted boil of a man. So by saying that she lay with a piece of shit like you, and claiming that her child is yours, of all disgusting things, you have insulted her. And that will not go unanswered. So Walfert, Lord Mayor of Lennox, *former* member of The Seven, and walking piece of human excrement, I challenge you. Fight me, man to man, you prissy fuck, and let's see how your blades do against someone who's taken the worst this world can throw at him. Fight me and leave the games to the children where they belong."

"Games?" Walfert asked, his voice rich with amusement. "Games? Leshru, I haven't been playing games. I've just been stalling until the last of my guardsmen could make their way up the back stairs. Come on, men, let's clear this rabble out. I'll pay an extra ten gold for the man who cuts off Brokeblade's cock and brings it to me. I think I'll hang it over my desk."

Walfert looked around, then drew a dagger and slammed the hilt into a nearby stone wall. The hilt rang like a bell, and doors all along the landing opened, with men in guard uniforms moving forward.

And falling flat on their faces, dead, as the thieves and assassins behind them let go of the bodies they were holding up. Tarisa grinned at the gobsmacked Lord Mayor and said, "Deacon sends his regards, but the offer you made him was...how did he phrase it? Ah yes, your offer was 'insufficient to outweigh the deleterious effects that cockwart's presence has on my business operations.' Seems my boss doesn't like you any more than this lot does."

Leshru grinned and rolled his head from side to side, loosening up his neck muscles. "Come on, Walfert," the big man said. "Let's dance."

CHAPTER FIFTY-FIVE

Qabil took half a step forward, but a thick hand on his shoulder froze him in place. He looked up at Celia, who just shook her head without speaking. He opened his mouth to protest but stopped when he caught Torgan's eye. The dwarf also gave one firm shake of his head, then pointed to where Leshru was advancing on Walfert.

The cocky thief twirled a dagger around his index finger, flipping it into the air and catching it by the hilt again and again. After every third or fourth toss, he feinted throwing the weapon at Leshru. The big man never flinched, never adjusted his pace as he stalked Walfert. The distance between them wasn't great, maybe fifty feet, but it grew as Walfert kept backing up, finally ducking through a door into another, larger room. Leshru and the others followed, stepping into a Great Hall with a massive open space in front of dais where an ornate chair sat. It wasn't quite ostentatious enough to be called a throne, but it wasn't far off, either. Just that tiny little bit of gilding away from being ridiculous, the chair had gems set into the arms and legs, thick cushions on the seat and back, and four feet carved into dragon's claws.

"Nice chair," Leshru said, amusement coloring his voice. "You always wanted to be seen. Well, no one will miss you sitting on that monstrosity. Hope it's at least comfortable."

Walfert gave a rueful smile. "Not in the least. The cushions are lumpy, and it's just enough too tall that only my toes reach the ground. I have to either use a footrest or look like a fucking toddler when I hold audience. I cut the maker's throat after delivery. But it is pretty, isn't it?"

"No, you fucking moron. It's huge and ostentatious and stupid-looking, and it shows yet another reason Tara wouldn't have touched you if you were the last swinging dick in Relhye. You're a tasteless twat, Walfert, and no amount of money will make you anything but a half-reformed gutter rat. You might have these people fooled into thinking you're some hot shit Lord Mayor, but you and I both know different. You're still the scrawny little fuckwit who tried to pick the wrong pocket and would have been dead in a ditch if Tara hadn't spoken up and asked me not to crush your fucking throat."

Qabil looked at Torgan, who nodded. "Walfert joined us when your mother kept Lesh from killing him."

"Be better for her if she hadn't," Thallis muttered.

"But worse for Lesh," Torgan said, giving the thief a dark look. "Murder comes with a price, even when it's done for good cause. And being annoyed with a street rat is almost never a good cause. Almost." He stared at Thallis for a long moment on that last word, driving it home.

Walfert and Leshru circled each other, wary, measuring. It was obvious the two men knew each other, had studied each other, and had sparred. But it was equally obvious that this was no sparring match. There was no lighthearted banter, no teasing, just two men staring holes into each other and watching, waiting for an opening, the tiniest mistake.

"You weren't this cautious in the old days," Walfert said.

"You were this chatty. Another reason I never liked you."

In response, Walfert sent one of his knives whipping across the space between them, tumbling end over end at Leshru's chest, barely missing him as the big man turned to one side. Walfert let out a sharp whistle, and the knife vanished to once again reappear at his side.

"That's really useful," Thallis murmured.

"Only if you're in the habit of throwing away your weapons," Celia said, her voice equally low. Footsteps echoed behind them, and she turned to see a blood-spattered Prynne limping into the room. Torgan bent to the side to look past her, then turned a quizzical look at the archer. She didn't speak, just shook her head once.

She stared past the rest at the two men slowly testing each other's defenses. "Oh, for fuck's sake, just kiss already!" she shouted, and both men turned to her.

329

"Prynne? But where's..." Leshru's question faded into the air as he saw the woman's stony expression. "Oh."

"Did poor old Nipural's heart finally give out? Did he put too much energy into one of those fireworks shows he was so fond of? Or did Bothun just carve out his guts?" Walfert's singsong tone was mocking, light, and yet still vicious.

"Did you challenge this mucksucking sheephumper, or can I shoot him without pissing you off?" Prynne asked, staring daggers at Leshru.

"I challenged him. So please don't shoot him unless I die. If he kills me, I won't give a fuck what you do to him."

"That's not terribly chivalrous," Thallis murmured.

"You see any fucking patents of nobility hanging around Lesh's neck?" Torgan asked, his voice thick with emotion at Prynne's revelation. "We're not knights, boy, and this is no tournament. This is life and death. Well, certainly death. For at least one of those two. Maybe more."

Leshru turned his attention back to his former companion. "Well, Walfert. Are we going to do this, or am I just going to snap your neck and throw you into the moat with the rest of the keep's sewage?"

Walfert's reply was a dagger thrown straight at Leshru's face, followed by a screaming charge as the smaller man barreled toward him. The thief whistled, calling his blade back to him, and he drew it again as he closed with the unarmed brawler.

This dance was very different from his match against Qabil. Much closer, with more grunts and thumps of fists and knife hilts slamming into bodies. A sharp *crack* split the air as Leshru slammed an elbow into the hinge of Walfert's jaw. A loud *oof* from Leshru as Walfert buried a knee into the big muscle of his thigh, knotting it up and making it harder to move.

Walfert's blades barely made it into play, with Leshru too close to allow him their full use. Every time Walfert thrust, Leshru stepped into the strike and slightly to the side, turning a potentially killing blow into a long scratch, painful but not debilitating. Likewise, every finishing blow Leshru swung, Walfert managed to duck and weave away from, sacrificing ribs and shoulders to protect his face and head.

The turning point of the fight happened in an instant, so quick that everyone watching missed it. It was a tiny slip, just the slightest overextension on a punch Leshru thew at Walfert's solar plexus. He overbalanced just a touch and couldn't recover quickly enough to get out of the way of Walfert's riposte, which opened up a gash along the underside of his right arm from his elbow to his armpit. Blood flowed freely, spattering on the white marble floor in haphazard patterns that matched the men's ongoing dance.

It was one of those spatters that proved Leshru's undoing. He planted his foot to push off with a massive leaping punch at Walfert's face, but his foot slipped, dropping him to one knee in front of his former companion. Walfert didn't hesitate, driving his right-hand dagger into Leshru's broad back, burying it to the hilt in the big man's right side. Leshru threw his head back in agony, letting out a howl of pain and rage that rattled the doors in their hinges. As he snapped his head back, he tore the knife from Walfert's grip. It was wedged tightly between two ribs, so firmly stuck that even Walfert's magic whistle couldn't pry it free.

"No bother," the thief said. "That's why I always have a spare. Oh look, you've got my Mercy stuck in your back, so it's only fitting that Judgement is the one I have left. Time for my judgement to come for you, Leshru."

"Go fuck yourself, Walfert," Leshru said, a foam of blood bubbling up from his lips. He reached around to his back, but he couldn't reach the dagger to pull it out.

Walfert drew his other blade and stepped up to stand before his former companion. "I am truly sorry, Leshru," he said, and there was a hint of real regret in his voice. "I had hoped you would come work for me, but I know after things didn't work out with Eltara that you would never understand."

"I understand," Leshru said, a slight cough masking his words. "I understand she wouldn't fuck you, so you murdered her, and now you've stabbed me in the back. Ironic, since she and I were the only two that ever trusted you. Nip always said you'd bury a knife between my shoulders if I ever gave you an opening. Guess he was right."

"Too bad he's not here for you to tell him that," Walfert said, raising the dagger named Judgement.

"Too bad indeed," Leshru said, his voice suddenly hard and strong. Where seconds before the big man had sounded like he was two steps on the wrong side of death's door, now he moved with the agility of a man decades younger, a man who hadn't been tortured for the better part of a day and a night, a man who didn't have a knife sticking out of his back. "Qabil, throw me that sword."

The stunned Qabil froze, not understanding the concept of Leshru Brokeblade calling for a weapon, so Thallis yanked Eltara's blade from her son's scabbard and flung it across the room to the brawler, who snatched it out of the air and spun it around in a practiced arc.

"W-w-what?" Walfert backpedaled as he watched Leshru take a few experimental swings with the unfamiliar blade, then switch it to his left hand, where the knife sticking out of his ribcage would impede his movements less.

"Just because I *don't* use a sword doesn't mean I *can't*, you stupid piece of shit," Leshru said, contempt dripping from his tongue. "It's right there in my name—Brokeblade. If I broke it, I must have had a sword at one point, right? Well, now I've got another one, and it's only fitting that the blade Tara used be the one to send you to the afterlife. Pray to whatever god protects idiots and traitors, Walfert, because you're going to meet them soon."

He took one step forward, lunging with the sword, but as Walfert frantically tried to parry the blow, Leshru let go of the sword, flipping it up so the hilt flew at Walfert's face. The confused thief threw a hand up to block the onrushing steel and took his eyes off Leshru for just an instant.

Which is all the big man needed. He stepped inside Walfert's reach, trapped his remaining knife hand with his left arm, and wrapped his right hand around the scrawny thief's throat. Walfert beat at Leshru's wrist and arm frantically, flailing with his one free hand, but the big brawler's grip never slackened. The treacherous thief's face turned red, then purple, then finally, as Leshru grunted and lifted him off the ground one-handed, Walfert's eyes rolled back in his head and closed.

Leshru lowered him to his feet, then released his grip. The dead thief stood there for a long second, balanced perfectly in front of his former companions like a life-size doll, before an arrow sprouted from his left eye and he collapsed backward to the marble.

Everyone turned to stare at Prynne, but she shook her head and pointed at Thallis, who stood with his short bow still held high.

"What?" the young thief asked. "I didn't like the way he was looking at me."

With that, everyone broke into motion, as Torgan and Celia rushed to catch the collapsing Leshru, Qabil walked slowly over to the corpse of the man who murdered his mother and destroyed his life, and Thallis and Tarisa did what any two thieves set loose in an ornate mansion would do. They robbed the place blind.

EPILOGUE

"He was a good friend." Leshru spoke slowly and simply, but his words were heavy with emotion. We stood on a small hill outside of Talberg, overlooking both the city where Nipural has crafted a new life for himself, and the road that was so much of his life before Talberg. Everyone was there—Leshru, Thallis, Prynne, Celia, strumming her lute in a mournful dirge, and Torgan, the gruff dwarven cleric who kept using the end of his beard to wipe away tears. His beard was dripping from overuse.

"Probably the best I ever had. Certainly the best I'll ever have from here out. We rode together for a lot of years, and we were apart for almost as many, but when we met again, it was almost like no time had passed. Except my knees hurt more."

"And his back ached," said Torgan, reaching again for his beard.

"And his temper was even shorter than it used to be," said Prynne with a rueful smile. She stepped forward and put a hand on the big man's shoulder. "He loved you like a brother, Lesh. Probably better, since his only sibling put an arrow in him once."

"He loved you, too, Prynne," the big man replied. "Even after the arrow thing. He said he deserved it."

"He did. Still probably shouldn't have shot him," she said, and took a long draught from the wineskin in her free hand.

"He was the closest thing to a father I ever had," said Thallis, his unruly brown hair flopping down loose and masking the piercing intelligence in his eyes. "He took me in when I had nowhere to go, taught me how to read and write, how to do sums and keep books, and how to spot counterfeits and stolen merchandise."

"And how to steal it?" I asked, my tone gentle.

"Nah, that I picked up on my own. Stinno...Nipural didn't allow it if you lived under his roof. Said running a nest of snot-nosed pickpockets would draw too many eyeballs, and he didn't need any more attention from the Watch than he already got. I didn't know he had a whole 'nother reason for wanting to fly under their notice. But he never turned a street kid away, no matter what we'd done. If the guards were on your tail, you knew you could run to Stinno's and if you could get to the bolthole under the floor of his storeroom before the Watch spotted you, then you were safe. He wouldn't rat you out, and they never pushed too hard if he told 'em there was nobody there. He was a good'un. One of the few I've known."

"He was the smartest son of a bitch I ever met," Prynne said, taking another drink. "No offense to our mother, but she was. A stone-cold bitch, I mean. And Nip was too smart for his own good, even from the time we were little. He got me in more trouble with his 'experiments' than I ever did fighting. And I got in a *lot* of fights growing up."

"Can't imagine," said Thallis, earning himself a cuff upside the head for his troubles.

"He knew he was dying," said Torgan. All eyes locked on him, and he shrugged. "We talked about it one night while I stood watch. He had some kind of lung rot. He thought he might have picked it up from the dragon way back when."

"You mean the dragon that..." Celia's question trailed off.

"Aye, my love," the dwarf replied, reaching out and taking his wife's hand. "The dragon that made him Nipural Wyrmrider. He thought that was where he caught whatever was killing him. He'd used spells to keep it at bay as long as he could, but over the last few years, he felt it growing inside him. He said it felt like his lungs were tight, that breathing was like walking through three feet of snow. I asked him when he thought he'd ever seen three feet of snow, and he laughed so hard he had a coughing fit. He never mentioned it again, but he knew this was his last ride."

For all we knew, it was all our last ride. Would have been Prynne's for sure, had Nipural not sacrificed himself for her. Probably would have been all ours but for the spells he spent with abandon, knowing he wouldn't need them any longer. But there we were, standing over his grave, all alive and mostly in one piece. Leshru's wounds had healed. The ones on his body, at least. No telling about the ones on his soul, but I wasn't going to ask Leshru of the Broken Blade to discuss his feelings with me. I'd survived one suicide mission. I wasn't keen to take on another.

"Goodbye, old friend," Leshru said, kneeling in front of the plain marker he'd erected. There was no name, no dates, just a stylized number seven with a dragon twined around it, and a gold coin set into the stone by a wizard in Lennox who owed us a favor and had no love for Walfert. He was more than happy to pay tribute to one of those responsible for freeing the city of its corrupt Lord Mayor.

Leshru drew back his fist, clad in the metal bands he wore in battle, and slammed it into the stone just below the seven. The metal rang like a bell, and it was almost like I felt it deep within my soul, like I resonated with it.

Then he stood and walked away without another word. I watched him go, walking east as the sun set behind him, and although I had questions, I let them die on my lips. I found him once. If I decided someday that I needed those answers, I could find him again.

And that, my dear Stinnip, my beautiful boy, is the story of the last ride of The Seven, and the parting of The Six. I hope that I'm here to tell you this story myself when you're old enough to hear it, but if not, know that you bear the name of heroes, Stinnip Leshgan Celprynnis, son of Qabil the Deposer. You shall do great things, because it is in your blood. From your grandmother, to your mother, to all your aunts and uncles, you have greatness within you. But no matter what lies within you, only you can decide what path that greatness will take. But whatever you decide, know that your mother and I are proud of you, and love you very much.

All my love,
Father.

335

Qabil closed the book and put his quill down, massaging his hand then reaching for the mug on his desk. Finding it empty, he looked around and saw that the fire had burned low and the lamp on his desk was the only light in the room. "Gods," he muttered to himself. "I must be getting old. I wonder what time it is."

"About two hours before dawn," said the young man sitting before the fire. He leaned forward, that unruly brown hair falling down over his eyes again. "No point in sleeping now. Let's get the horses saddled and we can be halfway to Talberg by sunup. There's biscuits and ale in a sack already hanging by the door."

"Okay," Qabil said. "Just let me kiss Tarisa goodbye and we can be on our way."

"Don't dally," Thallis said, a teasing grin twitching up one corner of his mouth.

"Why not?" Qabil asked. "She's my wife, I'm not allowed to dally with anyone else. Besides, it's not like she can get any more pregnant."

The young thief-turned-pawnbroker laughed, rose from his chair, and began buckling on his sword and checking his pack. "Just don't be too long. It's time this is done."

"Don't worry. I'm a brave man, but not near brave enough to wake a pregnant woman from a sound sleep," Qabil said. He ducked into the back of the house he and his wife shared, then reemerged a few moments later without the journal he'd been writing in.

"The last ride of The Seven, eh?" Thallis asked. "Guess we'll have to call this new band of idiots something different."

"Maybe let's wait and see if we're alive in a week, then start thinking up names. Besides, I thought you'd be perfectly happy if you never saw a horse again in your life."

"I would have, but circumstances made me act. That bastard has gone unchecked too long. It's time to do something about him."

"And this wouldn't have anything to do with a certain bartender at a certain tavern in Bedtev, would it?"

Thallis's ears flushed pink. "Shut up and ride, Ears. We've got a guard captain to kill."

ACKNOWLEDGMENTS

This book took longer to write than anything I've ever worked on, beginning right as COVID-19 sent the world into lockdown and bouncing between burners on my creative stove for four years between then and now. In that time a lot has changed in the world, and in me, but one thing that remains, and shall remain, is our desire for stories, and for heroes.

Our world is complicated, and often confusing and dangerous. My hope is that this book, and all my books, help you escape to a simpler world, where the heroes do good things and the villains are punished. It's a little simplistic, but when everything around you is complex, a little simplicity is often what's called for. I hope my simple tales can bring some clarity, and some escape, to you.

This book wouldn't have happened without Natania Barron and her amazing artwork, and without Melissa McArthur to tell me where the commas go. My Patreon patrons got to read pieces early, and their feedback kept me going when I didn't want to write. So did my mortgage, but I'm not thanking my creditors in my acknowledgments.

Thanks to Darin Kennedy for having the idea for the Kickstarter to produce this book, along with his trilogy and Patrick Dugan's new release. His friendship has been steadfast and unwavering for a lot of years now, and he's earned his "Ride or Die" merit badge many times over.

Thanks to all the fantasy authors who have influenced me, in ways great and small over the years. Raymond Feist, Tad Williams, Wesley Chu, Joseph Brassey, David Eddings, Robin Hobb, Nicholas Eames, and so many more have moved my work in different directions just by doing what they do so well. I appreciate all of you for your work and your talent, and thank you for being part of my life, even if we've never met in person.

SPECIAL THANKS

A special thank you to all our Kickstarter Backers!
You helped make this happen, and these books are for you!

Sheryl R. Hayes, Kiersten Keipper, Bill Feero, Chuck Teal, Beth Wojiski, Kerney Williams, Dino Hicks, Jessica Bay, Rowan Stone, Josh Minchew, V. Hartman DiSanto, Hope Griffin Diaz, April Baker, Princess Donut, Allison Charlesworth, Shanda, maileguy, Joelle Reizes, Alexandra Corrsin, Joseph Procopio, Kevin A. Davis, Robert S. Evans, Eric P. Kurniawan, Amber Derpinghaus, Andy Bartalone, R. David Grimes, Patti & Joan Holland, Scott Casey, Asha Jade Goodwin, Chuck & Colleen Parker, Jessica Nettles, Sarah J. Sover, Joe Compton, Brendan Lonehawk, Tera, James & Hannah Fulbright, Chris Fletemier, Carol B, A. L. Kaplan, Joey & Matt Starnes, Wanda Harward, Dennis M. Myers, Evelyn M, Nick Crook, Bob!, Bill Bibo Jr., Karen Palmer, Dina Barron, Charlie "Kaiju Mapping" Kaufman, Nancy E. Dunne, Rachel A. Brune, Noella Handley, Sara T. Bond, SM Hillman, C Keeley, John L. French, Anthony Martin, Lynn K, Fay Shlanda, Cristov Russell, Candice N. Carp, Samuel Montgomery-Blinn, Susan Griffith, Vee Luvian, Randy Cantrell, Gail Z. Martin, Tawni Muon, Caryn S, Jimmy Liang, Preacher Todd, Casey & Travis Schilling, The King of Rhye, Ruth Brazell, Melisa Todd, Vic Chase, Tom Sink, Nicholas Ahlhelm, Donna Berryman, Richard Novak, Liz Lamb, Angie Ross, Jonathan Casas, Christy Wilhelm, Robert Claney, Carol Gyzander, Ollie Oxxenfree, Ángel González, Caitlin Wright, Michelle Botwinick, Ashley & Cody, Amelia Sides, Nicole Rich, Ardinzul, Scott Valeri, Richard Dansky, Josh Bluestein, K.H. DeNeen, David Price, Mair Clan, Leonard Rosenthol, Vikki Perry, RHR, Jennifer & Benjamin Adelman, Everette Beach, Charlie Hawkins, Zeb Berryman, Julia Benson-Slaughter, Jesse Adams, Ash Peeples, Susan Ragsdale, Tina Hoffmann, Robert Osborne, A.M. Giddings, Michelle LeBlanc, Amanda, Ken St Clair, J. T. Arralle, Alec

Christensen, hemisphire, Marian Gosling, Zack Keedy, Dee Kennedy, Andrea Fornero, Allison Finch, Sandy Reece, Maya Barb, Shirley Kohl, Ronald H. Miller, Adrianne McDonald, James Ball III, Louise K, Elyse M Grasso, Steve Ryder, Debbie Yerkes, Brendon Towle, LB Clark, Jenn Huerta, Emily L, Eric Guy, Reverend Trevor Curtis, Jim Reader, Shauna Kantes, Stephanie Taylor, Kyla M, Micah Cash, Eric R. Asher, Cindy & Scott Kuntzelman, Avery Wild, Wes "nothing clever to say" Smith, Tamsin Silver, Steve Saffel, phoenix17, Mike Dubost, M.C. Jordan, Sarah Thompson, Cursed Dragon Ship Publishing, Venessa Giunta, Drew Bailey, Sue Phillips, LaZrus66, Scott M. Williams, William C. Tracy, Larissa Lichty, David Scoggins, Mari Mancusi, Jim Ryan, Seth Keipper, Marc Alan Edelheit, Dr. William Alexander Graham IV, Perry Harward, Liam Fisher, Jessica Glanville, Susan Roddey, Regina Kirby, Jeremy Bredeson & Leon Moses, Misty Massey, Janet Iannantuono, Regis Murphy, "Yes That Mark" Wilcox, Berta Platas, Kristen Clark, Matt, B. Y., Theresa Glover, Carol Malcolm, Dr. Keith Hunter Nelson, Adam, Leigh A. Boros & Robert A. Hilliard Jr., Aysha Rehm, Gary Phillips, Tom Savola, Audrey Hackett, Michael J. Sullivan, Annarose Mitchell, Karen M, Patrick J. Blanchard, Kayleigh Osborne, Chris Oakley, Andrea Judy, Casey, Helen Gassaway, J. Matthew Saunders, Carol Mammano, Danielle Ackley-McPhail & eSpec Books, and Jared Nelson.

ABOUT THE AUTHOR

John G. Hartness is a teller of tales, a righter of wrong, defender of ladies' virtues, and some people call him Maurice, for he speaks of the pompatus of love. He is also the award-winning author of the urban fantasy series *The Black Knight Chronicles,* the Bubba the Monster Hunter comedic horror series, the Quincy Harker, Demon Hunter dark fantasy series, and many other projects.

In 2016, John teamed up with several other publishing industry professionals to create Falstaff Books, a small press dedicated to publishing the best of genre fiction's "misfit toys." Falstaff Books has since published over 300 titles with authors ranging from first-timers to NY Times bestsellers, with no signs of slowing down any time soon. He is also the founder of the SAGA Genre Fiction Writers' Conference, where students hone their business and craft skills to write better books and make more money.

In his copious free time John enjoys long walks on the beach, rescuing kittens from trees and playing *Magic: the Gathering.* John's pronouns are he/him.

ALSO BY JOHN G. HARTNESS

THE BLACK KNIGHT CHRONICLES

The Black Knight Chronicles - Omnibus Edition

The Black Knight Chronicles Continues - Omnibus #2

All Knight Long - Black Knight Chronicles #7

Lady in Black - Black Knight Chronicles #8

BUBBA THE MONSTER HUNTER

Scattered, Smothered, & Chunked - Bubba the Monster Hunter Season One

Grits, Guns, & Glory - Bubba Season Two

Wine, Women, & Song - Bubba Season Three

Monsters, Magic, & Mayhem - Bubba Season Four

Blood, Sweat, & Tears - Bubba Season Five

Swing Low

Unholy Ground

Wampus Rumpus

Shinepunk: A Beauregard the Monster Hunter Collection

QUINCY HARKER, DEMON HUNTER

Year One: A Quincy Harker, Demon Hunter Collection

The Cambion Cycle - Quincy Harker, Year Two

Damnation - Quincy Harker Year Three

Salvation - Quincy Harker Year Four

Carl Perkins' Cadillac - A Quincy Harker, Demon Hunter Novel

Inflection Point

Conspiracy Theory

Comes a Reckoning

Lost

Histories: A Quincy Harker, Demon Hunter Collection

Histories II: A Quincy Harker, Demon Hunter Collection

SHINGLES

Zombies Ate My Homework: Shingles Book 5

Slow Ride: Shingles Book 12

Carnival of Psychos: Shingles Book 19

Jingle My Balls: Shingles Book 24

Snatched: Grandma Annie and the Cooter of Doom: Shingles Book 29

Deader than Hell: Shingles Book 40

NSFW - The Shingles Collection

OTHER WORK

The True Confessions of Fandingo the Fantastical (with EM Kaplan)

Queen of Kats

Fireheart

Amazing Grace: A Dead Old Ladies Detective Agency Mystery

From the Stone

The Chosen

Genesis

Hazard Pay and Other Tales

Have Spacecat, Will Travel

Identity Theft

FRIENDS OF FALSTAFF

Thank You to All our Falstaff Books Patrons, who get extra digital content each month! To be featured here and see what other great rewards we offer, go to www.patreon.com/falstaffbooks.

PATRONS

Dino Hicks
John Hooks
John Kilgallon
Larissa Lichty
Travis & Casey Schilling
Staci-Leigh Santore
Sheryl R. Hayes
Scott Norris
Samuel Montgomery-Blinn
Junkle

Made in the USA
Middletown, DE
23 July 2024

57618205R00210